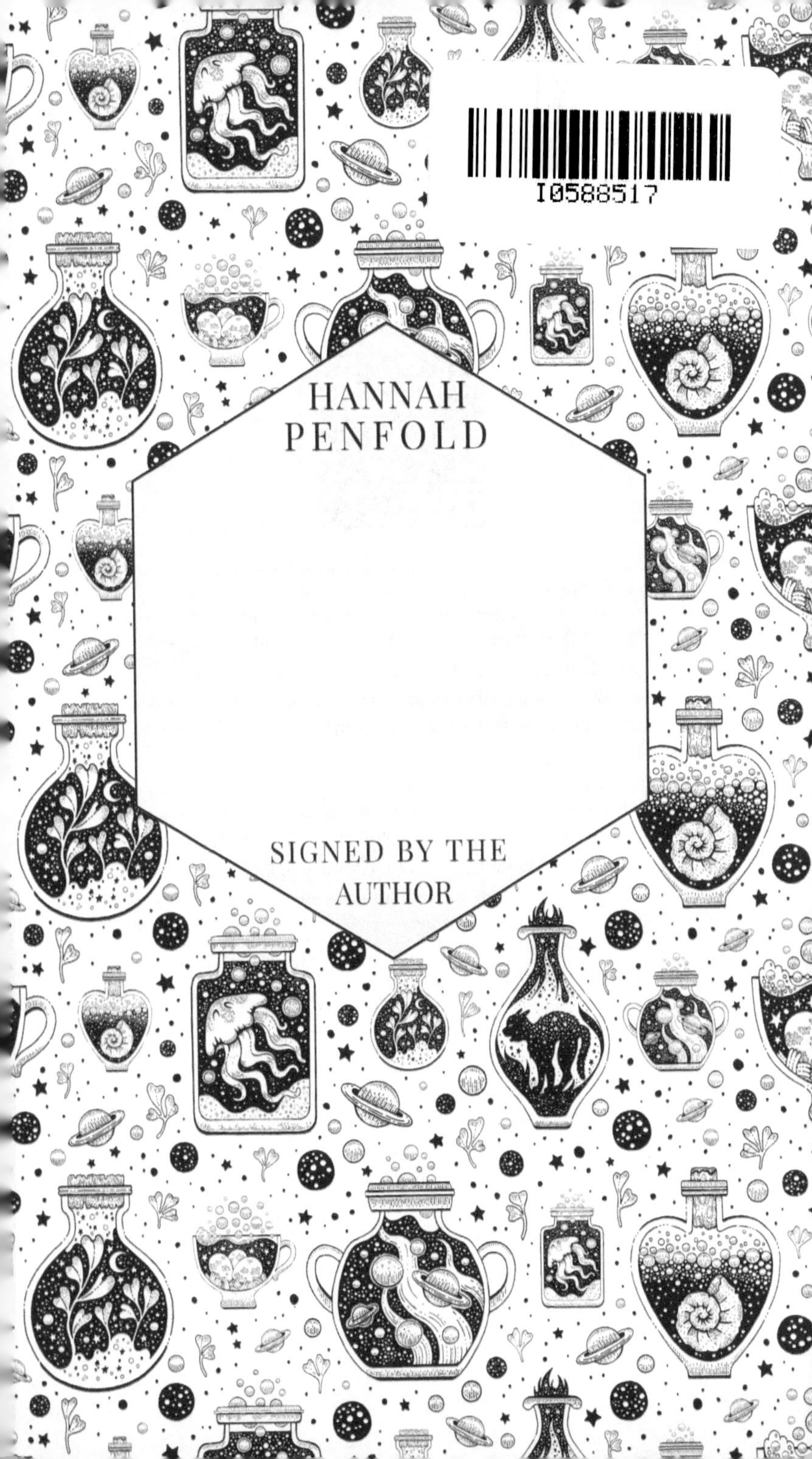
HANNAH
PENFOLD

SIGNED BY THE
AUTHOR

# CONTENT WARNINGS

This book contains material that may be triggering for some readers. Reader discretion is advised. For a complete list of content warnings please scan the below:

THE SAPPHIRE CROWN
Editing by Leonora Bulbeck
Cover Design by Miblart, www.miblart.com
Character Art by Ekaterina Vasilevna
Map by Danielle Greaves
Ebook ISBN #978-0-6455270-9-4
Paperback ISBN #978-0-6458468-0-5
Hardback ISBN #978-0-6458468-1-2

# THE SAPPHIRE CROWN

BY HANNAH PENFOLD

# THE HOUSES

<u>HOUSE OF RAVEN:</u>
RAVENS CONSIST OF VAMPIRE AND ROYAL BLOOD. THEY HAVE THE POWER OF HEIGHTENED SENSES, CONSIDERABLE STRENGTH & SHARP FANGS. UNLIKE VAMPIRES, RAVENS CAN SUSTAIN THEIR BODIES WITH BOTH NORMAL FOOD AND BLOOD. THEY ARE ABLE TO WALK IN SUNLIGHT WITHOUT BEING BURNT AND ARE KNOWN FOR THEIR RUTHLESSNESS.

<u>HOUSE OF BANE:</u>
NIGHTSHADES CONSIST OF UNICORN AND ROYAL BLOOD. THEY ARE WELL KNOWN FOR THEIR INTELLIGENCE AND THIRST FOR KNOWLEDGE. NIGHTSHADES CAN COME INTO CONTACT OR INGEST POISON WITH NO REPERCUSSIONS MAKING THEM EXTREMELY USEFUL ALLIES AND TERRIFYING ENEMIES.

<u>HOUSE OF SUN:</u>
CESLESTIALS CONSIST OF ANGEL AND ROYAL BLOOD. THEY HAVE THE POWER TO CREATE SUNLIGHT AND HEAT. THEY ARE KNOWN FOR THEIR DIVINE BEAUTY AND INCOMPARABLE FIGHTING ABILITIES. THEY ARE CLOSE COMPANIONS WITH DRAGONS WHOM THEY HAVE RIDDEN FOR HUNDREDS OF YEARS.

<u>HOUSE OF VELVET:</u>
SILKENS CONSIST OF SIREN AND ROYAL BLOOD. BEST KNOWN FOR THEIR SLY AND CUNNING NATURE, THEY ARE ABLE TO CONTROL A PERSON WITH THEIR VOICE ALONE. AMONGST THEIR ABILITIES OF MANIPULATION THEY HAVE A REPUTATION FOR BEING DECEITFUL AND SELF SERVING.

<u>HOUSE OF CREATION:</u>
BRIARS CONSIST OF FAE AND ROYAL BLOOD. DEEMED THE MOST MAGICALLY POWERFUL HOUSE OF THE SIX. BRIARS ARE A DANGEROUS KIND TO CHALLENGE. SLOW TO TRUST BUT EXTREMELY LOYAL, BRIARS' FAITHFULNESS WILL KNOW NO BOUNDS.

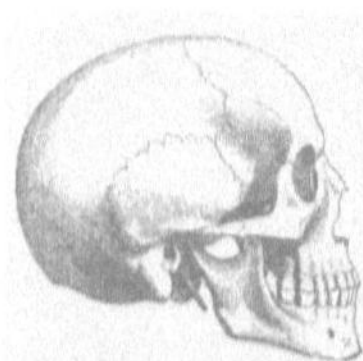

<u>HOUSE OF GLASS:</u>
THE SEVERED CONSIST OF DEMON AND ROYAL BLOOD. CLOSELY RELATED TO THE FALLEN ANGELS, THE SEVERED HAVE THE ABILITY TO SENSE DEATH  EVEN GOING AS FAR AS SEEING THE DEAD. HAVING DEMON BLOOD, THEY DO NOT HAVE SHADOWS THUS MAKING THEM EXTREMELY ARTFUL IN THE CONDUCT OF SPYING.

*The Hex consists of one representative from each House and will consist of three females and three males. If death occurs to a member of the Hex, they will be replaced at the first opportunity.

*This book is dedicated to my niece, Lara.*
*Be kind, trust yourself and always remember Aunty loves you.*

# GLOSSARY

**ALEX IRVINE** - Dameer

**AURA'S DRESS SHOP** - A woman's clothing establishment situated in Tealwaters

**ASH** - Eldest brother of Scarlet, breeder Raven

**BADGER'S SETT** - A fighting establishment situated in Rubien

**BLAZE** - Older brother of Scarlet and twin of Ember, fighter Raven

**BRANDE (Brand)** - Current Raven of the Hex, younger sister of Ruby Seraphine

**BRIAR** - Half fae, half dameer (royal blood specifically)

**CARMEN SPARK** - Mentor of the Hex, Witch

**CELESTIAL** - Half angel, half dameer (royal blood specifically)

**DAMEER** (Dah-mear) - A human born with magic

**DIMITRI THUNDERS** (Da-me-tree) - Scarlet's best friend, vampire

**ELDER RAVEN** - Leader and figurehead of the House of Raven

**ELDER NIGHTSHADE** - Leader and figurehead of the House of Bane

**ELLIS IRVINE** - Alex's younger brother, dameer

**ELSA** - Works at Aura's Dress Shop, human

**EMBER** - Older sister of Scarlet, fighter Raven

**FLEDGLINGS** - New Hex members still in the training phase of their career

**FOXGLOVE** - Nightshade, inventor

**GUARDIAN** - A dameer member to the Hex

**GWENORE FOREST (Gwen-noor)** - A magical forest who harms anyone who steps off her paths

**HAG'S SPITE** - Poison that causes the skin to melt away over time

**HALF-BLOOD** - Someone whose parents are different species

**HANRAH** - A kingdom found in the North known for its hot desert climate

**HEX** - A group of magical beings who protect and serve all people regardless of race, culture or influence

**HEX MANOR** - The residence of Hex members during their stay in Tealwaters

**HEX TRIALS** - A deadly competition to find the next representative of the Hex

**HONOUR TOUR** - An expedition of all kingdoms

**HOUSE OF BANE** - An army of Nightshades created to serve Tealwaters and its sovereigns

**HOUSE OF CREATION** - An army of Briars created to serve Envy and its sovereigns

**HOUSE OF GLASS** - An army of Severed created to serve Whitlocke and its sovereigns

**HOUSE OF RAVEN** - An army of Ravens created to serve Hanrah and its sovereigns

**HOUSE OF SUN** - An army of Celestials created to serve Maya and its sovereigns

**HOUSE OF VELVET** - An army of Silkens created to serve Siamoon and its sovereigns

**HUMAN** - Someone born without magic

**INKBERRY** - A berry that sends many species into a state of unconsciousness

**IVORY CASTLE** - The main residence to the royal family

**IVY WYNTERS** - Nightshade of the Hex

**JACK WILDE** - Guardian of the Hex

**JOLLY PEARL TAVERN** - A drinking establishment situated in Tealwaters

**JON'S DEN** - A men's clothing establishment situated in Tealwaters

**KING AIDEN** - King of Maya

**KING HECTOR** - King of Tealwaters
**LIBRARY OF WONDERS** - The largest library in the lands situated Hanrah
**LIQUID GOLD** - An alcoholic drink that tastes vile for anyone underage and delicious to those of age
**MARIE WILDE** - Current guardian of the Hex, Jack's mother
**MATE** - An extremely strong and unbreakable connection between fae who are deemed equals in every way
**MAYA** - A kingdom found in the South-West known for its mountainous climate
**MERLOT (Mer-low)** - Competitor of the Hex Trials, friend of Scarlet's
**MOLTEN SLAPPER** - An alcoholic beverage
**NIGHTSHADE** - Creations made from unicorn blood and dameer blood (royal blood specifically)
**NIMBLE LADY** - An alcoholic beverage
**OLIVE ATTERLEY** - The Severed of the Hex
**PERI BELROSE** - Silken of the Hex
**PRINCE ATHOS (Ah-thoss)** - Heir of Tealwaters
**PRINCESS LEONORE (Lee-o-noor)** - Youngest princess of Hanrah
**QUEEN ADELA (Ah-dell-ah)** - Queen of Hanrah
**QUEEN CAIDA (Kay-da)** - Queen of Maya
**QUEEN MELODY** - Queen of Tealwaters
**RAVEN** - Half vampire, half dameer (royal blood specifically)
**RED RAVEN** - The moniker for Brande Seraphine
**ROSALIE** - Mate of Rusty, Supreme Briar
**ROUX (Roo)** - Eldest sister of Scarlet, breeder Raven
**RUBIEN (Roo-bee-en)** - Underground city in Hanrah
**RUBY** - Mother of Scarlet, worker Raven
**RUSTY HASELWOOD** - Briar of the Hex
**SAPPHIRE CITY** - Capital city of Tealwaters
**SAPPHIRE SALMON** - A seafood restaurant situated in Sapphire City
**SCALE CITY** - Capital city of Maya
**SENNASTONE (Sen-nah-stone)** - A continent, or large mass of land that holds the six kingdoms
**SERAPHINE (Seh-rah-feen)** - Scarlet's surname
**SEVERED** - Half demon, half dameer (royal blood specifically)
**SILKEN** - Half siren, half dameer (royal blood specifically)
**SIREN** - Beautiful creatures who reside in the ocean with singing voices that can lure men to their death
**SOL XAVIER** - Celestial of the Hex
**SUPREME** - A child of the Elder Briar (House of Creation)
**TARRGON CASTLE** - Main residence of the Mayan royal family
**TEALWATERS** - A kingdom found in the West known for its tropical climate
**TELLIAN** - Language spoken in Tealwaters, name of the people from Tealwaters
**THEA SPARK** - Mentor of the Hex, Witch
**THE TEACHER** - Jack's fighting name at the Badger's Sett
**TROLL** - A giant creature with green skin
**VERMILION FANG** - The moniker of Ruby Seraphine
**WINELLA (Win-elle-ah)** - Competitor in the Hex Trials, fighter Raven

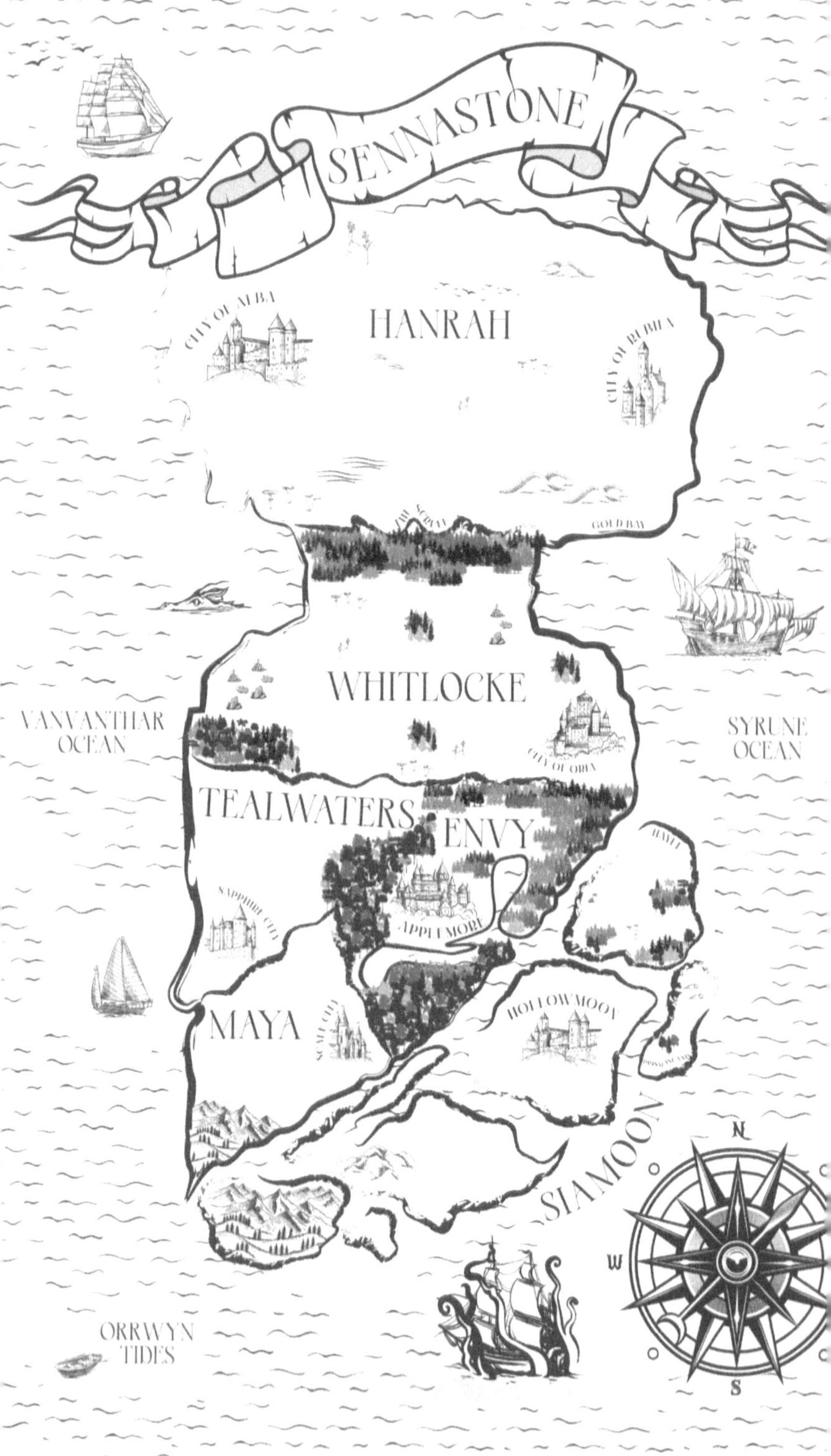

SENNASTONE
HANRAH
CITY OF ALBA
CITY OF RUBHA
THE SCHYAE
GOLD BAY
WHITLOCKE
VANVANTHAR OCEAN
SYRUNE OCEAN
CITY OF ORIN
TEALWATERS
ENVY
HAVEE
SAPPHIRE CITY
APPLEMORE
MAYA
HOLLOWMOON
SCALE CITY
SIAMOON
ORRWYN TIDES
N
W
S

# PART ONE

*House of Bane*

IVY WYNTERS

I

I roll onto my hands and knees, my back aching as I search my surroundings. The hot flames make it hard to see and difficult to breathe, but I don't care. I need to find Jack.

My right palm is covered in my own blood – my scar seeping with crimson – as I search the growing smoke for any traces of my guardian.

*You're in danger,* my scar tells me, but I curl up my hand into a fist and ignore the warning.

'Jack!' I shout, eyes snapping up at the fire that consumes the branches above me. Fear washes over my body as I get to my feet, leaning on the tree trunk for stability. 'Jack, where are you?'

The sound of cracking alerts me. I glance upwards just in time to find part of the tree I huddle beneath collapsing, its abundance of leaves seeming to fall in slow motion. My arms and legs move of their own accord, scrambling out of the way as heavy branches descend, different-coloured leaves streaming from the sky as they flutter to the ground where I once stood.

A rumble so loud echoes through my ears, the sound

not from the forest blaze but from beneath my feet. Bits of chipped bark upon the dirt floor vibrate by my boots. I look into the distance to see the ground rolling, as if a beast underneath the earth has discerned my presence. Without hesitating, I run.

The invisible threat doesn't let up, the moving terrain heading straight for me as I sprint through the trees, the forest's beauty being swallowed up by the terror that claws at my chest. I try to scream for help, but my throat is constricted, my voice coming out in fast breaths as I rush through the bush and approach a calm river.

As I close the distance between myself and the water, I leap with every bit of energy I can muster. I land on the other side – but only just, my legs giving out before I roll into shrubbery, pieces of woodland tangling in my hair. My chest heaves, trying to intake more oxygen as I roll onto my side to look behind me. The roiling earth stops at the water, seemingly annoyed it can no longer pursue me.

'Thank the higher powers,' I mutter, turning onto my back while I regain my breath, my chest rising and falling from the sudden exertion. My eyes wander over the upper-most trees, shades of green and orange dancing through the leaves. The smoke I was once encased in now fades as if a distant memory.

*This place is truly beautiful*, I can't help thinking.

'There you are.'

I'm on my feet in seconds, grappling for a weapon I don't have. My hands flex with unease as I subtly look for a stick or something else I can use to defend myself with.

The stranger is tall, muscular and looks like a fighter. He wears dark brown leathers that contrast with his glowing, sun-kissed skin and long fair hair, which surpasses even mine in length. He stares at me quietly, curious golden eyes watching carefully as I take him in.

'I wondered when you would arrive,' he says, his lips tugging up at the corners.

It takes my brain a moment to realise he is talking in Tellian, the mother tongue of Tealwaters. Which is not surprising, considering that's where the portal from the House of Raven was intended to lead when Jack and I stepped through. I am no longer in Hanrah, where I was born and raised, but much further south, where the sun shines all year round and the ocean is as blue as the sky.

Before I can answer, his eyes flicker to the sound of snapping, worry etched in his handsome features. 'We need to hurry back, or else Gwenore will kill us before you can meet the others,' he says, making little sense.

Before I can ask who Gwenore is, a tree so tall with a trunk so thick creates a strange creaking sound that grabs my full attention.

'We need to move,' the stranger frets.

It's only when his large hand yanks on my arm that I realise the tree is falling – straight towards us. My body is flipped into the air, my limbs flailing as the male chucks me onto his broad shoulder, and his grip is like iron as he starts running for his life.

'I don't usually handle new friends so inappropriately, but I feel this calls for an exception!' he calls out in apology.

'What is going on?' I yell, my stomach hurting from the motions of his shoulder digging into my middle. I watch as the trunk falls inch by inch, its colossal size causing dirt, leaves and even water from the river to splash across the forest floor like a tidal wave. 'It's going to get us!' I shriek as I feel the male lose his footing.

We tumble down a small hill, water crashing over the edge seconds after us. My shouts of dismay echo through the woodland, scaring four-legged animals and birds from their homes. I crash through bush and dirt until, after what feels like eternity, I roll to a definitive stop along a gravel pathway. A small stream of cold water trickles into my hair and along my shoulders, making the back of my shirt wet. My breathing hitches at the chilly temperature as I peel away a strand of my hair stuck to my face, tangled from getting caught in discarded sticks and undergrowth.

'Holy Hanrah,' I murmur, coughing up the soil I've inhaled during my tumble.

'You can say that again.'

I turn to see that the stranger looks just as battered and bruised as me – his clothes soiled, his cheek and forehead covered in grime. I can't help but bark out a nervous laugh when I see his golden eyes widen as the remaining water creeps near him too.

'Who are you?' I ask. I slowly push myself up into a sitting position, looking around us for any indication of where we might be. Nothing looks familiar, of course, now I've stepped into a new kingdom, and this puts me on edge. My only hope of getting out of here is the unknown male alongside me.

'My name is Sol Xavier. I'm from the House of Sun.'

My brows lift as I turn to him once more. So *this* is one of the other members of the Hex, a male that I am to work alongside as protectors of the land and its people.

'And you are Scarlet Seraphine, from the House of Raven. We were told to expect your arrival any day now.'

I ponder this a moment as we lapse into silence. I busy myself with removing a particularly sharp stone from underneath my leg as the male surveys our surroundings, looking much more relaxed now we are on what looks to be a path.

Sol staggers to his feet once he's done, and begins to wipe down his clothes. He looms over me but smiles warmly as our gazes meet. He offers a large tanned hand

and pulls me to my feet. I can tell he's extremely powerful and is used to hard labour from the calluses that line the underside of his hand.

'So, Sol Xavier,' I start, needing to fill the silence, earning an amused look from him as I dust away the twigs and dirt on my clothing. 'Why are you in the forest? Seems like a dangerous place to be alone in.'

'I wasn't alone. I was with Rusty – another teammate of ours. We got separated when the fire began. I heard shouting, and it ended up being you.'

'Do you think Rusty has my guardian?' I enquire, wrinkling my nose.

'I can't be sure.' The male shrugs unhelpfully, intensifying my worry for Jack.

What if he is hurt? How will I find him? His scent is *everywhere*. This whole forest smells of salt and fresh air, along with what I assume to be dirt, trees and something strong – medicinal. I wouldn't be able to track him down even if I wanted to.

'I'm sure he is fine. Hopefully, they've found each other like we did,' Sol says, shaking me out of my thoughts, seeming to note my sudden unease.

*I hope so too*, I think worriedly.

'Do you want me to dry your hair?' Sol asks. He grabs his own locks and trails his hands down them, a soft glow emanating from his palms.

I study him for a few seconds in awe before he shows me his large hands. Heat radiates from them and warms up my curious face.

'Unless you'd rather walk home *wet* ...' He winks, heating up my cheeks.

Reluctantly I allow him to take my hair. He slowly dries the dirty strands, my locks looking like blood across his palms. I peer at my scar, which is now closed, coated in dried crimson. Memories stir within me, flashes of blades, stains of red among ripped clothing. I blink to rid myself of the images before I begin to reflect on all the shit I've endured to get here.

'Where is all that blood from?' Sol asks, frowning down at my hand.

From here, I can smell something pleasant on him, something I don't know the name of quite yet.

'My scar.' I lift my right hand for him to see better. 'It opens when I'm in danger and closes when I'm safe.'

His mouth curls up on one side. 'That sounds helpful.'

'It is.' I nod, thinking of all the times it has saved me in the past. 'Can you only produce heat?'

'No. Like you Ravens with your shared heightened senses, all members of my House can create heat as well as sunlight. It's not called the House of Sun for nothing.' Sol smirks, making the corners of my mouth tip upwards slightly. He lowers a cupped hand for me, forgetting my hair, and a small ball of light glimmers within it. It grows in size until I have to look away from its brightness.

'That's amazing,' I gush, earning a bashful look from the male.

'I suppose for someone who hasn't grown up sharing this power with everyone else, it is.' He nods. 'But *my* power, something only I possess, is perceiving the memories of objects.'

I scrunch my nose up in confusion. 'Pardon?'

'Take this, for instance.' He reaches for the band around my wrist, bronze in colour. His body stills as if he is deep in thought as he grabs my wrist. 'I can see a female with bright red hair and fiery eyes. She used to wear this before you.' He looks up into my eyes. 'She looks like a relative – similar features but different colouring.'

I smile at the mention of Ruby. 'My mother. She gave

this to me,' I clarify, remembering her giving me this family heirloom before I left. She wore it herself once upon a time. The ruby on top, when pressed, activates a suit of armour that covers the wearer's body.

He nods as if this makes perfect sense. 'She used to be a warrior too.'

I open my mouth to ask what else he can tell me about my mother and her time wearing this bracelet, but shouts carry to us through the air, and my head whips towards them. My name. It's my name.

'Jack!' I yell, and I hear a faint sigh of relief.

Sol points into the distance, to two figures who travel along the same gravel path as us. Jack's silvery-blonde hair stands out in the forest scenery, his demeanour the first thing I notice. In an instant, I can tell my guardian feels uncomfortable, his shoulders unnaturally straight and body stiff alongside the unfamiliar stranger he walks with.

My eyes move towards the towering male, whose expression is unnervingly neutral. He wears similar clothing to Sol's, clothing that is suitable for combat, but instead of wearing shades of brown, like the male beside me, he wears mostly black and green. Along his muscular forearms, I can see small scratches across his dark skin, but his tight shirt covers the rest of his burly arms and broad chest. As he and Jack close the distance between us, I can smell the immense power the stranger holds, and I wonder if this is why he is so big.

Jack is by my side in an instant, leaving the towering figure behind as his sky-blue eyes roam over me with worry. His hands hold my arms gently as he inspects the damage to my face.

'Have you broken anything?' he asks, to which I shake my head.

'Have *you*?' I ask, noting Sol watching our every move out of the corner of my eye.

'No.'

As Jack's companion finally reaches our group, I suddenly feel on high alert. I thought Jack and Sol – similar in size and stature – were tall, but this male ... he's *massive*. I have to look up further to peer at his face, where he pushes away a chestnut strand of hair from his deep bronze eyes.

'Rusty.' Sol greets the giant with a slap on the back, his teeth incredibly white as he gives him a friendly smile. 'Glad to see you in one piece. I see you've rounded up the rest of the Raven party.'

'Likewise,' Rusty answers. As if sensing my surveillance of him, his burnished eyes meet mine. He is handsome, much like Sol is attractive, but in an effortless sort of way, a rugged beauty that only a few can pull off without it being too much. 'Hello. I'm Rusty Haselwood.'

'From the House of Creation,' Jack adds for my benefit, edging closer as he faces the males. He then turns to Sol expectantly, wanting an introduction.

Sol obliges, easing his features into a carefree smile. 'Sol Xavier, from the—'

'House of Sun,' Jack finishes for him, accepting the hand Sol offers him. They shake firmly, and it goes on for much longer than is necessary, the pair seeming to be sizing each other up. 'A Celestial and a Briar to welcome us to Tealwaters. What a treat.'

I sense my guardian is saying all this extra information for my sake. I, unlike him, did not train to be in the Hex all my life. I fell into this opportunity due to wanting to save my sister's life. I didn't think I'd ever work in the Hex, let alone work alongside those who had trained to be within the prestigious group.

Now, though, facing these strangers, I'm questioning

my lack of knowledge of the Houses and the vital information my guardian seems to have explored beforehand, which I did not read up on.

'A Celestial and a Briar?' I say, eyeing the males before me, letting Jack's body shield me for now. He's on high alert. I can tell by his heartbeat, but he does well to play it off in front of our current company.

Sol places a hand on his own broad chest, leaning forward as if wanting to tell us a secret. 'A Celestial is half angel. A Briar –' he looks at Rusty briefly – 'is half fae.'

I peer towards the Briar's ears, which poke out from beneath his chestnut hair. They're pointed at the top and unlike any ears I've seen. I drag my eyes away before my staring turns awkward.

'So, being part angel, do you have a halo?' I aim this question at Sol. With the subtle glow his skin emits, I wouldn't be surprised if he did have one.

'Being part vampire, do you have fangs?' he retorts.

'I'll show you mine if you show me yours,' I counter, admiring his long, shiny hair, imagining a circlet of glowing gold above it.

He seems surprised by my reaction but doesn't back down, his grin wide as he nudges Rusty's side. 'I knew she'd be a ball of fun.'

Rusty rolls his eyes. 'I suggest we head back. Carmen and Thea will be wondering where we have got to.' He aims a finger towards my face, and the hairs on my arms rise instinctively. 'And they'll want to check your wounds.'

I lift my hand to where he points and touch something sticky. My fingers come away covered in blood from a cut on my temple – something I must have earned from tumbling down a hill – but my palm, my once-silver scar, is open again. I look around expectantly for danger.

'Who are Carmen and Thea?' I ask, racking my brains to ascertain whether I should know these names.

'They are our mentors—' Sol begins to answer, but a whizzing sound catches my attention – apparently, Rusty's too, as we both look in the direction the sound is coming from.

Before I can figure out what it can be, something splats hard against my neck, a droplet of liquid hitting me at full force.

'What the fuck was that?' Jack demands, smothering me instantly. It's only when Sol grabs his shoulders and pulls him away roughly that my guardian's eyes glow bright blue in warning, his water magic ready to fight off any threat that targets me. 'Hands off me, Celestial.'

'Don't go near her, or you may be affected too,' Rusty instructs, a large hand pushing against Jack's chest, putting a safe distance between us before he turns to me with a calm expression.

Sol looks anything but composed, nerves rippling through his body.

'That looks like an inkberry,' the Celestial comments.

Rusty nods in agreement, watching me carefully.

'And what does an inkberry *do*?' I ask with a frown, finding it smells just as its name suggests – like berries.

'You'll see.' Rusty grimaces before my eyes begin to flutter, my arms becoming heavy.

'I suddenly feel very tired,' I murmur, finding my body swaying. 'What is ...?' My mouth goes numb, and my words begin to slur.

'Inkberries send vampires – and many other species – into a state of unconsciousness,' Rusty confirms, making me pout.

*How convenient*, I think before darkness claims me.

2

Voices grow louder as I open my eyes. The first thing I see is a row of beds along from the one I lie in. I still have my old and now-wrecked clothes on, but I'm partially cleaned up. I squint slightly as the sun shines through the window to my left. Two women are conversing animatedly, working at a desk that lines the entire length of the opposite wall. Along the worktable are bowls of cut-open and half-eaten fruit, pots of paint-brushes, metal tools that look somewhat clinical and even a pile of discarded newspapers.

Above them are shelves upon shelves of glass jars and substances that stand neatly in lines, while old and dusty books lie scattered across the messy and disorganised counter. I wrinkle my nose at the concoction of smells in here. I've never smelled so many things at once.

'Scarlet.'

I turn towards the bed next to me. Jack sits upon the crisp white sheets, his hands clasped together and knuckles white. The worry he displays is evident, and I go to reach for him, but he clears his throat, looking apologetically towards the desk. The sound alerts the two women.

'Hello, my sweet. How are you feeling?'

Both women are now staring at me with obvious interest. The one wearing all black approaches me slowly, as if not wanting to scare me. She leans over and feels my forehead, her warm hand making me flinch.

'Normal,' she confirms out loud, ignoring my reaction as she moves to the end of the bed.

The other woman gives me a reassuring smile. 'Are you thirsty, Scarlet?'

Without being prompted, she travels across the room, grabs a decanter and fills it with water. She places the decanter and a glass cup on a tray and brings it over to place it by my legs. She wears all blue, her dress elegant and feminine, the skirt flowing around her like water. This close, she smells of something floral with a hint of magic. I know then that these two strangers are both dameer – humans born with magical abilities.

I eye up the pair. The woman in black, who stands at the end of my bed, lifts a hand to her chest. 'I'm Carmen Spark.' She points to the woman in blue. 'And this is my sister, Thea.'

The pair of them are nearly identical, with their long dark brown hair and chocolate-coloured eyes. If they aren't twins, I'll be extremely surprised.

The one in blue – Thea – pours my drink and urges me to take a sip. 'How are you feeling?'

'Fine, I think,' I reply, glancing at Jack for any help, but he stays quiet. 'Are we supposed to be here?'

Thea smiles warmly, her face morphing into something sweet and magnetic. 'Of course! The boys brought you here so we could check you over. They were very concerned about you after you blacked out.'

I turn to Jack again, disorientated and confused beyond belief.

'Carmen and Thea are our mentors,' Jack offers, giving me a reassuring look. 'They are people we can trust. My mum has written about them often in her letters to me over the years. She's always spoken highly of them. There is nothing to be worried about.'

I nod slowly, absorbing his words. Jack's mother is Marie Wilde, current Guardian of the Hex. Having worked alongside my aunt, who is the Raven of the Hex, Marie would have many connections to those who reside outside Rubien. If she has approved of the trustworthiness of the women before me, I suppose I can too.

'We will be present for your whole Hex career, Scarlet. You can ask us *anything*. There is no such thing as a silly question. We know nearly everything at this point.' Thea leans forward eagerly, manicured fingers clenched together as if to keep them to herself.

Carmen studies me closely before flicking her wrist. A plate of biscuits across the room begins to hover and makes its way over to me. She motions towards it with a dip of her chin. 'Eat.'

I refrain from showing my surprise at her magic. Is it telekinesis or something else?

My scarred hand, which I note has been cleaned of blood, automatically reaches for the food. I don't want to know what will happen if I decline. Carmen seems more intimidating compared to her sister – her features somehow sharper, her dark eyes more observant.

'So, where are we?' I ask, munching on what I think is ginger. It tastes unpleasant, but I consume it without complaint.

'You're in the healing quarters at Hex Manor,' Carmen replies, noting my confused look. 'The manor is your home for the period of your stay in Tealwaters.'

'But you're in *here*,' Thea adds, motioning to the room we occupy, 'because we wanted to check you over.'

I scowl, earning curious glances. 'What happened?'

'You were hit by an inkberry – which without proper care can be very dangerous. We aren't sure where it came from, but we have our suspicions.' Thea pouts before remembering herself. 'Nothing to worry about now, though.' She beams as if to reassure me I'm no longer in danger. With lashes as dark as her gaze, she inspects me with her doe eyes, her stare roaming over my face, my damp, tangled hair and dirty clothes. 'You look like you've been to war, my sweet.'

'I've gone through worse.' I force a smile because it's true. The few cuts along my hands and face are nothing compared to what I've experienced in the past. From the expressions upon my new mentors' faces, they know I'm being truthful.

'You're safe here. Hex Manor is a haven for when you and Jack need it. No one will harm you within these walls,' Thea offers with a small, warm smile, my guardian giving her an appreciative nod.

*Only within these walls? How reassuring.*

Thea's eyes, however, look different – cheerless – as they lower towards my neck. I wear a high-necked shirt, but from the thinning of her lips, I know she and Carmen most likely saw my still-healing wounds from the Hex Trials while cleaning me up.

Carmen pipes up. 'You're safe unless you're training – we can't promise you'll feel in good shape after that.'

Thea shoots her a stern look.

'What? They need to know training will not be easy.' Carmen turns, aiming her words in our direction. 'Becoming the next Raven and Guardian of the Hex will be difficult. You may get hurt from time to time, and it may be painful or alarming, but you have to learn certain skills before you're allowed into the world by yourselves. Think of this as an introduction to the Hex lifestyle, if you will.'

'I think that's fair enough,' Jack answers.

I take him in, the light behind him making his frame glow. I peer over his shoulder, a bird having grabbed my attention as it flew past the window.

'Is that ...?' I slowly get off the bed to peer outside, enamoured of the sight.

Carmen comes to my side and opens the pane of glass for me, letting the soft, ocean-scented breeze tickle my face.

'We have lots of wildlife around here. Thea has several tables scattered around for the parrots and various other animals who live close by. We can show you sometime if you would like.'

I nod eagerly. 'Yes, please.'

Further up in the sky, a noisy flock of white birds flies overhead, their wings flapping. My mouth opens in awe. The clouds above them slowly move along the bright blue sky.

'Unbelievable.' My eyes snag on Carmen beside me, her dark eyes following my every expression. 'What?' I ask.

'It's been a while since I've seen a Raven so entranced by what we've grown up thinking is ordinary,' she replies. Behind her, I can see a similar expression on Thea's face. 'But it's nice to see that type of appreciation again. It makes me realise how lucky we are to live as we do.'

'You'll acclimatise to the surroundings eventually,' Thea chimes in, her hands entwined as if nervously. 'Everything in Tealwaters will be new and exciting to you, but you must remember to be cautious of beautiful things. Those of beauty can deal out the deadliest hands.' Thea's dark eyes flick to the garden outside, a blanket of colour surrounding the front of the manor. I don't think she means the flowers, but what do I know? I've not even been here a day.

'I'll be careful,' I promise them, finding Jack observing me closely, a tilt of his lips letting me know he feels more relaxed with these two females than with Sol and Rusty.

'Well, now you're awake, let's get you settled in,' Carmen says, making Thea grin with delight.

3

We are given a brief tour of Hex Manor, and it's much larger than I first expected. At the front of the premises is a beautiful flower garden with colours of every shade and two matching bird baths sitting among the blooms. Out back is Thea's vegetable patch, which consists of several massive boxes that are full of rich brown soil and tall sticks poking out of the ground with greenery curling around them. I'm told that there are pumpkins, tomatoes, carrots, parsley and a list of other things that I can't remember the names of but that sound equally delicious.

Inside the manor, the decor is tasteful, in various shades of blue – cobalt carpet and rugs, patterned midnight-blue wallpaper and pure white ceilings that are much higher than I'm used to.

The large foyer has a long, winding set of stairs that leads to an upstairs balcony, where we can look down on the reception space. On the second level are the bedrooms. We pass multiple doors lining the wall before we hit the one at the very end of the passageway.

'This is your room,' Carmen says, twisting the handle and pushing the door open.

My personal chamber is *huge*. If I hadn't known any better, I would have thought the room was to be shared with several others. As I step through the threshold, I see a theme throughout the space – red, and it's everywhere.

'Past Hex members have decorated their bedrooms in their House colours to help with homesickness,' Carmen claims, stroking the tasteful wallpaper. 'If you wish to change anything, we can have that arranged.'

Jack, who stands cautiously in the doorway, crosses his arms. He looks as impressed as I feel, his pale eyes darting around the room as if a threat will pounce at any moment.

'The last Raven of the Hex removed her belongings not long ago, so we've yet to redecorate,' Carmen continues, making my ears prick at the mention of my relative.

'Brande?' I murmur.

'Yes, that's right.' Thea nods. 'Brande will have much insight to offer you when she visits next. You'll be able to have some quality time together when you eventually cross paths.'

I've never met my aunt. My mother, Ruby, was in the Hex once upon a time. However, when she fell pregnant with me, having fallen in love with a human man – a sin in the eyes of our House – she was banished from the Hex, and Brande replaced her. Now I'll finally have the chance to see the younger sister Ruby grew up with.

'She's lovely, and I'm sure you'll get along like a house on fire.' Carmen's mouth twitches with amusement as Thea laughs at her sister's attempt at a joke – my family is known for its fire elemental powers. 'But yes, she'll visit soon enough if work comes up nearby. Other Hex members will also be visiting from time to time, so don't be alarmed if you see them too.' Carmen steps further into the room, motioning for me to follow. 'Come. Let me show you your wardrobe.'

She gathers me towards a door and opens it to a space that is larger than my old bedroom back in the House of Raven. I've never had a wardrobe, only boxes under my bed, so this is already far superior to what I'm used to.

My chest tightens as I think of my old room, which I shared with my two sisters, and what the room will look like now I'm gone.

I don't react to my darkening thoughts. Instead, I study the area. On the floor, I see my packed bag, a sack I gave to Princess Leonore days ago in preparation for having it here, ready for my arrival. Sticking out of it is a knife – midnight black with gold stars along the handle, the blade the colour of liquid gold. I recognise it as the one my friend Leonore – the Hanrae princess – cut my hand with to make my oath to the Hex. I smile, not surprised she's left it with me. The details in its design are beautiful enough to make it a grand gift. I grab it and admire it closely.

*You sneaky dameer*, I think fondly.

'Like your room, if you don't like your clothes, we can arrange to have some more made to your liking,' Carmen says as my gaze ascends and roams along the rails of mostly scarlet clothing.

I refrain from wrinkling my nose. I want my room to be anything but crimson, and my clothes to be anything but my House colour, but of course, I say no such thing. Taking in the fine materials used for my garments, I have a sinking feeling in my stomach. Only a handful of the clothing is long-sleeved or has a high neck. Instinctively I rub a hand along an arm, thinking of my burns on show for everyone to see.

*You'll have to reveal them eventually*, I think sourly.

'Thank you. This is all very nice,' I say, giving the sisters a polite smile.

Carmen's eyes narrow slightly, as if she knows what I'm thinking, but she doesn't comment. She leads me out of the walk-in wardrobe and towards a set of light, airy curtains. When she pulls them aside, they reveal two glass doors that lead out onto a small balcony, which can fit two people comfortably.

'This is your balcony. It looks out onto our vegetable garden,' Carmen says, allowing me time to take in the view. Below my balcony, connected to the manor wall, is a small area of wooden decking that overlooks the delicious-smelling garden. Upon the dark wood platform is a long table, which has a book opened halfway upon it – its reader is missing. 'We own all the land you can see. The field and the forest ...' Carmen trails off, motioning beyond the white picket fence that borders the back lawn. From the small gate, the land slopes down to a field of long grass, then a dense border of trees.

'You must be careful in Gwenore Forest,' Thea says firmly, looking at both Jack and me solemnly. 'She has already taken advantage of you both, and next time, you must be more prepared. The Elder Raven created her portal in a very dangerous and inconvenient spot.'

Carmen's gaze hardens, like she already knows what type of person my Elder is and isn't surprised by the events that unfolded.

'You say that as if Gwenore is a person.' My brows crease in confusion. Sol had also mentioned her briefly before we had to run for our lives.

'Gwenore is the forest itself, my sweet,' Thea answers. 'She is the spirit of the trees, and she harms anyone she can get her hands on. If you do not stick to the paths, she has the right to hunt you down.'

'Why would anyone go in there, then? Why did the Celestial and the Briar go in there?' Jack asks with pursed lips.

'Training,' Carmen states plainly. 'Gwenore is a good educational tool. She strengthens our Hex members and hardens them for the future. She is harsh, but she's taught our prior students well and is the reason we start our journey here, in the kingdom of Tealwaters.'

'We don't stay here?' I ask, feeling rather silly for not knowing anything.

Carmen places a gentle hand on my shoulder. 'No. We will be travelling through each kingdom eventually, but don't fret. We will explain it all in good time. For now, you should rest and get yourself settled. Dinner will be soon.'

They go to leave before Thea spins round to face my guardian and me, her dark brown eyes flicking between the two of us. 'Is there anything else you need?'

'No. Thank you,' Jack replies before facing me for my answer.

I ponder the question for a moment before nodding. 'Have we any stationery? To send letters?'

The female smiles at me fondly. 'I'll bring some up for you.'

After our mentors leave, I wander around the room, touching and studying everything within. I relax slightly once I'm convinced nothing will harm me. I find every possible item I can use as a weapon, just for peace of mind, and even find a secret spot under my bed, beneath a loose wooden floorboard, to hide the pouches of money Dimitri gifted me before I left.

With not a lot more scoping out of the room to do, I

stand beside my bed, stroking the covers fondly. It's quite substantial in size and very comfy-looking. I'd wager it would be big enough to fit all my siblings in, if they were here with me. My eyes prick with emotion.

'How are you feeling?' Jack asks, having watched me like a hawk as I flitted around the room.

'Like I've been thrown into a whole new world. You?'

He steps forward, and my heart hammers at the gesture, but I keep my features neutral as he shortens the distance between us, his large hand stroking the bed covers too. He smirks. 'I'm wondering why you're touching your bed sheets with such adoration.'

'Is that jealousy I detect?' I jest.

'If you want me to be honest ... then yes, I am rather envious of your bed.' He grins for the first time since stepping into this strange new kingdom, and I can't help but mirror him.

We stand there for a moment in silence, taking each other in. With Jack I think of nothing else, my mind empty except for him before me. His gaze softens as he watches me study him so intently.

'This must be a lot for you to take in, Scarlet.'

I nod. 'It is, but I have you to make it easier.'

'You do.' His hand rises and softly moves my hair behind my ear. His thumb runs over a small cut along my temple. I feel his touch through my skin, warming my cheeks. My eyes close briefly before an intimate memory of us comes to mind.

'Jack,' I murmur, voice low.

Before our last trial, we spent a moment together which consisted of locked lips. We had acted on a forbidden desire we had been harbouring for each other. But we knew if we were caught, like my mother was when she fell in love with my father, our careers and lives will undoubtedly be made much worse by the Elder Raven.

Too much had happened since then to truly talk through what occurred between us. What we should expect going forward.

'We should discuss what happened in the barn,' I sigh.

'We should.' Jack agrees, his hand dropping away from my face. 'Like you said, it was purely out of desire. What happened mustn't happen again. We may have left the House of Raven but that doesn't mean the Elder Raven is not watching our every move.'

'You're right.' My expression stays neutral as I nod in agreement. The affection I hold for Jack may be growing the more time I spend with him but that does not mean he feels the same way for me. 'She was not pleased we won the Hex Trials and we are more at risk here – being in an environment we are not familiar with. We will have to be careful with who we trust.'

He looks at me long and hard, those blue eyes silently debating. 'Come here.'

I look up into his softened face with silent questions. He no longer displays his protective act. With me, alone, he's himself.

Jack takes my hands in his and wraps them both around his waist, forcing me forward so our bodies touch. My head automatically lays on his chest, hearing his steady heart beat beneath his skin. Contentment fills me when he gently embraces me back, squeezing firmly as he moulds his body around mine. I could stay like this all day.

'We've got this, Scarlet,' he murmurs into my hair. 'As long as we stay together we'll be fine.'

I barely hear him, my mind swirling with how much of his body is pressed against mine. It's unexpected to be held so gently but the feeling is pleasant, and a rush of want shoots through my chest.

*Clear your mind of him, you are better off as friends.*

I take a deep breath, expelling any simmering emotions I have for what Jack and I shared in the barn. For our safety I need to rein in my affection for the guardian. I need to keep him at arm's length – even if it disappoints me to do so.

4

Wen dinner is ready, Thea comes to fetch Jack and me, finding us on my balcony. We exit my room and trail after her as she points to each door.

'You're next to a bathroom, Scarlet. Then we have Sol, Rusty, Peri, Ivy and Olive.' She knocks on each one, shouting for them to come downstairs.

Like mine, the other personal chambers are supposedly all coloured according to House colours – crimson, gold, bronze, violet, sapphire and emerald. Jack's room, however, which I note is at the other end of the passageway from mine, is decorated in various shades of white and blue, with timber features.

We descend the stairs to the foyer, and Thea, noting we are early, begins to show us other areas of the manor. The healing quarters – which we've already visited – are at the front of the manor. Then there's a study, a small library, three lounging areas, an armoury and lastly the kitchen, where we briefly meet two women who are cooking up a storm. My eyes wander over the ingredients they have ready to make dessert.

*I'm going to like it here*, I think giddily.

Eventually, we finish up at the back of the manor. Thea, Jack and I step into a dining room larger than my old house back in Rubien – the space is lavishly decorated, with a long table set proudly in the middle.

'This is our big dining room,' Thea says, waving towards the table, which is already set. Plates, bowls, cutlery and sapphire serviettes are laid upon the surface, while white candles in the middle are already lit for our arrival. The whole ensemble is beautiful and nothing like I'm used to.

'*Big* dining room? Does that mean there is another dining room somewhere else?' I ask with astonishment.

'This one seats us all.' Our mentor motions to the impressive cushioned chairs. 'The small dining room is attached to our kitchen and is used more for those that come and go. This space, though, is perfect to have big household meals together.'

'Are we allowed to sit anywhere?' Jack asks, pointing to the seats.

'Of course. Take whatever place you'd like. The others shouldn't be much longer. I'll go check if the cooks want a hand with anything.' Thea smiles and exits the chamber in a flurry.

Carefully Jack and I stand behind two chairs next to each other. We don't sit yet, deciding it may look rude without anyone else present.

'What do you think they'll be like?' I ask, but Jack doesn't have a chance to answer my question before we're interrupted by two strong voices arguing about something, becoming louder and louder until they finally stalk into the room.

Sol, who is now clean and looking rather dashing, wears an outfit of brown trousers and a white shirt that is open at the collar. He looks slightly flustered but also highly amused, his skin glowing and more luminous than I remember. His smile gleams mischievously as he turns back to his companion.

Entering behind him is one of the most beautiful females I've ever seen. She wears a long silver dress that looks stunning on her. The shiny pewter material clings to her curves, contrasting with her dark complexion. I feel immediately underdressed in the new black trousers I changed into and the red long-sleeved shirt I found hanging in my wardrobe.

My eyes travel over the female's long hair, coils of lustrous green tumbling down her back to her waist, while shorter strands frame her feminine face. Meeting her emerald gaze, I realise I'm staring at the female, her observance of me bright and clearly pleased with my reaction.

'Friends!' Sol's golden eyes flicker to Jack before they land on me. 'Good to see you back on your feet.'

The female slides up to the Celestial's side and gives him a not-so-subtle elbow to the side.

He smirks at her. 'Always so eager.'

'Sol.' She gives him a stern look, and he motions towards me and my guardian.

'Fine. Meet our lovely Severed of the Hex – Olive Atterley. She is from the House of Glass,' Sol says, motioning to his female companion.

The residents of the House of Glass, from what Jack told me while I got dressed into something not stained or ripped, are called Severed because demon blood courses through their veins. Having once been angels, demons were thrown out of the heavens and fell straight here, to the land of Sennastone, where they dispersed through the six earth kingdoms. They are supposedly unpredictable beings but very powerful allies. I'm careful to keep my distance, in case I unknowingly displease her.

'Jack Wilde.' Olive smiles pleasantly, taking his forearm in her grasp. She twists it gently before letting go.

I lift a brow to Sol, but he only smiles. A normal Severed greeting, then, I assume.

My guardian's ears turn unnaturally pink from her touch, although he does well to pretend she has no effect on him. I try to hide my amusement when he eventually meets my gaze. His neutral expression hardens as if he is trying his very best not to give in to her pleasing appearance – his lack of trust in everyone and everything has been evident since arriving here in Tealwaters.

Finally, the Severed turns towards me, and I can't help the feeling of my body becoming more alert under her piercing gaze.

'And Scarlet Seraphine,' she says, stepping forward and reaching for my arm. Her delicate fingers skim my elbow. I do well to copy her, remembering the gesture for the future. Her touch is unexpectedly tender and warm. Her gleaming smile is infectious as she looks down at me. Her height, I note, is close to Sol's and Jack's. 'It's so wonderful to finally meet you.'

'Understatement of the year,' Sol scoffs, earning a razor-sharp look from the female. 'She's been prattling on about you for *weeks* now, Scarlet. I'm surprised she hasn't peed herself seeing you.'

Olive pulls back from me to slap him on the arm in a playful manner. 'For your information, Sol, I made sure to visit the ladies' room before I came to dinner.' She glances at me with an amused grin – far from embarrassed. 'Don't listen to him. He's full of drivel most of the time.'

'I won't.' I smirk mechanically, feeling my throat tighten slightly.

*They've known each other for weeks?*

Briefly I turn towards Jack, who doesn't seem to notice my inward doubt. These people have already been working and training together, while we strolled in without a clue about any of them. *Shit.* Talk about them having the upper hand on us.

'Olive will spin any tale to make me look bad,' Sol insists, waving his hands around.

The pair share a long look, and I feel a prickle of something between them. I smile unconsciously, sensing the buzz they no doubt feel too.

Sol is the first to break the connection, taking a seat opposite me at the table and making himself comfortable. Olive goes to sit next to him without missing a beat.

'Also, I wouldn't be too worried about formalities tonight. It's only us and the Spark sisters – the others won't be coming,' Sol announces nonchalantly.

I try not to show my relief as Jack asks, 'Why is that?'

Olive shrugs before sharing a look with Sol. 'Rusty went to investigate Gwenore Forest to find out what targeted Scarlet this morning with the inkberry. We all think Gwen was playing her tricks as usual, but he's not convinced.'

'I see,' my guardian replies, twisting his mouth in thought.

There is certainly a long list of people who would want to see me harmed, but the thought that they have followed me here is troubling.

Olive shrugs, giving me an apologetic look. 'The Briar is always on the move – unable to sit still. I'd wager he's being paranoid or enjoys the excuse of having some alone time.'

'A lone-wolf kind of guy?' my guardian asks.

'You could say that,' Olive confirms.

'As for the other two, you'll meet them soon enough,' Sol says, draping his arm across the empty seat beside him.

'Ivy may be back later this evening, maybe not. She's currently at home, making the most of having family around. Her House – the House of Bane – resides here in Tealwaters.'

I nod, feeling I'd do the same if we had all gathered in my homeland first. I'd make the most of my time with my siblings, my new niece and nephew and, of course, Ruby. Gloominess washes over me as I think of them all and what I'll be missing out on now I'm not there.

'And Peri ...' Sol hesitates, earning an encouraging nod from Olive. 'Peri is a mystery. He doesn't seem to like people very much – or crowds. So don't take his actions to heart – it's nothing personal, I don't think.' Sol offers us a reassuring smile, attempting to be diplomatic but also truthful about what to expect.

'Right,' I say with a curt nod. 'Well, I'm quite glad it's a small turnout, to be honest. Today has been absolute madness, and the thought of having to meet even more new people had me worried for a moment.'

Olive smiles knowingly, her emerald eyes sparkling. 'I'm glad I'm not the only one who felt that way. And I'm so pleased to see you finally arrive. I've been a bit lonely without another female around. The males have definitely taken over.'

'You only feel lonely because you never get your way,' Sol jests, making the Severed roll her eyes.

'Well, now Scarlet is here, you better watch your back, angel face. I'm sure I'll be getting much more of what I want in future.'

'You wish.' Sol wiggles his brows as Carmen and Thea enter, trays of steaming food in their hands.

'Dig in!' Thea calls out with excitement.

What I thought would be a tense and awkward evening meeting new people turns into something rather the opposite. Delicious food is served; a flavoursome, bubbly pink drink is poured into tall crystal glasses; and conversation flows easily across the table.

Hours later I find the tightness within my mind and muscles since arriving slowly easing. Subtly I turn towards Jack, who adds to the conversation timidly every now and then, the walls he's built around himself with these people lowering briefly. I imagine us in a few years' time, surrounded by people we trust, still together. I smile to myself.

Seeming to catch my affectionate surveillance, Olive studies me from across the table. She raises a brow pointedly at Jack before taking a sip of her drink. I stiffen, finding a secret smile upon her lips. My hand unconsciously twists the bronze bracelet around my wrist as if to remind myself of Ruby and her warning.

*Love always finds its way to the surface. It is a wonderful feeling to face but something you must hide if you ever experience it. The Elder Raven has spies. She has people undercover to stop anything that occurred from happening again.*

I relax my features and smile at the Severed, scolding myself for letting my feelings slip for the barest of moments. *Not again,* I tell myself. *It will not happen again.*

5

Early the next morning, I'm standing with Jack and Carmen at the front of the manor. Our mentor waves her hands, and the double doors, crafted from thick timber and painted a deep midnight blue, close by themselves with a definitive thud.

'Don't dally. We shouldn't be late,' she calls, walking along the front garden path, either side filled with an abundance of flowers.

Jack and I make haste to keep up with her.

'Where are we going?' my guardian asks as we come to a white picket fence.

Carmen opens the small gate for us and motions us through before facing down the road, where two horse-drawn carriages are waiting. 'To the House of Bane. A lot of our work and training will be conducted there. From experience, Thea and I think it benefits you fledglings to see the other Houses and to mingle with their residents. It's good to build positive relationships, as you never know when you may need them in the future.'

She gives us a knowing look, making my insides spark

with excitement. To be able to compare my House to others will be not only fascinating but favourable. The more I learn, the better I'll be as the next Raven of the Hex.

*And the House of Bane will likely not be underground either,* I think with satisfaction.

As we approach the fancy-looking transportation, I keenly watch the gorgeous geldings that stand patiently, their golden tails flicking from side to side to keep the flies at bay. Two coachmen feed them sugar cubes and chat to each other, patting the horses fondly.

Beside the carriages, giving them no notice, is the Hex – all five members – with Thea lingering beside them. My palms begin to sweat, as I know I'll be meeting the entire group today.

'Boys in one. Girls in the other,' Carmen instructs as she walks through the middle of the gathering, motioning for the males to follow Thea, who hops into the front carriage.

I find myself beside Olive and give her a polite greeting before my eyes land on the female I've yet to officially meet – Ivy. I admire her sapphire hair, the way it falls in soft waves to her shoulders. Then I meet her equally bright blue eyes, which study me with intense scrutiny. She wears a stunning outfit of pure white and deep blue that shows off her assets. She has a good physique, but it's her cold stare that intimidates me more than anything.

'Good morning,' I offer, but she simply ignores me and steps up into the second carriage.

Olive dips her head down close to mine, her voice low so as not to be overheard. 'Meet Ivy Wynters – Nightshade of the Hex and ice queen of Tealwaters.'

The rest of us bundle into the carriage. Olive and I are on one side, while Carmen and Ivy sit opposite. I try to keep my eyes averted from the Nightshade, her obvious distaste for my presence making me slightly nervous. I'm used to others not liking me, but I was hoping to make a good first impression.

As everyone converses about weapons and clothes, future training sessions and the glorious weather, I can't help but appreciate the intricate detailing on the inside of the carriage. My hand slowly runs over the grey cushioned seats we sit upon before rising to the white velvet ceiling, which feels soft to the touch. By the smell of it, the impressive and recently polished wooden flooring beneath my boots has been cleaned to utter perfection.

'Have you been locked in a cage your whole life?' Ivy asks, her voice devoid of emotion.

I peer up questioningly, thinking of all the better questions she could have asked that wouldn't have sounded so rude.

'You look at everything as if it's the first time you've seen it.'

'That's because it *is* the first time I've seen everything,' I respond, trying my best to stay civil. Ivy doesn't know my background, and I don't know hers, but the female's tone needs some serious improvement.

'You have never been inside a carriage?' the Nightshade asks, face screwed into horror.

'People in Rubien don't use the same methods of transportation as you do. The most we have is portals, and even then they are rare.' I shrug, feeling self-consciousness ripple through me with the way she stares with bewilderment.

The Nightshade shakes her head, her loose sapphire locks swaying around her unimpressed face.

*What is her problem?*

'Know this,' Carmen starts, turning to the Nightshade. Her dark brown eyes bore into her – a look I would shrivel under at that close proximity. 'Not everyone will be as priv-ileged as you, Ivy. Be kind to others, as you never know what their circumstances are.'

The females stare each other down, the darkest brown eyes meeting the most vivid blue. I'm observing them to make sure a fight doesn't occur when a flicker of movement causes me to study Ivy. Along her jaw blooms several miniature flowers on her skin, the sapphire blossoms unfurling slowly as if in warning.

*What the fuck is that?* I think wildly, finding myself edging away from her.

I glance at Olive, but she doesn't seem to notice.

'Privileged?' Ivy scoffs. How she isn't intimidated by Carmen right now is beyond me. 'You know nothing about me, Sorceress Spark.'

*Sorceress Spark?*

I tuck that little piece of information away but keep my eye on Ivy's face. The flowers trail down her neck and up to her temple, her skin slowly being taken over by the indigo blooms.

Carmen decides not to answer but gives the Nightshade one last lingering look before turning my way. 'Don't feel you need to hide your awe, Scarlet. Ivy will learn to get used to it.'

I glance at the blue-haired beauty to find she's already staring daggers my way – probably blaming me for getting herself in trouble. A small part of me is glad she received a scolding. Perhaps from now on she'll be more mindful of others.

'This carriage *is* rather luxurious, though,' Olive says, raising her hand as I did before and stroking the velvet lining. 'I've only been in a carriage a few times, and they have never looked as lovely as this.'

My mouth tugs up at her attempt to relate to me. She's doing her best to put me at ease with my inexperience, and I'm silently grateful for it.

'We're here,' Carmen announces, making us all look out the window.

*Thank the higher powers for that.*

6

We travel towards a large establishment with multiple levels, the front a mass of windows covering the stone structure, with green vines that trail in between and cover the entire building from roof to ground. Our carriage stops, and the door is opened for us. The coachman offers his hand as we all escape the tense confines of the cab.

The property looms high above us, looking imposing and extravagant. If I thought Hex Manor was grand, this place is magnificent. I can see why Ivy is used to splendour. With a home like this, it's no wonder she turns her nose up at anything less than lavish.

'Welcome to the House of Bane, ladies. Ivy, would you like to tell your fellow fledglings a little about your home?' Carmen asks, giving the Nightshade a stern no-nonsense look.

Something prickles between them, but Ivy doesn't bite back like I expect her to. Her jaw, once covered in flowers, is now clear, making me wonder if I imagined them.

'The House of Bane used to be a private school for the rich and noteworthy,' the Nightshade begins, as if reciting a textbook. She walks forward along the gravel path made up of light-coloured stones. The males and Thea join our group to listen in on her insightful speech. 'The structure was built hundreds of years ago by the royal family so their children could be educated in a place of high security close to home.'

Ivy points north. I follow her finger, and in the far distance, I can spot the tall spires of an opulent castle.

'That is Ivory Castle, residence of the royal family.' Ivy's face pinches slightly before smoothing out a second later. If I'd blinked, I would have missed the sudden flicker of sorrow upon her tanned face. 'We are a two-minute walk from the ocean. Our beaches are the most spectacular throughout Sennastone, and travellers come here to sit and watch the water all day,' Ivy continues, pointing west, where the breeze comes in. The smell of sea and salt is potent at Hex Manor, so I'm not surprised by how close we are. 'We come across many marine creatures, such as orcas, dolphins, seals and turtles. We've even had a visit from the occasional lost mermaid.'

The Spark sisters chuckle at this, perhaps having experienced such a thing before. But studying the group around me, I note only one person who doesn't join in the amusement.

The mysterious Peri.

He looks guarded, his dark violet eyes flickering over our surroundings as if he expects something to come charging at us. He's similar to Jack in build, but instead of fair locks like my guardian's, his hair is of the darkest purple, tied away from his face in a half-up, half-down style.

He appears well built, his covered arms corded like Sol's, but his obvious power is somehow dimmed by the clear apprehension written across his pale face. Considering he's been living at Hex Manor for weeks now, I would have thought he would feel some sort of camaraderie with at least one person. But from the distance he puts between himself and the group, it's evident he doesn't.

As if sensing my thoughts, Peri glances my way and quickly averts his violet eyes once he finds me inspecting him. *Interesting.*

'We are also able to marvel at the occasional ship that passes our shores from the top storey of our home,' Ivy says, not noticing my lack of attention. 'But be warned of pirates and sirens if you visit the beach – they are the creatures you *don't* want to come across, and they won't hesitate to cause you harm if you linger.'

'Sounds exciting,' Sol jests, earning a smirk from Rusty.

Ivy leads us towards the once-private school, and the extravagant front doors made of dark driftwood open by themselves as if expecting our arrival. I feel rather than see Jack's presence close by – a lingering shadow as we enter this new location.

A woman with long sapphire hair stands in the centre of the reception space, hands clasped as she waits for us to step inside. Her bright blue eyes watch us carefully, probably making assumptions about each of us, her sharp gaze lingering on each member of the Hex until it lands on me.

It's as if she's readied herself for this moment as she takes me in. Her breathing becomes shallow, and her hands clench slightly. With her subtle shuffling and the accelerating rate of her heart, she seems uneasy at the very sight of me.

'Welcome, fledglings,' she says, ending our tense moment, her voice strong regardless of her body's tells. 'And welcome to our lovely home, the House of Bane. I am the Elder Nightshade, and I am so thrilled to meet you all finally. Ivy has told me much about you all, and I am very excited to share your time here in Tealwaters.'

I scan the group until I find Ivy. Jack and I haven't been here long enough for her to spill her thoughts about us, but from our interactions in the carriage, I have lost any hope of gaining a favourable word from her.

The Elder Nightshade approaches Carmen first, shaking hands with our mentor before doing the same with Thea. They all look very comfortable with each other, the women talking quickly among themselves. I can tell from their relaxed demeanours that they've known each other for a long time.

'Let us start with a small tour. I will tell you all about the magic behind our House and what it means to be a Nightshade,' the Elder says, motioning for our group to follow her.

She wears a long cloak-like robe that has no sleeves but spreads out behind her like the train on a gown. Our steps echo around the high ceilings. The floor is made of light-coloured marble, and the various arched windows bring in lots of light.

Jack and I make sure to trail at the back of the group, a habit from the House of Raven but one that I don't mind keeping up. In a strange and new place like this, anything can happen, and having our backs turned to the wrong people can be deadly.

'Can anyone tell me what magic we Nightshades share? Something we are genetically born with?' the Elder asks, looking over her shoulder as we amble through a gallery – noticeably avoiding my gaze.

'Due to the unicorn blood you all possess which has healing properties, Nightshades have the ability to digest poison without harmful effects,' Rusty answers, earning a proud nod from the older female.

Sol gives him a playful thumbs-up.

'That's right. Like every House, we all share a power, and then we have our additional, unique abilities that set us apart from the rest. However, we are quite different from our fellow Houses. We do not possess any individual gifts until we hit adulthood.'

I lift a brow, having never heard of this before. In the House of Raven, we are born how we are to grow up. My family is blessed with fire magic, and as each member matures, they learn to wield the element – with some accidents along the way. I was born with a scar along my palm and was warned when danger came from as early as I can remember.

'Is this the same for dameer?' I whisper to Jack, who shakes his head.

'Not necessarily. I think it depends on the family lineage. Mine all receive their magic at puberty, but I have distant cousins who got theirs as soon as they could walk.'

As we travel deeper down identical corridors, we pass classrooms that hold row upon row of tables. Sitting silently are Nightshades bent over pieces of paper as they scribble away. Curious glances are thrown in our direction when they hear our presence.

Next, we peek inside a chamber that holds several small round tables with chequered boards sat on top, two chairs facing each other. It's full of people, groups cheering and others observing with keen eyes.

'This is our recreation room. As you can see, most of our youths are fond of chess. We excel at it naturally, but against each other, it's rather enjoyable to watch,' the Elder Nightshade says with a soft smile as she lets us examine the busy room.

'Have you ever played chess?' Rusty asks from behind, his figure looming over me as we peer inside the chamber.

The others – besides Jack – in our group have already wandered off.

'No. I don't really know what it is,' I admit.

'It's a game of strategy. I'll teach you sometime if you want,' he offers, making me blink in surprise.

'Okay.' I shrug, feigning nonchalance as the Briar stalks off.

Jack purses his lips. 'I can play chess.'

'You can?'

'Yes. My father taught me.' A flicker of his pale eyes lets me know he's thinking of Mr Wilde when he was alive.

'Perhaps you can give me a lesson one day, then.'

He nods, pleased.

I hide my smile, seeing his mood brighten slightly.

Finally we get to the end of a hallway where it seems busiest in the House of Bane. A set of white double doors opens up to reveal males and females, all with the same sapphire hair as Ivy, darting around the room, all wearing a variety of safety clothing.

'Welcome to the infirmary. We have everything a usual clinic in Tealwaters would have.'

The Elder waves her hand around the space, and it's a similar sight to the healing quarters back in Hex Manor, but ten times bigger. Clean beds line one side of the room, while tables of equipment and bubbling substances cover the other side.

'If the hospitals ever overflow for some reason, we are capable of taking patients here,' Ivy adds, enjoying all the impressed expressions.

We walk around the perimeter of the clinic, and my gaze roams over the beds that are occupied by Nightshades. They have a variety of wounds – most have burns, while others have welts and other strange skin rashes. I wrinkle my nose, wondering how they got them.

Along the walls are shelves stacked high with glass jars filled with unsavoury-looking substances, tatty old books that could be close to hundreds of years old and cages with a whole range of insects stuck inside.

'What are they for?' I ask, pointing to a small enclosure that holds several differently patterned moths.

My question catches the attention of a Nightshade who works nearby, her bright blue eyes peering up to see what I'm referring to.

'Those are a rare kind of moth, called the Loosro moth. They can produce silk which is hard to come by here.' The female lowers her attention to me, her heart pounding, but she pretends she's fine. I admire her ability to keep the fear out of her voice and make an effort to keep my distance for her sake.

'Do you catch them yourselves?' I ask, sensing the Hex watching our conversation. Jack is near my side, taking his role as guardian seriously with so many strangers around.

'Yes. Every member of the House of Bane migrates around the kingdom every year, and that's when we collect whatever we can for the next twelve months. Herbs and spices, insects and other small creatures, leaves and bark, copious amounts of animal bones and also an array of plants. Then we store them all here for anything we may need them for.'

'Bones?' I wrinkle my nose.

She nods eagerly. 'Yes. You would be surprised what crushed rabbit bones can do for a sore throat.'

My eyes widen at this piece of knowledge.

'Moving on,' Ivy mutters, giving the female an annoyed look.

To my delight, the female gives her an unbothered expression before turning around to her work once more.

'Thank you for explaining,' I whisper, ignoring the

Nightshade of the Hex. 'We don't have anything like this back in the House of Raven. This is all very different from what I'm used to.'

'You're very welcome,' the female murmurs back, eyeing up the group behind me.

They are now listening to what the Elder is saying about the rows of beds that are used for any patients that may require healing, and the concoctions that are most used.

'I'm Scarlet.' I don't offer my hand, suspecting she won't take it, but when she offers me hers, I'm happy to oblige.

'I'm Foxglove, but you can call me Fox,' the female answers.

'What is that you are working on?' I point to a small ball that is set in a dish. It's dark grey in colour and shiny in appearance.

'I'm working on a type of bomb.'

I blink. 'A *bomb*?'

She nods eagerly. 'We've perfected the smoke bomb and the explosive bomb, but I want to experiment and see what happens if I add different substances, such as metal or poison goo, to the device.' She chuckles at my horrified expression. 'It's all done in a safe environment, and I make sure to test them without any guests around.'

She says the word *guests* as if it's inconvenient that I'll be affected by her bomb if it is filled with some toxic gas.

'Is this something you do normally? Create things for the fun of it?'

'For fun and for work. Imagine,' Fox declares, eyes brightening with the opportunity to talk of her projects. 'You're the next Raven of the Hex. You take out this small ball.' She lifts the dark grey sphere from her work counter and acts out her story. 'And you smash it to the ground. It helps conceal your escape or, depending on the type of bomb, injures your opponents. The possibilities are endless.' She throws the ball in the air and catches it.

I flinch away, wondering what will pour out of it if she accidentally drops it. 'Wow.'

She nods in agreement. 'Wow indeed. Plus it helps that the sovereigns are backing my idea. Otherwise, I'd be working on something far less exciting.' She points to the table three over from where we stand. 'Oleander over there is working on non-melting butter,' Fox explains with a flat look, clearly unimpressed by the idea that she could've been in Oleander's shoes.

'The king and queen ask for all these things to be made?' I ask curiously, eyeing up the other inventions on her desk – they all look as harmless as the small bomb, but I suspect they aren't.

'Or their son, the heir. Prince Athos comes by more often than our rulers.' Fox rifles through some papers on her desk, looking for something. 'We have been outlining projects for years now for all sorts of marvellous gadgets. Extendable chains, enchanted rope, blindfolds that also muffle sound ...' Fox finally finds the paper she needs and points to a drawing in the middle. From what I can gather, it's a suit made of some sort of colourful scale – from a fish, perhaps.

'Armour?' I guess.

'That's right. This is made from mermaid scales – super hard to obtain but very valuable. Their tails are made of one of the strongest materials in the world, alongside dragon scales. They cannot be penetrated by weapons such as javelins or even cut by the sharpest of blades.'

'Has this been made yet?' I ask, thinking of the poor mermaids who will be hunted for such armour.

Fox shakes her head, leaning forward and watching our

surroundings carefully. 'No, but between you and me, I'm quite glad. It's exciting to come up with all these unique ideas, but I don't want to go as far as killing creatures for our creations. Our House is here to provide a service to our kingdom and its residents, not to devastate it.'

I place my hands on my hips as she places her papers down. A pile of paper sits with several drawings on each sheet, arrows coming off the designs Fox has conjured up, explaining each part and what materials they will be made of.

'It seems strange a prince would be willing to chase mermaids down for something as trivial as this. I agree that protective gear is important, but not at the cost of the suffering of others,' I concur, making her nod in under-standing.

'It may be strange, but he's asked for all sorts of wild and wonderful things. I personally think he enjoys the creation aspect more than utilising them.' Fox shrugs.

We lapse into silence for a moment before I point to a small design in the corner of one of her pages of notes. 'Is this something else you've come up with?'

She shakes her head, chuckling as if I've amused her. 'No. It's just a symbol I saw once.'

'Looks like a flower,' I say, making the Nightshade tilt her sapphire head. The drawing is of three triangles, each connected by a point, all facing the same direction.

'What flowers have you seen?' She snorts. 'I thought it looked more like the head of a windmill.'

I mirror her and twist my head to see if the new angle will help. 'Nope. It's a flower,' I jest, making her laugh.

The Hex starts to move on, so I wave the Nightshade farewell. 'Well, it's been nice chatting to you, Fox. Good luck with the bomb.'

'Don't be a stranger, Scarlet,' Fox calls out before I race to catch up with the group.

## 7

The Elder Nightshade leads us into a separate room off the infirmary. Here it's quiet, and several tables are arranged in a classroom-like manner.

'This is one of many labs you'll see throughout the building,' the Elder says, patting the nearest table and watching as Carmen and Thea take a seat together at the front. 'Today your mentors and I thought it would be a good bonding exercise to get you experimenting with some substances and see how much you know already.'

My eyes flicker to Jack, thinking of a time we had a rack of deadly potions in front of us that I had to drink. He seems to be remembering the same thing, as his silver-blonde head slowly turns my way.

'Pair up, and we can get started.'

Instinctively I head for Jack, but Olive stands in my line of sight.

'Can I go with you?' she asks innocently.

I don't have the confidence to say no, nor a good enough reason to turn her down.

*It will benefit you to make allies*, I tell myself. So I nod good-naturedly and end up sitting next to the Severed.

We are handed racks of tubes, bowls of smooth lotions and unusual-smelling liquids in a dish. The green-eyed female and I exchange inquisitive looks.

'Do not fret,' the Elder Nightshade says. 'All the ingredients you have been given cannot harm you. The worst you can do is give someone a lingering headache if you give them your creation. The best that can happen is giving them glowing skin.'

The room laughs, my lab partner included. Everyone shuffles into place and begins their task. My eyes gaze sidelong to my fellow Hex member, watching her graceful movements.

'I can feel you staring.' Olive smiles when she meets my gaze, leaning forward slightly. 'I don't bite, Scarlet, ask me your burning questions.'

My mouth tugs up in answer. 'Who says I have questions?'

'Your face shows your immense curiosity. I would be surprised if you didn't.'

'All right, I do have at least *one* question I've been wondering about.'

'Go on,' she encourages.

'When we were travelling in the carriage, did you happen to notice any flowers on Ivy's face?' I study her closely out of the corner of my eye, wondering if I was in fact imagining things or if Ivy revealed a Nightshade trait.

'Oh, them. Yes,' Olive says with a casual wave of her hand. 'The flowers on Ivy's skin are poisonous – one touch, and you'll drop dead in minutes. When she gets testy, you'll notice them springing up. If you don't touch them, you have nothing to worry about.'

'Her flowers can kill people?' I blurt, earning a glance from the Nightshade herself. I can tell by her sour expression that she knows we are talking about her.

'Yes, so I suggest you keep your distance if you ever see her flare up,' Olive confirms. 'I heard she nearly killed a dameer who got too close for comfort once.' She peers at Ivy, and I follow suit.

'Do all Nightshades have that gift?' I ask, finding relief when Olive shakes her head.

'No. That's her unique ability, which is terrifying when you know what she's like.'

I purse my lips before eyeing the Severed. 'And what about you? What can *you* do?'

'I can create and manipulate glass.' She shrugs as if this isn't the most impressive thing I've ever heard.

'*Pardon?*'

'Glass,' she repeats, pointing to the row of windows along the room.

'So you could shatter them without touching them?' I gape, looking between them.

'I could. Or bend them to my will.'

'I'm officially very envious right now.' I pout, earning a chuckle from her.

We sit in silence for a few moments before the Severed asks, 'Have you any experience with this type of thing?' Olive glances at me briefly before taking a tube of gold liquid.

I take hold of a tube the colour of Gwenore Forest – deep green with flecks of orange – and make sure to avoid the red vial that gives me the jitters. 'I've never been too handy with potions and poisons. The best I can do is tell what plants to eat and what ones to stay far away from – but only in Hanrah. It seems I've yet to learn about Tellian nature,' I answer, thinking of the inkberry incident.

I study the Severed's delicate fingers as they pick several items to mix together. She looks like she knows what she is doing.

I take a spatula of dirt-brown cream and blend it with my green liquid. It starts to thicken, and small black dots appear. I frown. It doesn't look right.

'If what you say is true, that surprises me,' Olive admits, chuckling softly. 'I thought Ravens would be naturally talented at everything.'

'I'm sure they tell everyone that, but no. We are just like anyone else.'

She snorts. 'You are *not* like anyone else,' she says, elbowing my side playfully. 'The House of Raven is made up of *vampire* blood. Do you know how amazing that is? I'd love to have the heightened senses you all have.'

I've never wished away my ability to see further, to hear from longer distances or to smell the faintest of scents. Olive is right. It is quite the impressive quality to possess.

'All right, you got me there,' I confess with a bashful shrug.

Olive forgets her concoction, lifting her spatula up and pointing it my way. 'And don't forget you can drink blood as well as normal human food. You can survive in *any* situation. All my House can do is sense dead things and locate graveyards.'

I turn to face her fully. '*What?*'

'As half-demon beings, we can sense those who have died or are close to death. So I can point you in the direction of the closest cemetery just from a feeling I get in my stomach.' She places her hands upon her middle, clutches a roll of skin and shakes it.

I give her a questioning look, refraining from actually saying the question I have spinning through my mind out loud.

She sighs. 'The closest cemetery is a short walk north-east.' She points for good measure, making me break out into an impressed grin.

'You make it sound like that couldn't be useful,' I reply, trying to brighten her mood.

'What use do you have for a graveyard, Scarlet?'

I ponder this a moment, finding my mixture is starting to smell strangely pleasant. I sneak a look at the other tables, and the other concoctions are, to my relief, similar to mine in texture but have turned out different colours.

'It would be good if you had a dead body you needed to dispose of quickly,' I offer.

'Yes. So helpful.' Olive rolls her eyes playfully.

'It would be in the House of Raven.' I force a smile, but her body tenses, becoming instantly wary.

'I don't need you to confirm whether your House is as brutal as people say, but is it frightening living there? Or is it normal for you?' she asks, leaning in as if somehow knowing I'd not want others to listen in.

'Frightening? Yes, it is at times,' I answer honestly, thinking of all the occasions when I wished to run away and never look back. 'Is that normal? Unfortunately, also yes.'

Olive's mouth twists in distaste.

'How is everyone going?' the Elder interrupts. She strolls over to each table and comments on each substance. 'These all look great. But now we must test them out. If you can please dip your hands in and smear your concoction on an area of your skin ...'

Silence.

'It's safe,' Thea promises, smearing her mixture of dark blue onto the back of her hand. When she's done, the dark substance seems to harden, spiderwebbing across her knuckles.

'What you have in front of you is different-scented skin remedies made of natural ingredients. Like I said, you may walk away with a minor headache if you don't agree with the scent, but you'll have glowing skin.' The Elder chuckles as she watches each of us muster up the courage to follow our mentor's lead.

'I dare you to smother your face in it.' I point to Olive's yellowish-brown mix.

'Only if you do it first.' She's delighted by my comment for some reason, and I find I enjoy her reaction, her emerald eyes glimmering with merriment.

I dip my hands into my dark green mix and smudge it over my cheek dramatically, finding Olive staring at me with utter glee.

'You look like a troll,' she blurts before releasing a strangled laugh, covering her mouth with a hand to try to keep it contained.

'Charming. And here I was about to compliment your looks,' I huff with good humour.

I take a lump of her concoction and slap it on her forehead, causing her body to shake, a howl of laughter escaping from her lips.

8

It seems every day I will find something new to explore. Today I find myself standing in front of a barn. Hex Manor, to my delight, has its own set of stables, and the moment I learn of its existence, I'm rushing off in search of it. Jack opens the doors, and inside are some of the most beautiful horses I've ever seen, with honey-coloured coats that shine like polished wood and hair as golden as Sol's. I'm instantly approaching each of them and introducing myself, hoping we will be fast friends.

Jack watches from the entrance with his toned arms crossed, his ocean-blue gaze roaming over the structure as if at any moment it may collapse.

'Lighten up, guardian,' I call out from inside a stall, checking the feet of a mare. Her hooves look in pristine condition, and I wonder if we have workers here on the premises who also take care of the animals.

'It's my job to keep you safe. I'll lighten up when I know for a fact we are far from any danger,' he answers calmly.

I peer over the stall door to watch him. Since leaving the House of Raven, he's been more reserved – not with me personally but in general, and noticeably with the others.

I'm used to the Teacher and his ease, to his witty quips and casual demeanour. But now I observe him as suspicion coats his features even when he approaches a stallion in its pen.

'Tell me what worries you,' I say, earning his attention. I lean my forearms on the door. The horse behind me – who I've learned is called Mira – nudges my leg, sniffing intently for treats.

Jack turns slowly and gives me a pointed look. 'Everything.'

'Be more specific,' I press.

He wanders over and places his hands on either side of me. His face is near mine, and I can't help but let my eyes trail down to his pursed lips. He doesn't notice my perusal of him, appearing deep in thought.

'Since setting foot here in Tealwaters, I've felt nothing but uneasiness.' Jack shuffles and averts his eyes. 'All these new people and places ...'

'It's a lot to process. No one expects you to feel comfortable straight away,' I assure him, placing a hand on his. 'Trust me. I know better than anyone what it's like to suspect the company I hold of something sinister. I think after everything we have been through, it's normal.'

I can tell he is processing my words, the cogs in his mind turning. Eventually, he faces me once more, content to stare straight at me. I feel his gaze heavy on my face, his curiosity evident.

'Say what is on your mind, guardian,' I murmur, allowing my gaze to wander over his features. Sapphire stares back at me, unexpected doubt filling them. 'We are in this together, remember?'

'I trust you with my life, you know that right?'

The words make me pause. My heart flutters with nerves.

'Yes and you know that I trust you in return,' I offer.

He nods thoughtfully. 'Being here, with you … I'm trying to relax, trying to fit into this new routine but I feel so on edge *all* the time. All I can think about is who will harm us next, who will potentially rip us apart again.'

My eyes lift to meet his. I swallow. 'I wager that feeling will never end with a job like ours, Jack. We are always going to have enemies.'

'I know,' he relents, finding the truth behind my words.

'This is new for both of us. Take your time to adjust. I know I certainly am.'

'It's all so different to Rubien, isn't it?' He ponders, eyes roaming over the barn we stand within. 'The climate for one, the noises, the constant smell of the ocean.'

'I lay awake at night just listening,' I admit, making my guardian lean closer. 'They have so many different types of birds here and I can't wait to learn what all of them are.'

'I'll learn them all with you,' he offers, making my cheeks heat.

*Holy Hanrah.*

I clear my throat, needing a moment to distance myself from his intense gaze. Turning back to Mira I readjust her saddle, feeling my guardian's eyes on me still. 'I've come to realise there are so many dangers in this world. But there are also many *beautiful* things too. Maybe we should focus more on those instead of dwelling on the "what ifs".'

'I'll try my best,' he muses, amusement lining his words.

'That's good enough for me. And besides we won the fucking Hex Trials. If we can do that, what *can't* we do?'

We share an uncertain moment, the trials something we've not spoken about since arriving in Tealwaters. Does Jack have nightmares as often as I do? Do small things remind him of the times we nearly lost our lives? Or is it only me that feels so afraid of remembering those times that I try my best to block them out in hopes I'll eventually forget them all?

'I know something we can't do,' Jack counters, bringing me out of my thoughts.

I lift a brow. 'And what is that?'

'We can't fly,' he says, his head tilting in thought. 'We also can't read minds ...'

I narrow my eyes in feigned annoyance. 'Why must you ruin—'

'I don't know about you but I can't touch my toes either,' he interrupts with a grin.

'Urgh!' I turn my back on Jack, hiding my smile from him.

'We also can't—'

I spin so fast and open the stall door with such force the gate nearly comes off its hinges. Jack's face splits into laughter at the sight of my expression.

'One more word out of your mouth—' I proclaim in warning as I chase him, the two of us running around the outside of the barn until we are both puffed out and sweating. Of course I could catch him within moments but I pull back, enjoying the display of contentment my guardian shows.

Jack, like me, was thrown into this new role with no real expectations. He has his troubles, has his worries and that's all right. But I know deep down, together we will conquer them all, together we will hold each other's hands for support and come through the other side stronger than ever. Because that's what our bond was built on from the beginning – trust and belief we can do anything we put our minds to.

9

I'm halfway through adjusting my stirrups when Olive and Sol enter the stables. I sit upon the mare Mira – who I've become quickly attached to – while Jack throws a leg over a tall stallion called Bolt.

I hear the Severed and Celestial chatting before they come around the corner, the couple strolling in casually as if they, too, had the idea of going for a ride. They wear proper riding boots and tidy apparel that rival even the House of Raven's. I find myself wanting a nice new pair of boots, remembering the tatty old ones I left behind in Rubien.

'Are you both heading out?' Sol asks, pointing to our steeds.

'Indeed we are,' I answer. 'Do you want to join us?'

I sense Jack stiffen in his saddle, anxiety drenching his body immediately. I feel guilty for putting him through this but know deep down we need to scope our fellow Hex members out. We must determine who is trustworthy, who we can learn to rely on.

'Sure, we'd love that,' Olive replies with a gleaming smile.

For a second, Sol seems mesmerised by it, watching intently until he seems to remember himself. It wouldn't take a genius to know he feels *something* for her.

Within half an hour, we are walking through Gwenore Forest, making sure to keep to the pathways, which apparently Gwenore has no jurisdiction over when it comes to harming us. I'm mesmerised by everything as we pass through the trees, the sunlight shining down in patches across the forest floor. I see the occasional bird, but most of the other creatures I assume are around can probably hear our loud presence and choose to stay out of range.

Olive wiggles her way through the group and rides next to Jack, forcing him to separate from my side. She's not had much time with my guardian, and she seems eager to know more about him. He answers each question reluctantly, hesitant to give her too much information.

'What's your weapon of choice?' the Severed asks.

'Bow and arrow,' Jack replies.

I ease Mira back with a subtle manoeuvre of my reins, watching the conversation unfold, silently wishing for Jack to loosen up. He stays arrow straight in his saddle, never turning towards Olive when he speaks, but I can tell the guardian is on high alert, just in case.

'Is he always so guarded?' Sol murmurs, steering his horse to ride beside mine. The mare is much older compared to the rest of our horses and slightly slower, but the Celestial doesn't seem to mind, letting her walk at her own pace without complaint.

'No. He's still adjusting – as I'm sure you all did when you first arrived.' I give Sol a pointed look, trying to make him recall his first few days. I want Jack to feel comfortable sooner rather than later, but I don't want him to feel rushed or pressured – even if it feels like I'm making more progress than him. 'I think it will take us some time to ease into the Hex lifestyle you all seem so comfortable in.'

'I'm not judging anyone,' Sol protests, putting a hand up in apology. 'I only wonder if even Olive's charms can crack his walls. I tried approaching him after our initial meeting, but he seemed cautious. I merely wanted to make amends in case we got off on the wrong foot.'

The Celestial looks guilty. In the forest, Jack and Sol had met under abnormal circumstances. I know my guardian wouldn't have felt so intimidated if we'd been trying to navigate this strange new place alone, but to have to trust two strange males straight up ... even *I* thought it was unnerving. We had been through the Hex Trials knowing we'd go through some troubling shit, but that trauma doesn't leave a person the moment it ends. It lingers, and Jack's way of coping is doubt and distrust.

'Give him time,' I assure the male. 'Let him adjust at his own pace, and I'm sure he'll come to you. You'll be fast friends after that. Just you wait.'

Sol raises a brow but doesn't argue. He simply turns forward once more as we head for an unknown destination. His skin glows subtly, as if the sunlight above rejuvenates him, and the warmth radiating from him, even from this distance, emanates pleasantly.

'Do you glow all the time or just when you are feeling content?'

The Celestial peers down at his bare arms before shrugging. 'Both?' he answers, making it sound like he's never thought about it before.

'Because I've noticed you glow a lot when you're around Olive.' The moment the words escape my mouth, I wince.

*Way to be subtle*, I scold myself.

Sol smiles as if knowing my angle but doesn't seem mad about it. 'She relaxes me, so I'm not surprised if that's the case. I suppose her presence is comforting – as is yours.'

My cheeks flush at the compliment. We've only known each other for a short amount of time, but I get the impression he's never struggled making friends in the past. His charm alone does a good job of swaying people to favour him. But his friendliness – his willingness to put himself out of his comfort zone to make others feel comfortable – shows those new in his life he's willing to make an effort. Much like he is with me, being honest and open about his feelings when he could be shielding them from me.

'If I had a gold coin for every person who said that to a Raven ...' I say, earning a grin.

'I'm not sure if you're tricking me. Would you be surprisingly rich or dirt poor?'

'I'd have one gold coin,' I confirm, making him laugh.

Jack turns in his seat to see what all the fuss is about. I try to play it down, but Sol is glowing much brighter now, and I find myself squinting slightly.

'What dirty joke did you tell him?' Olive jests. 'He never shines that bright unless it's highly inappropriate.'

'No jokes needed,' I tell the Severed. 'I'm just naturally witty.'

She smiles in approval. 'I can't argue with that.'

A snap of a stick makes me jerk in my saddle. My gaze flickers towards the sound as I pull Mira to a firm stop, the reins tight in my white-knuckled hands.

'It's all right. It was probably a deer,' Sol says in reassurance, stopping his horse too.

But my eyes land on the exact spot I know the sound came from. The stick in question lies by itself in a clearing where no bush surrounds it.

'And how fast do deer run?' I ask the Celestial, earning a quizzical look.

Olive and Jack finally notice we have paused and begin to turn back. Jack's expression of unease is clear as he takes in my rigid demeanour, knowing instantly how on edge I am.

'What is it?' he asks.

With this question, Olive and Sol seem to sober up, realising something isn't right.

'I think something is there, watching us.' I motion towards the clearing, the snapped branch lying on the ground, taunting me with instinctive trepidation. 'A deer I would have spotted, but nothing moved. I think it's still there, waiting for us to pass by.'

Without another word, Jack lifts a hand. His eyes glow bright blue as he creates a tidal wave of water towards where I pointed. I expect something to happen, for a figure or an animal to come into existence, but I'm sorely disappointed.

'Perhaps we should head back,' Jack suggests, riding by me.

I give him a reluctant nod, turning Mira around, but my gaze trails back to the space. I'm unconvinced.

'Let me check, to be safe,' I murmur before Jack protests.

Sol catches my reins, making sure Mira doesn't run away as I land on my feet, and I walk towards the vacant area. My steps are slow and quiet as I make sure to listen for any other movements. My scar doesn't bleed, so I press on. I stop by the stick and stare at it, hoping it will give me answers. I kneel down and pick it up, smelling deeply, but nothing abnormal comes back. If it were a deer, it should smell animalistic, but this – it's lacking in *any* scent.

It can't be Ravens, I surmise. I don't know any with the ability to cloak themselves, and if they were here, watching my every move, my scar would bleed for certain. Their intent would give them away.

I hesitantly get back to my feet, throwing the stick away.

'False alarm,' I call back, knowing full well it's a lie. I head back to my horse, jump on with ease and kick her on. 'I must be paranoid after the inkberry incident,' I explain, earning understanding looks from everyone besides Jack.

He gives me a *we'll talk about this later* face, and I nod.

IO

I sit on my balcony with a cup of tea and a full belly. For dinner, we came together as a team, with the wine flowing, several conversations happening at once and a sunset to die for. We stood outside on the wooden deck to watch the bright rays disappear behind the horizon, observing the pink-and-purple sky darken. It was the most beautiful sight I've ever seen.

With the full moon out, hanging in the dark blue sky, I finally decide to head to bed. I discard my cup on my dressing table and remove the excessive number of pillows from one side of the bed. Just as I pull back the sheet, I pause.

A prickle on the back of my neck alerts me. I peek at my scarred hand, but it's closed.

I stand up tall and head for my wardrobe, where my gold-and-onyx dagger lives. I tell myself to stock up on more weapons tomorrow before I unsheathe my blade and look across my empty room. I step barefoot across the floor with a deathly silence only a vampire can muster, and creep back to the balcony. It's here that I feel the sudden sense I'm being watched again.

Regardless of my scar being clean of blood, I don't take a chance. I throw my dagger, trusting my instincts. The golden blade flies before disappearing into thin air. I hear the thud of steel embedding itself into something soft.

*Where did it go?*

'Fucking seal balls!' someone hisses, making my body move into action without second-guessing.

Despite being in my nightgown, I'm clambering over the railing and jumping off my balcony. My feet sting from the hard ground when I land, but I don't dare stop. I head for where the curse came from in hopes of pinning down the assailant. Throwing an arm out, I'm lucky to connect with a large form. They fall to the ground, flicking back into view.

*Invisibility.*

'Who are you?' I demand, yanking my dagger out from his shoulder and pressing it against his neck. Blood dribbles out from his wound, and I make sure to press on it painfully with my free hand to make him talk.

'Mother of pearl,' he wheezes, pain lining his words. He looks down at my thin and flimsy attire, his Tellian blue eyes widening with something between discomfort and curiosity. 'Oh, why, hello there,' he drawls, his demeanour casual but his scent revealing his underlying fear.

In any circumstance, I'd be embarrassed by my clothing in front of a stranger like him – especially with the burns along my arms and legs showing so starkly under the beaming moon. But at this moment, I don't care. I know without a doubt this is the someone I knew was watching us in Gwenore Forest today. This male – this dameer with the power to render himself unseeable – was observing us. But why?

'Who are you?' I press, edging my face closer to his, my sharp fangs on show to elevate his apprehension. By the sound of his hammering heart, it's doing the trick, but he hides his panic well.

'Alex Irvine,' he replies with a sigh, as if he's had a long and rough day. He tries to shuffle from under me, but I don't let him move a muscle. 'Now lower the blade.'

'If you shift an inch, I'll cut off your ear, and then I'll move on to your nose. Now tell me why you were there in the forest today, and don't deny it. I know it was you keeping tabs on us.'

He considers me a moment, arrogance consuming his features, before he accedes to my demand. 'I've been following you and the other Hex members because I need your help. I was going to approach you before, but I heard Ravens can be quite ...' He glances down at the wound I've given him – the puncture has now stained his shirt and cloak with a dark patch of blood – before motioning with his light eyes towards the dagger across his throat. He grins wickedly, feigned amusement filling his stare. 'Aggressively hands-on.'

It's getting late, and I have a fool with a clear death wish under my knife. 'State your business or be gone, dameer.'

It's as if he flicks a switch within himself. His smirk morphs into distress, the lines in his face deepening with concern. 'My brother is missing. He was taken from his bed, never to be seen again. No one knows where he was taken or why.'

'Are you sure he didn't run away?' I ask, lifting my knife only slightly. 'How old is he?'

'Twelve,' Alex answers with a shake of his head, his hood falling down to reveal silver-blonde hair. 'He would never leave like that, not without taking me with him.'

Sorrow and hard determination fill the dameer's stare, and a twinge of something twists inside my chest. I don't dare release Alex, though. I keep the facade up in case this is all an act.

'And what do you want me to do about it?' I ask calmly, letting my voice lower so no one inside the manor wakes up to this charade.

'I need help finding him. I thought he was the only one, but I've been getting friendly with some of the locals, and a similar thing has happened to other children as well. And to further my suspicions, they are all *dameer*.' He says this as if it's a clue.

I tilt my head, unsure, but my grip is unwavering.

'Are you really going to let an innocent civilian bleed to death in your back garden, or are you going to let me go and hear me out like a Raven of the Hex should?' He huffs brazenly, a challenge in his gaze.

The title clangs through me, and I release him almost immediately. I will have to become used to the unconventional ways people will approach me now I'm to be a member of the most reputable group in the whole of Sennastone. Some will feel uneasy enough to scope out the situation first – Alex being a prime example of this – or come to me or one of the other Hex members in some other strange or peculiar way.

'Let's get you cleaned up,' I say, noting my scar is still silver and deeming him harmless. 'But next time, approach me like a normal person. This sneaking-around business will only get you killed.'

'Noted.' He nods, reluctantly taking my offered hand and getting to his feet. He cringes at the movement of his body, his shoulder evidently hurting him.

I lead him over the back deck and open one of the double doors that lead into the big dining room, where the expansive table sits. Alex barely looks around as we head towards the healing quarters. I open the curtains to the spacious room to let the moonlight in and rummage around for a match. Alex makes himself comfortable on a bed. Once I've found a small box in the chaotic organisation Carmen and Thea think is appropriate for their sickroom, I light two lanterns so we can see better.

Alex is broad, like a swimmer, his shoulders wide, and his now golden-blonde hair is messy from our scuffle. His body language shows slight nervousness, and I feel a twinge of curiosity about the dameer. Perhaps I shouldn't have been so brutal with him, but he doesn't seem offended by my reaction to his visit.

I search the messy counter and several cluttered shelves for any helpful tools. Bringing back a tray of several random items, I motion for him to remove his shirt.

'I know we had an instant connection, but to demand I strip on the first meeting? I thought you were classier than that, Raven.' He wiggles his eyebrows as I sit on the bed opposite him. I give him a deadpan look, and he rolls his eyes. 'You're no fun.'

Without hesitation, he takes off his bloody cloak and his dark shirt beneath. I have a better view of his body, and I study it with mild interest. To my annoyance he is a sight to behold.

Against his tanned skin, the wound looks stark. His chest is toned but in a subtle way, the hairs on his muscled arms rising under my inspection. Pulling my attention away from his build, I study the slashed skin – it's not as bad as I was expecting, but it won't stop oozing crimson.

'Are you checking me out, Raven?' He glows with merriment, his teeth showing as his smile grows, but his heart still hammers. It seems I'm dealing with a dameer who needs humour to deal with his emotions.

'Don't flatter yourself, dameer. You look like every other male I've come across.'

This gets him, his smile faltering for a second. 'Oh, ouch. That hurt worse than the stabbing.'

'Good,' I mutter, unable to hide the lift of my lips. He's funny – I'll give him that.

I take my dagger and cut across my unscarred palm, letting it drip into a glass cup I found. I'm not sure if the goblet is clean, but it will have to do for now.

'Tell me about your brother while I fix you up,' I instruct.

Alex starts without delay, watching carefully as the cup progressively fills with my blood. 'Over a month ago, Ellis went missing. We are close, he and I. We lost our parents just over a year ago, and we've become much closer because of it. But he would never run away. He's as happy as a kid can be at this age. So when I walked into his room to find his bed empty and the window slung wide open, I knew instantly it was kidnap.'

I gaze up at Alex, letting my hand curl into a fist as I finish with my blood, the final drops echoing between us. I offer him the cup, and he holds it with a quizzical face.

'Drink it,' I say, making him scowl.

'But it's your blood,' he protests. He leans forward as if to tell a secret, his bare chest coming closer, with the scent of vanilla and something woodsy. 'This isn't some Raven kink, is it?'

I huff to cover my amusement.

*The audacity of this male.*

'I am part vampire, and vampires have healing properties within their blood. Drink it,' I insist, shoving the cup towards him.

He tips the cup up and swallows the blood down in one. He makes a show of tasting it before handing back the cup with surprise across his features. 'That tastes rather nice. Perhaps if we add a splash of liquor ...'

He smiles when he notices me rolling my eyes for what feels like the fifth time tonight. I wave a hand, wanting him to carry on with his story. 'Keep going.'

'My aunt and uncle – who we live with – were beside themselves with worry at first. Ellis was nowhere to be found. Eventually, the urgency to find him faded, their belief now that he ran away and has decided not to come back home.' He shrugs, playing down his emotions, but I can hear the faint sound of his heart skipping at the mention of his sibling.

'Now you want to try other means to get him back,' I guess.

'My family are not cruel people,' he says, as if to convince himself. 'They tried. They really did, but they are busy people, and I've come to realise if I want an answer to Ellis's whereabouts. I need to find those who will help me get it.'

'The Hex,' I state, getting a clean-looking cloth.

I wash his gash with disinfectant to prevent infection. He curses colourfully when I dab it along his skin, cleaning his wound. I can see that my blood is already working its magic, the injury slowly stitching itself back together.

'I wasn't sure if I had to ask for an audience or if I should approach only one of you ...' Alex trails off, looking down with mild surprise at his improving shoulder. 'I decided I'd follow you, see what you were like before I introduced myself. But you noticed me when I was supposed to be safely hidden, and it scared you.'

I don't answer, not wanting to admit he's right. I was fearful. Fearful that whatever it was would change its mind and attack us – an invisible foe with an obvious advantage.

'So you decided to visit me at night? To scare me half to death before I tuck myself into bed?' I give him a *see where that got you* look.

I bandage up Alex's injury, knowing by morning it will be fully sealed again with the potential of scarring, but he can see a healer to take care of that matter.

'I was going to knock on your window,' he claims, but I cut him off.

'What part of that plan made you think it was a good idea?' I scoff.

He frowns. 'I was thinking—'

'No, you weren't,' I counter. 'Next time, use the front door.'

He looks down at his entwined hands and shakes his head. 'No, definitely not.'

'Why not?' I ask, glancing at his soiled clothes. I hand his shirt back to him, grimacing at the smell of blood upon it.

'Look. Can you help me or not?' Alex asks. 'If Ellis has been taken, he could be in any kind of trouble right now, and the longer I wait …' He doesn't finish his sentence, only swallows thickly. He dips his eyes before mumbling, 'I need you. I need you to believe me and to help me bring my brother back. I made a promise to my mother to look after him, and if something happens, I'll never forgive myself.'

I purse my lips. I know my answer without having to think it through. If my brothers or sisters went missing – whether they'd been taken or had run of their own accord – I'd want answers too. I would comb the lands for them to make sure they were safe.

'I'll help you.'

He looks up so quickly I almost jump back.

'You will?' he murmurs, pure hope written over his tanned features. His hands reach for my head, and he kisses my cheek. The move makes me stiffen, but he doesn't notice.

'Thank you!' He grins, sitting back on the bed.

'But on one condition,' I say, making him pause. He evaded my question about why he wouldn't come to Hex Manor's front door. I assume he wants to keep the hunt for his brother quiet for now.

'And what is that?' He sags slightly on the bed, as if readying himself for a blow to his new-found hope.

'I won't do this without my guardian,' I declare, making him nod slowly, light eyes squinted.

'That's it? Sure. Fine. Whatever you want.'

I give him a nod in return. He sits there watching me intently. The silence grows awkward, and I feel the need to fill it.

'I'm sorry about your shoulder,' I mutter, motioning to his wound. 'My instinct was to act first and ask questions later.'

He shakes his head, amusement lining his lips. 'It's fine. I understand why you reacted that way. I suppose if I'd acted the same way for any girl in the city, they'd all be rather alarmed too.'

'Ravens do not become *alarmed*,' I scoff, mirroring his confidence.

'No?' He chuckles, giving me a superior smirk. 'Could have fooled me.'

I roll my eyes, knowing this debate could go on if I let it. 'I need to rest.'

'Here,' Alex says before rummaging in his cloak pocket. He pulls out a ribbon of bright blue and hands it to me. 'If you need to speak with me, tie this to your balcony, and I'll visit as soon as I can.'

I raise a brow but don't comment. He notices my blank look.

'You'd be surprised how many women need me, especially late at night, but I'll make sure to make you my priority.' He winks.

I give him a look of distaste. 'Charming.'

Carefully I take the sliver of material. It feels silky between my fingers, making a memory of me upon a fire-breathing dragon come to mind. My heart spikes, and my fingers stiffen unconsciously around the strip.

'Are you all right?' he asks, leaning forward, a surprisingly confident hand upon my knee.

I pretend not to hear and attempt to shake the thoughts away, as well as his warm hand. 'I'll make a visit to the city as soon as I can. Perhaps I can find some information as to why your brother's disappearance has been kept so quiet. In the meantime, try and find anything you can about Ellis, any clues from his bedroom or anything that looks amiss from that night.'

He nods. 'I will. Thank you, Scarlet.'

I tilt my head, hoping I'll be as much help as he hopes I'll be.

'Don't thank me yet.'

## II

The Hex is asked to meet at the House of Bane for training. When the other members have all chosen their horses, I hear complaints throughout the barn about the tack and how to put a bridle upon a horse's head.

I peer round the corner, having finished getting Mira ready, to find Rusty grumbling while trying to untangle some reins.

'Do you need a hand?' I offer, shutting Mira in her stall for safekeeping. 'I used to work in a stable. I can show you how to put everything on if you like.'

Rusty gives me a grateful look as I reach out my hand. He obliges and surrenders the bridle to me. I explain how the saddle fits, how to hold the reins and that the metal bit of the bridle goes *in* the horse's mouth, not around its chin.

'You certainly know your stuff,' he muses as I watch him swing up into his seat. His long, muscular legs dangle down, and I help him adjust his stirrups.

'Years of practice.' I smile, patting the stallion – named Hali – on the neck. 'Does the House of Briar not work with horses much?'

Rusty shakes his head. 'Rarely. We rely on portals for travel, or we tend to walk – we enjoy the exercise when possible.'

'Must be nice to have that option,' I say, finally done with his tack. Not sure what to do with my hands, I rest them on my belt, which is stocked up with knives and throwing stars. 'You and Hali are all set.'

Rusty smiles down at me. 'Thank you.'

'You're welcome.'

A while later, I sway in the saddle, my hands relaxed upon Mira's neck. The carriage on our first day here in Teal-waters was a luxury that Thea had rented for us to make the journey to the House of Bane. Apparently, from now on we are to travel on horseback – not that I would complain. I enjoy the slow-paced trip much more than the stuffy carriage ride, especially because it means I don't have to travel with Ivy again.

Jack and I stay at the back of the group, making sure to keep our voices low as I tell him about Alex's impromptu visit, his missing brother and how I want Jack's help. My guardian is quick to accept, which isn't surprising. This is his dream, after all, to help others, which is something he and his now-passed father spoke of him doing one day.

'But what of the others?' Jack asks as we enter the House of Bane's premises, the barn much larger than Hex Manor's. He jumps off Bolt's back and hands him over to a stable boy.

I do the same with Mira, the young sapphire-haired boy patting her fondly on the neck.

'Look after her,' I tell the youth, and he smiles timidly in answer, his heart picking up the moment I pay him any attention.

Ignoring the wash of bother, I turn towards Jack as we trail across the front of the property towards the school's entrance. 'I suppose we should scope it out first, to see if it's worth asking for extra help. It could be a case of a child running away from a bad household, for all we know.'

He nods in agreement, looking me over. 'You look tired. Did this Alex guy keep you up long?'

I detect a hint of suspicion in his tone, and it brightens my mood.

'Some advice my dear guardian, never tell a lady she looks tired, it's considered rude.'

'*Scarlet*,' he groans in frustration. 'Did this guy keep you up long?'

'All. Night. Long.' I jest, watching his reaction. His eyes darken slightly and I can't help but laugh.

'Is that so?' He asks, too intently.

'He *is* rather handsome,' I muse, finding his interest rather entertaining. If I didn't know better, Jack looks slightly jealous of my encounter with the dameer. 'I get the sense you're not worried for my safety but something else.'

My guardian's demeanour changes ever so slightly. Sapphire eyes turn to me, an intensity that makes my heart skip with giddiness making me grin sheepishly.

'I assure you, Raven, I am not bothered that he spent one short night with you.'

'No?' I say coyly.

'No,' he answers with confidence, his voice light with jest. 'I'm certain that after a night with me, you'll find it difficult to remember his name afterwards.'

I swallow thickly. From his tone I know he is joking with me but my heart races all the same. If I imagine myself having one uninterrupted night with Jack ...

*No. Don't you dare go there.*

I inhale deeply. 'You certainly have a large ego to think so.'

'That's not the only large thing about me,' he murmurs with a wink before entering the building.

The moment he steps through the door, his face smooths into neutrality, and his body straightens to show his dominance. The surrounding Nightshades don't linger, don't watch him closely as he strides through the marble foyer. They would never know he implied some very suggestive things to me seconds earlier.

'Oh, there you are,' Olive says, swiping her forehead with playful relief. 'I thought you got lost.'

'Only in conversation,' I reply, realising the others had gone off without us. We were so immersed in each other we didn't realise they were leaving us behind.

The Severed's emerald eyes flicker between us, noting Jack's steelier-than-usual gaze and my bashful smile. Placing her hands on her hips, she leans forward. 'Well, I suggest you make haste. Carmen is hosting our training session today, and she hates latecomers. The last time, she turned Sol into a toad for an hour.'

'A toad?' I gape. 'She can do that?'

Olive nods and motions for us to follow her. We hasten towards the second storey, heading up a set of marble steps. We pass windows as high as the walls themselves, looking out onto the grounds – Nightshades in groups are travelling to their next classes or relaxing upon the well-kept grass areas underneath the shade of the palm trees.

'Oh, sure. She turned me into a cat once, and it was the strangest thing I've ever experienced,' Olive admits, laughing at our horrified expressions. 'Don't look so troubled. She didn't transform me for punishment. I asked her to do it.'

'Ivy called her a sorceress. Is that what Carmen and Thea are? Witches?' I ask, scrunching my nose up and thinking of all the times they've used their magic. I thought at first they had telekinesis, but this is much more impressive.

'That's right.' Olive nods in confirmation. 'They have some impressive tricks up their sleeves.'

She reaches a door in the hallway and pushes it open without hesitation. Inside is everyone we lost on the way from Hex Manor. What makes me raise a brow, though, is the Hex members all sitting on the floor – the tables moved out of the way to make enough room.

'What's this all for?' Jack asks, sounding as confused as I feel.

'Sit down and I'll explain.' Carmen waves her hand for us to hurry up.

Olive sits next to Sol, and the only spaces left are next to Rusty and Peri. Jack and I shimmy between them, my guardian sitting next to the Briar, while I'm left beside the latter.

I shuffle nervously being this close to the mysterious male. He doesn't give me any indication he cares besides when I sense his body stiffening the moment I settle.

'Now we are all here, let us begin,' Carmen starts, flicking her wrist in a sharp movement.

A chair across the room hovers as if under her command and makes its way over to her. A second chair follows the first, and the Spark sisters sit together outside the circle we Hex members make on the floor.

'The Hex was created when one kingdom started the trend of having a supernatural army. Does anyone know which House this was?'

'The House of Raven,' Ivy answers, earning a nod from our mentor. She meets my glance and scowls as if the mere mention of my House is displeasing to her.

'That's right,' our mentor confirms. 'They started out because of the beloved Hanrae princess and her vampire lover. As some of you may know, female vampires are not able to conceive, but males, if they have a human partner, *are*. This happens very rarely and occurs seldom only with dameer as powerful as the royal family.' Carmen shuffles in her seat slightly, leaning forward and seeming to enjoy going back in time. 'Can anyone tell me what House was created next?'

Blank looks surround me within the circle.

'The House of Velvet?' Jack guesses, to which the Spark sisters nod in elation.

'Precisely,' Thea says. 'The House of Velvet was created because the ruling king of Siamoon saw it as a warning. He thought if Hanrah had a magical army, he'd make his own.'

'The Silkens,' Rusty murmurs.

'Yes. Peri and his Silken brethren were created, excelling in many things, but being part siren they are most famous for their swimming, as they are so closely connected to the ocean and their love of her song.'

I steal a brief peek at the male beside me. He doesn't react, doesn't move at the mention of the House of Velvet – his home. Instead, he looks sombre, slightly lost.

'After that, the Houses of Glass, Creation, Bane and Sun followed their lead, till all the kingdoms were equipped with a powerful army of hybrids they had chosen and fashioned to be their perfect weapons,' Carmen says, sitting back in her chair. 'Once every kingdom had assembled its own army – all unique and special in their own ways – they made a treaty. One person from each House would represent the whole of their lands, swearing their life to Sennastone with a blood oath. Since then, we have had many of your kind roaming the lands, fighting for peace.' She clasps her hands over her knee. 'Since then, we have been training fledglings like you to become your best selves, to prepare you for the outside world and the future you've signed up for.'

*Signed up for*, I refrain from scoffing. *Yeah, right.*

'Are there any questions?' Carmen asks, looking around the circle.

No one answers.

'Great. Now, today we are going to be talking about our abilities. It is very important we know what everyone can do magically and how that can help the Hex in certain situations.'

Our mentor snaps her fingers, and within our circle, a crystal ball larger than my head appears, propped up on a stand so it doesn't roll away.

'This is my personal crystal. What I want is for each of you to touch the underside of the ball. Ivy, you can go first.'

The Nightshade leans forward as instructed and gently places her hand under the crystal. Immediately the clear orb begins to turn a shade of purple, and tendrils of smoke waft from it, the glass portraying a scene within. I find myself peering closer – as everyone does – to see what it's showing us.

A female with sapphire-blue hair and matching eyes sits at a table. Before her is a goblet filled to the top with clear liquid. She sips on the drink and nods her head appreciatively, as if enjoying the beverage. A female with blonde hair and brown eyes – a human, no doubt – comes along and takes a sip from the same cup, but the moment she swallows, she drops dead.

The Nightshade who drank the beverage without harm is approached by a male, who seems livid at the sight of the dead body. He looks to be shouting at the Nightshade, making her recoil in fear. Flowers bloom across her skin, cobalt petals covering her arms and face. The male goes to touch her, to yank her arm, but the moment he comes into contact with the blossoms, he begins to wither, and he clutches his throat before dropping dead himself.

My eyes widen at the display. *Holy Hanrah.*

'The House of Bane,' Thea announces. 'The first scene shows the Nightshades' shared ability to consume or encounter poisons or toxins without harm.'

Silence envelops our group as we absorb what has been shown. Ivy takes her hand away from the crystal ball.

'The second scene is Ivy's unique ability. She is able to produce poisonous flowers along her skin and infect anyone who comes into contact with her. A protective mechanism to keep her safe from harm.'

'Well done, Ivy,' Carmen says before pointing to me.

I go rigid. I don't have any powers, so will it show a scene?

I slowly reach forward to copy Ivy's previous actions. The glass ball is cold to the touch, and the moment my hand is in place, it's stuck – as if the ball itself is holding me in place.

Violet puffs of smoke flow from it once more, covering the Hex's legs. The crystal ball goes dark, though, nothing showing except utter black. I observe for a moment longer, but nothing happens. It remains dark.

I glance up at Carmen and Thea, scowling. They seem as perplexed as me.

'No matter.' Thea notices my gaze and smiles reassuringly. 'We can try again later. Peri may go next.'

And so on we go, watching intently as the crystal presents Silkens with the shared ability to take over the mind and body of someone by merely talking or singing, much like sirens can.

My eyes trail sidelong to Peri as his scene displays itself. Everyone's expression is full of admiration and a sliver of fear, but to my surprise, that's all it shows.

*Perhaps Silkens don't have their own abilities,* I ponder.

The House of Creation can do as its name suggests – create anything. While Rusty himself has the strength of a troll – which doesn't surprise me – I find envy swirling through me. The Briar is no doubt the most powerful of us all when it comes to magical abilities. I already know he will be a valuable asset to the team.

Sol – as he told me in Gwenore Forest – can see the memories of objects, as well as produce sunlight and heat on command.

Olive, who looks rather sheepish touching the crystal ball, watches intently as it displays her House's connection to death and those who are near to experiencing it. Glass fills the orb to reveal her personal capability in creating and manipulating glass – a gift I learn is what the founder and first Severed was born with, which brought about the name of the House.

And lastly, Jack is asked to join in, his water magic shining beautiful shades of blue as the calming element fills the ball, marine animals swimming around the orb as if encased.

The list of amazing and powerful magic makes me start to feel sorry for myself.

'Now try again, Scarlet,' Carmen insists.

I lean forward to find the crystal showing nothing but the depths of darkness anew. There is no hint of movement inside the ball, no scene playing out like all the others, and I feel slightly embarrassed, as if I've broken the crystalline piece.

I sigh heavily before removing my hand.

'What can you do, then?' Ivy asks with exasperation. 'Or is this a hint you can't do anything at all?'

She is cold and thoughtless with her words, but I don't bite.

'I have this scar that can tell me when I'm in danger.' I show the group my right palm, letting their eyes roam over the jagged silver gash. 'It's not as impressive as all your skills, but it has been a lifesaver for me, so I guess it's advantageous.'

My words are more to convince myself my power isn't lame. But from the looks I receive, I know they are feeling various amounts of sympathy for me right now. I find Jack glancing my way, and I give him my best attempt at an unfazed smile.

Without hesitation, he reaches over and squeezes my knee closest to him. The gesture doesn't go unnoticed, Ivy's eyes narrowing in on the movement, and the moment my guardian realises what he's done, he looks close to panicking.

'That's it?' Ivy asks, genuinely disappointed. 'A bleeding cut?'

Carmen shoots the Nightshade a warning look. Ivy reluctantly shuts up.

Sensing the rising tension, Sol smiles at me. 'I guess we should have seen this coming ...' He points to Carmen's crystal ball. 'Get it? Crystal balls can see the future ...'

Olive groans in answer, and I can't help chuckling at the Celestial. He winks before cracking some more atrocious jokes that ease the strain of the training session.

*Thank you*, I mouth to him when the group finally moves on from my abominable performance, the conversation swaying back to history.

## 12

Sol turns to me, his grin as wide as mine, his teeth so white I wonder if he could make them glow in the dark if he wishes. 'Ready for your first physical Hex training session? They can get quite brutal.'

It's the first time I've seen the back of the premises. The House of Bane is built in a U-shape, with the space in the middle made into a personal training area for Nightshades. Along the edge that is free of stone walls are bushes and palm trees that give the property a sense of privacy from the public. A single path leads from the building to a golden beach and expansive ocean, which takes over the horizon.

The salty smell is potent but refreshing here, reminding me of Jack and his elemental magic. The sound of crashing waves relaxes me as I stare out into the distance. I take a total of ten minutes to gape with awe over the stunning scenery before I'm nudged in the side by the Celestial – no doubt still taking pity on me for my crystal-ball fiasco.

'Brutal?' I echo, feeling Jack step slightly closer to me.

My guardian seems to be taking his words literally, but I can tell Sol is half joking from the eye roll Olive gives me. Regardless, concern starts eating away at me. What if I'm not as good a fighter as I think I am? They must already have low expectations of me.

'I'm sure Scarlet can handle it,' Olive says loyally.

'I'm not afraid of a little work, Celestial. What about you?' I ask, feigning confidence. 'Are you going to be all right with getting your lovely hair messed up? Perhaps a little tangled?'

Sol runs a hand through his long strands, curling a golden end around one of his sun-kissed fingers. I can tell even Olive is briefly admiring Sol's long, silky locks, her emerald eyes roaming over the expert plaits that keep the hair away from the male's face.

'You think it's lovely?' Sol asks, the lack of jest in his voice catching me off guard.

'I'd wager I'm not the only one who is envious,' I reply.

Rusty snorts, entering our little group. 'Don't encourage him, or it will be the only thing we hear about for weeks on end.'

Sol shares an infectious grin, my own growing. 'I think you're right, Raven. He *does* sound envious.'

Before Rusty can protest, Carmen calls our attention with two firm claps, distracting some nearby classes in which Nightshades are dealing with weapons. 'Gather around, people. We will start with stretches.'

Everyone suddenly moves in sync, voices surrounding me, bodies all around of varying types, and I quietly enjoy the moment of chaos. As we gather together on a training platform made of seashells, I note I'm the shortest by a significant amount. Jack, Sol and Olive stand at similar heights, at least a head taller than me. Rusty and Peri are even larger, the Briar dominating as the largest person present in the House of Bane today. Ivy, not quite the same stature as Olive, is still lean, her legs long and toned, while I stand the same height as our mentors, the three of us looking like children's dolls in comparison to the rest of our group.

'Don't be nervous,' Thea whispers, her body sliding close to mine as she catches me inspecting my feet, admiring the shells beneath my boots. The colours and various textures have grabbed my attention. 'Everyone was in this same position when they first arrived. You'll do fine.' She smiles, squeezing my shoulder.

I frown slightly, watching her walk away, wondering if I look so aimless as to need reassurance. Perhaps the crystal-ball debacle meant much more to my mentors than I originally thought.

Taking a spot in between Jack and Rusty, I begin to copy the others in the group. They warm up every muscle meticulously – my guardian included. Ravens don't usually warm up – our bodies are naturally ready to be pushed to their limits without the need to loosen our muscles – but it feels good to stretch, regardless.

'Right, that's enough,' Carmen instructs.

I watch and follow as the participants all reposition themselves around the edges of the platform.

'Today I want Jack and Scarlet to watch. I want you both to see where we are in training, to get a feel for the group, as you've yet to *really* get to know each and every one of your teammates,' Carmen says directly to us, making me pause. 'The group has learned many of its strengths and weaknesses already, whereas you'll be going in blind.'

'Unless you want to challenge yourself,' Thea pipes up. 'Then that is your choice.'

'First pairing I'd like to see is Ivy and Sol. No magic this time.'

I narrow my eyes, feeling the sisters are purposely working everything around me.

Sol and Ivy head to the centre of the dais without hesitation. When the latter walks past Olive and me standing together, she gives me an icy look as if I've done something to offend her.

'I assume you now understand what I felt being constantly overruled by the males,' Olive whispers, shuffling closer. 'As you can imagine, I've tried being approachable, but it's as if making friends is a strange concept for her.' She pouts, and I give her a questioning glance.

'She seems nice to me.' I shrug, feigning indifference, earning an incredulous look from Jack.

The Severed leans back as if momentarily astonished, before realising I'm being sarcastic. She smacks my arm lightly and grins to herself. 'You had me there for a second.'

I grin. 'How well does she fight?'

'She isn't bad, but she'd rather be doing something incredibly impressive, like curing some disease or something. She's what you'd call the brains of the team.' Olive gives me a look as if to say, *You know, the smart type that makes us all feel horribly simple-minded in comparison.*

My eyes roam over the stern Nightshade and the smiling Celestial, who looks eager to prove himself. As they begin to fight, I already know Sol will win – his form is better and his competitiveness is obvious. He enjoys winning, whereas Ivy looks like she wants this to be over as soon as possible.

'Sol, on the other hand, is an excellent fighter, but in training he can sometimes become arrogant, and that is his biggest downfall.' Olive smiles like she knows what it's like to see him lose.

'You've beaten him?' Jack chimes in, making Olive look around me to answer.

She nods. 'Several times.'

'Remind me not to get on your bad side,' I reply, making her smirk with delight.

As I predicted, Ivy loses the fight, her arms pinned behind her back in a painful manoeuvre. She yields without reluctance, and Sol instantly lets go. The Nightshade's eyes are cold as she rubs her wrists, giving him a disdainful look as she stalks off.

'Sol, choose your next opponent, please,' Carmen instructs, watching Ivy as she sits on the edge of the platform and turns her attention away from us.

Sol ponders for a moment before pointing at me. 'Would you do me the honour?'

13

Carmen sighs. 'Did you not hear me specifically say I wanted Scarlet to *watch* this lesson?'

'I thought you, or more specifically Thea, said she can join if she *chooses* to,' Sol replies tartly, hands on his hips, mimicking her to a T.

Thea looks to be attempting not to reveal her amusement. Her sister notices with a narrowed stare.

'Fine. Scarlet, do not feel obliged to fight, but you can if you wish.' Carmen aims these words at me, a dark stare conveying not to give in to Sol.

*No pressure.*

Several pairs of eyes watch as I debate. I should wait on the sidelines and observe, like Carmen suggested. But a part of me doesn't want these people to think I can't take a challenge, that my lack of magic means I'm weak.

'Don't doubt yourself,' Jack whispers from behind me. 'You're the next Raven of the Hex. You're certainly capable of beating him.' His face shows no suggestion of a lie – not that I think he would be dishonest with me.

'If I lose, I'll be blaming you, guardian,' I answer playfully, stepping forward.

Thea claps her hands in delight, and I find even Peri nodding his approval.

'Take it easy on me, will you?' I ask Sol, giving him my best innocent look as I take centre stage. Strangely enough, I feel somewhat nervous, even when I know this isn't anything life-threatening.

'Sure.' Sol nods politely.

With the approval of Carmen, we begin.

I expect him to attack me with full force to deny my request, but he seems to have listened as if I had been serious. Minutes go by of him jabbing and kicking and me keeping my full capabilities on a leash, wanting to learn as much about his fighting style as I can.

'Step up the tempo, please,' Carmen orders, seeming to sense my reluctance to reveal anything.

I briefly notice that around the platform, Nightshades are gathering to observe the fight. Sapphire heads circle us, and I try not to let them distract me.

*This is like any fight at the Badger's Sett*, I tell myself. *Find your opponent's weakness, and home in on it.*

Sol does as he is told, and I realise this male is happy to take orders – his skin luminous and radiating a pleasant heat. He is perhaps someone who needs structure in his life – perhaps even a routine to keep to. I ponder whether he keeps to certain moves with his fighting.

*Only one way to find out.*

I snap out a hand and tug his long fair hair – not roughly, but enough to let him know I'm fooling with him. His eyes glow, golden orbs dancing with the challenge. He snakes a punch towards my stomach, hoping to wind me, but I grab his wrist midway and quickly change its direction – straight into his own cheek.

'That's got to hurt,' I hear Rusty say with unrestrained delight.

Sol stumbles for a moment before shaking his head. 'What was *that*?'

'What?' I smile coyly. 'I didn't hurt you too bad, did I?' I'm genuine in my questioning, but I know from what Olive said that the Celestial can be uncharacteristically arrogant during combat, and that's what I need right now. 'I mean, Jack can handle it, so I assumed you could manage it as well.' *Lie.* I have never done such a thing to my guardian, but Sol doesn't need to know that.

The mention of Jack seems to spur him on. Sol launches himself at me, using brute strength in hopes of overpowering me. He no longer plays nice. He uses his full body to manipulate mine, and for now, I let him. He smiles, thinking he's got me entangled, my hands behind my back, like he had Ivy's.

The audience cheers at Sol's victory, no doubt thrilled he's triumphed over a Raven. A part of me knows that for some reason, the fear they associate with me is why they don't want to see me succeed. I try not to take it to heart, but as Sol speaks, I can't help but want to show off in spite of them.

'Do you yield?' the Celestial asks from behind, his elated voice giving me the impression he is grinning.

'If I did, it wouldn't be much fun, would it?'

Without hesitation, I fling my head forward, tucking my shorter legs up as I roll my body tight into a ball. Thankfully, his arms don't waver as they keep a firm grip on my wrists. Otherwise, this would never work.

When my body is vertical, I stretch out my legs and wrap them around Sol's neck. It's a problematic position to be in, his head so close to my crotch, but I don't care. As I hang around his neck, I force my legs out towards the ground and roughly roll him over me, releasing my legs to let him land in a heap. His grasp finally loosens on my arms, and I bolt to my feet. The fight ends up with him on his back, looking up at me as I smirk down at him, a finger at his throat.

The crowd, once loud and excited, goes quiet with shock. Their sapphire eyes widen at my finishing move.

'Holy seal balls,' I hear someone say.

'Mother of pearl,' another whispers.

'My dagger, if I had one,' I explain, enjoying Sol's dazed look, pretending to cut his neck with my fingernail. 'I think that means *you* yield, correct?'

## 14

I receive many different expressions from everyone watching as I stand up straight. Surprise. Concern. Nervousness.

'Well played, Raven,' Sol finally says, getting to his feet and wiping himself down.

I turn to our mentors, and they are the only ones to seem bemused by my method of combat. Their smiles are sly but carefully kept in check, watching our interaction.

'Where did you learn to fight like that?' Sol asks.

'Did I hurt you?'

He shakes his head, his smile broadening as he runs a hand over his hair, tidying it up. 'Only my ego,' he jests, poking my arm lightly. 'You caught me off guard. I'm astounded you got out of my hold.'

I shrug bashfully. 'I learned quickly how to escape unyielding hands.'

This seems to be the wrong thing to say, as his gleaming smile and glowing skin dim significantly. Golden eyes trail over me with a new sense of understanding, and I feel suddenly self-conscious.

'Don't.'

'Don't what?' he murmurs.

'Feel sorry for me.'

'I didn't—' He sighs. 'My first thought was you in the grasp of someone cruel,' he admits with the twist of his mouth.

'I grew up with this being normal. I know no different. You don't need to pity me,' I insist, giving him a cheerful smile – more for his sake than mine. 'I'm stronger because of it.'

'That's the thing, Scarlet. It's *not* normal. It's ruthless – merciless,' Sol replies before stopping himself abruptly. He forces a smile, seeming to sense the gloomy direction of this conversation. 'You won. You get to choose your next opponent.'

I glance at the people watching us still with their expressions of bewilderment. The smell of fear taints the air. They are afraid of me – now more than ever.

'Is it all right if I have a moment to …?' I try to find the right word for my mentors. *Get myself together* is the best phrase to explain my feelings, but for some reason, I don't want to admit that out loud. I end up waving my arms unhelpfully.

'Of course. Take your time,' Thea says.

I smile gratefully. The moment I go to step off the seashell platform, I feel Jack behind me like a shadow. I lift a hand, stopping him mid-stride. 'I'll be back soon.' It's a silent request to be alone. For a brief moment, I think he will refuse, but he reluctantly nods.

'I'll be right here,' he offers. 'Don't stray from my sight.'

I stop myself from making a joke or rolling my eyes. He needs my confirmation as a sign I understand his worry. We've been through a lot together already, and this is one way I can ease the tension that coils within him.

'I'll be right there.' I point to the path, and the end of it, which leads into sparkling blue water. 'I'll be fine.'

He nods but lingers for a moment. I get the sense he wants to say more, or to reach out and touch me. Instead he turns away to leave me to my thoughts.

The gravel path slowly brings me to the golden sands of the beach. The urge to take my boots off is immense. Instead, I bend down and take a handful of the loose granules and watch them fall through my fingers, remembering the feel so I can detail it out in my letters to family and friends.

I step closer to the ocean, the various shades of cobalt pooling before me. Nightshades in various states of undress are in and around the waves. Needing space, I decide to sit away from them all, enjoying being a distant presence while they move throughout their daily routines.

A prickling sensation washes over my arms as I rest, the sunshine warming me. I steal a look behind me, peering between the bushes towards Jack fighting on the platform with Olive. They look fairly equal.

I see Foxglove, who I met in the infirmary, walking my way. She wears a white dress perfect for the warm weather. She spots me looking in her direction and waves, her hand and arm dressed in a bandage.

'Hi there,' she says, plonking herself down beside me. 'Taking in the view, are we?'

I nod. 'It is quite spectacular, I must say.'

'I agree. You can see why we have so many travellers come to our neck of the woods. It's a great place to stop and think, to reset the mind and find a new perspective.'

I give the Nightshade a quizzical look. 'Are you speaking from experience?'

She twists her lips in thought. 'It gets quite manic sometimes, and I find flopping on the sand really helps. It's as if the ocean air sweeps the worries away.' She motions to the subtle breeze around us before gesturing to it flowing away to the horizon.

'I would have liked a place like this to escape to every once in a while,' I admit, thinking of all the times I needed a relaxing place to sit and think in utter peace. An image of bubbling lava springs to mind, replacing the ocean before me, and I find myself scowling at the memory of my prior home. 'But I'm glad I get to see it now.'

'Positive thinking. I like it.' Fox smiles as if trying to stay cheerful for my sake.

'So, what happened to your arm?' I ask with a frown. My hand feels wet, as if ... blood is welling in my palm, a red flag telling me I'm in danger.

Fox glances down at her bandage with a rueful look. 'I was experimenting with ...'

A small twanging sound distracts me from the rest of Fox's sentence. I instinctively jerk to my feet without hesitation. Where I sat before lies an arrow that has sunk into the sand. Dread fills me, and I glance at my companion with panic as she slowly absorbs the shaft beside her.

'Where did that come from?' she blurts with alarm before I spring into action.

'Move!' I order, grabbing Fox and yanking her good arm, my blood coating her skin. I hurl us both into a sprint across the beach, the sound of a bowstring being released louder inside my skull. 'Run faster!'

Nightshades catch us escaping, their apprehensive looks spreading as they examine their surroundings. They start to search for what's spooked us and begin their own getaways.

'What is going on?' Fox yelps as another arrow nearly catches my shoulder.

'I don't know!' But a part of me does. I have little doubt

this assailant is the same person who shot me with the inkberry in Gwenore Forest. My guess is a Raven has finally come to get me, as per the Elder Raven's last wishes. But what do I really know? Ravens aren't the most loved race. It could be anyone.

'We need to split up,' I say, letting go of Fox's arm, her breathing ragged compared to mine. 'Run back to the House of Bane, but take the long route. Tell the Hex the area is compromised.'

'What? I'm not leaving you!' Fox protests, trying to grab my wrist, but I slap her hand away.

'Do it *now*, Fox. I needed backup two minutes ago.'

Realising the trouble we are in, she doesn't hesitate this time to escape, and she heads for the front of the school. I keep travelling along the beach, looking back to see if any other arrows have been aimed my way. Once I think I'm finally out of range, I try to catch my breath. I see the bronze bracelet around my wrist and scold myself for forgetting about it. I could have given it to Fox for protection.

*Next time*, I tell myself before asking, 'What the fuck is going on?'

Understandably, I'm wary of everything around me, so when a small circle sparks in mid-air upon the sand a short distance away, I pull my dagger free from my belt. The portal opens, and I expect the Elder Raven to step through, but instead, it's Rusty with an amused look upon his tanned face.

'You leave us for a few minutes,' he jests, to which I smile timidly, glad to see a familiar face.

'I have to keep you on your toes somehow.' I shrug, peering around him into the portal. The House of Bane's barn lies ahead, the other Hex members in a group, talking loudly over each other as panic ripples through them.

Carmen and Thea are huddled together, unease etched into their features, as they watch Rusty and me. They must have made a portal to come and retrieve me. Relief floods my body at their swift thinking.

My guardian, having noticed me, sprints over and jumps through the floating opening with little effort. He's around me in seconds, studying my body with panic written all over him. Rusty meets my eyes as I'm manhandled but doesn't deign to comment.

'What happened? Are you hurt?' Jack demands, shaking me roughly by the shoulder once he's deemed me unharmed. 'What were you thinking? You were sitting right there!'

'I didn't *do* anything,' I reply. 'I was minding my own business when a volley of arrows came flying for me. I did what I had to do – I ran.'

*Ran like a coward*, I think with a grimace.

My guardian is breathing hard as we stare madly at each other. His ocean-blue eyes hard as he stares. It hurts that the usual expression he deals out to strangers is being dealt to me at this moment.

'What is your problem?' I growl.

'You are always in the midst of trouble. Can you not for *one* day be mindful of your safety?' he hisses, running his shaking hands through his messy mop of hair.

'You say that as if I were *looking* for trouble.'

'At this point, it seems like you *are*,' he bites back.

I jerk away, the sting instant and lingering. I turn absently, momentarily speechless. I expect an apology from him for lashing out, but none is offered as I face my guardian once more. I go to speak, but nothing comes out. Instead, I ignore him, walking around his frame and stepping into the portal. I step inside the barn and feel my chest tighten with a pang of something sharp.

Everyone is busy preparing their horse for our journey home, Carmen clapping and shouting demands for us to hurry up. I stand by numbly as I watch a Nightshade run into the stables to inform our mentors the House of Bane has been searched. No one was found with arrows on their person, but they were able to pick up a shaft that was found discarded on the beach.

'And?' Thea asks the male, her eyes round.

The informer briefly gives me a once-over, his heart skittering at the sight of me. 'The arrows were laced with poison. I think they intended to kill the Raven rather than simply maim her.'

Thea's hands automatically clamp together, her knuckles turning white, but she keeps herself composed with a gracious nod. 'Thank you for letting us know. I assume it will be tested in the lab.'

The Nightshade nods. 'It's already on its way there.'

'Good.' Carmen chimes in.

The portal closes behind me, the sensation of Rusty and Jack staring at my back crawling up my neck. I move away in a state of silence, going to Mira in her stall to tack her up. She neighs softly as if to see how I am, but I'm a mess of emotions. A storm of anger, hurt and frustration.

Our mentors are instructing us to go home, the pair staying behind to see if the Elder Nightshade requires their aid, but I hardly hear them.

My eyes stay on the road ahead as we travel, the Hex all riding home as a unit. When we arrive back at Hex Manor, I stay in Mira's stall, watching her eat from a bucket of hay. I can barely feel my body, my mind churning with questions.

'Are you hurt, Scarlet?'

It's the first time I've heard him say anything. Peri looks over the door, his violet head popping up, and he lays his gaze on Mira, admiring her from afar. He doesn't turn my way to confirm if I've heard but rather waits for an answer.

'I came away unscratched,' I respond finally.

He nods once. 'Good.'

We fall into silence, the deafening sound shifting my emotions into guilt and doubt for what happened. If it weren't for whoever was hunting me, all the beachgoers would have been safe. I put them all in danger – put *Fox* in danger by merely associating with her.

'Do not blame yourself for what happened today,' Peri says, as if reading my thoughts.

'I don't.'

He flinches, which makes me pause. Finally the Silken turns to me, violet eyes narrowing. 'Don't bother lying to me. I can see straight through the charade.'

'I'm not lying.'

He flinches again.

'Why does that happen? Why do you flinch every time I answer?'

'When you lie, I'm ...' He shakes his head. 'Never mind.'

I watch him carefully as he trails his eyes over Mira once more.

'I am half angel,' I whisper, loud enough for him to catch.

His expression hardens, his eyes closing at my untruth. I realise then what is happening, why every time I lie, he reacts as if I've hurt him. 'You're a truth-teller. You feel pain when someone tells you falsehoods.'

He doesn't reply, but the worry etched across his features is enough of an answer as he storms off, leaving me alone once more.

Why did Carmen's crystal ball not present this hidden power of his?

## 15

Not surprisingly, the House of Bane is full of gossip the next day. Whispers of what happened – and what definitely didn't happen but everyone believes happened – echo through my skull. Jack and I have hardly spoken since his outburst, neither of us willing to apologise for our quarrel yesterday.

The Elder Nightshade leads us into a grand hall, or rather, a massive library of books that are stored on shelves as high as the ceiling. My eyes widen at the copious number of tombs stored here, the two levels full of busy Nightshades, all with sapphire hair and matching blue eyes, in various whispered conversations.

'This is our personal library,' the Elder announces, reaching her arms out to the expanse behind her. 'As you can see, our library is one of the biggest in Sennastone, the biggest being in the capital city of Hanrah, the Library of Wonders.'

My attention spikes at the mention of my homeland. This library is massive in every sense of the word. If this didn't rival the one in Hanrah … I cannot even imagine how many books that would mean.

'We value knowledge and intelligence in the House of Bane,' the Elder continues, sweeping a hand across the collection. 'We strive to learn more, to help others and to become the best versions of ourselves. You'll note this room is the most used. If you ever need to borrow a book, please do not hesitate to let us know. Usually they aren't allowed outside the library doors, but you have special allowances, being in the Hex.'

Thea steps forward to stand beside the Elder Nightshade, her hands clasped together in front of her as she engages with us. 'We are going to be staying here for most of the afternoon, my sweets. We have some theory work to get through, so choose a section each, and don't distract any of the others. Carmen and I will come around and check on you all in case you need any help.'

Carmen suddenly holds several wads of paper she didn't have before. She hands them out to each of us, our names written clearly at the top of the first page.

As I go to grab mine, I can't help asking, 'How do you do that?'

'Be more specific,' she states, not unkindly, tilting her head.

'Make things appear out of nowhere,' I say, earning a smile in response.

'Thea and I have many skills, and one of them is transporting items from one location to another, much like making tiny portals and passing objects through them.' She lifts her head, the dark locks falling away from her face.

'I thought as much.' I nod, looking at my stack of paper. 'An exam?'

'You will be tested often on different topics throughout your training. We need to know how well versed you are so we can get a sense of where you sit among the group and the progress you need to make. Don't worry. The others have done this test as well.'

To my dismay, Jack has already headed off by himself, so I traipse further inside, watching as the group disperses into different caverns of the library. Peering up, I admire the ceiling, depictions of stained story pages, scrawled handwriting and divine beings all over it – all lit up by the expansive windows with ornate bronze frames that line the two levels.

Bridges connect the upstairs level every so often, and my curiosity leads me towards the upper storey. I come across a spiral staircase hidden behind an aisle, books stored in the column of it with spines of every colour peeking out as I make my way upstairs.

Nightshades who are also working among the collection of books observe my every move. When I greet them, I'm answered with silence or hurried escapes. Like their Elder, their racing hearts display their obvious fear of me. I try to put them at ease with a friendly smile, but it does nothing for their nerves.

Frustration seeps into me, but I keep my face pleasant and hands relaxed.

*They'll come around eventually*, I tell myself.

I finally stumble across a section where a table sits empty and the stacked shelves either side are free of Nightshades roaming around. I take the one chair where I can look out the window and see the fluffy white clouds above. As seems usual with Tealwaters, the sky is as blue as Jack's eyes on its best days – but also on its worst. After a full ten minutes, I pull myself away from the beauty and try to focus on the papers in front of me.

'This is going to take me forever,' I mutter to myself, taking in the stack and flipping through its pages. It's a huge wad, and I wonder how long it will take to get through it all. An ink pen suddenly appears beside me, startling me into a yelp.

'All right, I get it,' I utter, picking it up and starting on the first page of questions. They aren't particularly hard, but I soon realise my knowledge of this subject – Tellian history – is rusty at best.

'The classic history test,' a voice pipes up, making me look up.

Sitting on the table, leaning on his hand, is Alex, the cloak he wore on his last visit gone and his attire looking much more suited to daytime ventures. He looks rather handsome with his windswept hair and dazzling smile. 'I used to always pass them with flying colours back in the day.'

'What are you doing here?' I ask in bewilderment, keeping my voice low as I peer behind me to see if anyone has spotted him. 'How did you get in? Are you even *allowed* in the House of Bane?'

He shrugs. 'There is no sign saying I'm *not* allowed here.' His smile is jolly, bordering on uncaring.

I roll my eyes in response. He doesn't seem to be any different from the last time we met. Still arrogant. Still full of himself.

'So is there a reason for your presence? Or am I suffering with your ego for nothing?' I ask with a lifted brow.

He smirks, seeming to enjoy my bite today. 'Besides from seeing your lovely face, I had to ask you an important question.' He leans forward, and I unconsciously mirror him. 'Do you know if any other Ravens were sent here besides you?'

I shake my head with a frown. 'My guardian and I were the only ones who stepped through the portal the Elder Raven made. I saw it close behind us.'

Alex nods, deep in thought, no longer smiling.

'Why?' I ask, getting to my feet and coming around the table to him. Has he somehow heard about the beach fiasco yesterday? Does he know if the assailant involved is a Raven? 'What did you hear?'

'It's not what I heard; it's what I *saw*,' Alex replies. He crosses his large arms, his light eyes intent on me. 'I was snooping around, as I do, and came across some individuals that looked very similar to *you*. Red hair, red eyes ...'

'Really?' I frown.

He nods slowly as if gauging my reaction.

*Ravens are in Tealwaters. They are here to get me*, I think wildly, my theories coming to the forefront of my mind.

'Do you think they are involved in whatever happened to Ellis?' Alex asks, his brow creasing.

I blink.

'You think *Ravens* took your brother?' I ask incredulously, not sure if that would be something the House of Raven would undertake. I would be the first to say the Elder Raven is a dreadful person, but why would she care about one dameer youth?

'You don't think they're capable?' Alex asks, not in a judgemental way but with open curiosity.

I shake my head with puzzlement. 'No, they are capable of anything. But why steal a single child?'

'I told you that others have been taken too,' Alex reminds me.

'Which I will make sure to confirm. But it's still not the Elder Raven's usual approach. She would certainly do something dangerous and stupidly risky to prove our House can do the impossible. But this ...' I wave a hand as I try to explain. 'It seems too simple for something she'd be interested in. The Elder Raven would never agree to something like this unless she was getting something *major* in return.'

'A whole lot of money?' Alex asks, wrinkling his nose.

I purse my lips. 'My gut answer is no, but—'

'Raven. Carmen wants you to—'

I spin on my heels and try to stand taller to hide Alex from sight before I remember he has the power to turn invisible. Ivy stops in place and studies me intently, sapphire eyes narrowing with uncertainty.

Having expected my dameer companion to have escaped before he gets caught trespassing, I squirm slightly at the sudden and cold exhalation of breath across the back of my neck – as if he is stunned by something. I come to the realisation that everything in Alex's current state is cloaked, his heartbeat and his smell. It's alarming. Not even I – a Raven with the ability to perceive both – can sense him right now.

*An asset indeed.*

'What have you done?' Ivy demands, scepticism evident in her tone.

I tilt my head in confusion, easing slightly into a more relaxed position. 'What? Nothing. Why do you say that?'

'Because you look extremely guilty right now.' She steps closer but doesn't seem to notice another presence. I watch with curiosity as the Nightshade snoops around the table for something. She peers under the desk, even pulls out each of the chairs tucked beneath it.

'What are you looking for?' I ask.

I copy her as she searches beneath the table. I meet her sapphire gaze beneath the counter, and she scowls deeply.

'I'm looking for the property you've either ripped, spilled ink on or otherwise damaged in some way.' She starts to look over the books on the shelves either side of the table.

'I've not touched any of them,' I reply with a huff. 'You simply caught me off guard.'

'Hmm.' She turns to glance at me. A single flower of

cobalt blue blooms on the side of her neck, it unfurls intimidatingly. I refrain from reacting. 'I don't trust you,' Ivy says.

'You and everyone here,' I retort, earning a penetrating gaze of defiance.

'It looks like you're hiding something.'

I pause, watching the cogs in her brain turn.

Ivy and I stare at each other for several moments, the Nightshade none the wiser about my churning thoughts, before she says, 'Carmen wanted me to tell you that drinks will be served downstairs in ten minutes.' Her eyes narrow once more before leaving the space.

I count to twenty before letting myself relax.

When I turn around, Alex is nowhere to be seen, but left on the table, hidden from Ivy's view, is a small note.

*Meet me in the barn tomorrow afternoon.*

16

I'm the last one to arrive when we gather for drinks. Thea patiently waits for me before leading us out of the library and down several hallways. White walls with blue decor seems to be the theme here – much like at Hex Manor.

Uncharacteristically, Thea is quiet, her demeanour tight and suspicious.

'Is everything all right?' I ask her, noting the way her eyes take in every door and every window like it's a possible threat.

'I'm merely making sure we don't have a repeat of yesterday,' she replies kindly.

Guilt swells within me. Do Carmen and Thea feel obliged to guard me now? What does this mean for my visit with Alex tomorrow? Will they let me out of their sight?

Together we step outside. The fighting platforms we train on are full with duels. The Nightshades look impressive, their schooling as formidable as the Ravens'.

Along the perimeter of the large area are several eating places that offer a variety of poisonous foods that would no doubt make me drop dead in seconds – the food looks and smells delicious when I walk past.

I notice for the first time that bordering the training area are multiple fountains of clean water, which are used to top up the Nightshades' waterskins. My face receives a pleasant spray of the element as the wind catches it, which is nice under the balmy sun.

Thea turns left and leads us towards a small drinks bar where several Nightshades are shaking up colourful concoctions behind the counter. Carmen and my fellow fledglings are sitting with a variety of vibrantly coloured drinks on the table.

I take the last remaining seat, which is next to Sol. He smiles up at me. He leans back in his chair and places both hands on the back of his head. He glows under the sunlight, and a subtle warmth radiates from him.

'I thought you'd got lost in there.' He grins.

'For a moment there, so did I.' I grin back.

'Scarlet, would you like a drink?' Carmen asks, offering a tray my way. 'We have alcoholic and non-alcoholic choices.'

'Alcohol on the job?' I tease, finding my gaze trailing over to my guardian. He does a good job of averting his stare, sipping his cocktail absent-mindedly. But once I glance away I can feel his sapphire stare upon my skin like a blanket.

'A treat. Don't get used to it.' Carmen motions for me to choose. 'We need a moment to unwind.'

My eyes search the tray for something familiar, but it's all different from what I'm used to. I pick a blue option, and from the look on my mentor's face, I've chosen an alcohol-filled drink.

'Drink wisely,' Thea sings, picking a glass of pink liquid.

Of course, it's a joke, as Ravens cannot get drunk. Alcohol doesn't affect us the way it does humans and dameer – but from the slightly dopey look on Olive's face, it seems the Severed do not come under the 'unaffected' category.

I rest back in my chair but feel eyes on me as I sip the fruity concoction. I turn to see Sol staring at my occupied hand. I trail my eyes over his choice of drink. He, to my surprise, has chosen water.

'Do you want to try a little bit?' I ask him, motioning to my glass. 'I think it has pineapple in it, but I can't be sure.'

His eyes lift to mine, his golden gaze seeming to clear before he shakes his head quickly. 'Oh, no. That stuff is bad for my health.' He smiles ruefully, lifting his shirt to reveal a very nice stomach of pure muscle. He gives it a gentle pat before lowering his shirt once more.

I almost choke on my drink. 'I don't think one beverage will change *that*.'

Sol smiles, no doubt delighted with my reaction. He gives a one-shoulder shrug, going back to his water. 'I'm on a special diet.'

I would have thought our conversation funny had I not counted throughout our break how many times he's glanced at my cocktail. It's a total of seven times.

When we all go back inside, I watch the Celestial closely. The further we walk away from the bar, the more I observe him visibly relax – as if the drinks were a threat he did not know how to fight.

When I'm back at my spot in the library, my paper and ink pen ready and waiting, I can't stop thinking about Sol's reaction – how my drink seemed to dull his usual warmth with just its presence.

It doesn't seem right.

So I do something that could be seen as sneakily clever or rather mean. I find a book of recipes and go in search of the Celestial. He's chosen a location near the library entrance but tucked away into a corner. He's sitting in a leather armchair when I find him.

'Why, fancy seeing you here,' he says, his white teeth on show. The glow he was lacking before is now firmly back in place. His body shines brighter, and I feel the guilt coil inside my stomach.

*You need to know the truth*, I tell myself, greeting him as brightly.

'I got bored and thought I'd see how everyone is doing,' I say, reaching the window and sitting on its sill. My bum can just about fit on it as I let my legs dangle beneath me.

'I can see that.' He points to the book in my hands. 'What have you got there?'

Silent relief fills me. He's brought me the perfect conversation opener.

'A recipe book.'

'For ... baking?'

I shake my head. 'No. It's for cocktails. I'm not used to Tellian drinks, so I thought I'd have a quick look through. Do you know the blue drink I had is called a nimble lady?' I turn the book around to show him a depiction of it as if he's asked to see it.

If I were human, I'd never have noticed the quickening of his breath or the unblinking eyes staring at me right now. Only small tells like the burning of his ears and the thick swallow lets me know this is not a normal response.

'Anyway,' I continue, seeing what I've come to find and not wanting to make him even more uncomfortable. 'I'll leave you be. I can see I'm being a distraction. See you later?'

'Yeah, later,' he murmurs, waving half-heartedly as I exit the space.

As I walk back to my workstation, I peer over my shoulder at him. He leans forward, his book discarded on the floor beside his feet as he cradles his head in both hands.

## 17

I knock on the door to the healing quarters. A faint voice inside grants my entry, and I step in to find the Spark sisters fiddling with several items along their desk.

'You wanted to see me?' I say, feeling confused as to why they have invited me here.

'Come sit down, my sweet.' Thea motions to a bed, and I do as I'm told.

It's a contrast to the first time I was here – unsure and worried about my company. Now I'm confident in the trustworthiness of the ladies before me. They are devoted to bringing us fledglings up in the real world, teaching us the fundamentals of becoming a respectable Hex member, and coaching us in everything we will need to know when the day finally comes for us to fly the nest.

'How are you, Scarlet?' Thea asks as Carmen continues to flit around. Glass clinks, and I ponder what she's doing.

I force a smile. 'Fine, thanks.'

She doesn't believe me. I can tell by the expression on her striking face.

Thea tilts her head, her dark eyes boring into me. 'Are you really?'

I sigh. 'I've yet to receive word back from my family, which is strange as my mother is always sending out letters and I've recently become an aunt.' My shoulders sag at the thought. I had told myself time and time again that I wouldn't be getting a letter for weeks at a time and to be patient. But when I started receiving regular written correspondence from both Dimitri and Princess Leonore ... 'An update to how my niece and nephew are faring would be nice. But I'm starting to wonder if my letters are even getting to the House of Raven.'

'Well the post does take much longer when it crosses kingdoms,' Thea explains, her hands lacing together. 'But perhaps your letters aren't reaching them like you said.'

My eyes narrow. 'Hmm perhaps you're right.'

I wouldn't put it past the Elder Raven to have taken my letters and ripped them up before they could get to Ruby. That would also explain why Dimitri and Leo are the only ones answering me – their mail isn't overseen by a particularly evil Elder.

Thea nods thoughtfully as if sensing the wheel inside my mind turning. 'Is that all that clouds your mind? I have noticed a slight distance cast between you and our guardian,' she says, to which I twist my mouth in distaste.

'He thinks I'm reckless.'

'And are you?' Thea asks with genuine interest.

'No,' I retort before conceding. 'But I do attract a lot of trouble, it seems.'

She nods slowly as if understanding. 'And how are you coping since the beach incident?'

'I'm not a stranger to people wanting me dead.' I shrug. 'So yes, I'm okay, I suppose.'

It's harsh but it's true.

Thea answers with a terse nod. 'Your mother and aunt had the same thing happen to them when they first started in the Hex,' she confesses. 'Someone always has an animosity towards you Ravens.'

I stiffen. I've never mentioned to anyone in this manor – except for Jack – my relation to the previous Ravens of the Hex. But in seconds, Thea Spark has confirmed she knows two things – I am related to the Vermillion Fang and the Red Raven, and I'm a half-blood.

I peer up, expecting scrutiny, but she tilts her head.

'Did you not think we would figure out your heritage?' Thea asks.

Carmen walks over now with a tray of drinks and puts it on the bed beside her. The sisters sit opposite me, and I get the sense this has been done on purpose. They watch me like a pair of lionesses waiting – for what, though, I'm not sure.

'I don't boast about what I am,' I finally answer as Carmen hands me a glass of water.

'Well, anyone with working eyes can see you're a child of Ruby Seraphine,' Carmen counters. 'The Seraphine women all have that same look.'

I frown, not understanding.

'They look as if they want to prove something,' Carmen explains, making the edges of my mouth tilt up at her pointed look.

'Did you know my mother personally?'

The witch nods. 'We've been working with Hex members for a *long* time,' Carmen replies, giving me the impression this is absurdly true. But the sisters look slightly younger than my mother. The facts don't add up.

'How long is *long*?' I probe, lifting a brow.

'Since the very first female was appointed Raven of the Hex,' Thea answers, watching my reaction carefully.

I jolt back with disbelief. The first Raven was generations ago. How could they be …?

'You're *immortal*?' I gape.

'No. We are cursed,' Carmen amends with a sigh. 'We were young when we displeased an extremely powerful person and were punished for it. We were told we'd live as long as we trained the land's future heroes.'

My eyes widen at the revelation. 'Wait. So you trained the Elder Raven – I mean, Garnet Cerise,' I blurt out in bewilderment.

I only know the Elder Raven's full name due to a visit to Rubien's library with my sister Roux. There we found out about Ruby being a member of the Hex from a newspaper that had printed the story, and the scandal that was my birth.

'Indeed we did.' Thea nods timidly. 'But Ruby was something entirely different. She walked in here and told us she was through with abiding by the Raven rules and regulations. She carried so much trauma from the Hex Trials that she wanted to live a life she wanted, not the life the Elder Raven expected her to lead.'

My brows lower at the reminder that my mother went through some serious trauma to get to the position I'm in now. We both did.

'My mother has always been true to herself,' I reply proudly.

Ruby has always spoken her mind, has let herself show emotion around me when Ravens do no such thing. She doesn't care if her peers call her a whore for sleeping with a human or if they speak badly of her – she ignores them all without so much as a retort.

'She has,' Thea agrees. 'And it's been a nice surprise to finally meet her infamous daughter. Which is why we asked you here to the healing quarters.'

The sisters share a quick glance, which puts me instantly on edge.

'When you shared your power with the crystal ball,' Carmen starts, pointing briefly to the orb upon one of their cluttered shelves, 'it showed us darkness. Do you know what that means?'

I shake my head as she goes to grab it. She places it in my hands, and the usual clear colour slowly turns inky. I scowl down, finding only my reflection in the glass staring back at me.

'It means something is blocking the power from your body to the crystal ball,' Thea clarifies, motioning to the connection between my skin and the magical artefact.

'Or because I hold no power,' I offer, earning unconvinced expressions.

'If we hadn't known of your history – of your mother's history – we wouldn't have come to this conclusion, but we think you may be harbouring dark magic within,' Carmen says, pursing her lips in thought.

'*Dark* magic?' I scowl. 'That's not possible. I can't do any more than bleed when I'm in danger.'

'Dark magic doesn't necessarily mean you are able to wield it. It can be implanted or forced upon you, like we have experienced,' she says, motioning towards herself and Thea. 'But you're right. That scar is an enigma. What Raven only bears a power of such little impact compared to her kin?'

'I'm a half-blood Raven. I'd expect to be less powerful than my brethren,' I say.

Thea shakes her head. 'No. Ravens are powerful regardless of diluted blood. Plus you've proven to have all the other abilities Ravens have – heightened senses and healing properties in your blood.' She leans forward and reaches for my scarred hand before pausing. 'May I?'

I don't hesitate to surrender it, and I watch as her pale fingers trail over the silver line across my palm. I imagine darkness flowing within. I almost laugh at the thought.

'I think this is the entry point,' Thea mutters to her sister, whose dark eyes narrow slightly. 'I can feel it.'

They lift their gazes, brown – nearly black – eyes staring at me in puzzlement.

'Scarlet, if you had the opportunity to obtain a new gift – a much more powerful gift – would you take it?' Carmen asks, her tone sharp and serious.

I nod slowly. 'Yes. I would.'

Who wouldn't want to gain power? Who would say no to a question like this?

'If that's the case,' Thea says, getting to her feet swiftly, 'we may ask you to swing by every now and then for some tests. We have a lot of work to do if we are to make this possible.'

'Tests? A lot of work? What are you talking about?' I press, looking to Carmen for answers.

She twists her lips but doesn't hesitate to reply. I can rely on her to always be precise with her words.

She rests both her hands on her lap. 'Scarlet, you cannot have been born with that scar, due to magic being the reason for its presence. Therefore, we believe it's the mark left behind from when you were cursed.'

'Cursed? By who?'

The moment the words leave my mouth, I know who would go to such lengths.

'Our theory?' Carmen says. 'Most likely the Elder Raven.'

# PART TWO

*Sapphire City*

## 18

I stand in the barn alone, tapping my foot with impatience. Alex should be here by now.

'If you are present, show yourself. I'm not in the mood to play around today,' I say into the quiet afternoon air, hoping but not expecting an answer. I glance down at the scar upon my hand.

Before I left the healing quarters, the sisters had taken several samples of my blood and promised to update me on anything they may find. I wrinkle my nose. Is it true, what Carmen and Thea said? Is this scar blocking whatever power I was born with from showing its true colours? Will I one day be able to wield fire like my brothers and sisters and finally fit in?

I shake my head.

*Do not expect anything too grand, and you won't be disappointed by the outcome if it's not what you hoped for.*

I sense movement outside. Pale blue eyes land on me, my guardian strolling into the stables, wearing his daily attire, but he is adorned with very noticeable weapons.

'What are you doing here?' I blurt, lowering my hand.

'I'm assuming you're meeting that dameer here.'

I don't answer.

'I'm here to make sure the meeting goes swimmingly,' he says, voice hard, but his eyes are gentler than I've seen them in days.

I tilt my head. The anger that burst out of him seems to have faded since the day at the beach. His body seems more relaxed, his hands unfurled and holding his belt, which is stocked with small knives.

'So you're keeping an eye on me now,' I reply, earning an eye roll.

'I'm your guardian. It's my job to keep you safe.'

'You're *everyone's* guardian,' I remind him. 'Guardian of the *Hex*, not guardian of the *Raven*. Go find someone else to look after.' I cross my arms as he steps closer, his ocean scent wafting towards me, the lapping waves coming to mind with it.

With our bodies this close, I can hardly think straight, his lips right there – taunting me. I force myself to look away. I'm still angry at him, and I'm willing to be stubborn enough to wait for an apology before I play nice.

'Look, Scarlet,' he says, hands out in surrender. His fingers caress my arms, sending a shiver shooting through my spine at his touch. I expect an apology, but like before, none comes. 'I'm coming whether you like it or not.'

I grunt my disapproval before I feel a prickling sensation at the back of my neck. Jack is talking but I'm not listening, instead watching the entrance of the barn. I know my guest has arrived when no one comes into sight.

'Jack Wilde, meet Alex Irvine.'

Jack spins to find thin air before him. He scowls as he turns to look at me over his shoulder. 'You're being petty now.'

I tilt my head forward, motioning for him to look again. Before him stands a tall, lean male with effortlessly done blonde hair and Tellian blue eyes. The males have similar features, except for the strands of silver through Jack's locks.

Alex, I notice, wears particularly nice clothing of white and midnight blue, but unlike Jack, he wears a thin cloak. It's warm all day every day, so I don't understand his choice of attire, but I don't comment on it.

'Holy Hanrah,' Jack mutters, jolting back before assessing the newcomer.

'I've heard many things about you, guardian,' Alex says, offering a strong hand. 'Mainly your good looks, but I think the Raven still has you beat.' He peers over Jack's shoulder and gives me a flirtatious wink. 'Hello, Scarlet. Miss me?'

'And yet I've heard nothing about you,' Jack retorts, his protectiveness on show as he takes the dameer's offer, Alex's hand turning white from the firm handshake.

'Easy, guardian. I need my hand in good condition.' Their hands unclasp, and Alex flexes his, massaging it. 'If you know what I mean.'

Jack doesn't laugh, but Alex seems unfazed by his lack of humour.

To save us all from the growing tension, I say, 'Great. Now the introductions are over, let's get going. I don't want us to ride back in the dark.' I clap my hands and head for Mira's stall. The mare is already tacked up, so I lead her outside. 'Do you want to borrow a horse, or are you coming with me?' I ask the dameer.

Alex's grin widens, but before he can respond, my guardian has his say.

'Not a chance.' Jack snorts from inside Bolt's stall.

'Is there a problem?' I ask sweetly, heaving myself into the saddle.

'He's a stranger.' Jack hauls Bolt outside and adjusts his bridle in a rougher manner than is necessary.

'No, he's someone who needs our help.' I turn towards Alex and give him the option. 'Your choice. You can ride on one of our horses here, ride with the guardian or ride with me.'

He nods towards me without much deliberating. 'I'll never turn down an invite from a pretty lady. I'm definitely riding with you.'

I smile with fangs. 'I thought as much. Hop on.'

19

After riding through Gwenore Forest, keeping strictly to her pathways to prevent her from harming us, we finally come to the end of the path. Jack has been silent the whole trip, while Alex and I have conversed quietly, keeping in line behind him, the dameer directing us to our destination.

'I had different expectations for when I met the guardian. I thought he'd be more agreeable.' Alex has his hands around my waist – probably to piss Jack off. A pointed look from the guardian causes the dameer to tighten his hold on me significantly, his chest warm pressing hard against my back.

'Don't mind him. You caught him on a bad day,' I say, bobbing my head towards the sulking figure in front of us. 'Jack is in a grumpy mood, but he won't bite.'

'You sure? I can see him eliminating me the moment you leave us alone,' Alex mutters, eyeing the guardian with curiosity.

'I give you permission to put him in his place if it comes to that.'

We stride out of the sheltered forest and onto the sun-filled cobblestone pavements of Sapphire City. In the distance, the royal residence stands tall, the multi-spired castle glinting like polished pearl under the sunshine. Ivory Castle has a light, iridescent exterior that complements the metropolis, which consists of mostly white stone buildings and sand-coloured roofs.

The streets, I note with approval, are exceptionally clean – full of pedestrians, carriages and horse riders. We even pass several water roads, on which people in boats are taken from one destination to another. I marvel as elementals use their magic to give rides to locals.

'This place sure is beautiful,' I say, surveying the civilians milling around the shops and food vendors on either side of us. We are given a few glances, mostly from curiosity rather than concernment, and I'm glad. I don't want to be gawked at like I am in the House of Bane – or be constantly putting people on edge.

'She is,' Alex agrees cheerfully, his voice close to my ear.

He points to an establishment that looks much older than the rest, its exterior looking as if it has never been updated. But upon closer inspection, I find it has character and charm only an old building can carry off. It looks like an antique compared to the shops around it, but the sign clearly states it was one of the original stores in the city.

'Once upon a time,' Alex starts as I nudge Mira forward, weaving our way down the main street, closer to the gleaming castle, 'our sovereigns were avid sailors. They would come back with bags full of pearls, along with other treasures they would find on their travels, and they would give them to the people of Sapphire City on special occasions. That's how we chose the kingdom's emblem, the oyster pearl, as that's where our wealth originally came from – selling the pearls off to the wealthy, who admired them and demanded to wear them round their necks.'

I look over my shoulder at the dameer, his face bright and open as he talks of his kingdom's past.

He finds me watching and grins. 'Did I give away my love for my kingdom's history?'

The way he says *my kingdom* makes me smile. It's as if the territory belongs to him, and in many senses of the word, I suppose it does. The people I've met so far seem to love their home, love their city, and it belongs to each and every one of them. I start to wonder if the civilians of Rubien feel the same way, if they, too, think of the city as *theirs*, even when they are trapped underground with minimal sunlight.

'I get the impression you had a good education growing up.'

Alex nods, light blue eyes averted. 'Yes. I was very lucky.'

I wait for more, but he seems content with that as an answer. I nod to myself before finding Jack coming to a stop. He jumps from the saddle, and I motion for Alex to follow his lead. A long leg of his swings over Mira's behind and lands perfectly beside her. I can tell he has experience with riding, which I assume isn't abnormal here in Tealwaters. Horses seem to be the main means of transportation after boats, but his elegance makes me pause.

'Is your family wealthy, Alex?'

He looks up at me with puzzlement. 'My, aren't you full of questions today?' he says, mildly amused. 'But yes. They are somewhat comfortable. Why do you ask?'

'You seem confident around horses. I thought perhaps you'd had lessons.'

*You don't look like a warrior getting off his steed*, I think, *but rather a rich man getting off his prize stallion.*

'I knew some people who owned horses. They had a whole stable of them, and they were nice enough to let me ride whenever I wanted. I don't do it as often any more, but when I'm back in the saddle, it's as if I've never been out of it.' Alex watches as I ready myself to jump off Mira's back. 'Is *your* family wealthy?'

I shake my head, reining in the scoff at the absurdity. 'Holy Hanrah, no.' I laugh as I land on my feet. I take the reins over Mira's head and tie her to a wooden rail where other horses have been left. I don't want to give Alex too much information, so I switch topics, motioning to the street around us. 'So, where first?'

Jack, who has secured Bolt to the hitching rail, strides over, his face neutral as he joins the conversation. I can't help but notice the way he studies our surroundings – most likely calculating any and all threats nearby. I smile at the sight of him before remembering I'm still annoyed with him and focus my attention back on the dameer.

'The Dashers' residence,' Alex replies, putting his hands on his hips, squinting slightly under the sun's warm rays. 'I was horribly drunk when I last saw them, the grief particularly bad that day, and I think they took pity on me. That's when they admitted they had heard of more children going missing.'

'Sounds like a promising start. Lead the way.' I wave him on, and he moves without further prompting.

The first home we approach is two storeys high but rather narrow, as seems normal for this part of the capital. The curtains are parted, and a downstairs window is open, the smell of something savoury wafting out into the street.

'Good sign someone is in,' Jack murmurs before knocking on the door.

Alex disappears behind me as I hear him say, 'Just in case.'

*Just in case of what?*

But before I can voice my confusion, the door swings

open, and a man steps forward, his light blue eyes and blonde hair shining under the sun, which streams through his home.

'Can I help you?' he asks, looking between my guardian and me with a creased brow.

I take note his gaze lingers on me for a while longer.

'Hello, Mr Dasher. My name is Jack Wilde, and this is Scarlet Seraphine.' He motions towards me, and I give the man a small smile, making sure to keep my fangs hidden.

Mr Dasher's fascination with me is evident as he leans forward, eyes roaming my face.

'We wanted to ask a few questions,' Jack says, getting his attention back. My guardian's voice is light and friendly, his demeanour having changed considerably since our ride. He now portrays himself as a trustworthy neighbour and friend. 'Have you heard of any children going missing from their homes? Say, in the last month or so?'

The man's heart spikes, but he plays his part well, shaking his head with a baffled look.

'Missing children? Around here?' he asks, crossing his arms over his chest.

*A gesture of defence*, I note.

'We have heard of a young boy going missing, and we wanted to make sure no others have also been taken,' Jack offers, hoping to loosen the man's lips, but the Tellian does not yield.

'Sorry, no. I've heard nothing of the sort.' He shrugs as if that's as much as he can give. Jack dips his head in thanks, and the man closes his door. When we return to the horses, we gather around the side of Bolt.

'I know I was impaired, but not enough to make a whole conversation up in my head,' Alex grumbles, coming back into view. 'He must have been lying.'

'He was,' I confirm, earning a frown from Jack.

'Why do you say that?' my guardian asks.

'When you mentioned the missing children, his heart rate changed. He may not know about which children are going missing, but he certainly knows *something*.'

'Then we keep going and hope someone decides to give us a vital piece of information,' Jack replies, putting a foot in a stirrup. 'If we have a case of more missing children, this could be much bigger than we originally thought.'

I grimace, looking at Alex. His light blue eyes are downcast, his tanned skin looking slightly paler. I can tell he is uneasy, but when he spots me watching him, the cockiness is back, along with a straighter posture and reassured demeanour.

*An act*, I've come to realise. This part of him is a facade to keep his true feelings at bay.

'Don't worry, Scarlet. That's only the first house. We have more to check out,' he insists, pulling me towards Mira.

A prickle of awareness flares through me. Subtly I scan the perimeter of the street but find nothing amiss. When I turn back to Alex, he seems deep in thought.

'Hey,' I murmur, stepping closer to the dameer. 'Whatever happens, I won't stop until we find answers. We *will* find Ellis.'

He lifts his head and gives me a firm nod, his gaze hardening slightly. 'I know we will.'

## 20

We try several homes. All our questions receive the same answers.

'We haven't heard of any missing children.'

'Missing children? In Sapphire City? That doesn't seem likely.'

'Sounds like you're trying to spread rumours. Get out of here.'

All these responses but no true answers to why Ellis Irvine may have been taken. But a common thread that links them all is the change of the speakers' pulses when Jack says the words *missing children*. It's as if their hearts squeeze with silent fear. But I don't understand why none of them reveal they know of something.

'Because they are scared,' Jack declares when I share my thoughts.

'Yes, but *why*? Are all these families missing children, or do they simply know *of* them? Why wouldn't they say anything? If I was a mother, I'd be shouting from the rooftops for any hint that someone had seen or heard something of my child.'

'Perhaps they are fearful it will happen again to them or someone they know,' Alex chimes in as we walk to our next destination.

Jack knocks on the last door, our routine of him asking questions, me standing by as a silent observer and Alex behind us, invisible. This time a woman, Mrs Kapper, appears, and she's heavily pregnant. She cradles her stomach protectively, and an image of Roux comes to mind, my older sister, holding her twins before the Hex Trials.

'Good afternoon, Mrs Kapper.' As before, Jack introduces us, and we start our usual line of questioning.

'I'm sorry.' She shakes her head, acting well even as her heart hammers. I can see small patches of perspiration on her temples – a sign of her nerves. 'I've heard nothing of the sort.'

'I'm sorry to have wasted your time, then,' Jack says, offering her an annoyed but soft smile before letting her go, like the gentleman he is.

'Mr Dasher and his wife mentioned several households they suspected knew about the disappearances, and they are all pretending otherwise,' I hear Alex whisper behind me. 'What is going on?'

As the woman goes to close the door, a wave of frustration hits me full force. Several people have lied to us. Several people have kept information to themselves, and we are getting *nowhere*.

Before I know what I'm doing, my foot is stopping the lady from closing the door fully. She shuffles nervously, holding her belly away from me, making me realise she thinks I'll hurt her.

'Are you being threatened?' I murmur, leaning forward so she can hear my lowered voice. 'Because your silence is helping no one. If children are disappearing in Sapphire

City, we won't be able to help get them back. We can't do *anything* unless someone tells us what is happening.'

Mrs Kapper clutches the door tighter, swallowing deeply. 'Leave, before I get my husband to kick you out.'

'You hold a child.' I motion to her stomach, making us both look down at its roundness. 'Do you not wish for any threats to be dealt with by the time he or she is born? Think of the parents who have suffered with the loss of their children. Imagine this baby being stolen from the comfort of your home. Would you speak up? Would you help us then?'

She blinks, tears gathering in her eyes. 'You don't understand.'

I nod in agreement. 'You're right. Because no one will take the time to tell us what they know.'

We stare at each other for a long time. Her light blue eyes gaze into dark crimson.

'I'm here to help you. To help the people of Sapphire City. But we have no leads, no new information, and without that, these children will be lost forever. Please help us,' I implore her, letting my emotions come to the surface, letting this stranger, this woman who will be a mother, see how ruined we will be if she does not help.

We stand in silence. The males behind me say nothing, do nothing.

'If you are being threatened, we can protect you. We can find the people responsible for this,' I press, my voice low in hopes this will spur her into talking.

'I'll ask you one more time to leave,' Mrs Kapper murmurs, her voice shaking.

I straighten, defeated. She sees the visible change, and her features become sorrowful.

'I apologise for overstepping. We won't bother you again,' I state flatly.

I remove my foot from her home and move back to Jack's side.

Mrs Kapper doesn't immediately close the door, her eyes catching mine one more time.

'I wish you all the best with the birth,' I say, thinking of Roux. 'I recently became an aunt, and it's the best feeling in the world. So I can only imagine what being a mother will feel like.' I force a smile, then turn to my guardian. 'We are done here. Let's go.'

As we walk back to the horses, I feel Alex squeezing my arm.

'Thanks for trying.'

I motion for him to get back on Mira, but he shakes his head.

'I'm closer to home here.'

'Where do you live?' I ask half-heartedly, trying to act normal. 'I can take you.'

'No, it's fine. I'm only up there.' He jerks a thumb over his shoulder, towards the main street, Ivory Castle glinting in the distance, where the wealthier and more lavish houses reside.

'Get home safely,' Jack says, his tone as tired as I feel.

'I will.' Alex nods before facing me. 'Scarlet. It's always a pleasure.' He bends to kiss my hand, his lips brushing my knuckles.

I feel Jack bristle beside us.

Alex smiles smugly up at me, seeming satisfied by my guardian's reaction, before stalking off, turning invisible.

I lift myself into the saddle, Jack and Bolt waiting patiently.

'Are you okay?' my guardian asks, to which I shake my head faintly.

'We are no wiser than we were this morning,' I reply

glumly. I can try to hide my true feelings from him, but he knows me too well for that.

He grasps my hand in his, warmth spreading through my fingers. 'Look at me, Scar.'

I do as I'm told, those ocean-coloured eyes holding mine. Hope and something else – something more intense – within them makes me want to lean forward and press myself against him, to feel his comfort.

'We'll try again tomorrow, and the next day and the next,' Jack says, with no room for debate. 'We won't give up because of *one* little bump in the road. We've gone through worse, and we'll come out stronger than we were before.'

A part of me wonders if he is talking purely of Alex's brother going missing, but I nod nevertheless.

'I don't want to be a failure,' I whisper, looking up into the sky to stop the tears from falling.

'You have *never* been a failure,' he reassures me, his thumb tracing circles on my knuckles.

I swallow thickly. Jack is uncomplaining as I compose myself.

'Shall we head back?' he asks when I finally take a deep breath.

I nod, wanting to go back to normal. Wanting the relationship Jack and I had before our little argument on the beach. For the time being, I forget about it and straighten my shoulders.

'I'll race you, guardian.'

Jack smiles timidly, and the sight of it makes my chest tighten. 'I don't want to upset you when you lose.'

I snort before kicking Mira into action, looking behind me as I get a head start.

'Cheater!' I hear him shout.

21

Training is cut short today. Carmen and Thea hurry us home from the House of Bane so we can all bathe and dress for the afternoon. We gather in the foyer of Hex Manor when our mentors finally announce why our usual day of theory and physical training has changed.

'We are going shopping together in the city,' Thea says with excitement. 'Then we have a dinner booked afterwards at my favourite restaurant.'

'Shopping? Whatever for?' Sol asks. He looks to Peri, who stands next to him. 'Do *you* know?'

The Silken shakes his head, seeming to hate the sudden attention, as he averts his gaze.

'We have been invited to an evening with the royal family and their friends tomorrow night, and we have to look our best,' Carmen explains, earning various expressions from our group.

'What's the occasion?' Rusty asks.

'They want to give you a warm welcome to their kingdom,' Thea pipes up. 'It will be a night of impressing the wealthy guests and sovereigns with your many talents. First impressions are *everything*.'

'So we are buying dresses?' Olive asks, her voice becoming high-pitched, her hands clasped at her chest.

'Yes. The girls will be coming with me to Aura's Dress Shop, and Carmen will be taking the boys to Jon's Den.'

I've never heard of either establishment, but I assume they both sell clothing.

The Spark sisters direct us outside, where two carriages are ready and waiting. As before, one is for the males, who will be riding with Carmen, and the other is for the females, who will be escorted by Thea. Before we all step inside our transportation, our mentors confer to decide on a time and meeting point within the city when we're all finished.

'See you later,' Jack murmurs, giving my arm a soft nudge before setting off with the others.

I watch his back until he steps into the carriage, my guardian winking before stepping out of sight. A familiar flutter warms my chest. We have slowly come to be on speaking terms, our beach argument having faded away into the backs of our minds.

'Come on,' Olive urges, pulling me away.

For this journey, I'm sitting next to Thea, with Ivy opposite me again. I make sure to keep a neutral expression, having been told off by the Nightshade last time we rode in a carriage together, keeping my awe of the new landscape tightly restrained.

'Oh, look, it's the theatre,' Thea points out with excitement.

People line up outside a large building in droves as several jugglers and magical acts entertain the guests while they wait.

'We'll make sure to see a show sometime. You'll love it.' The sorceress glances at me briefly. 'The ladies get to dress up in their finest gowns, and the men always look so hand-some.' Thea smiles with recollection. I wonder when the last time she visited was.

'I do like to dress up,' Olive murmurs happily, her eyes scanning the streets outside.

It isn't long before we are dropped off outside Aura's Dress Shop, the sign above the white-framed door painted a dark pink. We all shuffle inside. Thea obviously knows the workers, given how easily they converse.

'Elsa, my sweet.' Thea greets the lady at the front counter, both of them hugging with fond expressions. 'This is Ivy, Olive and Scarlet. We need to find them some appropriate outfits for meeting the royal family.'

Elsa is a true Tellian local, with long blonde hair that curls around her tanned face and light blue eyes. She dips her head in greeting. 'So lovely to meet you all. I have the best variety of beautiful dresses that would look marvellous on you all. Please come this way,' she says, waving for us to follow her.

We are escorted to the back of the dress shop and into a room that is pink and white. It's very feminine but nicely appointed with fancy furniture. The oil paintings on the walls show ladies all in glamorous gowns, while several very expensive-looking vases of brightly coloured flowers complement the room with their floral scents.

Elsa must have prepared for our visit today, as within minutes two other workers enter the room along with racks and racks of glorious dresses. On the rails are small tags, our names scrawled in neat handwriting on them to show who each collection of dresses is for.

'I've already picked out some options for you to choose from,' Elsa says, eyeing up the glorious materials before us. 'Thea gave me some ideas about what she thinks you may like to try. If you have any gowns you're not sure about, I'm happy to swap and change them around.' Elsa smiles, motioning for us to have a look.

To my dismay, all my dress options are red. I peer over my rack to see Olive's rack is full of green dresses, and Ivy's are all different shades of blue.

'Is there a reason we have only one colour choice?' I ask, trying my best to sound polite and not ungrateful.

'We thought it would be fitting for you to represent your House in front of the royal family. They will clearly see who is from where, then,' Elsa replies, thankfully not taking offence at my question.

Ivy waves Elsa over, asking her about certain fabrics, before I can say much more.

Thea comes to my side and delicately touches a gown with ruffles on it.

'Won't they know who we are by our features?' I motion to my dark red hair and my matching red eyes. 'I mean, if they can't figure out I'm a Raven, they will the moment I open my mouth.' My tongue sticks out and touches a sharp fang for emphasis.

'Do you not want to wear your House colour?' Thea murmurs with an understanding look. She can probably tell I want to say no, but I get the sense that among company, she has to be diplomatic.

'Do the others have to wear their House colours too?' I ask, referring to our male counterparts.

'Yes.' She nods. 'This is the only event where you are asked to wear certain garments.'

I purse my lips. This is her way of saying, *You only have to do this one time.* After this evening, we can choose our own outfits without complaint.

Nodding in understanding, I say, 'I can suffer with red for a night, I suppose.'

She smiles thankfully. 'I think you've suffered worse than a colour constraint for your dress.'

Absent-mindedly I let my fingers roam over a chiffon gown of dark crimson – a similar shade to my hair. It's beautiful with its gossamer sleeves and cuffs of silk at the wrists. It's tight around the bust area with its sweetheart neckline and corseted waist. As I trail my gaze downwards, I find the skirt fans out, any slight movement making the small gems across the skirt glitter under the light.

'Try it on, Scarlet. I think it would look lovely on you,' Thea urges, taking the long, flowy dress off the rail.

I look at the feminine gown and nod slowly.

'Come on. I want to try these on together,' Olive urges, stepping into one of the large fitting rooms. She pulls a cream curtain across to prevent anyone from seeing her change.

Ivy gives the gown in my hands a brief look but says nothing before taking a silk dress of her own in to try on.

*My choice is obviously not horrible, then,* I think with amusement.

It takes me a few minutes to get my dress on and button up the back – the material is airy and surprisingly comfortable, but the beauty of the dress is ruined by one thing.

'What's taking you so long?' Olive asks, her voice so close to my changing room curtain I flinch.

'She probably doesn't know how to use buttons, let alone put a proper gown on,' Ivy says, making Thea tut audibly at her.

Annoyance runs through me. I take a deep breath and step out into the open, letting all the females finally see the final product. My arms hang awkwardly by my sides, my skin, which bears the marks of the fire-breathing dragon, peeking through the sheer material. My chest, which is also covered in still-healing burns, and a raw-looking neck, however, are on full show. My disastrous throat, the result of my Elder's hatred for me, is on full display in all its glory.

All I hear is silence.

'Oh my,' I hear Ivy murmur, her sapphire eyes wide like saucers as she takes me in. For the first time since I've met her, something other than judgement etches her features.

I tense my jaw to keep myself from shedding tears. I want to look beautiful in this dress, but my skin – my injuries – ruin it. I take in Olive's gown, ruffles surrounding her. I look down at myself and feel the need to cover up.

'Should I pick something else?' I ask, voice trembling. I scowl at the betrayal of my evident emotions.

'No. You look absolutely beautiful.' Olive gawks, making me frown.

'I agree. You look wonderful, Scarlet,' Thea chimes in with a soft smile.

I turn to Ivy, knowing if anyone will give me an honest answer, it's her.

She purses her lips, putting her hands on her hips.

'Do you feel comfortable in it?' she asks, staring into my eyes.

My hand lifts to my neck as I battle my thoughts. I want to not care about my skin, but I also don't want people staring at me.

Before I can answer, the Nightshade goes to my dress rack and starts rummaging through it. She finds what she needs before she comes my way. She holds a bright red piece of silk that was meant to go with another dress as a sash. She comes over to me and slowly ties it round my neck.

'This hides your scars,' she murmurs, fiddling with it without looking at me.

I smile timidly as she ties the fabric into a bow for me. 'Thank you, Ivy.'

She finally glances up, and she gives me a hard look. 'Don't think this means anything.'

'Of course not,' I answer, her statement cheering me up immensely. I turn towards Olive and Thea. 'Better?'

'You looked lovely before, but you seem more confident like this,' Olive observes with a satisfied nod. 'I think it's a winner.'

'Well, I want to try some more options,' Ivy announces, sighing loudly at her attire. 'I don't think this is right for me.'

'I want to try some more on just because I *can*,' Olive confesses with a grin, earning an approving nod from our mentor.

'We have time,' Thea declares.

For an additional hour, Thea and I sit on a comfortable sofa, watching as Ivy and Olive work through the dresses on their racks. So many fabrics, so many shades of sapphire and emerald. Thankfully, they both find the perfect dresses. Thea and Elsa are more helpful than I could ever be when questions about certain cuts, body types and fabrics are voiced.

'We are going to look *amazing*.' Olive beams as we pay for our gowns.

I leave the dress shop smiling along with my companions, feeling like we've bonded on a new and deeper level.

*This is only the beginning*, I tell myself, smiling brightly as we leave Aura's Dress Shop.

22

Thea's favourite restaurant, the Sapphire Salmon, resides in the heart of Sapphire City – hence its name. The building, like most around it, is double-storey and is made of sandstone. What sets it apart, though, is the balcony big enough to accommodate several circular tables, which look out onto the city square. In the distance, I spot the pearly-white castle we will soon be visiting, while behind the structure is the ocean, which sparkles under the sunlight. It is breathtaking, with waves crashing into the golden sandy shore, and even from this distance, I can detect the strong smell of salt in the air, which makes me sigh happily.

*I love this,* I can't help thinking with a grin, taking every detail in.

On the restaurant tables are blue-and-white-chequered tablecloths, candles already lit, with wax melting down the sides, and flowers of pink and yellow decorating the centre. Taking in all the small details, I distractedly take the first empty chair I come across, unable to take my eyes off the setting and the stunning city panorama.

'Look at this view,' I gush.

The Hex and our mentors are sitting and conversing while we wait for our food. Rusty sits on one side of me, Peri on the other. The sky is full of fluffy white clouds, and I can't look away, enamoured of everything Tealwaters has to offer.

'How lucky are we?' I aim this question at Peri as our drinks arrive and are passed around the table. I'm given a bright yellow drink that smells sour — supposedly something healthy and with lemon. I sip it and raise a brow. This stuff is *exquisite*. I peer across to find Jack with the same beverage, while Sol, beside him, has water again.

Peri nods in a sort of daze at my question, keeping to himself, as per usual, and I find myself deflating. Is there a reason he barely talks, or is it because he's not found common ground with anyone yet?

*Perhaps he does not engage for fear he will feel pain if someone lies to his face*, I think, realising this could be a large factor in his asocial behaviour.

'This weather must be quite different from the cold you're used to,' I say to the Silken, his posture rigid and eyes averted from everyone on our table.

I know that the House of Velvet resides in the south. In the south-east of Sennastone, Siamoon is known for its snow, frost-covered trees and ice fields. Its summers consist of sunshine, like they do in any other kingdom, but with temperatures so cold you'll lose your fingers if you fail to remember gloves.

'Yes, very different.' He shifts in his chair.

I note he wears his shoulder-length hair down most of the time, only the top part pulled away from his face, which, with the perspiration that covers his temples, seems strange. Unlike the other males, he wears his sleeves rolled down, and most of his body is covered up, like mine. Wouldn't a male who is used to the cold be hot in a kingdom like this, where the sun beats down on us all day every day?

'A dunk in the ocean would help with keeping you cool. I can always come with you if you ever want company.' I smile even though I can't swim to save my life, but I don't mention this, expecting him to reject my offer anyway.

'Thanks,' he answers with a tight nod.

I purse my lips, determined to find some shared interest.

Jack meets my gaze from across the table, Sol telling him some story about grapes, I think. My guardian seems to be slowly warming up to our fellow fledglings, but he doesn't give this away, his face neutral and his answers forcibly polite.

*Are you all right?* he mouths, to which I nod.

*Are you?* I mouth back, and he rolls his eyes when Sol acts out something.

'You can manipulate people, can't you?' I ask Peri suddenly, recalling the reveal of all our powers. I think from the slight jerk away from me, he thought I was done with him for the time being. 'Can you make Sol suddenly sing or dance?'

He quirks a brow. 'You want to see that?'

'Don't you?' I challenge.

'I don't use my powers for pleasure.'

I turn fully to him. 'Does it cause you pain to use your magic?'

He leans away, his body taut as if he expects me to strike him at any minute, but he gives me his full attention, violet eyes boring into me, unflinching. 'No, but I don't like using it. Especially to get my own way.'

'I'm glad. An ability like yours is rather intimidating. It's nice to know someone as powerful as you has an awareness of others.'

He nods but doesn't comment.

Our conversation is paused by a waiter who brings out large dishes of seafood, beady black eyes and scales galore. The sight of the sea creatures makes me twist my mouth in uncertainty. I've never eaten such a variety of food, but when they stare up at me ...

'You may enjoy it,' Rusty says beside me, taking what he tells me are prawns.

'I guess I won't know until I try it,' I agree, filling my own plate.

I watch the Briar eat, copying his movements for the dishes I'm not sure about. He smiles down at me when he notices, but instead of judgement, he simply starts instructing me.

'You don't eat the heads,' Rusty says, pointing to the slimy creatures. 'You have to rip them off.'

'Oh, lovely.' I laugh, slightly disturbed when I behead the poor creatures.

He puts one in his mouth and smiles, motioning for me to do the same.

'That's interesting,' I comment while chewing, having thought they'd taste saltier, but the flavour is sweeter than expected. 'Why do people eat these?'

'Good for strong bones,' he says, making me hum in answer.

People around us begin to rise to their feet, pointing out from the balcony. An increase in voices makes me turn towards the commotion. Something interesting is happening.

Carmen and Thea stand along with them, and we fledglings take no time to imitate them. I finally spot what all the fuss is about – in the distance, a large swarm of colourful birds flies through the city streets. They squawk and flap their wings, making me gasp as they head towards the ocean. The people below in the streets look up to watch the spectacle.

'Are those parrots?' I ask, having seen them in Thea's gardens.

'Yes. A whole load of mail has arrived, it seems,' Ivy answers, her sapphire eyes admiring the scene.

I turn to Jack questioningly.

'They use parrots to send their mail,' he answers without prompting.

I quirk a brow in pleasant surprise. In the House of Raven, we use ravens. It didn't occur to me that other species would be used elsewhere.

Our heads turn as they surround the balcony, a flurry of rainbow colours shooting past us. Peri even watches the show beside me, craning his neck so he doesn't miss it. It's only when the birds have flown into the distance and we all settle back into our seats that I see it.

The Silken's head turns back towards the table, his hair moving ever so slightly back from his neck. My eyes dart to the large scar that peeks out from his shirt collar. Long and silver with spots of dark surrounding it. They look like tiny burns in the process of scarring.

Sensing my attention, Peri twists and finds my eyes still on the side of his neck. He looks alarmed, lips tight as if I've intruded on something personal. He grabs the arms of his chair and simply stares, willing me to say something.

I try to choke out words, blinking away the horror of what I've come to realise.

We wage a war as we study each other.

Finally I whisper a question, hoping no one else can hear. 'Who did that to you, Peri?' Because he couldn't have done it himself, with the way the lesion curves towards the back of his neck. He would have to be extremely flexible.

He, like me, has been hurt before. That much is obvious

now. The reason he covers up is the same reason I do – we bare scars we want no one else to see.

The Silken notices my reaction, and his features change – disbelief into suspicion. 'Why do you care?'

'Because I … do.' I'm not sure what to say, but knowing someone has given him such a large mark makes me want to grind the abuser to dust. It's not enough of an answer for him. He turns away and begins to ignore me again.

I can't help it. I stare because I don't know how to move on from this, how to make my mouth move to make conversation. My mind is filled with how a wound that prominent came to be on my fellow Hex member's neck.

'What?' Peri snaps into defensive mode. He leans forward, so close to my face I can sense people watching our encounter.

I don't move away but rather move closer, looking deep into his plum-coloured eyes.

'Who was it?' I press, needing to know, needing a name so I can put them on the list of people I want to one day destroy.

*They can go one below the Elder Raven and Winella,* I think, grinding my teeth together.

'Why do you care?' he repeats, shaking his head in confusion. 'Why ask? Why do you want to know?'

I realise it must be strange for him, a person he barely knows wanting to know about a potentially dark moment in his life. I don't know how to explain it to him, that I feel a sudden need to shield him like no one was able to for me.

A stray thought shoots through my mind. *Perhaps we can be that person for each other.*

So I do the only thing I can think of and pull down the neck of my shirt. I reveal the most painful part of me, which holds on to the memory of the most terrifying moment in my life. His violet eyes trail down, seeing my ripped skin, and he swallows. I replace the material of my shirt before anyone else can see.

'I *care* because I think you'll understand when I say it is dreadful being made to feel so small and weak. To be defenceless and to suffer in silence – to feel alone in all your torment.'

Emotion fills the Silken's gaze, raw, unfiltered bitterness flashing through his dark eyes.

I take a deep breath to calm the growing fire in my heart, the spark of hatred I have when I think of the Elder Raven and the masters who enjoyed torturing me throughout my childhood.

'My family did it,' I hear him say, so low only a vampire could hear, before he gets up and walks away.

My heart sinks as I watch him leave the restaurant.

'What did you do now?' Ivy asks, shaking her head.

'Nothing,' I insist.

'Hmm, it doesn't *look* like nothing.' She goes back to her meal with a disapproving look.

## 23

My reflection stares back at me. She wears a grimace as her dark crimson eyes trail over her bare and exposed skin. The burns are a faint pink colour, while the texture looks inflamed and sensitive still.

*I can do this*, I tell myself. *It's only skin.*

I wear a short-sleeved top that displays my arms and neck. To any other female, the shirt is conservative – unrevealing – but to me in my current state, it's something I've been preventing myself from thinking about. I know that eventually I will have to stop wearing the long sleeves I've been clinging to recently, but seeing Peri's wound ...

A part of me feels like I need to prove a point, show him that we can be ourselves even with the scars. They do not define us; they only show our strength. That we are *survivors*.

'I will go out there and show them it does not bother me,' I tell my reflection, a determined expression plastered on my face, my hand nervously playing with the bronze band around my wrist. 'You can do this.'

I head for my bedroom door before I can second-guess

myself. I walk steadily down the passageway, passing everyone's door, and head for the back garden, where we are to meet. I keep my mind blank, counting my steps to think of anything but my growing doubt.

It seems I've wasted more time debating in front of my reflection than I first thought, as I'm the last to arrive. As I step out from the big dining room onto the wooden deck, all eyes turn to me. Heat rushes to my cheeks, but I don't back down. I approach the group and let them stare, taking the details they need in.

To my shock, no one seems surprised. Sol even gives me an approving nod before glancing towards our mentors.

Jack lifts a brow in question as I come to his side.

'Turning over a new leaf, are we?' he asks, and I nod.

'Something like that.'

I meet Peri's eye and smile tenderly, silently telling him everything I wished to say at dinner in the city yesterday.

*I can do this, and so can you.*

'Right, everyone,' Carmen says, having not given me a second glance. 'Let's get going.'

We walk out of the vegetable garden and down the slope through the long grass. An arm links through mine. Olive smiles down at me, not caring about the feel of my skin against hers. She's already seen my body when we went dress shopping, saw it and accepted it without hesitation.

'Brave, resilient and remarkable. Will you ever cease to amaze me?' the Severed says with a tilt of her emerald head.

'I'm only keeping up with the high standards we Ravens hold.' I smirk, earning a chuckle.

'Being serious for a moment, I think you doing this is wonderful. I could tell in Aura's Dress Shop your wounds are something you've felt the need to hide, but I'm glad you've decided to give them some sun. I think you look like a true warrior.'

'Thank you. To be honest, I feel extremely uncomfortable right now,' I admit.

'Oh, of course you'll feel that way at first, but you're doing great,' she reassures me, earning a nod from Jack.

My fingers fall down to feel the long tendrils of grass that are as tall as my thighs. Jack's hand grasps mine for a brief moment and squeezes. In the gesture, I can feel his pride, his respect for me and what I'm doing. He lets go too soon, making me wish for his touch again.

The Hex stands facing Gwenore Forest. Her dark shadows taunt us from within, promising harm if we so much as step inside. Instead of training at the House of Bane, we are being schooled in our back garden.

'You want us to go back in there on *purpose?*' My guardian motions towards the dense trees lining the grass field.

I'm obviously not the only one who still has lingering uneasiness when it comes to the dangerous woodland.

'That's correct.' Thea nods. 'Okay, fledglings, your partners are as follows.' Her eyes rise to the sky as if recalling a memory. 'Ivy and Olive, Jack and Peri, Sol and Carmen, Scarlet and Rusty. I will be around to help if anyone is in need. You have thirty minutes, and you will hear a horn when you are allowed to travel back to the safety of the paths. Good luck!'

I glance towards Jack, who looks apprehensive as he

approaches the Silken. The pair stand together awkwardly, neither male wanting to be the first to make conversation. I shake my head at both of them.

Before us is a long path that winds its way through the greenery, a fork in the distance separating it into four different trails. I've only been down one, knowing it leads to Sapphire City, but where do the others lead?

Thea instructs that each team must pick a different track and not go looking for each other – she will be close by if anyone needs urgent help.

My confidence plummets. I've experienced this forest before, and it feels too soon to be visiting again, but everyone grabs their designated partner.

'Are you ready?'

I turn to find Rusty looking out into the thick brush. The other teams are already making their way inside. My nerves rise as I watch Peri leading Jack to the leftmost pathway, his lithe body on edge as my guardian follows.

'Jack will be fine. Peri is probably the best person to be with in a training session like this,' Rusty reassures me, his voice low and soothing as we choose the last path available – the second from the right. 'He and Gwenore seem to have an understanding. She won't be too vicious with him around.'

This calms me for only a second. 'So she'll be dreadful to us?'

'Most likely. She seems to really dislike me. Carmen reckons it's because of my magic – Gwen supposedly detests powerful people.' He shrugs like this is normal.

*A forest hating a person.*

That is *not* normal.

'She'll love me, then,' I mutter under my breath. With only a scar that bleeds when I'm in danger, Gwenore may take pity on me. Then again, she didn't the last time I visited, so why would she do so today?

*Perhaps it's the dark magic within you*, I think with a jolt, peering down at my scarred palm.

We walk in silence along the pathway. The only sounds I can hear are the occasional animal trudging unaffected through the trees, the crunching of the gravel beneath our boots and the steady rhythm of Rusty's heart – mine, in comparison, pounds like a drum.

'Scarlet,' the Briar says quietly, bronze eyes briefly taking in my burns before darting away to the trees. 'Tell me if this is inappropriate to ask, but what did you have to do to become the next Raven of the Hex?' He is excellent at hiding his feelings, but I sense his concern.

I hum thoughtfully, keeping up with his long strides. I don't usually want to talk about my past, but now that I've got my scars on display, it's likely that people will ask questions.

'I had to compete in a set of trials, all of them deadlier than the one before.'

'How did you beat them?'

From his belt he takes out a small knife and offers it to me. I shake my head and bring out my own dagger of gold and midnight in answer. He studies it with interest, his bronze gaze roaming over the star-studded handle and pure-gold blade. Leo would be extremely pleased with herself if she saw his reaction.

'I beat each challenge with determination and pure dumb luck,' I answer honestly. He appears to not believe me, so I go on. 'I was never like my brethren. I didn't grow up to fight and train to be a warrior. I worked in a stable and was given the lowest pay imaginable.'

'Does your Elder force Ravens to compete in these trials?' Rusty asks quietly.

'No. She did, however, use something we needed against us. In my case, my older sister needed medicine that would save her life and the lives of her unborn children when she gave birth.'

Rusty gives me an alarmed look.

I nod in agreement. 'As you can imagine, I jumped at the opportunity, hoping to save her, because the alternative wasn't an option for me.'

'That must have been terrifying for you,' Rusty murmurs.

'It was,' I agree. 'What about you? How did your House choose you as the next Briar of the Hex?'

He shakes his head glumly. 'I was simply next in line.'

I frown. 'You make it sound like a royal bloodline.' I pause. 'Wait, are you Briar royalty? Have I been missing the opportunity to bow to you every time I see you?'

He smiles at my attempt at humour. 'It's similar, but no. We have a male Elder, much like yours, who is the head of our House. His children are what we called the Supremes. Any male heir will be next in line for the Hex, while in their absence, any female heir will look after our tribe until the male heir retires and becomes the next Elder,' he explains, leading me further into the forest.

'So that means your father is the Elder Briar?'

Rusty shakes his head. 'No. This is where it gets complicated. My mate, Rosalie, is a Supreme. She was the firstborn female of the Elder Briar. As her mate, I am her equal and thus as powerful as her.'

*Mate.*

I remember Jack explaining that having a mate is very common among the fae. It's an extremely strong and unbreakable connection with a person who destiny, or some other magical entity that the House of Creation believes in, deems their equal in every way. So Rosalie must be very powerful, given Rusty's abilities – magically *and* physically.

Rusty continues, not sensing my internal thoughts. 'Rosalie's older brother was supposed to be the next Briar of the Hex, but due to his … absence, I had to take his place.'

He grimaces, and I wonder what it felt like to have that pressure put on him. To be paired with the most powerful female in his House and to one day be pulled away from her because of duty.

'Do you resent that tradition? Would you have stayed home if you'd had the choice?' I ask sympathetically.

He hesitates before giving a very diplomatic answer. 'I would do anything to be beside Rosalie. But without her brother to protect the lands, I must step up. It's not ideal, but we have the ability to see each other whenever we want, so I am luckier than most.'

I don't have the chance to ask what he means before a horn suddenly blares, echoing through the branches of the trees above us. My head snaps up to the sound, wondering what it is.

'That's the signal for us to begin,' Rusty says, making me frown.

'Begin what, exactly?'

'You'll see,' he murmurs, cautiously stepping off the safety of the path and into the trees.

## 24

Gwenore Forest irks me. It's somehow colder today, even when the sunlight streams through the treetops. My steps are quiet and careful, as if the moment I stomp around, Gwenore might wake up and attack us.

'So for half an hour, all we have to do is stay alive?'

'Basically, yes,' Rusty answers. 'But don't let the apparent simplicity of the task fool you. We always go in teams for safety. Gwen can be *very* dangerous.'

A bush nearby rustles, and I jump back in panic, aiming my dagger at the sound. I find a small fawn stumbling out towards us, a twig of berries in its small mouth. I stare at the creature, having never seen one in real life before.

'It's so *adorable*.' I gawk, wanting so badly to get nearer, but from books, I know they can be skittish, and I don't want to scare it away.

Rusty's brow lifts with silent amusement as he watches me study the creature. It's only when I slowly bend down, leaning on one knee to get level with the creature, that I reach out to let the animal sniff at my scarred hand.

'I think it likes me.' I smile, adding this experience to

my mental list of things to mention in my letters to family and friends. I know when Merlot finally receives my messages she will love hearing about this and will tell her guardian all about it too.

My throat feels tight at the thought of my friend who still has not replied.

*She* will *recover, the princess said so herself,* I remind myself. *Merlot will wake up when she is ready.*

'I don't trust it,' Rusty says, hooking me out of my darkening thoughts. 'Make sure it doesn't have razor teeth before you stroke it.'

Rusty's eyes zoom in on my outstretched hand, and I stifle a laugh. My scar is still closed, so I know I'm safe for the time being.

'Deer have fangs here?' I ask with bemusement.

'No, but you never know what surprises *she* has in store for us.' He motions to our surroundings before he pauses and listens.

A soft rumbling sound begins, and my hackles rise. The fawn dashes off as if sensing the danger lurking too.

'Something is coming,' Rusty says.

I peer around at the ground, knowing the last time I heard a similar sound, the earth tore apart and lifted as if a monster moved underneath. But nothing shifts now.

Suddenly my hand turns damp. I peer down to see my scar bleeding, blood oozing down between my fingers. I jerk to my feet so I can turn in circles, hoping to find the threat before it hits us.

'Rusty ...' His name lingers in the air, panic washing over me as I cling on to my weapon, the feel of it now too small for what I suspect is coming our way.

'Your hand. It truly does tell you when we're in danger?' Rusty's frown is prominent as his bronze eyes flicker between worrying over my bleeding hand and fretting over our hazardous surroundings.

'Not you, only me,' I correct.

He grumbles something under his breath.

My eyes land on something behind my training partner that makes my heart drop. 'Holy Hanrah!' I shout, pointing into the distance at clouds of rising dirt. 'A stampede!'

Animals of all shapes and sizes race across the forest floor towards us. Some of the creatures I have seen before, remembering them from books, but others are much larger and much more terrifying than I thought they'd be in reality.

'Stay behind me,' Rusty orders, pulling at my arm roughly and pushing me behind his hulking body.

We stand there watching intently as the mass quickly approaches, my heart beating faster and faster the longer we wait, my hands shaking with the rising panic growing in my chest.

'Are we going to let them trample us, or can we go now?' I practically shout at the Briar, my feet itching to run, to find a tree to climb until the charge passes.

'No,' he answers cryptically, his voice calm and commanding. He has yet to take out his weapons. What is he waiting for?

*They'll be upon us any second now.*

My hand reaches for Rusty's shirt and tugs it firmly, the fear in my voice evident now. 'I don't have any other magic to defend us, so either do something right *now*, or I'm getting on your shoulders.'

As if in answer, his muscled arms rise, hands circling in the air, the tang of magic enveloping me like a heavy blanket. I expect him to create something, something to ward off these creatures, but instead, colourful sparks fly from his hands as large circular portals open in front and behind us, their dark green edges rustling like leaves. They are nothing like the Elder Raven's portals, which crackle like blazing fires – no, these are calm and benign.

'How are you doing this?' I marvel out loud, stunned. I think back to the one that found me on the beach – I had thought Carmen or Thea had created it, but it must have been the Briar.

I watch with wonder as the animals that charge us run into the portal before us and come out behind us, passing us completely. They don't stop, seeming to be in a craze as they quickly fade into the distance.

Minutes pass, and the magic finally softens around me.

*It's not ideal, but we have the ability to see each other whenever we want, so I am luckier than most*, Rusty said when talking of his mate, Rosalie. Now I understand. He can see her whenever he wishes by creating a portal to the House of Creation.

Envy slices through me, thinking of the number of visits I'd make home to see my new niece and nephew – to see if everyone I care for is okay back in the House of Raven.

'Are you all right?' Rusty asks. He seems to look healthier somehow, his eyes clearer, his skin glowing and flushed with colour. Is this the effect using his magic has on him?

'I didn't realise you could create portals. That must be a valuable ability to have.'

Slowly we begin to walk back to the path, hoping training ends soon.

'As my House's name suggests, I can create anything that isn't living. With portals, though, I can only make them to locations I've been to before, so as long as I've been once, I can travel anywhere I like.' He shrugs as if this type of skill is ordinary. Perhaps in the House of Creation, it is.

'I have so much to learn about your kind,' I murmur with wonder. 'A House that can create *anything*?'

'Anything not living,' Rusty repeats.

'So you can make ...' I think for a moment before getting excited. 'Weapons?'

He takes my dagger – the gift from Princess Leonore – and studies it intently. Light flares from his palms before he lifts his hands. In each, a golden blade with a black hilt decorated in shimmering stars shines menacingly. I gasp, unable to tell which is the original.

'I marked mine so you wouldn't confuse them,' Rusty explains, pointing to a symbol engraved in the blade. A stag, so small I wouldn't have seen it unless I had been searching for it.

'It's beautiful,' I murmur in awe.

'It's yours.' Rusty offers me the blades.

I take them with a grin and twirl them between my fingers. 'Thank you so much.'

'You're welcome.'

I sheathe them in my belt, the pair looking dangerous and perfect.

'So, what about food?' I continue, enamoured of his abilities. I knew he was powerful, the very scent of him giving him away, but this? This is more than I ever could have imagined.

'It's difficult to muster up tastes, but technically, yes. As long as I've seen something before, or in this case tasted it, I can replicate it if need be,' he says, tilting his head left to right as if weighing his answer.

'Liquid Gold?' I ask with excitement, thinking of my favourite drink from when I used to fight at the Badger's Sett.

'I've never seen or tasted Liquid Gold before, so no.'

I visibly deflate. I love the drink – the alcohol doesn't

affect me like it does humans, but it always reminds me of my best friend, Dimitri.

'I'll have to find some for you. It's delicious,' I say, seeing the path up ahead. Relief floods me with the sight.

'I'd like that,' he answers, looking down at me with a warm expression, but I see a glint of something in his bronze eyes.

A horn blares, making me jump.

'And that's our training session done for the day,' he says, not commenting on my quickening pace.

## 25

When we arrive back at Hex Manor, I head to my room to retrieve some fresh clothes. I find a small envelope on my bed. On the front is written *To the Raven*.

My frown deepens as I open it up. Inside is a piece of paper that's been folded in half. It smells faintly of smoke as I begin to read, the handwriting different from the envelope's.

YOUR SILENCE WILL BE THE KEY TO YOUR DAUGHTER'S SURVIVAL.

IF YOU TELL A SOUL ABOUT HER DISAPPEARANCE, WE WILL KNOW AND WILL ENSURE SHE IS PUNISHED FOR YOUR LACK OF OBEDIENCE.

DO NOT FRET. SHE IS NOT ALONE, NOR WILL SHE EVER BE.

A gasp escapes my lips before I jolt into action. I head for the door and swing it wide, only to find myself face to face with the Nightshade.

Sapphire eyes widen in alarm. I shove the letter into the back of my trousers before she notices.

'Ivy!' I greet her with too much enthusiasm. 'To what do I owe this pleasure?'

Never has she come to my chamber, let alone knocked on my door, but she gives me a cool look before motioning to her occupied hand.

'Delivering the dresses for tonight, obviously.' She shoves my crimson gown into my chest and gives me a quick look-over. Eyes narrowing, she says, 'You have that same look on your face. Like you've done something, and you are waiting for someone else to finally realise it too.'

I shrug. 'I think you're imagining it.'

'Whatever it is you're hiding, I'll figure it out.'

'I'm sure you will.'

She frowns but doesn't reply, instead walking off with a final look over her shoulder.

After throwing my gown onto my bed, I walk calmly to Jack's room, watching as Ivy strolls downstairs. I don't bother to knock on my guardian's door, instead letting myself in.

He is half-dressed and wearing an annoyed expression before he registers it's me. I close his bedroom door behind me before stopping in my tracks.

'Oh,' I murmur. My observance lingers, taking in every detail of him. The low-slung trousers that he's yet to button up. The toned body and strong arms that hold a crisp white shirt. His hair is damp from a bath, and his ocean eyes soften at the sight of me.

'Oh?' he quips.

I tilt my head. 'I wasn't expecting you to be ...'

My guardian purses his lips as if to stop himself laughing. 'Half clothed?' he supplies.

'I can come back later,' I offer, turning for the door. A hand stops me, his large fingers grasping my wrist before I can leave. Warmth shoots up my arm, making my body hyper-aware of his proximity.

'You're here now. Stay.'

My eyes close briefly before I turn to glance at him. Those light eyes of his are mischievous as they roam over my face, as if sensing every delicious thought I'm having about him.

'All right, I'll stay.' My eyes try to focus on anything but his chiselled chest but my traitorous gaze flashes back every so often to absorb the sight of his muscled arms and glistening hair that falls over his forehead.

Jack chuckles softly, seeming to note my awkwardness, making no effort to put distance between us. 'Why are you nervous, Scarlet? Does my nakedness affect you?'

'No,' I blurt, gritting my teeth. 'You look like every other man I've seen.'

This seems to make him more curious. 'And how many other men have you seen?'

My arms cross against my chest – mostly to hide my shaking hands but also to keep them away from his *very* tempting body.

'Enough to know this ...' I motion with my chin to his chest. 'Is average at best.'

Jack's brow rises in challenge. 'It seems I must work harder to gain your favour, Raven.'

*Please no. I don't think I could handle it.*

'Don't bother,' I say with more confidence than I feel, moving towards his window and opening it to let some air in. The breeze makes me feel instantly better. That is until his large body looms behind me, his nearness making me feel hot all over again.

'But I enjoy seeing you flustered,' he murmurs, his hand tentatively brushing over my hip. A quiet breath escapes me at the caress but I don't move. We agreed to keep our relationship platonic but if I turn around he'll know my thoughts are anything but friendly. 'I especially enjoy seeing your cheeks turn pink.'

'You flatter yourself, guardian,' I mumble, spinning on my heel to face him. And there before me stands the Teacher – confident, strong and a force to be reckoned with.

Every part of me wants to stand on my tiptoes and steal a kiss from him. Instead I drag a hand gently down his stomach – the way I did in the barn – and smile as my guardian bites his bottom lip to keep himself from reacting.

My hand drops away before it reaches his unbuttoned trousers, the heat in his gaze making me feel victorious.

Jack shakes his head. 'You are playing with fire, Scarlet.'

'I'm not the one without a shirt,' I counter before realising what I've said.

My guardian's eyes narrow in triumph. 'I do love knowing that I affect you, Raven.'

*You sure do.*

'But I must confess ...' Jack leans forward, brushing his lips against my temple. His hands wander across my hips once more, coming around to my lower back. The feel of him is consuming, the need for him a throbbing sensation I swear I can hear within my skull.

*Touch him. Touch him. Touch him.*

My breath tickles his neck as I allow myself to inhale his ocean scent. His smile grows slowly, becoming predatory as he traces my cheek with his lips.

'You are like forbidden fruit. I can't seem to stay away,' he utters, making my pulse race. My guardian's arms wrap around me, pulling me closer to him. Our frames melt into one, mine fitting his perfectly.

'What's this?' he suddenly asks, a crinkling sound pulling me out of my daze. Jack raises a small piece of paper in the air between us. The crinkle of his brow makes me remember the whole point of me being in his chamber.

'Shit.' I move out of his grasp, distancing myself from him so I can think more clearly. 'That is what I came to see you about. I think it was Mrs Kapper, the pregnant lady, who sent it to us. I found it lying on my bed.'

My guardian takes his time to absorb my words before narrowing his eyes. He slowly pulls away from the window we stand at and reads the contents.

I silently scold myself for being so foolish. The other fledglings are nearby, Sol's singing being indication enough that we could have been overheard.

*And someone is in need*, I remind myself, mentally slapping myself back to sense. *Focus on the important matter at hand.*

'So she *is* being threatened,' Jack mutters, taking in every inch of the paper, even the back. He frowns deeply. 'How many other families have received this same note?'

'Who knows?' I shrug, shifting myself to sit on the window ledge. The soft breeze cools me down, allowing me a moment to steady myself again. 'That's obviously why they reacted the way they did. They know more than they are letting on but can't divulge any details, in case their missing children suffer the consequences.'

I shake my head with dismay, thinking of poor Alex's brother and how terrified he must be.

'This is bigger than I first thought. And for them to admit they are taking more children ...' Jack trails off, making me nod glumly.

'We need to let Alex know,' I reply, recalling the blue ribbon he gave me.

## 26

We arrive at Ivory Castle, the royal invitation in Thea's hand as our carriage waits in line behind several others. The sky is no longer as bright and sunny. It is quickly darkening while displaying streaks of pinks, oranges and purples as we trundle through a set of pearly white gates.

The grand entrance quickly fills with people who not only are dressed in their finest outfits but are clearly *very* rich. As I exit the carriage, my eyes glide upwards with awe, the castle spires so high I can't believe they don't touch the clouds.

'It never seems to get old, no matter how many times I study it,' Thea says, peering up to the extraordinary sight before us, appearing just as impressed as I am.

As the Hex is escorted into the castle with all the other arriving guests, I stay close to Jack's side, making sure not to lose him in the expanse of people. His hand snakes out and grabs my elbow, leading me through the reception area, which echoes with chatter.

My first thought while walking through the castle is that it is extremely grand, and its decor is even grander.

With lanterns made of crystal and the floor made of something pearlescent, I can't help but gape at the opulence.

'Close your mouth,' Carmen murmurs, pressing the side of her finger under my chin.

I do my best to keep my features neutral, but the moment we get to a giant archway that leads to the back of the stronghold, I pause to take it all in.

A lavish set of ivory stairs spills onto a marvellous view of a luscious green lawn. On the far side of the well-maintained grounds is a small group of musicians playing their instruments. Behind them are colourful fruit trees that line the huge area and cover up a stone wall that separates us from the ocean, its waves crashing along the shore beyond.

I beam brightly as I imagine living here, having this as my back garden. It's such a wonderful thought that my cheeks begin to ache.

'I don't think I'll ever get used to seeing you experience new things,' Jack says in my ear, meeting my gaze when I look up at him.

'Is this real?' I ask him quietly, pinching my hand to see if I'll wake up.

'Sure is.' He nods, thanking Thea as she offers him a drink.

I'm then handed a drink of bubbles within a crystal flute. It shines pink and blue as I twirl it, the light catching the glass. Everything here in Tealwaters is so *pretty*.

*Those of beauty can deal out the deadliest hands*, Thea told me once, and her words make me pause briefly.

Our mentors gather us around, our group creating a circle.

'Remember,' Carmen says, as if we are her children. 'Be on your best behaviour tonight. Don't drink too much, and don't fondle any of the guests.'

I wrinkle my nose at that. She gives us all an *it's happened before* look.

'And remember that you only get *one* first impression,' Thea urges before she shoos us away and she and her sister head for a group of ladies. 'Go. Impress them all.'

Upon the grass area are several tables covered in silver cloth. Each one is stacked with dishes, plates and bowls of punch and delicious-smelling food. The dessert table grabs my attention immediately. I search hurriedly for Olive and grab her hand.

'Olive, do you see what I see?'

She scans the garden, and her emerald eyes widen with delight.

'A chocolate fountain?' She squeals, making Sol jerk away with his hands covering his ears. 'Do we have to wait, or can we fill our plates now?'

'I suggest you mingle first before stuffing your faces and potentially ruining your gowns,' Rusty says, motioning to our attire.

Olive looks down at her emerald dress. It has sequins all over and hugs her curves with incredible allure. I've already spotted several men and women looking her up and down since our arrival. She shrugs the Briar off before stalking away, dragging Sol along with her so he can apparently hold a second plate for her.

'I tried,' Rusty mutters to anyone who will listen before following them.

I look around to see where Peri has gone, but he seems to have disappeared into the shadows. If he is uncomfortable around a handful of people, then a large crowd like this would certainly be enough to overwhelm him.

The Nightshade of the Hex, however, seems quite content fitting in with a group of Tellians, her smile broad as she greets those she clearly knows, their conversations flowing easily.

I find myself slightly envious at how easy she makes it look. In response to my inner unease, I puff up my skirts, smooth out my hair, and make sure the fabric tied around my neck is perfectly in place.

*You can do this.*

Jack notices my preparation with eagle eyes. 'I'm not used to seeing you in a dress but you made a fine choice, Raven.'

He offers his arm as we descend the stairs. I place my hand into the crook of his elbow before we head for the dessert table, where the Severed and her companions are piling food onto their plates.

On the other side of the party, where the band plays, the music is upbeat and loud as guests drink without limit around the pearl-coloured dance floor. One man is ogling the female violinist, who is doing a good job of avoiding his eyes. Couples dance already, colourful dresses swaying and twirling around.

'Thank you. You look rather dashing yourself,' I answer, having to keep myself from staring. He wears no specific House colours, the choice seeming to be entirely his own. But shades of blue – which I assume represents his elemental magic – wrap around his waistcoat in what seems to be swirls, bringing out the colour of his brilliant eyes.

Jack meets my gaze but promptly drops my hand the moment we tread on the last step. I stop the scowl that forms on my face before anyone notices.

'We make a fine looking pair,' he muses, not seeming to notice the sudden spike of yearning that shoots through my chest at the statement.

'We certainly do,' I utter back.

'Can I stand with you?'

I peer around to see Peri awkwardly standing off to the side, hands in his pockets as those dark violet eyes roam the garden with suspicion. He looks handsome in his waistcoat, embroidered with delicate silver silk moths – a motif of the House of Velvet. I realise then I'm not the only one who was probably forced into certain attire tonight.

'Of course you can,' I answer, swallowing my feelings down as I move my body so he's included in our group. 'Jack was about to get us some refills. Do you want one?'

My guardian gives me a quizzical look, peering down at our practically full glasses.

I swallow mine all in one and hand it to him. 'You said you wanted to walk around and get a *feel* for the people. Peri can look after me. Right?'

The Silken gives me a reluctant nod when I turn to him for confirmation but refuses the refill, not having a drink to start with. When my guardian strides away, Peri shuffles nearer.

'Why did you send him off?'

*I need space to clear my head which is filled with a male I should not be holding affection for.*

'I thought you'd feel more comfortable with just the two of us.' I can feel his gaze burning through my skull, and I hesitantly turn and meet his look. 'Was I wrong?'

'I can manage a party.'

'Can you? Where did you disappear to at the beginning, then?'

He averts his gaze and says nothing. 'I went to relieve myself.'

'You went before we left Hex Manor. Why did you need to again?' I ask, earning a scowl.

'How do you know—'

'You don't have to hide your feelings from me, Peri. I

may not have the power of truth detection, but I know when someone is nervous,' I murmur, keeping my voice low.

He twitches with surprise, seeming uncomfortable.

'If it makes you feel better, I'm nervous too.'

A set of trumpets sound, and I startle. Peri's pale hands encase my arm, preventing me from stumbling. I give him a grateful look.

'It seems the royals have arrived,' he utters.

## 27

I watch along with everyone else as the royal family enters the garden. Upon the grand steps, as lavish as I would expect them to be, is the very handsome King Hector and his utterly stunning wife Queen Melody. They are slow in their descent, letting their guests soak up their overwhelming wealth and prestigious presence. Their smiles are unexpectedly bright and welcoming, their hands lifting up in greeting as they approach the crowds.

Guards I never noticed before now surround the premises as well as the sovereigns, keeping a short distance from them in case of trouble.

The king and queen both have the usual Tellian blonde hair and stunning light blue eyes that I would never complain about having. They wear matching attire of silver, with dark blue adorning the queen's gown, and the king wears an extravagant seashell-and-pearl crown.

A male, who I assume is their son and thus heir to the throne, follows them down the stairs. He wears garments of deep cobalt and a matching ocean-themed circlet upon his head, making him comparable to the darkening sea as the sun begins to disappear from the horizon.

I watch him with interest, as Fox has mentioned Prince Athos before. She has worked closely with him for years, bringing his inventions to life. Besides that, though, I realise I know very little about the future king of Tealwaters.

The royal family members are surprisingly social, not taking a seat on the three silver thrones that have been placed for them but instead taking the time to welcome each assemblage of guests to their home and stopping to converse.

'It's nice to see them make an effort to engage with their people,' Peri says, making me nod as we watch the trio wade through the partygoers. 'If this were my king, he'd be sitting by himself like a scolded child with his miserable wife beside him.'

I lift an amused brow. 'Your king sounds delightful. I can't wait to meet him.'

'Hmm. You jest but you'll see.'

As future Hex members, we will travel to each kingdom, not only to meet its royal family and other important figures but to learn about its land and culture. The sudden pressure in my chest makes me feel dizzy, the understanding that I'll have to attend parties like this for a while longer before we are allowed free rein in the world.

'Do you ever think of the future?' I ask quietly. 'How we will be in years to come?'

The Silken shakes his head. 'I can't afford to think that far ahead. I only think of the present.'

I peer sidelong at him, but he watches the guests intently. As much as he tries to seem casual, his stiff shoulders give away his unease.

'If you want to escape, I can make up a story about seeing you around.'

'That's not necessary.'

I shrug, unconvinced. 'If you're sure.'

We stand in silence for a while, until the royal family turns towards us. They aim straight for where we stand as they take each group in their stride.

'Oh, shit,' the Silken utters, his hands removing themselves from his pockets. All the casualness he's feigned since being here turns to straight-up panic.

'Stay calm,' I murmur, taking his arm in my grasp. It bends in answer, my fingers peeking through his white shirt as his free hand comes to lie on mine. He's cold, oh-so cold, and I refrain from flinching from his touch. When I look closely at his fingers, I see faint lines of red across them. I scowl at the sight.

The prince, who seems to have spotted Peri and me standing alone, beelines for us, an easy smile playing on his tanned features. His pearl-and-seashell circlet glitters under the lanterns, and my eyes can't help but study the beauty of it.

'You must be Scarlet and Peri. It's a pleasure to meet you both,' he says, as if this is a normal conversation, as if he isn't the most highly regarded bachelor in the whole kingdom. 'I've heard many things about you two. My name is Athos.'

The heir to Tealwaters extends a hand to me, and I reach out without hesitation. He takes my fingers and bends over to kiss my knuckles. His lips leave a whisper of warmth behind, making my cheeks feel unnaturally hot.

'Your Highness,' I answer, making a dismal effort to curtsy.

He doesn't seem bothered by the lack of grace but rather beams with amusement. He turns to my companion and touches his forehead with his fingers. Peri mirrors him, violet eyes wary. I assume this must be a traditional Silken greeting, if the prince knows it.

'I hope you are enjoying the festivities. Your fellow fledglings are enjoying the music, I see.' He motions towards Olive and Ivy, dancing along with some other guests, who seem thrilled by their presence.

Sol and Rusty mingle on the sidelines with my guardian. As if sensing my gaze, Jack looks my way. I smile. He winks.

'Just wait until you see this guy on the dance floor,' I jest, tilting my head towards Peri.

He doesn't react, but the prince laughs, filling up the awkward silence.

'I can certainly imagine.'

A servant approaches Prince Athos with a tray of beverages. The heir takes two and hands them over to us. To my surprise, Peri takes his flute, albeit stiffly, but he doesn't make a move to drink it.

Prince Athos stands taller, his next words catching me off guard. 'May I take the Raven away for a moment? I'll bring her back in one piece, I promise.'

Peri turns to me with a questioning look, ignoring the prince and only focusing on me. *Do you want to go with him?* he silently asks.

I smile in reassurance, squeezing his arm gently. 'I'll be right back, and then we can have some of that delicious cake over there.'

Peri observes the dessert table before giving me a firm nod.

Prince Athos offers his arm, and I take it. He walks me around the garden, our pace slow but steady as we watch the party unfold before us. I feel my nerves waver, wondering why he'd ask me, of all people, to accompany him alone.

'I'm sorry to take you away, but I wanted to speak to you privately.'

'Oh?' I ask, tilting my head.

'I've heard a great deal about you from our mutual friend, Foxglove. She mentioned you were intrigued by her work when you visited the infirmary. It piqued my interest that you were curious about our projects, so when I saw you here, I couldn't help but approach. I'm so fascinated by your kind. Ravens are a brilliant and formidable race.' The prince's words are rushed, as if he's been planning what he's going to say to me.

I smile with quiet delight that a future king would find my presence to be noteworthy.

'We are certainly one of a kind,' I answer, not knowing how to respond.

'No other creature compares to you. Your vampire ancestry entails such strength and agility. I've met a Raven before, but I was captivated by your personal story.'

He looks sidelong at me, pale blue eyes studying my reaction. People around us watch the prince, taking in his finery, his grace. He doesn't seem to notice, or perhaps he is used to being stared at.

I straighten my shoulders before saying, 'My story?'

'I know what happened in your trials,' he admits.

I frown deeply.

He notices my questioning expression. 'Do not worry yourself. It's all confidential. My family was given the profiles of you and the other fledglings, so we know what to expect when we inevitably meet. To know your background is important for creating strong bonds.'

'So you know *how* I won the trials?' I ask quietly, the feeling of something cold washing over me.

'I know that you fought your own sister, Ember Seraphine, that you fought to the death with her but chose not to participate in the way the other finalists did.' He stops and turns to face me fully.

All of a sudden, I feel lost for words.

He absorbs my reaction and continues. 'I wanted to tell you I admire what you did. I don't think there are many people – certainly not Ravens – who would have had the courage to do what you did.'

'Courage?' I whisper with confusion. 'How could you describe it as *courage*?'

*I was scared out of my mind*, I want to admit, but I keep my thoughts to myself.

'How else would you explain it?' he asks, seeming genuinely put out by my words. 'A normal person would do many things to stay alive, even at the cost of loved ones. But *you*, Scarlet Seraphine, are strong of heart. When I heard of your triumph, I couldn't stop thinking about it. I knew I had to meet you.'

I blink. What does one say to that?

He laughs then, loud and uncontained. 'I apologise. My cousin says I will talk anyone's ear off if they are nice enough not to stop me. I see he's correct. Let me get you that slice of cake you wished for.'

He leads me to the table of desserts. He cuts me a slice of some chocolate cake that looks to be popular among the choices. As he serves me, I wonder if it's appropriate for him to be feeding a commoner and not the other way around.

'I hope we can meet again, Scarlet. Foxglove and I are in the midst of designing some amazing things, and I feel you'd have some valuable input to offer. The Nightshade also tells me she would love you to try her creations out in the field sometime. I said I'd help persuade you if it comes to that.' He gives me a pointed look as if this is an inside joke we all have together.

I smile, feeling at ease with the prince. He doesn't seem self-absorbed or snobbish, like I originally thought he might be.

I curtsy with a fork halfway to my mouth, the chunk of cake smelling delicious. 'Of course. I'd be honoured.'

He grins, and I can't help but mirror him.

'I cannot wait to see what you do with the world at your feet. It must be a nice feeling, being let out of the cage after being stuck underground for so long.'

I nod without hesitation. 'It's different, but I'm certainly not complaining.'

'I feel with you becoming the next Raven of the Hex, we will be in capable hands, Scarlet. I know special when I see it, and you ...' He motions to my attire. 'You are that and more. Together I hope the Hex and I can build Tealwaters to reach its greatest potential.'

'We'd like that, Your Highness.' I smile, finding his ambition admirable.

## 28

We all tumble into the foyer of Hex Manor. The music is still ringing in my ears as I watch the tipsy residents head to their respective rooms. Olive giggles as a sober Sol helps her up the steps, her face creasing into a dopey smile.

'Goodnight, everyone!' she calls, and she is gifted with several murmurs back.

I make my way towards the kitchen to grab myself a cup of water before heading upstairs to the bathing chamber. To my delight, I discover Jack waiting for me, as I requested.

He turns and smiles. 'Is everything all right?'

'I need help with something.' I shrug gingerly before putting my glass down. I turn towards the luxurious tub and prepare myself a bath. After the night I've endured in the high shoes I've been wearing, hot water will be the perfect way to end the evening.

'With what exactly?' Jack wonders eying up the pleasant smelling liquids I pour into the tub.

'I need a hand undoing all these buttons,' I admit, turning around to show him the long line of crimson fasteners down my back.

'Ah I see,' he chuckles, eyeing the gown I wear with understanding.

I clutch my skirts as he approaches from behind, his touch gentle as he begins with the top button. My head lifts to watch our reflection at the window. Jack appears thoughtful as he carefully peels away my dress, one button at a time.

'This dress is beautiful,' he whispers, the feel of his fingers against my skin making me shiver.

'Indeed it is.'

I found myself enjoying the festivities and forgetting to worry what people thought when they noticed my skin. It was a wonderful night, a wonderful dress and a wonderful memory to keep.

'This is the first time I've truly *felt* beautiful,' I admit, looking down at myself with approval.

'You have always been beautiful,' Jack declares quietly, the backs of his knuckles slowly sliding down my spine. I find myself exhaling a shaky breath, his heart beating as quickly as mine now.

The window's reflection reveals his hungry gaze as his fingers skim my lower back now, my hands now having to keep up the material of my heavy gown against my chest.

'Thank you, Jack.'

My guardian lifts his gaze and discovers me watching him. My cheeks burn at being caught staring but he doesn't move away – doesn't tease me.

'Anytime.' He presses a kiss against my bare shoulder, eyes never leaving mine as his large hands hold my waist.

It feels like an age that we stand there, observing what the other will do. My body itches to move, to face him and take what I want from him. The pounding of our pulses seem to get louder and louder in my skull until I can't stand it anymore. I take a deep breath and release my hands of material, dropping my dress and letting it pool around my feet like blood.

Jack's gaze snaps down, unabashedly letting himself take in every part of me that is on display for him.

With more confidence than I feel, I say, 'Get in the bath, guardian.'

The water is steaming hot as bubbles fill the bath to the brim. I check the temperature and throw my guardian a timid smile. As the bathroom is between my chamber and Sol's, we have to be quiet, which only adds to the thrill.

*We mustn't make a sound,* I silently say putting a finger up to my lips.

Jack doesn't need prompting to strip his clothes off. He does so the moment the water is turned off. He stands naked before me, his arms toned, stomach hard like stone. I can't stop as my feet move towards him and my hands roam over his skin. His body shivers under my touch, his hands coming to my waist and pulling me near.

He kisses my temple and along my jaw, all while taking his time to explore my body with his hands – something I've dreamt about too many times.

Slowly he leads me to the bath, helping me step into the warm water. We sit facing each other, and Jack hums with contentment as the water washes over him. Unable to keep my distance, I lean forward and reach out. Beneath the water, I trail my hands up his legs towards his thighs. His face shifts, mouth open as I find what I'm looking for.

I smile shyly at my guardian, and he grins back.

I wrap my hands around his length and softly play with him. He drops his head back against the bath rim, biting his lip to stop from moaning. I gain momentum, quickening the pace as I get onto my knees to find a better position.

Bubbles – some as small as my fingernails, some as large as my hand – begin to rise and float up from the tub. There are only a few at first, until the air is filled with iridescent orbs. My eyes flicker between the spectacle above me and the sight lying in the bath before me.

Before Jack can reach his limit, I stop, and his head springs up, all the bubbles in the air popping. I beam with delight, his magic as mesmerising as the first time he used it around me. Leaning forward I lay my naked body on his, feeling hotter than ever with every plane of him beneath me.

'Get on your knees,' I whisper in his ear, biting his lobe. His cock twitches with the feel of my tongue.

'Gladly,' he murmurs back.

I sit back and watch him obey. Before me is the man of my desires, staring down at me with such passion I can't help but feel giddy with excitement. He runs a hand through his hair, making it damp, and mirrors me, his eyes lighting up.

'Now what?' he mouths, enjoying my mischief.

Leaning forward, I wrap my hand around his cock once more and bring it towards my mouth. His hands find my hair and pull gently as I get a taste of him.

The water in the tub begins to bubble then, his magic smelling of the ocean. I use my tongue to tantalise him, to make his grip on me harden through my locks. I want to make him moan, to make him cry out in ecstasy. He's close, so close to climaxing, and his eyes glow a bright blue as the bubbles increase, letting me know how just a swipe of my tongue will finish him off.

'Come for me, Jack,' I whisper huskily.

His body shudders seconds after as he finds his release, his legs wobbly as I listen to his hard breathing. My ears try to pick up any other sounds but our surroundings are quiet. With some luck everyone is deep in sleep from the long night we've had.

Slowly Jack lies back in the bath. I stare at him, proud to make him feel how he looks.

He indicates with his fingers for me to come closer. I go back to lying on top of him, my head resting on his broad chest, our legs tangled together.

He hums, beginning to play with my hair, massaging my head with his strong hands.

'What a dangerous mouth you have, Raven,' he murmurs.

I refrain from laughing out loud but my fanged grin is enough to let him know I'm pleased with his statement. Slowly, his fingers start to roam over my back, my hair tossed to the side for his hands to slip over my body. His hands curve under my bum, and they pull me further up his body so we are face to face.

'Hi,' I murmur.

'Hi,' he answers, giving my chin a peck. He moves his kisses along my jaw and up to my temples. My eyes flutter closed as his lips move along my face. 'You are a vision, Scarlet.'

'Sure I am.' I play along, earning a smirk from him.

He kneads my arse, pressing me against his stomach, until his hands begin to wander. Hunger fills my guardian's gaze, and a quiet gasp escapes me as his fingers plunge between my legs.

'My turn,' he whispers, kissing me deeply.

I lean into him, spreading my legs further to give him better access, and he moans quietly against me in thanks.

I'm wet from before, but now, with him touching me, rubbing against me, I'm soaked.

Water creeps over my hips, making me shiver as it roams up my spine of its own accord. I don't stop kissing the master of the element as it wraps soothingly around my scarred neck and across my scalp, making me jerk with pleasure. His fingers play with me expertly. All the stroking makes me tremble, my nails digging into his shoulders.

'Don't stop,' I plead breathlessly.

'Get on your back,' he orders, pushing me away suddenly. The water threatens to spill over the edge of the bath with how quickly Jack manoeuvres me, eager to have my back against his chest. 'Open your legs,' he says, kissing the side of my face as he slides me up his wet body so my head leans back on his shoulder.

His hands are greedy as they cup my breasts, cup between my thighs and send me to oblivion. His water magic has a mind of its own, trickling over me, tickling me in the exact spots that make me arch my back, wanting more.

With nothing to stop my mouth from crying out, my fangs long and sharp from the pleasure rushing through me, I ball my hand into a fist and bite down on it. Driving into me, one finger turning into two, Jack makes my body shudder with need, tense with the building sensation that tingles through my fingers and toes.

'Come for me, Scarlet,' he murmurs, repeating my words back, and so I do. He rumbles with satisfaction beneath me as I find my peak, my body becoming limp. 'That's a good girl.' He strokes over my sensitive nipples, water circling them, and I shudder under his touch. 'Good?' he asks, and I can sense he is grinning from ear to ear.

'So good,' I confirm as we lie in the bath. 'So fucking good.'

We lie there until the water gets cold.

29

Days later Jack and I stand in the dark within the confines of our meeting spot. We patiently wait for Alex to arrive, several minutes late, as seems usual for him. In the distance, I hear a panting sound, and not long after, the dameer comes running round the corner, nearly knocking into me.

'Are you all right?' I whisper to Alex, watching him lean up against a wall, clutching his chest, his breathing erratic.

'I don't have the lung capacity of your kind,' he huffs, taking a moment to catch his breath as he keeps a keen eye on the streets. 'But I think a kiss would make me feel better.'

I watch him carefully, his eyes darker and demeanour stiff. I play along with his facade, knowing he probably needs the humour right now. 'You can't help yourself, can you?' I snicker.

'With you, no, I really can't.' He grins.

I see Jack roll his eyes in my peripheral vision.

'Did you sneak out of home or something?' I motion to his state, wondering where he lives if he's this puffed out and if his aunt and uncle would kill him for putting himself in danger on our night-time missions.

He nods, words swift and breathy. 'Yeah, something like that.'

Sapphire City is quiet at this time of night. Households are dark, the families within them no doubt fast asleep while we hide in the shadows, waiting for something to happen.

'So where are we heading to?' Jack asks, eyeing the dameer as he recovers.

We have come up with the plan that each night we will patrol the streets. If children are being taken from their homes, we will eventually find who is responsible and who is sending the horrid notes to the poor families who wake up with one less child.

Alex waves his hand. 'If there is news of something dodgy occurring in this city, then this is the place to be. It's notorious for the congregation of thieves, fraudsters and outlaws. We watch who exits and follow them.'

'Simple,' Jack grumbles, earning a glare from me.

'It's the best plan we have right now,' I tell him.

He nods reluctantly. 'I know.'

I peer around the corner of the building we wait by, Alex motioning towards an old and run-down place called the Jolly Pearl Tavern. It smells disgusting even from a distance, and it's located in the middle of the industrial area, away from all the nicely presented homes and streets I'm used to.

We wait patiently for half an hour, standing around like fools, with no one in sight. I sigh, feeling the boredom kick in. 'Did you unravel the mystery of whether those figures you saw were Ravens?' I ask, growing progressively weary of our pursuit.

Alex nods, peering around, seeming as discouraged as I am. 'Yes. I believe there are two of them.'

'Did you catch their names?' If I could identify them, perhaps I could pinpoint their reason for being here and not back in the House of Raven. 'If they are spying for the Elder Raven, we may have a slight advantage.'

Alex shakes his head. 'No names were said out loud, but I'm not surprised I practically stumbled across them.'

'Where did you spot them?'

I don't receive an answer. A group of three darkly clothed men exit the tavern straight into the shadows. I receive a firm slap to the stomach from Jack, his features turning from aloof to excited.

'Ow!' I whisper, glaring at him.

He winces, moving his attention back to the strangers. 'Do you see their cloaks?' He motions to his own chest, making me search the clothing of each of them when they twist our way.

Upon the men's cloaks is a simple design made from red thread, consisting of a circle with lines through it, like a carriage wheel – only with fewer spokes. Recognition flickers through me, but I'm not sure why. Jack brings out the handwritten note we received from Mrs Kapper. He points to a small drawing in the corner I failed to notice before.

'It's the same symbol,' Alex states, looking between the men and the letter, making Jack nod eagerly. 'A red circle of sorts.'

'Let's follow them,' my guardian suggests.

The way the men move through the streets is suspicious, the group keeping to pockets of darkness rather than walking straight down the middle. When one of them begins to glance excessively over his shoulder and check every alleyway before walking past it, I have a good feeling we've got our targets.

'They look shifty,' I murmur, making sure the males don't make too much noise as we follow. I grab Alex and bring him closer, my voice low so it doesn't echo through the streets. 'Do they look familiar to you?'

Alex shakes his head. 'I don't think so, but I can't be sure from this far away.'

Keeping a safe distance from the trio, we observe their movements, taking precautions not to be heard as we dash madly from one alleyway to another.

The leader of the group stops suddenly while in a residential area, pointing up to a townhouse window with a confident nod. 'Greg, do your thing.'

A subtle dose of magic hits my senses as one of the other men – Greg – reaches for the windowsill, his body stretching so unnaturally tall that his cloak now looks minuscule on him. When he is finally tall enough to reach the window, he turns and waves for his companion.

'You're up, Morris.'

The second man begins to climb Greg's limbs with expertise, making me assume they've done this many times before.

'Don't dally,' the leader warns, keeping watch.

In minutes, Morris has broken open the window, snuck inside the room and has come back with a sleeping child that looks limp in his arms. Morris passes the kid through the window to Greg, who then hands her over to the leader, who flings the small body over his shoulder.

Alex shuffles beside me. 'The man who went inside must have rendered the girl unconscious, or she'd have woken up by now.'

I nod in agreement. 'If we engage, we need to be careful

Morris—' I start, but the look on my companions' faces is pure perplexity.

'Morris?' Alex's face crinkles with confusion.

'As a vampire hybrid, I can hear what they are saying,' I remind him. 'We need to be careful Morris doesn't send us to sleep,' I say to my guardian, who dips his chin in acknowledgement. I turn to Alex, earning wide eyes. 'What? You didn't really think I'd watch a child be kidnapped without doing anything, did you?'

'I mean, no, but we don't have any weapons,' Alex counters, patting his body as if hoping a blade will miraculously turn up in one of his pockets.

'Speak for yourself,' Jack mutters, heading forward as the men in cloaks slink into the darkness again, knives in both his palms.

I do the same, bringing out my twin daggers and some throwing stars I took from the armoury back in Hex Manor. I hand Alex the stars. He doesn't protest as he takes them, but his look of unease doesn't go unnoticed.

As we traipse through the dark, I keep behind my guardian, watching his back. I reach a hand out to the dameer, who trails behind me, keeping my eyes on the kidnappers. 'Swap cloaks with me.'

Alex frowns in confusion but doesn't argue, giving me his cloak. I put it on, making sure to cover my hair with its hood, and in return Alex puts my cloak on, doing the same. It's too short for him, but it doesn't matter as long as we hide our features.

'Why am I wearing your cloak, Scarlet?'

'Purely to make you look silly.' His unimpressed expression makes me smile. 'If one of them can discern I have no scent that might give away who I am. But if I smell like you they'll assume I'm dameer and nothing more.'

He nods. 'That makes sense.'

'Don't let them see you, and don't get too close. I'm going to get the girl back.'

Alex renders himself invisible before we trail the trio and the unconscious child further into the depths of the city, towards what I realise is Gwenore Forest.

'If they go into the trees, we will lose them,' Jack murmurs, as if reading my mind. 'The darkness will hinder our ability to track them.' He motions between himself and where he thinks Alex is.

'Don't use your powers,' I murmur.

'Why not?' He frowns.

'It's an easy identifier, and if they realise a Hex member is onto them, those kids will be in more trouble.'

He nods, finally understanding. 'I'll go round the side and make sure they don't split up.'

When my guardian hurries off, I whisper into the dark for Alex.

'I'm here,' he murmurs, so close I nearly jump out of my skin.

After warning him to stay put, I count to three before pouncing on the cloaked men. Before they can react, I run up behind the group and knock out Morris with the handle of my knife, knowing he'll be the biggest threat to me if he uses his power. He drops like a sack of potatoes, and this alerts the other two.

'What the—' the leader says in alarm before I reach him. I'm aiming to grab the girl, but a pair of thick hands wrap around my neck from behind and yank me back.

Greg – the stretchy guy – has a hold of me and won't let go. I choke on his firm grip before tightening my grip on my daggers and slicing at his hands. He howls in pain, staggering back, and I spin and kick his stomach, sending him into a stone wall.

The leader runs, the girl's arms flopping around across

his shoulder, her eyes closed and face serene as if in a pleasant dream.

'Let go of her!' I demand, but he doesn't slow down. He cuts corners trying to lose me, but I'm on his heels. 'You piece of shit,' I mutter before an invisible force smacks him across the face.

He stumbles, giving me the opportunity to catch up and grab the back of his cloak. I yank his free arm down with all my force, pushing him to the ground. He falls to his knees, making me wince at the bone-cracking sound. I grab the child from him before his eyes roll into the back of his head as another force hits him, making his face snap to the side, and he falls face first onto the ground.

Alex appears, a shovel propped on his shoulder as he looks down at the unconscious bastard. He wears a determined expression as he looks up at me.

'That felt good,' he admits.

'Where did you get *that*?' I ask incredulously, tilting my head towards the garden tool he's snagged, manoeuvring the limp child into a better position for me to hold.

'I took a shortcut and found it propped up next to someone's front door. They must have forgotten about it.'

'Didn't fancy using my throwing stars?'

He shrugs, prodding the now-unconscious leader in his ribs to see if he'll move. He doesn't. 'What do we do with them now?'

I peer around to see Greg, the man I'd cut with my knife, has run away. Morris and their leader lie on the alleyway floor, out cold.

'Check their pockets,' I suggest.

Alex bends over, searching through the leader's trouser pockets. He takes out several random items before coming across a piece of paper. His eyes glint with something like hope before holding it up for me to read. 'A contract for

Heath Arrington, Morris Yates and Gregory Hadaway. Now we just need proof of what that work entails. And look.' He points to the same circular symbol that is embroidered on their cloaks upon the paper.

'Good.' I nod, relieved we have some sort of reward from this evening's work.

My eyes catch movement from the alleyway and find my guardian dragging a body behind him. It seems Jack stopped Greg from his escape, his unconscious body stretched strangely.

'Nice catch,' I tell him.

He smiles, obviously pleased with himself. 'Likewise.'

I turn back to Alex and dip my head at the paper in his hand. 'Take that with us and keep it somewhere safe. We'll have to let them go for the time being and make sure we're here for the next time they want to steal a child.' I grimace, peeking at the young face in my arms. She's blonde, with freckles over her cheeks and nose. Too young to be caught up in a mess like this.

'Bastards,' Alex mumbles, putting the contract inside my cloak, which he still wears around his broad shoulders. 'I hope the kids get the justice they deserve.'

'Me too,' I reply as we head back to the girl's home.

## 30

I'm one of the first to wake up the next morning. I sit at the small table on the wooden decking, looking out onto the vegetable garden. The weather is balmy and has been every day since I arrived. My guess is this kingdom has only one weather setting – comfortable warmth, even in the evenings.

I'm eating a bowl of fruit that consists of much more variety than I've ever imagined eating. The choice in Teal-waters is so much better than back in the House of Raven. The most we get there is ruby-red apples and the occasional stone fruit, depending on what the food shipments can deliver into Rubien.

Another novelty is having cooks on hand in the manor. They work for us, employed with keeping us fed and watered here in Hex Manor. They kindly prepared this bowl for me, happy to feed my hunger, and made me promise to come back for more if I'm still peckish.

It's peaceful sitting here in my own company, listening to the wind and the birds. That is, until the two large doors from the big dining room open wide behind me. I turn to find Peri standing awkwardly for a second before reluctantly taking a seat. His dark purple gaze is daunting as he stares at me. In his hand, he has a full plate of breakfast, and he sits himself on the furthest seat from me.

'Good morning,' he murmurs. His voice is deep and a little rough, as if still waking up.

I notice this small step of progress, similar to the other night.

*He is approaching me of his own accord.*

'Good morning,' I reply, continuing to eat and take in the scenery.

Tealwaters really is a breathtaking sight. The very opposite of my old home, which is underground, in the deepest parts of a cave.

When I glance back at the male, I find him staring at me like I'm a puzzle he needs to figure out. I smile politely.

'How did you sleep?' I ask. I jab a piece of yellow fruit and pop it into my mouth. Its sweet juices flood my tongue, and I hum in pleasure.

'Better than you, it seems,' he answers.

I frown. 'Charming.'

'I only meant ...' He motions to the circles under my eyes. 'They are darker than usual. Did you not sleep well?'

'I slept very little,' I admit. Not because I *couldn't* sleep but because I was too busy running around the capital to be tucked up in my warm, comfy bed.

'I struggle to rest too,' Peri admits with a shrug. 'But that's nothing abnormal for me.'

I imagine him in a strange place. He sits alone and wary whenever he hears footsteps. His body tensing until the moment they fade into the distance.

How many sleepless nights has the Silken endured, thinking he's in danger?

'Are you happier here?' I ask, softening my voice. 'Do you feel less threatened?'

I'm toeing the barrier here. I know it. He's never been open about his personal life, except for the very small but very vital detail he confessed at the Sapphire Salmon – that his own blood had left the large, jagged scar across his neck.

Peri forgets his food for a moment, chewing mindlessly as his violet eyes glaze over. 'Yes. Although I fear the consequences when we visit the House of Velvet.'

'Consequences?'

He shakes his head, pursing his pale lips. 'I don't wish to discuss it.'

My body is on alert at his firm tone, but I take a deep breath and shrug. Quickly I get up and leave. He doesn't say anything as I go back inside the manor, just watches me like a hawk. I head for the kitchen to ask the cooks for the same breakfast Peri is eating, and I wait in the small dining room connected to the kitchen. It takes a little while as they cook up a storm. Then I head back outside and sit in the seat I occupied before.

I eat quietly, nodding approvingly at my plate. This is *delicious*.

'Is that ...?' Peri's dark gaze narrows on my food.

'Your breakfast looked too good not to try.' I scoop mouthful after mouthful into my mouth. 'Holy Hanrah, this is *divine*. I'm definitely having this every morning.' I grunt with satisfaction, taking in the toasted bread, soft butter, cooked balls of red that the cooks told me are tomatoes, scrambled eggs and some herb garnish they sprinkled on top of it.

I know from the suspicious look he's giving me that he thought I was going to push for an answer, to pry further into his past, his story or something just as private. But I know what it is like to want to keep parts of your life hidden. To want to prevent talking of it in hopes of forgetting it.

My mind wanders to the trials, to Winella plunging her sword into my friend Merlot's back. To the day I nearly lost Jack to a chamber of poisonous gas, and the blazing flames of a dragon just before they consumed me whole.

I put down my cutlery for a moment and interlace my fingers as I finish my mouthful. Once I've swallowed, I take the Silken in. 'If you fancy telling me about your life, Peri, that's your prerogative. But if not, I'm not going to pin you down and interrogate you. I understand you are suspicious of everyone here, but you'll eventually see I'm an ally.' I observe his straight posture, his pristine attire, his effortlessly done hair. He seems like a male who needs things in a particular way – neat and organised. I also get the impression he comes from a family of wealth, from the meticulous way he dresses himself, never far from appearing immaculate.

'An ally is only that until they want something from you,' he says with a faint scowl.

'And what could I possibly want from you?'

The Silken considers me for a moment. 'I'm still trying to figure that out.'

'Well, you let me know when you do. I'd love to know the answer.'

He pokes his fork into a piece of cooked tomato. I copy his movement, cutting mine into quarters and popping a piece into my mouth. It has a strange taste, and the juice spreads through my mouth, making me chew quicker.

'These are the tomatoes Thea grows in her garden,' Peri says, as if deciphering from my features my lack of knowledge of the fruit. He watches me intently as I nod in acknowledgement and keep eating it with a grimace. 'If you don't like it, don't eat it.'

I shrug, swallowing the next piece whole to try not to taste it so much. 'I don't like to waste food. You never know when your next meal is, right?' I smile, but he doesn't look impressed.

'Good morning!' Olive greets us with a large grin, tossing open the door. She plops herself down next to me. Sol and Jack are right behind her, and they also seat themselves at the table – Peri now forgotten.

I meet my guardian's eyes as he takes the seat beside me, giving me a small, welcoming smile.

'Morning, all,' Rusty says from the doorway. He expertly holds four plates of food within his large hands, and I gape at the amount of different foods filling them. He takes a seat next to Peri, who looks at him with equal amounts of concern and astonishment. The Briar places the plates in a particular order in front of him before tucking in, eating slowly.

'Do you always consume that much?' I ask, earning an unabashed nod.

'If you think Olive has a sweet tooth, you should see this guy. He's a pig for anything drizzled in caramel.' Sol laughs, making Rusty's eyes glint with amusement. 'Who knew the fae liked their sweet treats so much?'

I wouldn't have pegged the Briar as having a sweet tooth, and seeing him eat, I can imagine him scoffing whatever he's given, no matter the taste.

'So, did you hear the news?' Olive asks, her own bowl of fruit full to the brim with colourful slices.

'We've only just woken up, Olive. What do you think?' Sol drawls, earning a scowl from the Severed.

'I wasn't talking to *you*, angel face.' She aims her next set of words at me. 'The Nightshades have figured out the poison used on the arrow that was aimed at you.'

My heart spikes. 'What was it?'

'A fungus they call straimis.'

'Straimis?' Jack scowls, his ocean blue eyes flickering as if trying to recall any memory of the word.

Ivy finally joins us, a book in hand as she plops down next to Olive. She crosses her legs and props her chin on a fist. 'Straimis is a fungus that, when boiled and melted, can become quite poisonous to the touch. It can be found commonly in the depths of caves – but only caves in the *northern* realms.'

I bristle. She means Hanrah.

The Nightshade lifts her sapphire gaze, amusement flickering in it. 'It seems someone from back home isn't pleased with you, Raven. They want you dead.'

## 31

My mind wanders while I'm in training. We all sit in a line on the seashell platform outside the House of Bane, facing the beach. The sun is warm on my back, and I pretend to watch Carmen demonstrate the ideal posture while shooting an arrow. She releases the shaft, and it hits a fluttering blue ribbon nailed to a palm tree. She's talking, but I struggle to listen.

'Are you worried about being targeted here again?' Olive murmurs, giving me a side eye before trailing her emerald gaze to the bushes the attacker is thought to have been lurking in.

I shake my head. The honest answer is I'm *really* tired. Since our first night saving children, Alex, Jack and I have patrolled the streets most evenings. We have saved a total of four children so far, but it seems those working to steal the youth of Sapphire City come back regardless of our efforts.

'I didn't get much sleep last night,' I reply. 'I have lots on my mind.'

'Anything I can help with?' Olive asks, genuine worry

etched into her beautiful features. 'It always helps to unload your burdens onto friends.'

I smile. 'Thanks. I—'

'Perhaps you should go to bed earlier,' Ivy suggests mockingly, lifting her chin in a way that makes it clear she thinks I'm a fool.

'Thanks, Ivy. I'll give that a try,' I retort, earning a sly look back.

'What's on your mind? What's bothering you?' Olive asks, ignoring the taunts of the Nightshade, leaning into me as she lowers her voice.

My gaze flickers to my guardian, who I know is listening to our conversation but is pretending not to be. He, of course, knows why the bags under my eyes are growing – his have become more shadowed too.

I shrug, feeling a sliver of unease creep into my chest. Jack and I have yet to reveal to any of the others our late-night escapades. Guilt washes through me.

*Maybe another person in the know would help.*

Ivy chimes in again, grabbing everyone's attention. 'Perhaps you struggle to sleep because of the long evening walks you take.'

I spin towards her. She wears a scheming expression that makes my heart race.

*What does she know?*

The cogs in my guardian's mind turn as our gazes meet. His hard expression lets me know he's worried. If Ivy knows something ...

'I've been taking a stroll here and there to clear my head,' I offer, leaning back on my hands to feign casualness.

'Is that what they call it nowadays?' Ivy says, raising a brow in question, peering at Jack knowingly.

I don't bother to respond, my nerves fraying with how

much she may know and why she has decided to reveal her surveillance of me in front of everyone.

Someone clears their throat, and we all turn towards Carmen, who stands with a bow, her free hand propped on her hip and a look of pure irritation on her face.

'Now Scarlet will demonstrate, because she's clearly an expert at this if she's not paying attention.' Carmen stares down at me, giving me a stern look.

She's right. I've not been paying attention, but in defiance, I wave a flustered hand towards Ivy as if asking why she hasn't been called out. All I receive is a tilt of the head and a pointed glare.

'Fine,' I answer reluctantly, getting to my feet.

'Aim there,' Thea says, pointing to a set of blue ribbons three palm trees deep. They flutter in the faint breeze as I nock my arrow.

As I go to lift my bow, Rusty coughs, and Ivy elbows him in the ribs with exasperation in her unimpressed features.

I meet the Briar's gaze, and his bronze eyes flicker to the basket of arrows beside me. I lift a brow in confirmation, and he nods. As I pick out another arrow and nock that with the first, Rusty gives another pointed look to the basket.

*Three arrows?* I ask silently with a scowl.

He answers with a slight dip of his chin.

Three is an impressive number even for a Raven, but I don't hesitate to nock the third shaft, taking my time to get all three in the right position.

'Good luck,' Ivy sings, her snarky tone evidence she thinks I'll fail.

I pull the bowstring back, imagining where my arrows will land. I take a deep breath and remember every lesson I've had in the past on archery.

Dimitri fills my mind, his voice and his words swirling

around my head. A knot forms in my chest, a gaping hole that is missing my best friend making my watery eyes blink. Writing letters is nothing compared to being *with* him.

*You can do anything you put your mind to, Scarlet. All you have to do is believe in yourself like I do.*

I close my eyes briefly, the memory hitting deep before I let go. The arrows land three in a row, all lined down the tree's trunk. Each blue ribbon is pinned down with accuracy. I manage a grin at my effort, proud I landed them all on my first go.

'Lucky shot,' I hear Ivy mutter as the others appear impressed at my attempt.

'Mother of sunlight,' Sol curses with an impressed nod. 'I'm glad you're fighting *with* me and not *against* me.'

I wipe off some non-existent dust from my shoulder, enjoying the wide-eyed looks from my peers and mentors.

'Well,' Carmen murmurs, forgetting to be annoyed at me for not listening. 'Who's next?'

## 32

After lessons for the day, Jack and I ride home but decide to travel via the beach. Mira and Bolt tread the sand easily, their hooves being washed by the waves.

'I think we should tell one of them about Alex,' I say when we are finally alone. The other Hex members have cantered off, racing along the coastline with their clothes and hair trailing behind them like ribbons.

'Do you think that is wise?' Jack asks, looking at me with doubt. I shrug. 'We now know that children are being taken. But what for? By who? Do you think bringing in another person will help in finding these answers?'

'Alex mentioned the children all being dameer. We didn't have any of the families confirm that, but that's a potential lead if it's true. So in that case, it could be for their magic,' I reply, watching the others fade into the distance. 'I think bringing in another Hex member will benefit us. Another mind to puzzle all this out. We may be looking at this wrong or overlooking something. A fresh pair of eyes would help. I'm sure of it.'

'If you believe so, then I do too.' Jack nods, my idea apparently making more sense to him.

I nod along. 'We meet tonight in our normal spot and go from there.'

'Hopefully, it's the right move,' he murmurs before kicking Bolt into a canter, leaving me in his wake.

I choose to tell Olive in the end. She is the hardest person to keep bending the truth to, and with her unique powers, I think she will come in handy.

I tap on her chamber door quietly and let myself in, the manor well and truly asleep at this time of night. Her room is decorated similarly to mine but in all shades of green.

'Ready?' I ask her, and she nods. I can't see any weapons on her person. 'Do you think it wise to go without some sort of defence?' I motion to my belt of throwing stars and my sheathed twin daggers, the gold blades glinting in the light of the single lantern.

She smirks before conjuring up two glass blades in her palms. They look identical to mine but translucent, my curiosity making me lean in to inspect her work. 'Who says anything about being defenceless?'

'Good point.' I grin and take one from her. I expect it to be cold and flimsy, but the glass beneath my grip is strong and sturdy. 'Do they break if you stab something?'

'Not unless I want them to,' Olive answers, watching me carefully.

'I'm jealous – again,' I admit with a laugh.

'I can make *you* some glass knives if you'd like. We could

design them how you wish and build them to fit you perfectly.' Excitement lingers in her emerald gaze, and I can't help but feel it too.

*At this rate, I'll have a weapon from each member of the Hex*, I muse.

'I'd love that.'

'Brilliant. I suppose we should get going, or else Jack will be wondering where we are.'

Olive motions to her balcony. She climbs over the rail and jumps down. I follow closely behind.

Jack and I said we'd meet at the border of Gwenore Forest to keep any prying eyes from seeing us. When we approach the shadows, I see the last person I expect leaning against a tree, arms crossed over his chest and a golden sword I've never seen before glowing faintly in the darkness.

'Sol?' I ask, looking between him and Jack.

My guardian looks as confused as I feel as he discerns Olive beside me.

'Wait a second. Why is Sol here?' I ask.

Jack retorts, 'Why is Olive here?'

Olive shoots me an exasperated look before I wave my hands in perplexity. 'We agreed to tell one more person.' I motion to the Severed, her emerald eyes flickering back and forth between the guardian and me. 'I didn't realise you were bringing along some company as well.'

'I thought that's what you implied – for *me* to ask.' Jack frowns.

'No, *I* was going to ask.' I sigh.

'Do you want me to go back? Is this a subtle hint I'm not wanted?' Sol pouts, humour lacing his words.

'Oh, is the big, strong Celestial's feelings hurt?' Olive croons, going to his side and nudging him in the ribs.

He doesn't move an inch but smiles down at her, golden gaze bright with amusement.

'No. It's great you're here,' I quickly reassure him before giving Jack a pointed look. 'I wasn't expecting you, that's all. Your presence is a nice surprise.'

Olive dips her chin towards his weapon. 'Although I'm sure we will come across more surprises if you don't sort out your sword, angel face. If it shines any brighter, we'll be spotted in seconds on our undercover mission.'

Sol peers behind his shoulder at the sword strapped to his back and grins. 'Oh, yes. I suppose that won't do.' He places a hand on its hilt, and seconds later it dims, no light to be seen. 'Better?'

I nod with satisfaction. 'Good. Now put your hoods up. We're going hunting.'

33

Alex is surprisingly modest tonight, not a flirtatious comment or glance towards Olive or Sol when we introduce them. I give him an *Are you all right?* look, and he nudges me softly in the ribs while I offer him a handful of throwing stars. He's nervous – more than usual, it seems.

'I'm fine now you're here, Scarlet. Still waiting patiently for that kiss, though ...'

I roll my eyes. It seems he's only inappropriate with me.

Like before on our evening pursuits, we find our snatchers after an hour of waiting. Tonight, though, is different. A group of six men prowl the city, looking for their next steal. The three men we found before – Heath, Morris and Greg – are there, but they are accompanied by others I've never seen before.

They stop at a townhouse, their usual routine of Greg stretching his body tall enough to reach the top window and Morris knocking the child into unconsciousness before clambering down Greg's body. In this case, twins – a girl and a boy – are hauled out of the bedroom window, and

Heath, who is no doubt the leader of the operation, shoulders a child like before.

The other snatchers begin tossing around a large brown sack, a faint smell of potatoes coming to my nose. I frown, wondering why they have spuds, of all things, with them.

'It seems they've learned their lesson.' Jack smirks. 'Didn't like getting bested, and now they need a bodyguard each.'

I hum in agreement. 'They must be the main snatchers – their powers are invaluable in stealing the children in a quiet and swift manner.'

'I suppose they won't have any evidence on their person, as they lost their working contract the last time.' Alex crouches beside me, glancing at me sidelong as we all peer from the shadows of a shop alleyway. 'We'll need to change tactics. Otherwise, we'll become predictable.'

I hum in acknowledgement. 'Any ideas?'

'We need to let them take the children,' Olive blurts, making me jerk back in horror.

'What?' Jack hisses.

'Well, from what you've told me, Scarlet, you've found no new evidence since that pregnant lady you spoke to hand delivered us a note. If we don't go looking for clues, none will present themselves. So the next step in the plan is to let them do their job, think they've won tonight and see where it takes us.' Olive gives us all a lingering look, urging everybody to see reason.

Sol concedes first, which is expected. 'Let one more child be taken for the sake of saving many,' he murmurs, making Olive nod glumly.

'I don't like it, but she's right.' I wrinkle my nose but understand the Severed's logic. 'If we keep running after these men night after night, we'll never find where they've taken your brother.' I spin towards Alex and give him a questioning look, silently asking him if he's up for this new twist of events.

'Whatever it takes, I'm in.' The dameer nods, features serious.

I give him a grim nod before turning back to the snatchers. Six of them in total as they huddle together in the shadows of the streets. They split into three groups of two. Two groups have a child each, and one group holds the sack of spuds over a shoulder.

'Is that a decoy?' Alex asks, genuinely impressed.

'Holy Hanrah,' I mutter, realising they've upped their game. 'Change of plan. We need to split up. You three go catch up with Greg and the little girl.' I motion to Sol, Olive and Jack, who are already standing. 'Alex and I will deal with Morris and the boy. We'll meet in an hour back at the city square. If one of us doesn't return, we get the other Hex members and go searching.'

Sol nods like my plan is sufficient enough, grasping Olive without a moment's hesitation. Jack, however, is the only one who seems to dislike my plan.

'No. I'm going with you,' Jack insists, stepping to my side as if a shield.

'I'm fine,' I murmur. 'If anything happens, Alex can turn me invisible. Isn't that right?' I face the dameer, and he nods without hesitation.

'Let Alex go with Sol and Olive,' Jack urges, but I shake my head.

'Alex is my responsibility. I'm not letting him out of my sight.'

My guardian stares down at me, his blue gaze hard. Suddenly his finger is raised to Alex's face. 'If she has so much as a splinter ...' The threat lingers in the air between us, raising the tension.

'Easy,' Sol says, stepping between the males. The

dameer looks grateful for the backup as Sol gives our guardian an uncharacteristically stern look. 'Scarlet can handle herself.'

'Jack,' I say, pulling his arm roughly so he moves away from them, making him look straight at me. 'That is not necessary. I am capable of—'

Jack begins to protest, shaking his head. 'It's not about incapability.'

'Enough. You are not my mother. You are *our* guardian.' I motion to Sol and Olive. 'Don't do this right now. We are losing their trails, and if we let those kids slip through our fingers tonight, I will not forgive you.'

'Fine, but Olive will go with you two for backup.' Jack doesn't give the Severed time to argue. He rushes off, not bothering to look behind to see if Sol is following.

The Celestial reluctantly leaves us with an apologetic look.

'They headed down that alleyway,' Alex announces as I pull my angered face away from my guardian.

'Let's go,' Olive urges, dragging me into action.

We begin our pursuit, with Alex in the lead, Olive and me trailing behind. The Severed gives me a wary look when I catch her glance. I know what she's going to say before it escapes her lips.

'I thought by now Jack would be comfortable enough to leave you alone.' She appears saddened, like the display of protectiveness was more of a snub to her and Sol than an act of not wanting me out of his sight.

'I'm sure if he had his way, he'd keep me by his side for evermore,' I grumble.

'Were the Hex Trials *that* bad?' she asks with exasperation.

I stumble but catch myself, surprised by her comment. 'Yes,' I answer truthfully. 'They were.'

She huffs as we run round a corner. 'We are not done talking of this.'

Alex slows, and we follow his lead until we come to a stop by a bush nearby the gloom of Gwenore Forest, her footpaths barely visible to the human eye. We stick our bodies through the vegetation and peek through the leaves, observing the pair we have followed – Morris and his companion – hauling the little boy into a carriage. The transportation looks normal, with its fair-coated geldings patiently waiting – the vehicle something a wealthier family would own. If someone so happened to glance outside their window at this time of night, they'd think little of it.

'We need to get on that carriage,' I whisper, making Alex's eyes widen. 'Not scared of a challenge, are you?' I taunt, giving him a once-over.

He opens his mouth, a glint in his eyes, before remembering Olive. He closes it again, refraining from his retort.

'No, of course not,' he decides to say.

Olive smiles reassuringly at the dameer, tilting her head. 'Under we go.'

She rushes off as the door shuts behind Morris, his companion getting in too.

Before Alex jumps into action, I grab his arm. I frown, wondering who will be directing the horses, but no one else comes into view, and I can't smell anyone else nearby. 'Be careful. Something isn't right.'

Alex sprints for the carriage, approaching the back as the Severed crawls beneath it. She waves a hand for us to hurry, but before Alex and I can crouch down, the horses nicker – a sigh in response to their commencement – and a tang of magic wafts through the air.

*Shit.* Morris's companion must be able to control or speak with the horses.

'Olive, hold on,' I hiss before wrapping an arm around Alex's waist. I jump onto the back of the carriage, the ledge only big enough for the balls of my feet to stand on. It thankfully holds my weight and Alex's when I drag him on.

'You just wanted an excuse to get up close and personal with me, didn't you?' he jests, but I can see the layer of unease beneath his humour.

I roll my eyes. 'Yes. I couldn't help myself. You're looking ravishing tonight.'

'I knew it.' He smiles as the ground beneath us suddenly begins to whizz by, the trees of Gwenore Forest now surrounding us. Alex's features become shadowed in darkness, dark enough I know he can't see anything with his human sight. Fear washes over his expression, which I know he only allows as he doesn't realise I can see him.

I nudge his side gently, hoping to distract him. 'I told Olive you had a smart mouth, but she didn't believe me. Can you believe that?'

'I like to pick and choose when to ooze with charm, it seems,' he answers, grasping on tightly, his muscled arms surrounding me as we grip the edges of the carriage.

The smell of smoke fills my nose. Fire begins to light up the woodland, and I quietly warn Alex that we'll need to jump to safety soon. Shouts echo through me, the clanking of chains and even the scent of blood registering in my brain.

The carriage stops, and I grab Alex. Where are we?

*Do not move yet*, I whisper, and he nods quickly.

I listen closely. Morris and his companion are shuffling around inside, no doubt trying to manoeuvre the uncon-scious boy. I point to the nearest line of trees, off the path we are currently on. My concern creeps in. What if Gwenore decides to attack us when we need to stay hidden?

*No time for doubt. The children need you.*

Without hesitation, we sprint for the safety of a large trunk and kneel down on the dirt floor. Not far behind us, Olive runs our way, choosing a tree next to ours. She gives me a thumbs-up and a questioning look. *All good?*

I nod. *All good.*

All we can see from this viewpoint is the carriage and a large canvas tent. Without moving, we are none the wiser as to where we've been brought.

A whip cracks, and a heart-wrenching cry rips through the air. Alex's hand is fast to grab my shoulder, and he peers over me to see where it came from. His grip is tight, so tight I find my skin twinging with discomfort.

'Alex, ease up.'

He obeys but doesn't let go. If we want to see where the children are being taken, we need another vantage point.

I motion to Alex the direction we'll be heading in next. 'We need to get closer. See where they are taking the boy.'

I rush for Olive's tree before he can protest, and she whispers, 'Have you seen Jack or Sol?'

I shake my head. 'No, but I'm sure they're fine.'

Taking our time to move from tree to tree, we head around the perimeter of the tent and come to the last thing I expect to find. When the three of us stand behind the same, extremely thick trunk, I can't help but gape.

'Holy fucking seal balls,' Alex mutters with horror. 'What is this place?'

Olive grimaces as I meet her eyes. 'It looks like we've found a prison camp.'

## 34

'We need to get them out of there,' Alex says.

The shouting of several guards makes my heart spike. A line of children, all in a state of tears and distress, are led from the tent. Across their wrists and between their ankles are long, thick shackles made of black metal. My face pales with realisation.

'They're using obsidian chains,' I mutter in dread.

Olive glances my way, puzzlement in her features.

I lean closer to explain. 'Obsidian chains stop all magic, so the wearer cannot use their powers. Any abilities the children may have are useless when they are wearing them.'

'How do you know this?' Olive whispers.

'Jack and I have experienced them back in the House of Raven.' I wince at the memories that invade my mind. The pillar I'm chained to, readying for the whip that cracks along my back. The wire that sparks with electricity when looped around Jack's neck when he tries to defend me. 'For those who rely on their magic, it's fucking awful. You are turned human.'

She blanches, no doubt thinking of all the ways to keep

herself away from the terrible metal. 'We need to get inside and scope more of the place out.'

Alex nods. 'I can get us in there, but I'm not sure I'll be able to manage turning all three of us invisible at once. Not unless we can walk the perimeter in under ten minutes.'

I grimace. I don't want Alex getting anywhere near the camp. If he's hurt or, worse, taken, I'll never forgive myself. But in a situation like this, he's an asset we need.

'What do you want to do?' I turn to Olive.

Her emerald eyes crinkle in thought before peeking up at the tree before us. 'I'll climb up one of these and keep watch over you. If you so happen to flicker back into view, I'll make sure to be ready to bring down anyone who comes near you.'

'Are you sure?' I ask, and she nods.

'I have unlimited weapons, so I'll be the best support. You have your scar to know if someone can sense you, and Alex will have to go in regardless.' She shrugs. 'I got your back. You'll be fine.'

I turn to Alex. 'We go in purely to scope out the layout. We do not have the resources to help any of those kids escape tonight. Do you understand?'

He stares for a full minute, eyes flickering with something I can't explain. He seems to debate my words, churning over their true meaning.

*If we see Ellis, we cannot help him tonight.*

Finally he sighs. 'I understand.'

'The moment I tell you to run, you run. If you see me in trouble, don't turn back. Do you understand?' I add, making sure we are on the same page when we set foot into this establishment.

He dips his head, a sound of frustration escaping his lips. 'Yes, Scarlet.'

I offer my hand to him. 'Don't let go until I say otherwise.'

He takes my hand slowly, the both of us turning invisible. I look down, and I cannot find or sense my own body. I move my leg and observe nothing. I shake my head with silent bewilderment.

Olive's eyes flicker around with amazement, unable to see us any more. 'In and out. No funny business.'

I pull Alex along, making sure to dodge any sticks or debris that looks loud enough to make a sound if we step on it. Heading for the first tent, I peel a knife from my belt with fumbling fingers and press it to Alex's chest. He silently takes it without a word.

As we sneak along the tent, I look to see if we produce any shadows from the lanterns inside, but there is no sign of our existence. Upon the ground, something faint shimmers. I pause to take a closer look and realise it's a shield – much like Queen Adela's, which I came across back in the House of Raven.

'The place is shielded,' I declare, earning a soft grunt from my companion.

We turn the corner and find three males standing guard outside. A slit in the material is the only opening I've seen so far that is not secured by magic.

I squeeze Alex's hand to let him know that's our entry point. He tightens his grip in answer. Slipping past the tall, lumbering men, I hold my breath. One shuffles on his feet, making my heart hammer wildly, but thankfully, he doesn't give an indication he knows of our presence.

Once inside I let my breath out slowly, making sure to keep a firm grip on the dameer. We sidestep along the edge of the tent, finding cages of all sizes covering the ground, children confined either alone or in groups. Some are silent and rock themselves back and forth, blindfolds over their faces. Others sob quietly to themselves, wearing the same strips of material over their faces, but they shout when they speak, as if they can't hear anyone. My throat constricts when I spot some that have puddles of urine beneath them, no one finding them sitting in their own filth to be an issue.

'Barbaric,' I hear Alex hiss under his breath as Morris enters from behind us. He dumps the boy he's stolen on the far side of the tent. A metal eyelet stands proudly from the ground, and Morris makes quick work to bind the boy to it with rope. When the kid wakes up, he's going to be terrified.

'Are you sure we can't save *him* at least?' Alex whispers, his breath on my ear.

'If we risk it, they might double their security,' I reply, hating my words but knowing I'm right.

The tent houses many children, but I have a feeling the worst of it is outside.

As we move towards the smell of fresh air and unclean skin, a large gravel area opens up before us. Thick wooden slats close off the camp from the outside world, so the shield I saw before is an extra layer of protection from intruders.

That explains why the devilish spirit Gwenore hasn't decided to harm these bastards – they are technically not in her domain.

To left and right, there are several identical tents and a few areas in use, fenced-off zones that crackle with blue fire. Alex doesn't need persuading to get a closer look. From where we examine them, the younglings inside these zones wear no restraints – all they have are coils of what looks to be silver rope around one ankle. Guards who look like soldiers bark out orders, forcing them to use their magic.

'See the restraints they wear,' Alex murmurs, making my eyes flicker to the silver rope again. 'It looks like rope, but if the child undoes the knot, it will automatically retie itself.'

'How can it be conquered?'

'I presume either by killing its master – most likely one of the guards – or with a sorcerer's spell.'

*So we'll need Carmen or Thea.*

One boy has the power to manipulate metal. Steel arrows are released from his palms and shoot through a line of dummies full of hay. Every time the boy hits a mannequin's chest, he's rewarded with a biscuit, which he gobbles down in seconds.

'They are starving them, but why?' Alex wonders, as perplexed as me.

We move on. Children with power over the elements, teleportation, shadows and even shape-shifting fill the pens. They, too, are rewarded with food and water, and they react to the sustenance as if they've not been taken care of in days – which doesn't surprise me, as most of the younglings seem to have weeks' worth of dirt on their skin and clothes.

'What is the reason for this? Teach the kids to use magic and do what?' Alex ponders as we circle back around another cluster of tents.

A scream comes from one, making my heart race.

My eyes take in every detail, every guard that stands watch and every possible entry and exit from the establishment. My heart thunders more the longer we linger, and I hold my breath when travelling past those who are working for this vile operation, my hand sweating in Alex's.

It's only when my arm is tugged back that I stop. Alex holds firmly enough that I can't move on, towards the entry we came through and back into the safety of the trees.

'Alex?' I whisper.

An invisible presence holds my chin and turns it

towards the fence. It takes me a while to look over the barrier of the camp and peer *behind* it into the blanket of leaves above. I spot Olive, who crouches in the crook of a tree branch. She handles two long blades made of dull glass, ready to aim when necessary.

'I see her. What's the issue?' I ask, wrinkling my nose.

His hand swivels my head to the left, and I audibly release a sharp breath. Three trees along, a female with silky red hair and shiny, long fangs sits looking into the premises. She's yet to spot Olive but is armed with a bow and arrow and other weapons over her dark suit. She looks like a creature of the night.

'Fuck,' I mutter. 'Is she one of the Ravens you saw before?'

'Yes. Although I'm worried now we'll come across the second Raven any moment.'

'Why is she here?' I'm thinking out loud, but deep down I know the answer. If she's the assailant who tried to kill me off at the beach, she's somehow trailed me here. But how?

'We need to leave. Right now.'

'And warn Olive somehow,' Alex says.

Nothing around us brings any ideas of how we can do this. Until I think of the throwing stars I gave Alex.

'Don't mind my wandering hands,' I utter as I touch the dameer's chest. My hands lower, and he stiffens. Ignoring his body's reaction, I feel around his belt, where something sharp brushes my fingertips.

'You've been thinking of an excuse to do this all night, haven't you?' he utters.

*If humour is his way of coping, then so be it.*

'You make it sound like I have some secret infatuation with you. I think someone has a high opinion of themselves.'

I grab a throwing star and release it from its holder. I

toss it near to Olive, the metal coming close to her ear. She looks in alarm to where it's embedded in the trunk beside her. Flicking her emerald head in our direction, she seems to debate what it means.

'Come on,' I urge, needing her to look beyond the star itself.

'Throw another,' Alex instructs.

'Have you not had a female touch you in a while? Is that why you are so eager for me to grab another?' I tease, but I do as he says. The second star lands right beside the first.

Olive's understanding is as clear as day. Her eyes widen at the figure hiding in the treetop along from her. But unfortunately for the Severed, the sound has alerted the Raven to Olive's presence too.

## 35

'No!' I hiss, and I drag Alex along.

I don't hesitate as we storm past the cages, back into the musty tent and back through the split canvas. The sound of metal clanging pierces through me as we race towards the trees. Guards inside the camp begin to shout, sounding their alarms as they come to realise intruders are near their borders.

'Run!' I order, shaking Alex's hand off mine. My body flashes back into view as I wave him off. 'Go now while their attention is off us.'

'No. I'm not leaving you.' He roughly pushes me forward, now visible to the world himself, but doesn't make a show of slowing down. I don't argue, knowing we have little time and Olive's life is at stake.

'Then hide in the trees. Throw those stars when you can, and make sure no one sees where they are coming from,' I order, my bronze bracelet around his wrist before he can protest. I push the ruby jewel on top with force and shove him towards the darkness and safety of the dense trees, Ruby's garnet-and-gold armour covering him like a second skin.

My legs carry me through the woodland, my head turned up to see where my friend is. Arrows fly from inside the prison camp, trying their best to kill the supposed invaders. A branch snaps, no doubt the work of Gwenore, and both the females fall to the ground in the distance. Olive rolls elegantly before getting to her feet, whirling around to find her opponent. I rush to the Severed's side, earning a growl as she whirls on me.

'It's me,' I pant, hands out in surrender.

Without comment, she pushes two glass daggers into my hands before two more materialise in her own. The emerald eyes I've become so used to have disappeared, and inky blackness fills the colour with nothing but lethal intent. I shudder at the sight.

'Olive, your eyes ...'

'The demon,' she explains coldly, her voice not her own.

I don't understand what she means, but she doesn't seem to notice my confusion.

'The bitch plays dirty,' she says, tilting her head towards the forest where the Raven is recovering. Black blood trails down Olive's temple.

I nod, figuring we'll talk of this later, and turn to the crunching of leaves.

The Raven is not someone I recognise, her form tall and lithe, her face soiled but determined. She's older and most likely an experienced spy for the Elder Raven, from the design of her fighting suit. It's nothing like any outfit I've seen before.

'State your purpose,' I command, earning a fanged smile in return. It doesn't take a genius to know what her answer will be when my scar begins to bleed, a stream of crimson dampening my right palm.

'I'm here to kill you, of course.'

'You're the one who shot me with the inkberry,' I say.

She smiles slyly. 'Oh, no. That was not me.'

She laughs as she advances, taking no time to dally. Now I'm in the picture, she doesn't care about Olive in the slightest, her fiery-red eyes only on me. She swipes with a long sword, having lost her bow, it seems, slicing the air milliseconds after I dodge her blade. She's quick and extremely talented with her weapon. I know I won't be a match for her.

'Olive!' I clench my teeth as the sword slams into my twin glass knives. A part of me expects them to shatter, but as my friend told me, they stay solid until their master commands them otherwise.

'The Elder Raven will reward me handsomely,' the Raven says, delight ringing in her voice. 'I cannot wait to bring her your head.'

The Severed attacks from the back, and the Raven has to fight an opponent from both sides. She looks far from worried, instead looking full of glee at the challenge.

'You think you can outmatch me? I was a warrior before you were both born!' The female laughs, looking to have the upper hand.

'You're outdated, then,' Olive retorts.

We parry, the sound of guards approaching making me feel caged in. I know we have little time to dispatch the Raven, her experience far surpassing Olive's and mine combined.

Suddenly a throwing star flies our way, aimed at the Raven's stomach. Unfortunately for Alex, his throw isn't hard enough to do any damage. The star merely pings off the female's outfit and falls to the ground with little effect. Olive takes the small moment of distraction to create a spear of glass.

'I thought I smelled a strong bloodline,' the Raven sneers, fangs shining in the moonlight.

Before I take a strike, Olive's glass spear penetrates the female's head, the long weapon making a disgusting squelching sound as it pierces bone and organ. The Raven stops as if momentarily stunned and gapes, blood gushing out of her forehead. Blood-red eyes flicker to me. Such hatred fills her gaze before she falls forward onto her front and lies motionless.

My horror is evident as I glance up at Olive.

Shock sets in. Not from seeing such a gruesome death – I've witnessed many of them in my lifetime – but at the lack of feeling or remorse on Olive's face. Midnight eyes bear down on the pale body, mouth widening in silent satisfaction as her glass spear dissolves into sand.

Hands wrap around my wrist, and Alex is there, his armoured chest crashing into my shoulder as he loops his arms around me. 'Scarlet,' he pants, reaching for Olive, rendering us invisible. 'Don't make a sound.'

The prison guards encircle the Raven's body, weapons covering them – all their soldiers ready to fight. Alex slowly shuffles us away, back towards the carriage and along the gravel path, and we eventually find ourselves back in Sapphire City.

My mouth tries to form words, but my mind is foggy. Everything I've seen tonight is still being processed. The dameer looks ashen, sweat coating his temples, the exertion of using his magic on three people taking its toll on him.

'Alex, are you all right?' I ask, squeezing his hand gently. 'Do you want us to walk you home?'

He shakes his head. 'I need time to digest all this,' he admits, handing back my bracelet. The bronze metal looks dim under the night sky as I take it and place it back where it belongs on my wrist. 'I have a lot to think about, and I'd prefer to be alone.'

Unhappy with the decision but understanding his predicament, I reluctantly nod. 'Fine, but no shortcuts.'

'Yes, Mother.' He smiles half-heartedly down at me, squeezing my shoulder.

As Olive and I walk towards the city square, where we are to meet Jack and Sol and update them on our night, I peer sidelong at my friend. Her emerald eyes gradually seep back to their usual appearance, and her features soften the further we travel from the prison camp.

I grasp her wrist and tug on it. 'Where did you go back there?'

She peers down at my touch, sorrow and dismay in her expression. She doesn't meet my eyes, shame and something else lining her words. 'Tomorrow. I'll tell you everything tomorrow.'

## 36

The sky is still dark when Jack, Sol, Olive and I climb the small slope towards the white picket fence around the manor. We briefly spoke of what we experienced. Sol and Jack were led around most of the city before losing their quarry, while Olive and I found everything we needed.

Upon seeing everyone's weary face, we promise that we'll talk more in the morning.

Approaching the manor first, I open the back gate and motion for my friends to come into the garden, where the vegetables smell most potent. Not wanting to risk the door of the manor and waking our mentors up, we all sneak back through our rooms, climbing the walls and landing on our balconies with softs thuds. I meet Jack's gaze from his balcony. A silent question lingers in his expression. I dip my chin, and he dashes inside.

Before my guardian visits, I clean myself up at my dressing table. My reflection displays a tired and grief-stricken face. Wiping away the night from my skin, I think of everything I've observed, everything those children must be suffering.

The door behind me opens and closes softly. Hands rest on my shoulders, and I feel their warmth spread through me. Two thumbs dig into my back muscles as they massage away my churning thoughts and soreness.

'Do you want to talk about it?' Jack asks, his voice low but clear.

'Which part?' I don't have to say out loud what I mean. *When you were an overprotective prick? Or the prison camp I had to witness and leave behind without saving one child?*

'You have every right to be angry at me for how I acted, but I will never apologise for caring, Scarlet.'

I close my eyes, letting his words wash over me.

'I nearly lost you once, and I forbid it to happen again.'

My throat tightens as his arms wrap around me, pulling me closer into his chest. Without thought, I trail my fingers over his broad arms, needing their proximity, tipping my head back to lie on his chest. He rests his chin on my head without a second thought.

'Ember – the Elder Raven,' he corrects himself, 'had you pinned down, and your arm was hanging limp. She ripped your throat out with her bare teeth. Your blood was *every-where*.' Jack turns me on the stool I sit upon, caging a hand of mine in between his. Tanned fingers caress mine as if needing to soothe not only himself but me. 'You died before my eyes.'

'I understand. I really do,' I say quietly, my voice rough. 'But I cannot flee from one cage to fly back into another. I'll always be in danger. I'll always be at risk. That will never change.'

*Please let me make my own decisions. Do not make them for me*, I silently urge him.

He tenses, letting me go suddenly. His absence makes me shiver, a sudden coldness washing over me from his lack of heat. Blue eyes blaze with fury, with hurt, with grief, and I'm rendered speechless as he leans over me.

'Your throat pulsed and gushed with blood, Scarlet. Your body was trying so hard to stay alive.' He looks away, running his hands through his hair. A heavy sigh drifts through the room as he sits on the edge of my bed.

I stand up and manoeuvre myself so I can face him while I gently rub his back. This is the first time we've truly opened up about the trauma we have faced. We have bottled up all our painful memories, attempting to push them deep down so as not to remember the horrors we endured.

'I'm sorry you had to see that,' I murmur, not knowing what else to say.

I've never imagined what it was like to see the end of the Hex Trials. Unlike me, Jack came away conscious, seeing things he may never forget in his lifetime – things he obviously thinks of often.

'I watched over your body, waiting for someone to come save you. Princess Leonore finally took me away, telling me I had to stop looking – but I *couldn't.*' He peers up into my face, his beautiful ocean eyes taking in my every feature. My heart swells at the sight. I reach out and pull us into a firm hug, not caring if he'd rather I keep my distance but his arms wrap around my hips without hesitation.

I eventually shuffle into his lap, and we stay there for a long time.

'They'd have to do better than that to keep me away from you, guardian,' I murmur into his hair, feeling his arms tense at the words. I kiss him wherever I can reach, trailing my lips along his shoulder. 'I'll fight through life and death to get back to you. I swear it.'

Hair tickles my cheek as he lays his head in the crook of my neck, his fingers trailing across my skin. We no longer talk. Rather, we sit through the emotions, letting the darkness wrap around us, letting the memories slowly fade until eventually we lie back on the bed.

'I never want you to feel like I'm caging you in, Scarlet. There is nothing more I want to see than you free from all the horrors in the world. But I don't know how to give that to you.'

'You don't have to. All I ask is that you hold my hand through it all.'

Jack reaches for my hand and slides his fingers through mine. His grip is strong – firm and a sign for as long as he lives he'll never let me go.

'Jack,' I whisper, our heart rates now calmer, more in sync than ever.

'Yes?'

'Can you make me forget?' A moment of silence envelopes us. I twist my head to face him, some emotion I can't decipher lining his features. 'Can you make me forget everything, if only for a moment.'

'Gladly,' he murmurs, placing a tender kiss on my mouth, taking his time to bite my lower lip. 'Gladly.'

## 37

My thighs straddle him as I reach over and take off his shirt. Moonlit skin welcomes me, warmth radiating off his bare chest as I lie upon it. I kiss the line of his collarbone towards his throat, earning large hands that press my body closer.

'Scarlet,' he murmurs, the vibrations of his voice running over my skin.

Distracting my mind with his mouth, I take the time to taste him, my tongue eager. He pushes back, the urgency between us growing as if any moment we'll be torn apart, and this moment will shatter into little forgotten pieces.

My fingers tangle with the buttons of his trousers before I drag them off and fling them onto the floor. My own clothing follows close behind, and the feel of his bare skin against mine makes me giddy, my breathing quickening, my heart pounding in my chest.

I knead his growing cock, his eyes fluttering at my motions. He's quiet as he rolls his hips, his teeth dragging over his bottom lip.

'I don't know why we thought staying away from each

other was an option,' he says quietly, his blue gaze pinning me down. 'It was never going to work out.'

'A fool's hope,' I agree, bending forward to capture his lips once more, enjoying the feel of him, his scent of need sending me into delirium.

Fingers curve around my hips, tightening at my waist before they trail beneath my bum. My breath catches as he begins to tenderly rub the wetness between my legs, a shudder of pleasure lancing through me. Together we rub and tease and taunt until we are both breathing hard into each other's personal space, the hunger growing with every second.

'That's enough,' he grunts, tightening his grip on me before rolling us over.

He slides his mouth to my jaw and lines kisses across it before dipping down to my breast. I wither beneath him with every swirl of his tongue on my sensitive skin. My thoughts are mush at this point, consumed with Jack and what he's doing to me. He sucks hard on my nipple, and my back arches in response. He moans, and it heats me from within.

'Don't make me wait any longer,' I breathe.

'As you wish,' he answers, taking no time to lower himself into me, the size and sudden pressure causing me to bite my bottom lip. 'You feel so good.' He hums with pleasure as he slowly thrusts into me, his arm muscles on either side of my head bulging as he moves above. 'So tight. So good. I can't get enough.'

I clutch his arse, urging my guardian to quicken his pace. Our quiet sounds of pleasure mingle as we kiss each other messily, my lips on his throat, his lips trailing across my shoulder.

'Don't ever stop,' I whimper as my body tightens, the

overwhelming feeling of him coursing through me. 'I don't want this to end.'

This spurs him on, causing me to moan. His hand is over my mouth in seconds, to stop the sound echoing through the manor.

'Be quiet, or else someone will hear you,' he warns, his own body swift and damp with perspiration as he thrusts into me, his hand on me firm and delicious.

'Damn you,' I whisper through his fingers as we finally have our release, my body at its peak as it trembles under his weight. My teeth bite gently into his fingers, marking them as mine. Shivers course through my spine as our love-making comes to an end.

Too soon Jack reluctantly slides off me to lie beside me with a dreamlike look of satisfaction. His fingers trail over my stomach, making me tremble with sensitivity.

He takes my hands and kisses them, taking his time with each of my knuckles. 'I could kiss you all day.'

'If only you would,' I say, watching with interest, eager to know what he'll aim for next. But my tone seems to change something for him. 'What?'

'We can never have a normal relationship.' His demeanour droops as if this realisation that we can never be together in public is finally occurring to him. That if we ended up together, I'd be punished like my mother was – most likely worse. 'Could you live with this being a secret?' he murmurs quietly, motioning between us.

Ignoring the emotions that swell inside me, I say, 'Yes. But maybe one day we won't have to hide these feelings from the world.'

I shuffle onto my side so we are facing each other, curling my hand around the back of his neck. He doesn't put up a fight but rather enjoys my sudden neediness when

I pull him closer. I place a tender kiss on his forehead, then his cheek, and leave one upon the tip of his nose.

He gives me a warm smile, but it doesn't reach his eyes. I can tell by his expression his mind is working away, the cogs whirring with deep thoughts. My fingers slide through his hair, my nails running over his skull. I bring our mouths together once more, entwining our tongues in hopes of making the doubts within him fade away. He seems to understand my thought process and deepens the kiss.

'I don't know what I'd do if anything happened to you,' he utters, making my heart skip a beat. 'Scarlet.' He moves away slightly, making a sliver of cold press between us. I refrain from frowning.

His mouth opens. Then it closes again before opening once more.

'I want you,' he tells me. 'I'll always want you.'

Somehow I know this isn't what he originally wanted to say but I'm becoming too weary to think much of it.

'And I you,' I whisper, lifting my hand to his face and cupping his cheek.

## 38

'Another late night, Scarlet?' Ivy asks, taking a seat far from mine.

Peri and I are sharing breakfast again this morning, and I can barely keep my eyes open. What with an eventful night and a solid finale, once my head hit my pillow, I was out cold. I woke up first, as per usual, to watch the beautiful sunrise with a cup of tea, happy that we don't have training but a full free day.

*The perfect day to tell the royal family what is happening under their noses.*

'Spying on me again, Ivy?' I retort, earning a snort in answer. I glance over at her. The Nightshade's sapphire hair is rippling in the subtle breeze. 'Some might say this is obsessive behaviour. Should I be worried?'

Cobalt eyes roam over me coldly. 'You put yourself on a mighty-high pedestal, Raven. I'd be more worried about *that.*'

I shrug, leaning back in my chair, closing my eyes against the already bright sun. I have little energy to clash swords with her. She has her ways, and I'll figure out her angle eventually, but right now I require rest. I need to look and feel my best when visiting Ivory Castle. I cannot appear haggard in front of the king and queen, or else they may turn me away.

I close my eyes for what only feels like a few seconds before a finger is tapping my shoulder. Squinting, I find Carmen before me, sitting at the now-empty table. I look around in confusion, only to have my mentor chuckle.

'We debated on whether to wake you up, but you seemed so content we left you to it.'

I sit up straighter in my chair, wiping at my face. At the back of the manor, in the vegetable garden, are Olive and Thea, tending to some pumpkins that look nice and big.

Peri is on his balcony above us, reading an old and tatty book as he sips on a cup of what I assume is tea from the smell.

'Where are the others?' I ask.

Carmen takes a seat with me, turning towards her sister. 'Ivy went home for the day to spend it with family, while Jack, Rusty and Sol have gone into Sapphire City. The Briar said he needed to stock up for tonight. What that means I do not know, nor do I intend to ask.'

'Oh.' A part of me feels left out, that they didn't bother to ask if I wanted to come. But I quickly realise Jack is finally making an effort with the other males and actively chose to go without me. That's a small step in the right direction. I smile. 'A boys' trip – minus one.' I peer up at the Silken again with a scowl. 'Why didn't you go to the capital with the others?' I shout up at him.

As if only now realising my presence below him, Peri leans over his chair to see me, violet eyes piercing in the bright daylight. 'Because I don't need to buy any alcohol.'

'Alcohol?' I scowl deeply, expecting an explanation, but I receive none.

'Yes, alcohol.' Peri goes back to his book.

*Fine, then.*

'Like I said, I will not be asking,' Carmen repeats, leaning back in her chair. 'Your free time is none of my business.'

I ponder over her presence for a moment, letting the silence envelop us.

'Did you wake me up to tell me something? Or just so I didn't sleep all day in the sun?'

Carmen turns her head towards me, slowly, like she's about to drop a bomb on me. 'We tested your blood.'

I perk up at the topic. Having given a few samples of my blood to the Spark sisters, I've been waiting patiently for the results.

'We tested it with all sorts of weird and wonderful concoctions, spells and runes but have come to a very disappointing and fruitless conclusion.'

'Which is?' I prompt.

'We cannot puzzle out how to reverse the curse on you. We have tried everything in our power to purify your blood to its original state, but nothing works.' She grimaces, going back to observing Olive and Thea who now tend to some purple vegetables I couldn't name even if my life depended on it.

'Nothing?'

She shakes her head. 'Nothing else we are willing to try.'

'Such as ...' I press.

Dark eyes land on me, any emotion in her features now gone. 'I wish for us all to be free of our curses, Scarlet, but some things are better left untouched. Dark magic can be *life-threatening.*'

The wheels inside my head turn, marvelling at her words. 'I have to die for the curse to be lifted?' I guess.

She stiffens but doesn't correct me.

I snort. 'Isn't that obvious? Dead people can no longer be cursed. They're ... dead.'

She rolls her eyes, a gesture I've never seen her make before, and it amuses me.

'Many have tried putting themselves in life-threatening situations to then be resurrected by a close accomplice,' Carmen explains. 'Some have succeeded, while others ... the resurrection part of their plan did not go as intended. But that's not the most of it, dark magic must be used for the cause of death. Supposedly it can balance itself out, dark magic devouring dark magic.'

I open my mouth to voice an opinion, but my mentor points a long, delicate finger my way.

'This will not be a risk we are taking with you. You are too important. So unless we find another way, you'll have to face living as you are.'

My shoulders slump as I absorb her words. To have my scar be cured of the Elder Raven's curse, I'd have to die at the hand of dark magic and be brought back to life. I shudder thinking of the pressure that would put on the people who would save me. No matter what power lies beneath my scar, I don't think I could let anyone do such a thing – as tempting as it may be.

'That's no bother, Carmen. My hopes for this –' I wave my hand in the air – 'were exceedingly low. I won't go off and try my luck. You have my word.'

She nods before knocking the tabletop. 'Good. Now go make yourself useful.'

It's not a request, I realise. My mouth twists.

My gaze travels to Thea and the Severed once more. The latter seems to make a great effort not to look my way. I don't blame her, considering the evening we shared, but I won't let that deter me.

I stalk towards the pair, letting my steps be heard. 'Do you need a hand?'

Thea smiles gratefully and begins to point out jobs to do in the garden. They aren't too hard labour-wise, so I get stuck in. When I find myself alone with Olive an hour later, our mentor having gone off to get drinks, I finally grab her attention.

'Do you want to talk about last night?'

Olive sighs, wiping her forehead of sweat. 'I suppose. You've been more patient than I thought you'd be.'

'It helps that I slept most of the morning away,' I jest, earning a shadow of a smile.

She flings off her gardening gloves and walks to the wooden deck to sit on the edge. She pats the spot beside her. 'Come. I'll tell you everything.'

## 39

'The House of Glass, as you know, is made up of half-demon beings. We have the ability to sense death, and some can even *see* those that have passed.' Olive peers at me sidelong, watching for my reaction.

I nod to let her know I'm listening.

'Being part demon, we are very different from the other Houses. We don't have souls. Our blood runs black, and when we feel threatened, our demon side rises to the surface. It's a defence mechanism we are all born with.' She sighs as I sit quietly, letting her think over her next words.

'Last night I was afraid, Scarlet. When I saw that Raven ... my demon reared her head. She shielded and protected me against the female, and I'm glad she did. But with our demons comes little feeling – they know right from wrong, of course, but they do not feel guilt or remorse like a normal human does.'

At the camp, Olive's eyes turned black as the night sky, her face neutral as if her usual bubbly personality was being smothered. Now I know it wasn't truly her but another being *within* her that was in control at the time.

'You don't have souls?' I ask, making her laugh nervously.

'From everything I said, *that's* what you focus on?'

'I don't understand how that works. How do you know you are soulless?' I scrunch my nose up in confusion.

'We are like vampires. We look into a mirror and see nothing. We stand in the sun, and no shadow follows us.'

My head tilts, my gaze flickering to my lone shadow upon the wooden deck. How have I never noticed it before?

I stare at the Severed, eyes trailing over her long emerald hair – the tight curls tied up away from her attractive face.

'You think your kind is soulless because you can't see your *reflection?*' I utter with exasperation. 'That's the most foolish thing I've heard in my life. Why in the higher powers would you think that?'

Emerald eyes widen in offence. 'It's a fact, Scarlet.'

'No, Olive,' I counter with a huff. 'You compare yourself to a vampire, but clearly, you know nothing about them. Yes, vampires do not have reflections once they are turned, but that does not mean they have lost their souls. *Time* corrupts a heart, not being a vampire – or in your case, a Severed.' I shake my head.

'I didn't mean to offend you.' Olive's hands are open in surrender, watching me closely as I take the time to breathe deeply.

'It wouldn't usually bother me, but my best friend back at home is a vampire, and to hear you say he is soulless because of *what* he is doesn't sit well with me.' I take a shaky breath before turning to her with a grimace.

'I'm sorry, Scarlet. I really am.' The female's entire face droops as if ashamed of herself.

Guilt trails its claws around me as I try to answer.

'You must really care about him,' Olive says before I can muster up words.

I nod without hesitation. 'I do. He's the best thing to have walked into my life. He's saved me more times than I'd like to admit. I wouldn't be here without him and his kindness.'

'He sounds nothing like the vampire stories I've heard.'

'That's because people only tell stories about the shitty vampires. Dimitri remembers being human, remembers his strengths and makes sure not to use them to his advantage. He is the best person I know.' I smile to myself, wondering what he's up to. A pang of sadness hits me right in the chest, making me rub a hand over the pain.

I miss him. I miss him *so* much.

'I'd like to meet him one day. He sounds like a catch.'

My surprise doesn't go unnoticed, the Severed's eyes sparkling with timid amusement when I peer at her. I've never thought of Dimitri in such a way, but I know if Olive ever met him, she would be impressed – not just with his dashing good looks but with his warm personality too.

'He *is* a catch,' I agree. 'But I don't think Sol would like that very much.'

I'm prying, but I don't care. A change of conversation is exactly what I need. And from the interactions I've seen between the pair, I know *something* is going on between them.

Olive smirks. 'Sol does not own me. I can be with whoever I wish.'

I nod once. 'Too right. But you must see the effect you have on him. You can't be that blind.'

She nudges my side bashfully before she confirms, 'I see it.'

'And you're not interested?' I press, finding her smile growing.

'You are such a busybody!'

'I am,' I agree, making her laugh. The sound is natural, more light-hearted now, and I'm glad we are slowly getting back to our easy dynamic of jokes and quips.

'Sol is charming, highly attractive and really funny ...' She trails off, and I wrinkle my nose.

'Those are all positives, yes?' I wonder what the problem is.

The Severed's face softens into neutrality, the humour from before quickly vanishing.

'Or are you unenthusiastic about those qualities?'

'They are all positives, but that's what I'm afraid of. An angel and a demon, it would never work. He is perfect and virtuous, while I am ... not.'

Comprehension dawns on me. Olive thinks she is unworthy of Sol, that being part demon, she does not deserve a divine being's love.

'Olive,' I murmur, shuffling closer. Her hands are warm when I tug them towards my lap, my grip firm as I address her. 'You are kind, intelligent, honourable and witty. Your presence brings joy to those around you. Your loyalty alone is admirable, and the courage I've seen from you is inspiring. Sol would be a lucky male to have you. Do not ever think yourself unworthy of him – or anyone else, for that matter. I simply won't stand for it.'

She sniffs before nodding, emerald eyes piercing through me.

'I wouldn't say it if I didn't believe it. Everyone would vouch I only speak the truth.'

An impulse to ask Peri for proof of her worries rises to my lips, but I shove it back down. His truth-detecting ability is his own secret to reveal when he is ready.

'I believe you,' Olive says finally, wrapping her arms around me. I hold her tightly, the feeling briefly reminding me of being in the clutches of my sister Roux. 'Thank you. I'm so happy I met you, Scarlet.'

'I'm happy to have met you too.'

In her embrace, I realise Olive is my friend, a true and honest friend that I can rely on and talk with about anything. We have an understanding and much to learn about one another, but as long as we are together, I don't mind. It's an adventure I'll be glad to have.

We move apart and sit on the deck for a while longer, the sound of a door opening and closing behind us alerting me of Thea's imminent arrival.

'Can I ask you something?' I blurt.

Olive nods briefly, looking towards Thea, who makes her way over with a tray of drinks.

'I have to go to Ivory Castle. Would you come with me?'

The Severed leans forward. 'Are you going to tell them about the prison camps?'

I nod. 'It doesn't feel right to keep it to myself any more.'

She straightens, squaring her shoulders. 'Of course I'll come. I'm sure they'll be eager to hear what we found.'

I squeeze her hand, appreciating the backup. 'Thanks, Olive.'

'Anytime.' She smiles, vibrant eyes glistening.

Ivory Castle gleams as if it's been recently polished from ceilings to floors. My attire looks out of sorts in this pristine scenery, my burns looking anything but flawless in this impeccable stronghold.

A servant escorts us to the foyer, then leaves us to find a member of the royal family. My hands sweat with nerves, and Olive seems to notice as I wipe them on my dark trousers.

'Don't be anxious. They're people just like us.'

'Those in power aren't necessarily the same as us commoners,' I counter, an image of the Elder Raven coming to mind.

Olive purses her lips, seeming to silently agree.

It doesn't take long for the same servant to come back to where we are waiting and wave us forward. 'The king and queen are unavailable at the moment, but Prince Athos is happy to have an audience with you both.'

Our steps echo through the marble passageways, the blue-and-white decor flowing through the residence. We come to a grand door framed in silver. The servant knocks, and a voice from behind allows us entry. Olive motions me to go first, so I open the door and come to an abrupt halt, nearly stumbling when the Severed walks into my back.

'Death almighty, Scarlet,' Olive curses quietly before seeing what I've come across.

The chamber is a masculine office, crafted of driftwood and marble. It's slightly darker than the rest of the wood found in the castle, but it suits the young prince's space well. He sits at his desk, hands steepled as he leans forward, his blonde hair shiny beneath the ornate seashell crown he wears.

Across from him is a similarly dressed male. He wears an immaculate uniform of midnight blue, a smaller but just as impressive circlet upon his golden head and a familiar smirk across his face that falls the moment he notices us.

Prince Athos stands with his hands out wide in welcome, a smile growing over his face at the sight of Olive and me.

'Miss Seraphine, Miss Atterley, please come in. Let me introduce you to my cousin Prince Alexander.'

# 40

P*rince Alexander.*

The male peers back, his emotions neutral so as not to give himself away.

Prince Alexander – cousin of Prince Athos, heir to the Tellian throne – is Alex Irvine.

My eyes widen as they take in the dameer's fancy attire, the pearl circlet and his unfaltering expression. I'm paralysed with disbelief as he acts as if this revelation hasn't flipped my world on its axis.

Olive blinks but thankfully saves me from answering.

'Your Highnesses,' Olive says with a bow. Her hand grips mine and firmly tugs me into motion alongside her. 'Thank you for seeing us on such short notice. We have some important matters to discuss with you.'

'Of course. Please come in. Alexander was just leaving for another appointment,' the heir says, making his way around the large desk and shaking hands with his cousin. 'I'll speak with you later. Dinner as usual?'

Alex nods before they say their farewells, their demeanours showing their closeness. Alex – the prince – walks past us, his voice so low only I can hear it.

'Don't leave without seeing me.'

A shiver rushes down my spine as I watch him leave, his pale eyes peering back at me, urging me to follow his request.

*Holy Hanrah! What the fuck just happened?*

'Take a seat, ladies. What can I do for you?' Prince Athos motions to the two armchairs of deep grey velvet before his desk. With a smile, he makes himself comfortable in his own seat, hands resting along the arms of his robust chair.

Olive takes no time to explain our late night visit to Gwenore Forest. 'We believe that an operation to steal children is in motion,' she says, making the prince's brows furrow.

'Please explain,' he says, not seeming surprised by our news.

I lean forward, shaking the sudden unveiling of Alex being a royal from my mind to focus on the matter at hand. Prince Athos *must* understand the urgency of what we are saying. The children's lives depend on it.

'Younglings have been taken from their homes in the dead of night,' I say, thinking of the ones I've seen being stolen from the safety of their bedrooms. 'They are then transported to a prison camp situated in the middle of Gwenore Forest, where they are violently abused and forced to live in shocking conditions.'

'We believe they are being taken for their magic. Perhaps an army of sorts, as the common thread between these children is that they are all dameer,' Olive adds, perched on the edge of her seat.

We discussed our theories with Jack and Sol the night before, and I hate what we concluded. This isn't simply a runaway youth, as I first suspected when Alex came to Hex Manor; this is a full-fledged attack on the people of Sapphire City – perhaps even the neighbouring areas.

'They also all seem to be under the age of fifteen,' I add, which earns a heavy exhalation from the heir. 'The perfect age to be influenced and moulded if in the wrong hands.'

Prince Athos considers this before asking, 'Do you have proof?'

I blink. 'Proof? Do you not believe us?'

The prince leans forward, his voice filled with patience. He rubs his eyes before showing his palms as if in apology. 'Unfortunately, you are not the only people who have come to see us about this matter.'

'What?' Olive gapes, disgust lining her features. 'And you've done nothing about it?'

'No,' the prince admits, face smooth with openness.

'Can I ask why? Shouldn't a royal be concerned about the disappearances of their people – their youth?' I ask, curious about his reaction. Surely he should be horrified – distraught, even – but only calm oozes from him.

'Because, Miss Seraphine, every time we've asked for proof, they have been unable to provide it. We have been shown by multiple people where they think they've seen this camp, and none has been present. Once we come to the location they think the camp is situated in, it has miraculously disappeared.' The heir lifts a shoulder in a quizzical manner, looking as baffled as I feel.

I scowl. 'How many people have come to you with this story?'

'Twelve if we are including yourselves.'

'So unless we bring some sort of proof this camp actually exists, you won't bother to come and seek it out with us?' Olive asks, eyes narrowing.

'The royal family has little time to waste on matters of hearsay, Miss Atterley. We searched for this establishment with the first seven people – we gave them the benefit of the doubt. But all those times, we came to find nothing but clear land.' He gives us a tired expression, his eyes lowering at the corners. 'I know Gwenore Forest is a menace at the best of times, but she cannot simply conjure up prison camps. I'm sorry to disappoint you.'

'So that's it?' I ask, my fangs slowly lengthening as my emotions get the best of me. 'That's all you can offer? An apology?'

Prince Athos gives me a gentle look, something like sympathy crossing his handsome features. 'My guards have scoured the entirety of Sapphire City for all and any information about these children and no one seems to know anything about it. And as you can imagine, I have the resources to make sure every stone is turned over but again, we found absolutely nothing.' He stands up and comes to our side of the desk, looking down at us with a troubled expression. 'We have come to the conclusion that someone must be playing a very cruel trick on some of the city dwellers. I truly am sorry I can be of no more help.'

My lips press together in frustration.

'I assume that was all you wanted to speak to me about,' the prince says. My legs are wobbly when I get to my feet, registering the obvious dismissal. 'I can escort you out if you wish.'

'Please don't trouble yourself. We can manage,' I say to him. Olive and I bow before exiting. 'Thank you for your time.'

'If you have any other worries, don't hesitate to visit. My office is always open to you and your fellow Hex members.' Prince Athos waves half heartedly before closing the door behind us.

Olive and I are quiet as we head down the passageway we came down. We arrive at a familiar foyer and head for the exit, our steps echoing around the high ceiling and the walls of my brain.

'What are your thoughts?' I ask Olive.

She sighs heavily, running a frustrated hand through her long hair. 'Why would he say the camp disappears? Is someone extremely powerful cloaking the area, or are they simply moving their operation elsewhere when they hear any hint of being found out?'

'I have to admit I'm perplexed, but I'm not convinced by the prince's words.'

We descend the steps and walk out into the bright sun to the pearly gates. Patiently we wait for our horses to be retrieved so we can leave the premises. All the exterior guards, I notice, keep a keen eye on us.

Sapphire City looms before us, the main street trailing all the way into the distance to a cluster of dark trees – Gwenore Forest. Memories of the children fill my mind, thoughts of their abuse, of the black-uniformed soldiers harming them when they disobey.

'I say we go pay Gwen another visit. What do you say?' I ask the Severed.

She nods eagerly. 'Sounds like a plan.'

'I hope you weren't leaving without seeing me, like I asked,' Alex calls out, his voice familiar but stronger somehow, as if having a crown on his head gives him more courage.

I turn around to find the dameer walking towards us. His regal jacket of midnight blue is no longer on, and instead, a nicely tailored shirt of white with silver detailing is on display. He looks every bit as princely as his cousin, and I make a face of distaste as he approaches.

'Your Highness.' I bow dramatically, my voice lined with affliction. 'We would do no such thing, in case you order your soldiers to lop off our heads.'

He grimaces, not a trace of flirtation or amusement in sight. 'Scarlet—'

'When were you going to tell me?'

He steps closer, and I back away, the move making him flinch. 'Scarlet, please.'

'You *lied* to me. When were you going to tell me?' I repeat, the hurt evident. 'You came to me needing help. I offered a hand to you, made myself responsible for you, and you were untruthful from the start. I let you walk into that camp.' I grab my head with realisation, thinking of all the possible ways our mission could have turned drastically bad. What if we'd been caught? Or worse, killed? 'If something had happened to you ...'

'This is exactly why I kept my background to myself. You wouldn't have let me come along if you had known of my supposed value,' Alex says, hands out as if to reach for me, but I evade them.

'*Supposed* value?' Olive snorts, crossing her arms in an obvious display of allegiance to me. 'After Prince Athos, you're next in line to the throne. Of course you're of value.'

Alex gives the Severed a *you're not helping* look, but she shoots him a *you dug this hole and now you must lie in it* glance back.

The prince pinches his nose as if trying to refrain from arguing further. His body sags with defeat, and he steps towards me once more. 'I apologise that I kept this minor detail from you—'

'Minor!' I whirl on him. 'Minor my arse. You are a member of the royal family. The king and queen would execute me if they knew I had willingly let you come along on our escapades. And if you had been harmed, they'd make sure to kill me again!'

He shakes his head. 'I am not fragile, Scarlet. I am not the heir; I am the *spare*. There is a huge difference.'

'I don't care. If something had happened to you, I'd never have forgiven myself,' I shoot back.

At this point, I'm sure the soldiers around the castle are debating whether to step in, our bickering louder than is probably deemed polite.

Hands on my hips, I glare at the prince, willing him to understand. I feel frustrated, annoyed and hurt that he has kept this hidden from me.

'I thought I was your friend,' I mutter, glancing away. 'I thought we had a mutual trust, and you've gone and turned out to be a fucking *prince*.'

Alex takes a deep breath, his heart calming slightly. A small tug of his lips shows his amusement, light blue eyes glimmering with something soft.

'I'm honoured you hold me in such high regard.'

I scowl but don't correct him. He's annoyingly right – a part of me does care for him, for some strange reason.

'I didn't mean to hurt your feelings, Scarlet.' He approaches slowly, wrapping me in his embrace, his arms tightly bringing me to his chest.

I don't allow my arms to do the same, standing there stiffly. I meet Olive's gaze, and she is doing well to hide her mirth.

'I had Ellis in mind. That was all. I did what I had to do to save my younger brother. You understand, don't you?'

I nod reluctantly. For my brothers and sisters, I'd scour the lands. I'd sail oceans and travel the kingdoms to make sure they were all right. I know better than anyone what the love of a sibling can make someone do. I went through hell and back for my own sister Roux, so Alex doing the same for his brother is something I can relate to.

'I do understand,' I agree with a sigh, finally lifting my arms to squeeze him back.

He lingers for longer than is necessary, or appropriate for a prince and a commoner, before pushing me to arm's length.

'But if you're keeping any more secrets—'

'I'm not. I promise,' Alex interjects, giving me a genuine smile. He looks over my shoulder at Olive. 'Will you forgive me?'

The Severed nods. 'I knew something was off about you. I had my suspicions.'

It seems I've missed a lot of telltale signs. All of Alex's answers to my questions have been vague, and his knowledge of the kingdom's history is stellar. Did I realise what he could be but didn't want to look deeper?

Alex peers at me next, tilting his head enough his crown looks near to falling off. 'Forgiven?'

I wait a few seconds before saying, 'I suppose.'

The prince beams with relief, nudging my side, the light I've come to enjoy back in his eyes. 'You suppose? I'll have to work harder to earn your forgiveness, it seems. No matter. I have some ideas.'

I groan. 'Please do *none* of the things you're currently thinking of.'

'You don't think they will be good?' He lifts a hand to his chest in mock horror.

'I know for a fact they'll be unseemly for a royal.'

He twists his mouth to hide his laugh. 'You lack faith in me, Scarlet.' Pale eyes flicker up and behold a servant standing by the castle entrance, looking expectantly our way. 'I better get back. I have a meeting I'm running late for.' He squeezes my arm before waving to Olive. 'See you soon?'

ALEX IRVINE

# PART THREE

## The Royals

## 41

'It's gone,' I mutter, unable to comprehend what I'm seeing.

Gwenore Forest is quiet except for the occasional bird singing and bush rustling. On our travels through Sapphire City, I searched for Jack, Sol and Rusty during their boys' time, but to no avail.

Side by side Olive and I stare in bewilderment. As Prince Athos suggested it would be during our meeting, the area is bare. No proof of human existence, let alone a child, in sight.

'Death almighty. What is going on?' Olive's emerald eyes roam the land before us, scanning from left to right in search of proof this area was used for nefarious means.

We find the tree the Severed was hiding in when Alex and I trespassed into the camp, and not a sign of our fight is left behind. No blood from the Raven, no broken branch from Olive's fall – it's as if we conjured up the whole night in our heads.

'No smell of blood. No smell of smoke,' I observe out loud. The scent around us is normal for Gwenore – dirt and eucalyptus. Nothing else lingers in the air to assume the place was once used to torture children. 'Those were both present when we visited last.'

Olive crouches down in a patch of dirt and runs her fingers through it. 'No footprints, no carriage wheel tracks. It makes no sense.'

'How is this huge operation setting up and suddenly moving within a day? It shouldn't be possible,' I grumble, frustration rising.

Olive shakes her head, defeat lining her words. 'What do we do now? Search the whole forest? What if it's no longer operating here? All those children ... lost.'

My mouth twists with disgust. Who is doing all this, and most importantly, why?

Hex Manor is quiet as the sky slowly darkens. Dinner is cleaned up for the evening, and now we sit outside in the long grass on wooden chairs we've taken from the deck table. In a circle, we all sit as a hot fire flickers in the middle, contained within an iron dish, logs piled beside it to keep it going throughout the night.

Surprisingly, every Hex member is present. Thea and Carmen are out visiting the capital, giving us leeway to do whatever we wish for the evening. So here we sit outdoors with the moon beaming down on us and the warm breeze that smells faintly of the ocean.

Originally I wasn't going to join, wanting instead to start our search for the missing prison camp, but after some persuasion from Sol and Jack, I came to the conclusion that a weary Raven was not a helpful one.

'We rest tonight and start fresh tomorrow,' Olive agreed with a firm nod.

When the boys bring out plates of food and bottles of alcohol, I watch as cups are filled and plates are covered with fluffy pastries. Jack, who sits beside me, hands over a bottle of blue liquid. I recognise it as the pineapple beverage I tried at the House of Bane – a Nightshade favourite – called Nimble Lady. I shake my head and pass it to Sol, who looks slightly uncomfortable, his cup unsurprisingly empty.

'You don't drink, do you?' I ask the Celestial.

'Not if I can help it,' he answers quietly, handing the Nimble Lady to Olive on the other side of him. Golden eyes land on me, and he stiffens slightly before giving me a large smile as if sensing my survey of him and hoping I'll lose interest.

I narrow my eyes, remembering him in the library after I'd spoken to him about cocktails. 'Do you have an unfortunate history with drinking?' My voice is low, my head leaning close to him so the others, who are chatting among themselves, can't hear us.

Sol averts his gaze, full lips rolling with indecision.

'I'm sorry, Sol. It's none of my business.'

'No. You're right. I used to drink, but I don't any more. I've been sober for ten months now, but I still have trouble at the best of times.'

My hand slips over his shoulder, giving it a firm squeeze in hopes of comforting him. 'Well, if you ever need a friend to slap away any drink that comes near you, I'm your girl.' I stick a thumb into my chest with a mischievous grin to try to lighten the mood. Thankfully, it works.

'I'd appreciate that.' Sol chuckles before accepting a peach iced tea from Olive. 'I try not to tangle with my past, but it's hard. I have good days and bad days.'

'We all do,' I agree. 'I have moments where I find myself slipping into past behaviours before reminding myself I no longer need to think that way.'

He tilts his head, his long, flowing hair rolling off his shoulder. 'Like what?'

I purse my lips. 'When Jack and I first arrived here in Tealwaters, I was suspicious of all those who were nice to me.' I motion to the group sitting in a circle, the people who had welcomed me with open arms on day one. 'I thought, being powerful, you must have ulterior motives. Powerful people always want more power.'

Sol squints. 'Do they?'

'Well, I've grown up with self-important, power-hungry individuals. It's what I experienced as a youngling, and that's a hard state of mind to turn your back on. But I'm taking each day at a time. That's all you can do.' I mirror the Celestial's secret smile.

'Wise words, Raven.'

Drinks flow and tongues loosen. Sol and I seem to be the only sober ones – even the Silken enjoys a whisky and some orange concoction Ivy hands him.

For the first time in a long time, I fully relax into my seat, content about where I am and who I'm with.

## 42

I've never before experienced a campfire or sitting around telling stories, but I decide it's one of my favourite pastimes.

Rusty is lounging in his chair when he startles, making Ivy beside him spill her drink.

'Watch it!' she barks, to which the Briar apologises.

His bronze eyes find me. 'Scarlet, I forgot!'

Frowning, I sit up straighter, not sure what the Briar is referring to. 'Forgot what?'

He doesn't answer but rather creates a small portal beside him, sticks his broad arm into it and brings out a bottle of something I've not seen in a long time.

'Liquid Gold?' I ask, watching as he sets the alcoholic beverage on his lap and brings out a second bottle from the portal before it closes. 'You got these for me?'

Jack leans forward, hands nearing the fire as he peers sidelong at me. 'We went to three different stores to find them.'

'Rusty said you mentioned it at training once. We thought it would be nice to try it together,' Sol pipes up, making me beam.

The Briar tosses a bottle my way, and I catch it easily. The label is familiar, its golden script one I saw often when fighting at the Badger's Sett. A lump sticks in my throat at the thought of that place. As dirty and smelly as it could be at the end of a busy night, it was a place I loved. I could go there to be safe, to feel strong and have no other Raven know where I was.

I meet Jack's gaze, his face expressing how I feel. 'Thank you. This means a lot.'

'Crack it open, then. I want to see what all the fuss is about,' Olive chimes in, spurring us all into action.

Glasses are filled with pure gold liquid and offered around the circle, the group's expressions amusing as they peer down into the thick substance. Sol holds his full glass so as not to look out of place but makes no effort to sip it.

Opposite me, over the crackling fire, Rusty's face lights up when he swallows. His bronze eyes meet mine. 'This is surprisingly good,' he declares before he gulps the rest of it down.

I finish my own drink and hand Sol my empty glass while no one is watching and take his full one for myself. I won't be feeling any effects of the alcohol, so we may as well help each other out.

*Thank you*, the Celestial mouths.

'Liquid Gold is my favourite,' I say, watching everyone else's reaction.

Peri looks alarmed by how much he likes it, his small, quick sips a giveaway. Ivy appears annoyed, like she was hoping to hate it.

'It changes flavour according to the drinker. It never tastes the same for any individual,' I explain, recalling Dimitri always saying his tasted of strawberries and cream.

'What does yours taste like, then?' Olive asks as I fill her glass up again.

'Mint chocolate,' I reply. 'What's yours?'

She takes a sip, this one bigger, and swirls it around her mouth. 'Apple pie.'

I can't help laughing at this. 'Really?'

She nods happily. 'We used to make a pie every week together. I have nine siblings, so it was a nightmare, but it was always good fun.'

'Nine siblings!' Peri gapes, and I can't help but mirror him. 'That's incredible.'

'And I thought I had a lot of siblings.' I laugh before nudging Sol in the arm. 'Do you have brothers or sisters?'

He nods, happy to be included. 'Yeah, three brothers. I'm the second youngest.'

'I got that impression from you, angel face,' Olive declares, making the Celestial frown.

'What is that supposed to mean?'

'You have a younger-sibling vibe about you. Determined to prove themselves and all that.' She waves a hand as if this makes sense. She points to me next. 'I'd wager you're the youngest out of your brood too.'

'Good guess,' I say, making her grin.

'How many are in your family?' she asks, leaning back in her seat, contentment on her face.

'Five including me. Two sisters, two brothers.' A pang shoots through me, and I cover my wince. The thought of a certain sister makes me shuffle with unease.

Olive notices my change in demeanour and makes a show of peering around the group, taking the attention off me, and she points at Peri. 'Only child?'

He shakes his head. 'I have a younger brother.'

She purses her lips. 'Not a good relationship, though. Am I right?'

Reluctantly he nods. He seems grateful when she moves on to Rusty.

'I predict you have sisters. You're not as boisterous as this one is.' Olive tilts her head towards Sol, amusement lining her features.

'You're right.' Rusty nods eagerly. 'Middle child. Two sisters.'

'Knew it.' Olive shakes a fist in the air with a sigh of triumph. 'And Ivy ...'

The Nightshade tenses but says nothing. This makes my brow lift with curiosity. Usually she'd be eager to divulge her thoughts, but she seems on edge.

'I have no idea. You give very little away. Maybe an older child,' Olive guesses, to which Ivy nods timidly.

'I have a younger sister,' Ivy confirms, making the Severed grin.

'And you, guardian, you're definitely an only child.' Olive points his way with a glint in her emerald eyes.

Jack's lips tilt up, the most warmth I've seen him offer to any of the Hex members. 'Indeed. They got perfection on the first try.'

I snort, nearly spitting out my drink. 'Wow.'

The group bursts into laughs and snickers. I can see Rusty, Sol and Jack have become friendlier on their boys' day, that my guardian has let down his guard to have this bonding time with them.

'So what made you want to be a guardian?' Olive asks him once the chuckles have died down.

'My mother,' Jack answers. 'She's the first guardian, and I wanted to follow in her footsteps. So I started in the traineeship and was thankfully paired with Scarlet.' He softens looking my way, and I smile shyly. 'Lucky for me, or I wouldn't be here today.'

'Are you referring to the trials?' Ivy asks, interest lining her face as she leans forward. For once she doesn't look ready to bite back with an insult. She looks genuinely curious – as does everyone else.

'Yes,' Jack utters. As if asking permission, he peers side-long at me.

I shrug. They'll all figure out what happened one day. What is the use of concealing the story?

'We have both been through some shit. I nearly died. Scarlet *did* die.' He averts his ocean-blue eyes to the beverage in his hand as if it's anchoring him, not wanting to face the people who watch us closely.

'What?' Olive blurts, looking aghast.

'Our last trial was a battle to the death,' I explain, feeling slightly uncomfortable – not because of what happened but because of what I know I'll have to reveal soon.

'Scarlet refused to fight,' Jack says, saving me from explaining further. 'But our queen favoured that behaviour. I suppose she wanted a representative who could see when fighting was the right course of action and when it was not. Anyway, she crowned Scarlet the new Raven of the Hex, and here we are.'

'Why didn't you fight?' Peri asks me, violet eyes piercing. Deep frown lines mark his pale face, as if he's genuinely angry with me for not defending myself. If only he knew.

'I couldn't bring myself to do it. My opponent was someone I cared for and didn't want to harm.' I shrug as if this is enough.

'Who was it?' Sol murmurs.

I purse my lips, feeling several pairs of eyes on me. 'My older sister Ember.'

Silence ensues. I suppose I expected such a response, but actually experiencing it is completely different. Not bothering to hide my resurfacing grief, I take in everyone around me.

'We fought illusions, people who were shifted into each

of us. My sister thought she was duelling me, and vice versa. When she killed the replica of me, the illusion faded. With my test, I refused to fight her, and I was pitted against the Elder Raven. She ripped my throat out and left me to bleed out.' I motion to the silver scar across my neck, their eyes taking in my skin as if studying it for the first time. 'But I'm fine now. It's all in the past.'

No one seems to believe me, especially when they know there are still those out there who are trying to kill me. Olive killed one Raven, but Alex mentioned another.

Olive sighs. 'Well, yours makes our trials sound pathetic.'

I give her a questioning look.

'I had to capture a cat. Whoever caught it first became the next Severed of the Hex.'

'You're kidding,' Ivy blurts, saying exactly what I'm thinking.

Olive shakes her head in amusement. 'No, I'm not.'

'So what did you do? Build a trap?' Rusty asks with furrowed brows.

Olive smiles slyly, bottle-green eyes gleaming. 'No. Everyone tried that. I realised after weeks of no one getting anywhere close to the creature that I had to think differently. So I attempted befriending the animal, getting closer to it each day and making conversation as if it was a close companion. On the last day, it came and sat on my lap, and I won.'

I peer over at Jack with an incredulous look. He, in turn, grins, humour filling his features.

'That's brilliant,' he says, a twinkle in his eyes. 'Utterly brilliant.'

Olive shrugs. 'You can call me the cat whisperer from now on.'

Sol snorts. 'It has a nice ring to it. When I was younger, they used to call me ...'

As conversation slowly turns to childhood nicknames, I lean over to Jack and breathe in his salty scent. 'It seems like a lifetime ago we were in Rubien, fighting for our lives, hatred filling the gaze of everyone around us.'

He hums in acknowledgement. 'I must admit I prefer it here.'

We share a moment, crimson eyes meeting sapphire. We've experienced a lot together, Jack and I. We've laughed and cried, been hurt and healed. I wouldn't have anyone else beside me, beside me now as the group shares stories. The urge to find my guardian's hand is strong, but I refrain, instead leaning over to whisper in his ear.

'I prefer it here too.'

## 43

Carmen and Thea sit together whispering, looking rather suspicious as we all eat breakfast together the next morning.

'What do you think they have planned?' I ask the Silken beside me.

Violet eyes roam over our mentors, his brain churning away. 'I think something important is going to happen today. Something we will most likely not enjoy.'

I hum in agreement, seeing the glimmering of excitement in Carmen's eyes.

*We're definitely in trouble*, I think glumly.

When everyone has finished with their meal, the sisters decide to announce today's lesson.

'So, some of you may know what these are, and some perhaps not.' Carmen snaps her fingers, and a long chain of metal lands in her palm. It looks heavy, and the colour is as black as night.

My heart thumps at the sight of it. I glance at Jack, whose face turns pale.

'Today we are training with obsidian chains. These are not your average restraints, however. They have been made to render the wearer powerless – meaning any magic you may have will be dulled completely.'

Thea motions around the table. 'We want to incorporate this today because it will force those of you who rely on magic to puzzle out alternative solutions when you face a problem.'

Carmen nods in agreement. 'You may come across an individual who can take away your power, who may muffle that advantage, and we want you to feel prepared.' She holds up another long, thick black chain, and my teeth mash together, memories stirring within my head. 'However, I thought we could change things up a little.'

Carmen rises from her seat and motions for Ivy to stand up. The Nightshade gets to her feet obediently, putting her book down on the table. The witch waves for me to come stand beside her. I reluctantly do as I'm told and shuffle on my feet beside Ivy with curiosity.

Thea comes forward and locks the obsidian chain around our wrists, my right connected to Ivy's left. 'Today you will learn to be with your partner and get through a day with them stuck by your side.'

Ivy and I share a look, her expression mortified, while mine is … blank.

'What if I need the toilet?' I ask, looking at the shackles with unease. 'Does Ivy have to be there too?'

'Yes,' Carmen answers without hesitation.

'What about me? I hope I'm not going to be paired up with one of them.' Olive points to the males.

'No, you'll be with me today,' Thea replies pleasantly.

Out of everyone, I feel Olive has been given the best option, until I think more into it. It will be rather strange sharing intimate moments with our mentor. I glance at Ivy to find her already staring daggers at me.

'Let's make some ground rules,' she says, yanking the chain roughly so I stumble closer.

The part of me that hates this idea is quelled by the fact that I know Ivy detests it even more. I smile because I can make her day so infuriatingly frustrating – I can't help but enjoy the prospect.

'No talking—'

I lift a finger before she can get any further. 'How about you pretend to like me, and we can have a marvellous day of fun and friendship?'

I hear Sol bark a laugh at that.

'I'd rather scoop my eyes out with spoons,' Ivy deadpans.

'Well, that sounds great. I'll be right here to watch you.' I beam brightly as I circle my chained hand around her neck to put my arm on her shoulder and pull her close to smush our faces together. 'We could do with some quality bonding time.'

'Please, no,' she mutters, eyes narrowing in disgust.

44

I'm being dragged along by a grumbling Nightshade who won't stop cursing at the Spark sisters for ruining her day. Personally, now that I've had time to absorb the task, I think it's rather hilarious. It's been obvious from day one that Ivy doesn't like me, and for reasons I may never understand. But Thea and Carmen did this on purpose – that much is obvious.

I break Ivy out of her rant. 'I think we'll have a delightful day.'

She glares at me, her plump lips pursed in repulsion, and keeps marching on through the streets.

When I asked where we were going, Ivy said she needed to do some errands and tough shit if I had plans – they weren't happening any more. Of course, I had nothing planned. In fact, I am enjoying seeing more parts of Sapphire City. The shops are open and streaming with customers. The water roads are filled with rowing boats. And the smell of delicious food wafts through the air, making me drool for a sweet treat.

'Can we stop for a pastry?' I ask, eyeing a bakery I've yet to visit that reminds me of the Tea Shop, back in Rubien –

its decor is pretty and feminine but is unsurprisingly ocean-themed, with white furniture and light blue tablecloths.

'No,' Ivy snaps, pulling on the chain between us, causing me to quicken my pace. 'I'm already late.'

'Late for what?'

'Well, if you put less effort into running your mouth and more effort into hurrying those little legs of yours, you'll find out sooner rather than later, won't you?' she retorts, giving me a pointed look as if *I'm* the problem.

I humour her and start to jog, rattling the chain for emphasis. 'Come on, then, Poison Ivy. Let's make haste.'

She tenses at the name but proceeds to glare at me.

I smile back.

'I don't run,' she declares, her piercing eyes looking down at me with irritation.

'You do now.' I grin and yank the shackles with full force.

I don't give her a choice. I pull her along by the wrist, imagining this as strength training while she shouts for me to slow down. 'We can't be late!' I remind her, and she finally finishes her tirade – probably regretting her choice of words.

It's a while later when I can hear the Nightshade's erratic breathing that I decide to slow to a walk again. Ivy's forehead is damp with sweat, and her eyes are bright from the exertion.

'Wasn't that pleasant!' I declare, but she pushes forward, bumping my shoulder as she overtakes me.

'I'm going to poison your drink when we have dinner tonight.'

'I can't wait,' I reply with heavy sarcasm.

She stops, and I take a look around to find we are near the House of Bane. As we approach she waves her hand to those on guard, and the gates to the school open. Ivy yanks me forward, and I dutifully follow closely, eyes roaming over the premises before us. No one is around, and a shiver shoots up my spine. It's eerily quiet as we enter the building, and the rooms we pass are all empty.

*Something is not right,* I can't help thinking.

'Where is everyone? Why are we here, Ivy?'

'Because we have a gathering today, and I can't miss it,' Ivy answers. Her voice is low, and something tugs at my mind.

*She no longer looks so good.*

'What is this meeting about?' My brows furrow.

She doesn't bother to answer as she pulls me through high-ceilinged hallways and past several laboratories that are bare and without a Nightshade in sight. Test tubes are left discarded in racks. Tables of paper and pens look to have been left behind. My senses prickle with mistrust.

Ivy pushes open a nearby door, and we travel down a hallway covered in framed pictures. Scanning each one, I note they are all drawings done by what I assume are children, the scribbles wobbly, the writing along some of them making little sense, but I smile nevertheless.

'This is rather sweet.' I wave towards the wall.

'Indeed.'

I don't bother trying to make conversation again. She's on a mission, and I'm not sure why. It's only when we get to a tall white archway with pearlescent doors that Ivy turns to me and puts a finger to her lips.

'When we go inside, do not talk. Do not make a sound. You're not allowed in this part of the House of Bane, but I have no choice but to bring you.' Her expression is hard, so serious I can't do anything but nod in confusion.

She swings open one of the pearlescent doors, and we are welcomed into a clean and rather sterile grand hall where the windows are tall and arching. The ceiling has the same paintings I saw in their extravagant library, and seats are situated in rows throughout the whole space. Every Nightshade I was expecting to see but couldn't find is here, sitting and listening to the figure dressed in blue robes at the front of the crowd.

The Elder Nightshade spots us immediately, pausing her speech and causing everyone to look over their shoulder at what has taken the older female's attention. One by one they all turn to stare with mixed expressions of horror, disturbance and nerves. Whispers echo through the hall, making me feel suddenly claustrophobic.

'What is *she* doing here?' someone whispers, making me wish I could crawl away.

Ivy speaks up – not to defend me but rather to explain, lifting the obsidian chain between us. 'I'm stuck with her. Deal with it.'

Whoever has doubts about my presence doesn't comment further, nor does anyone else as they hesitantly go back to giving their attention to the front of the room.

The Elder Nightshade continues, her sapphire eyes wary before she regards the audience once more. 'We gather here today to remember those we've lost at the hands of the Melantha vampire coven. We did not plan for the attack that day. Nor did we plan on losing so many good people.'

My body stiffens, and suddenly everything falls into place. I now know why the Nightshades look at me like some kind of threat, why their hearts race every time I pass them in the library or outside when getting food.

'We did not expect to lose so many souls. But with a heavy heart, I say they are dearly missed and will be remembered for evermore. Let us have a moment of silence,' the Elder announces, her voice echoing through the space.

Every head in the room dips, and I watch as, in unison, every Nightshade grasps their hands together as if in prayer. Ivy does the same, a tear spilling down her cheek.

No wonder she is pissed with today's training. She didn't want anyone seeing this private moment she and her House are experiencing – especially not with someone who reminds them of the very beings that caused them such obvious grief.

'May they rest in peace,' the Elder Nightshade murmurs sadly, making everyone raise their head once more, repeating her words back. 'Hemlock Boxelder, Haines Snakeroot, Castor Rosary, Oleander Mercury, Oak Wynters …' She lists names out as if by heart. Names upon names of people gone and never coming back. So many. *Too* many.

I pause.

*Oak Wynters?*

My eyes flick to Ivy.

*Ivy Wynters.* I recall Olive introducing me to the Nightshade when I first laid eyes on her.

Are they related?

The ceremony is over after an hour, and the hall clears soon after the Elder leaves. Ivy is quiet, and I let her take the time to absorb everything as others pass us, her steps small and silent as her teary eyes dip to her feet.

My stomach tightens at the thought of losing family. The strength Ivy shows is admirable – not that I'd tell her that. She holds herself well for someone who has lost someone to an attack so savage as this.

'Do you need a drink?' I ask her, my voice low so as not to startle her.

Ivy pauses and looks at me with confusion. 'Is that your way of asking if I'm all right?'

I shake my head. 'No. I can guess what you're feeling

right now is far from all right. I'm asking if you want to get shit drunk and forget everything for a few hours.'

She considers me intently, perhaps thinking of all the ways I could be manipulating her. But that's the thing – I'm not. Right now I'm offering her some time to numb the pain. To remove the emotions for a period and to feel nothing.

She nods finally. 'Yes. I would like that.'

45

The tavern Ivy chooses is apparently not her local.
'I don't want to see anyone right now,' she explains, and I can understand why.

The people here are all strangers to me, and seeing Ivy ease onto the bench beside me, I know it's the same for her. When a young girl comes by for our order, Ivy asks for a drink called molten slapper, and I have trouble trying to hide my amusement.

When the girl comes back with a jug of the darkest beverage I've ever seen, along with two small glasses, Ivy pours us both a small dose. Before I can grasp my glass, the Nightshade has tipped back a large mouthful. Her face contorts into a pained expression as she swallows, and she makes a disgusted sound after.

'Not good?' I crinkle my nose, sniffing at the alcoholic beverage.

'Tastes like crap,' she admits, pouring another.

This time I drink along with her, knowing full well I won't be getting an ounce of buzz from the alcohol, but I'm content to make Ivy feel comfortable by keeping up with her.

'Holy Hanrah,' I mutter, the disgusting liquid burning my throat. 'You're not kidding.'

It's after an hour of silence and the third jug that Ivy's lips loosen. Her body has progressively become limp over the table before us, her chained arm dangling between us.

'Oak was my twin sister.' Flowers begin to bloom across her skin, the petals fluttering as if caught in a subtle wind.

I refrain from shuffling away.

My heart races. *Twin sister.* I've been hoping the family member was someone older, someone perhaps more ready to greet death, but no. It's the very person she shared a womb with. *Fuck.*

'I can't imagine your pain,' I answer honestly.

'Our parents, along with everyone else in our House, used to call us the poison twins. Poison Oak and Poison Ivy.' The edge of her mouth tugs upwards at the memory, and I realise why she reacted the way she did when I used that exact nickname. 'When she was killed, I felt like my heart had been ripped out of my chest. Like the sun would never rise again, and I'd live in darkness forever.' Ivy fingers the rim of her cup, eyeing the dark liquid inside with such intensity I can practically see her thoughts swirling. 'She was the one who enjoyed this disgusting drink, but I make sure to toast her every year. It's the least I can do.'

'She had bad taste,' I offer, hoping she'll hear my joking tone. Thankfully, I'm gifted with a small smile – the first smile I've ever received from Ivy. But it feels wrong somehow.

'She really did. She was the one who wanted to be in the Hex – not me.'

My brows lift with this confession. It seems I'm not the only person in our group to have been put on this path because of reasons other than actually wanting to be on it. Rusty comes to mind, and I feel a pit of sadness well up that we are only now reaching out to one another and talking about things like this.

'She'd tell me stories of what she'd do when she was part of the team,' Ivy continues, a slight slur to her words now. 'Saving innocents, learning about new cultures and languages, falling in love with handsome strangers on her travels. She had such big and daring dreams I couldn't help but admire her fearlessness.' She sighs and knocks back her drink before filling our glasses up once more. 'Tell me if you want to stop.'

'I'm no quitter,' I answer, meeting her gaze. Sapphire meets crimson. Nightshade meets Raven.

'Oak told me about this project she wanted to present at the Hex Trials. Unlike in yours, we don't fight anyone – not physically, anyway. We strive for intelligence and sharing knowledge. Oak was the smartest person I knew. She would have made a brilliant doctor or inventor.'

'What did your trials entail? How did you win?' I ask.

'I used Oak's idea. She always loved the ocean and wanted so badly to be like the dolphins and whales we'd see migrating each year. After she passed, I found some plans she had drawn up of a special device that you place in your mouth, and it lets you breathe beneath the ocean waves.'

I must look impressed, because she nods animatedly.

'Clever, right?'

'That's really impressive. I wouldn't know where to start to create something like that.'

'Oak always thought outside the box. She was extraordinary. But she didn't live long enough to use her design, and so when the Hex Trials were announced, I decided to compete,' Ivy says with a shrug.

'How did your family feel about that?'

'They were always supportive of Oak's dreams. I think

deep down they knew I was competing in hopes of making her dreams come true, not because it was something *I* wanted to do. But they were fine with me leaving. I think we all needed the time to digest everything at our own pace. Our relationship was adequate at best before Oak passed, but now it's barely existent.'

I wrinkle my nose. 'You didn't have the trials at home?'

'No. Competitors are carted off to a secret location in blindfolds, and there we compete against one another until only one is left. Even now I have no idea where I stayed for those two years of my life.'

'*Two years?* Why that long?' I gape, imagining the House of Raven's trials going on for that long.

'It's a battle of the mind. If you can cope with relying on yourself, you're considered strong. If you are homesick and can't handle being away from civilisation, you are deemed unfit to become the next Nightshade of the Hex.'

'And you were fine all that time? You didn't miss your family? Your House?' I ask incredulously.

Ivy laughs sluggishly, the alcohol hitting her system full force now. She takes a swig of her beverage, scowling at it like she has at every other sip she's taken. Her voice is low, and her words begin to merge together, so I lean in to catch what she is saying.

'I missed home, sure. But I was so deep in my thoughts then. I had no aim in my life at that point. I'd lost so much that I thought the trials were better than being at home, wallowing in my sadness.'

'You had a goal there,' I guess.

She nods. 'Yes. My aim was to get the two years over and done with. I wished every day my feelings would go away by the time I saw my parents again, and we could somehow start over, start anew.'

'I bet that was very hard for you,' I say, thinking how I'd react if any of my siblings had been murdered.

*I would have ripped open the person who'd done it. I would have tortured them for what they'd done.*

'It was. The only way I could cope was to shut myself away. Pretend that part of my life was locked in a tiny box and leave it untouched for as long as possible.' Ivy peers between us at the chain lying on the bench, motionless.

'Well, if it works for you, then why not?' I shrug.

'Because it came with consequences,' Ivy mutters, her hands reaching for her glass again, but her fingers are unable to work properly, struggling to grip the sides.

I lean forward and move the glass away from her, my silent recommendation for her to stop drinking. 'Consequences?' I echo, earning an annoyed glance from the Nightshade.

'Yes. I became so detached from everyone around me. I became a bitch.'

I'm not sure how to respond, but her behaviour makes more sense to me. Her cold, aloof facade was made to keep people she cared for at arm's length. She doesn't want to lose anyone else and have to suffer with the grief that comes along with it.

'Understandable.' I nod.

'Are you done?' Ivy asks, jerking her chin towards the nearly finished jug. 'I think I need to be sick.'

I smirk. 'Yes, I'm done. Let's get you back to the manor.'

We stand from the bench, swinging our legs over. Ivy has a hard time coordinating her feet, and I end up helping. She slaps my hand away the moment she's upright, and we head for the tavern exit.

Bright sunshine and fresh air hits me, making me realise how stuffy the tavern was. My scar begins to bleed.

Ivy frowns down at my hand. 'Why is it bleed—'

Before she can finish, something cold wraps around my neck and roughly pulls me back.

## 46

Hands drag me away, but my assailant doesn't seem to notice I'm attached to a drunk Nightshade. Ivy squeals as we tumble into the shadowed backstreet beside the tavern, and I come face to face with a masked figure. They coil their petite hand around my throat and push on my windpipe as they force me against the stone building. Their scent is what alerts me first, their lack of smell concluding they are like me. A Raven.

'So you're the other assassin,' I choke out, my bleeding scar warning me she means business, the glint in her eyes enough of a clue.

I don't give the Raven enough time to answer or puzzle out why Ivy is partly on the ground, partly sprawled against the wall beside me. My dagger flies for my attacker, slicing across her stomach, but she's quick to jump away. Now with a small distance between us, I yank Ivy to her feet and circle the assailant, keeping the Nightshade behind me.

Everything but the Raven's eyes are covered, her hood doing well to conceal her forehead. Only menacing bright red eyes observe me.

'Who are you?' I ask, my body tense and ready to work when necessary.

She stays quiet, but I keep pushing.

'What has the Elder Raven ordered you to do? Just kill me? Has she offered anything for my demise?'

Again no response.

The female pounces, and I block her, the chain around my wrist jerking with Ivy's movements as she tries to stay out of range. The Raven seems to notice our connection and changes her angle, aiming for the Nightshade, who is clearly not capable of defending herself right now.

'Get down!' I yell before Ivy's sapphire eyes widen.

The flash of a knife, and Ivy's scream of terror echoes through my skull. I'm quick to respond, my body blocking the Nightshade's. A slash of pain across my chest makes me hiss in agony as something begins to sizzle.

*My skin*, I realise.

'It's poisoned,' Ivy mutters, disorientated, her gaze studying my gash before flicking back to the attacker.

The Raven lunges forward. I grab the black chain I wear and force her knife downwards, twisting the metal roughly so it contorts the female's gloved hand, eventually dislodging her weapon.

This seems to spur the Nightshade to act. Her tanned hand digs into her trouser pocket, and she throws a small grey ball to the ground. A loud boom goes off by the Raven, sending her and us flying into the air. Smoke billows through the alley, streaming into the air above us.

My body barks in pain as I land on my back, my chest now burning from the toxin that feels like it's melting my skin. I roll onto my side with a grimace, seeing if Ivy is in one piece. Thankfully, she's fine, her chest heaving, but her face is turning green.

'I'm definitely going to throw up,' she utters, clutching her stomach.

'What was that thing? And why did you have it in your *pocket*?' I demand.

She opens her eyes groggily, calming the storm within her tummy. 'I always have escape bombs on me. A Nightshade habit. Although it hurts more than I remember.' She winces.

Clutching my chest, blood oozing down my front, I get to my feet and roughly grab Ivy's arm. Yanking her up to wobbly feet, I see a flicker of movement from among the clouds of smoke that waft within the backstreet. The Raven is escaping.

'We need to chase her,' I tell Ivy, pulling her along, but she's heavier than I expected.

'No, we need to get you to a healer,' she rasps, pointing to my bleeding hand and wounded chest.

There is no use running after the assassin. She will get away regardless, and people from the streets have heard the bomb and are starting to investigate already, their curious faces peering into the alleyway with startled expressions.

Disappointment floods me. I sigh and observe as the Raven flees, her hood down now she thinks she's out of sight. Turning the corner, she looks once more over her shoulder, a smirk lifting the edges of her mouth.

'Maybe next time, half-blood,' she murmurs, and then she's gone.

## 47

I wake up to a waft of something floral – lavender, perhaps – that lightly perfumes the healing quarters of Hex Manor. I peer to my left and find Jack fast asleep in a chair beside my bed. His silvery-blonde hair shines before the window behind him, making it look like a pale halo.

'Holy Hanrah,' I mutter, moving my shoulders. They are stiff, and the bandages around my chest are tight, making it hard to shift into a comfier position on the bed.

'Who? What?' Jack jolts awake, looking ready to attack someone, but the moment he sees I'm awake, he's by my side, clutching my nearest hand and stroking it tenderly.

'Are you okay?' he asks, blue eyes studying me intently.

'Fine, I think. That poison was something, wasn't it?' I reply, assessing the dark circles under his eyes as I rub my chest gently.

'Some nasty stuff, that hag's spite,' he confirms as he strokes circles into my palm. 'Causes the skin to melt away over time. No wonder you were in so much pain.'

After I dragged Ivy away from the tavern, we stumbled back to Hex Manor. Carmen and Thea saw the state of us both and immediately got to work. I explained what had happened as they unchained us from each other. Without comment, they began to heal me with the help of some of their salves and a horrible drink before I fell into a deep sleep.

'How did the Raven retrieve such a toxin?' I ask out loud.

Jack's brows furrow. *'Another* Raven?'

I nod quickly. 'Yes.' When he doesn't answer, I add, 'Alex mentioned there were two, so it's unsurprising.'

My guardian gives me a pointed look. 'But Alex says a lot of things.'

I exhale, irritation flaring through me. 'What is your problem with him?'

Bright blue eyes observe me. They notice my heightened emotions, and Jack finally relents, not bothering to argue further. 'You've been through a lot. I wouldn't be surprised if your mind was playing tricks on you, that's all. If you saw another Raven, then that brings up a lot of questions.'

I hum in acknowledgement, pouting. 'I know.'

Lips are pressed against mine. Jack is leaning over me quickly as if trying to get in before I push him away. When he backs away sheepishly, I look up questioningly but without protest.

'What was that for?'

'I don't want you being angry with me. I thought it would be the quickest way to cheer you up.' He smiles, and I melt a little.

'How is Ivy?'

'She was a shaking mess when I saw her, but she calmed down after seeing you healed. She kept mentioning something about slappers.' He contorts his face into confused amusement.

'Oh yes,' I recall, thinking of the dark liquid we consumed in the tavern. 'Molten Slapper is a terrible drink we were sharing before we were ambushed minutes later.'

'Being drunk is not the best state to be in while chained to a poisoned Raven.'

I take a brief look at my wrist, at where the chain was. 'Ivy had her reasons for being in that state.'

Jack narrows his gaze intently, silently asking why the Nightshade was impaired.

I shake my head with an apologetic look. 'It's not my story to tell.'

'She's been very tight-lipped about it all. Although she was too busy vomiting to actually say much,' he muses before grimacing at the memory.

'It was a stroke of bad luck, that's all. She couldn't have helped the shitty timing of it all,' I answer, feeling strange for defending the Nightshade.

A tentative knock sounds at the door. Thea sticks her head in with a broad smile at the sight of me. Jack's hands are swift to move away from me, pretending he's not been holding my hand this whole time, breaking the bubble between us.

'You're awake.' Thea's bright pink dress swishes between her legs as she approaches the healing bed. 'I'm going to give you a check-over and rebandage that wound. Do you mind giving us a moment, my sweet?' She turns to Jack, who nods without hesitation, his eyes telling me he'll see me later.

## 48

Alex and I stand together in the darkness, peering around the corner of a building, hidden within the shadows. We have a perfect view of one of the many entrances into Gwenore Forest. The plan is if someone goes in, we'll follow closely behind.

'Tonight's the night. I can feel it in my bones,' I say, more for his benefit than mine. I can tell without the prince revealing a thing that something gnaws at him.

*Prince.*

It's still bizarre to think of him as royalty, as someone who wears a crown day to day, and only now, in the shadows, does he pretend to be someone else – pose as a commoner. It becomes absurd when I think about it too long.

'Someone will slip eventually, and we'll be able to trail them once more.' I keep talking, the pressure pressing against my chest. I promised Alex we'd find Ellis no matter what, but we come across block after block.

'I know what you're trying to do,' he remarks, peering my way. 'It's appreciated but not necessary.'

We've been searching for just over two weeks, and

we've yet to find the missing prison camp. We've searched every bit of woodland to no avail. Tonight, though, we've changed strategy – instead of searching the forest itself, we are now monitoring its borders.

Hours ago, when I was replenishing my belt with knives and small weapons of the like, I felt a flutter of hope. With Rusty now in the loop, making our search three teams of two. We can cover more entrances than we did before. The plan *has* to work.

'How does a whole operation simply vanish into thin air?' Alex wrinkles his nose as if in deep thought. He's got into the habit of mumbling to himself on our long evening escapades. I don't mind it, due to the long, tedious hours of waiting.

'We spooked them by leaving that dead Raven behind,' I reply. 'They know they're being watched. They've obviously been doing this for a long time. They're too good at hiding their tracks.'

As if on cue, two men in dark cloaks walk past our hiding spot. Clutching Alex's cloak, I pull him back so the darkness covers us. They don't notice us as they head for the cover of the trees. My hand tightens in Alex's cloak, silently telling him to ready himself.

As the pair enter Gwenore, I count to ten in my head before setting foot into the moonlight. A hand grabs me firmly and yanks me back before I'm seen.

'What—'

But Alex is pointing in the direction of another figure – hooded but alone.

'Who is that?' I mutter.

'Let's go find out,' Alex whispers, and we dash for the woodland.

We walk quietly, keeping to the edges of the path, close enough to sprint behind a trunk if need be but out of the grasp of Gwenore herself. The lone figure we follow doesn't notice us, doesn't even look back to see if they are being pursued – their gaze only falls forward, onto the pair of males further in the distance.

'We've been walking for over half an hour, and not once have any of them looked over their shoulders,' Alex states, curiosity lining his words. 'They're either very trusting or extremely foolish.'

A faint sound lingers in the distance, and I clutch for the prince's elbow. He whips his head towards me, and I put a finger to my lips before motioning to my ear. He nods in understanding, his eyes flickering at the sound he can now pinpoint.

The figure before us also senses a change and treads carefully into the bush, weaving through the tree trunks as the pair of men we all follow eventually come to a barrier – a shield. Its edges shimmer along the ground and up through the branches of the trees. Unlike Queen Adela's shield, which I came to learn about back in the House of Raven, this does not shine silver. It's a shimmering pink instead.

The men walk through the barrier without issue, slowing slightly but undeterred. The hooded figure stops and observes.

Without hesitation, I aim for the loner, slowly circling behind their back, Alex behind me. I release a gold blade from my belt and carefully approach. Peering out from behind the trunk, the figure doesn't hear as I step closer. In a flash, I have my dagger under their chin while pulling their body against me. Their hood falls off, and sapphire hair spills out.

'Ivy?' I hiss, eyes widening in shock. 'What are you doing here?'

She smacks my hand away. 'What do you think?' she

bites back, voice low as she motions to the shield. 'I'm trying to figure out how to get inside.'

Sapphire eyes pierce through me until they land behind my shoulder, surprise altering her features.

'Alexander?' Ivy blurts, finally off guard.

Alex looks uncomfortable suddenly, his hands not knowing what to do, his usually easy smile losing its confidence. His heart begins to speed up, the sound of it echoing in my ears.

'What are *you* doing here?' the Nightshade demands, as if his presence has ruined her night.

The prince attempts a sly but forced smile, his hands finding his pockets. 'You've always been a worrier, Poi—' He stops himself before clearing his throat. 'Ivy,' he corrects himself.

Ivy's heart spikes dramatically, and I know it's from the accidental mention of her childhood nickname. Poison Ivy. *How does he know that name?*

My eyes travel between the pair, and I sense something deeper between them.

The Nightshade makes a show of standing up straighter, her eyes blazing as she takes him in from head to toe. 'I am here on official Hex business. What is *your* excuse for being out of the castle at this late hour?' she snaps, looking anything but pleased to see him. 'Shouldn't you have your guards present?'

'Am I missing something here?' I ask with a raised brow, temporarily forgetting our evening's mission. 'Do you know each other?'

'No,' Ivy snaps as Alex says, 'Yes.'

I hum thoughtfully as I stare down the pair. 'Okay, well, tucking this little moment away for later ... Ivy, what are you doing here?'

'Like I said, I'm here on official Hex business.' She

crosses her arms defensively, glaring at Alex and me, her fingers fluttering beneath her arms with what looks like nerves.

'Doing what, exactly?' I press, not convinced I understand what justifies her being here.

Ivy huffs, crossing her arms. 'Peri may be happy to play ignorant while the rest of you go gallivanting off into the woods, but I'm certainly not. I'm here for the children, of course.'

'Well, that makes this easier,' Alex says, blue eyes lit with forced merriment.

Ivy scowls at him while I hide my surprise.

'Well, perhaps in future you can be more aware of who's tracking you while you're shadowing others. You were far too easy to follow,' I declare, earning an eye roll from the Nightshade. 'Aren't you concerned about your safety, walking around in the dark woods by yourself? Anything could be watching us right now.' I motion to the inky blackness behind us. The barest of sounds makes me feel jumpy, so Ivy must be even worse.

'I know Gwenore like the back of my hand. We have nothing to fear from her. I can sense she knows about the younglings and won't stop us from saving them.' Ivy observes the trees with an appreciation I've never felt. She waves towards the shield. 'I'm more concerned about how to pass their barrier.'

'You can see it?' Alex asks with a wrinkled nose.

She shakes her head. 'No, but it's obvious. They all slow their pace right there.' She points to where the males did exactly that. 'There must be a safety mechanism there that will trip if intruders pass, or even make them turn away.'

If that's the case, our time searching for the prison camp may have been thwarted. Without me to see the lines across the ground, the other Hex members may have found the shield and been unconsciously directed away without even knowing it.

I sigh. 'I think I can break the shield, but that may alert whoever made it.'

'Not a problem. I can sort that part out. We only need the means to enter,' Ivy states, heading for the barrier.

Keeping to the trees, we approach it, and Ivy watches me expectantly. 'Go ahead.'

Knife in hand, I cut my unscarred palm, my companions wincing at the sight. I smear my bloody hand across the shield and whisper my intent.

'Please let us pass,' I utter, hoping my blood deactivates whatever shield magic has been formed. I did it in the Hex Trials, and now would be a good time for it to work again. Thankfully, the shield slowly crumbles before my eyes. 'It's working.'

The Nightshade brings out a test tube from her belt. Inside swirls a light-coloured gas. She pops off the cork, allowing small tendrils of white smoke to leak out, and she blows them gently to the area of the shield I've touched. She hurries us through the opening before the barrier begins to stitch itself back together behind us.

'Is it fixed?' Ivy asks, and I nod in bewilderment.

'How did you do that?'

'I tweaked a healing solution I invented for lacerations of the skin. I didn't know if it would work, but it was worth a go.' Ivy shrugs, walking off.

Alex watches after her, no doubt having the same thoughts I'm having. 'This ought to go well.'

## 49

Several tents have been erected again, the canvas covering most of the torture and scared children. But instead of heading inside with the prince like I expected, I've been appointed as lookout. Ivy and Alex head inside, invisible to the eye. The Nightshade wants to see the condition of the children, to see if she can help or heal any of their wounds before we leave and plan our next course of action.

I climbed the highest tree I could find, much like Olive did on our last visit, and have been observing since, watching out for any danger. When the sound of rustling leaves comes from above me, I lift my chin to find Rusty stepping out of a portal onto a branch high above, out of sight of anyone in the camp.

'It worked.' The Briar smiles with relief, looking towards the small device hanging from my belt.

To anyone else it looks like a dark grey coin, but when pressed it sends out a signal to show where I am located – and thus the camp. Fox to my relief hadn't asked questions when I commissioned her to build tracking devices for me and the other fledglings.

'Where are the others?' I murmur as he climbs down to my side, well versed in such a task.

'They are guarding the perimeter. We suggested taking it in turns to guard the place, so if they up and move, we can follow them.'

'Good idea.' I nod.

'Where's the prince?' Rusty asks, peering down as if he'll find him on the forest floor.

'He's with Ivy inside there.' I motion, watching as a set of children are pulled along by a soldier. Long chains of obsidian metal are coiled around their wrists and ankles, and they are separated into different pens. Like before, they are uncuffed, and the blindfolds they wear are snatched off before they are given a different type of restraint – the inescapable rope.

'Ivy is here?' Rusty lifts a brow as I nod. 'How am I not surprised?'

'She's gone to see if she can help with any of their wounds.'

'And what are *you* doing?'

'Taking in the layout.' I wave towards the largest tent, five guards standing tall beside it. 'They keep most of the younglings within the tents. There are four exits, three carriages that come in and out with either supplies or children, and over sixty or so guards around and within the premises. Their powers range from replication to earth bending to camouflage ...' I trail off, having kept a mental list of any magic I see being used while I patiently wait.

'Sounds like you've been here a while.' Rusty sounds amused.

'You could say that,' I reply, our stares lowering to the operation once more. 'The Hex cannot bring down all of these people at once. We either have to stealthily remove these kids one by one and risk being caught and the base moving again, or bring down the whole place at once, but for that we will need backup.'

'I have an idea,' Rusty murmurs.

I peer sidelong at him, silently questioning.

'We need to visit the Elder Nightshade.'

The House of Bane is as busy as usual the next morning, Nightshades filling the passageways, the classrooms and, unsurprisingly, the infirmary.

I rode here on Mira, alongside Olive and Ivy on their own horses. Sol and Jack volunteered to stay behind to watch the camp, while Rusty has been put in charge of informing our mentors and Peri of what is happening within the confines of Gwenore Forest.

'The more people we tell, the better,' Rusty said, and I agreed wholeheartedly. This is no longer a mystery of one missing small boy; it is a whole camp of children that need saving.

Upon entering the school, we split up. Ivy heads towards the Elder Nightshade's quarters, while Olive and I head to the infirmary.

Before the Nightshade can get away, I grasp her wrist. Surprisingly, flowers do not coat her skin, but her scowl is deep, and her sapphire gaze pins my hand. I let go immediately.

'What?' she asks, a bite of impatience in her tone.

'How do you know Alex?' I ask, the curiosity too much for me to keep to myself any longer.

'You mean Prince Alexander,' she says, raising a brow.

'Come on, Ivy,' I say. 'Don't be shy with me now. I've seen you empty your guts. No need to play coy.'

She isn't impressed, but she sighs, hands resting on her hips. 'Oak and he were …' She swallows, considering her next word. 'Lovers.'

My eyes widen. 'Really?'

'Yes.' She nods grimly.

'So why the strange behaviour between the pair of you? Did you not approve of him?'

I know I'm pushing my luck, but I don't care. The interactions between them were strange enough to linger in my mind.

'My sister wanted to travel,' Ivy concedes reluctantly. 'The prince wanted her to stay. It got messy.' She grimaces before stepping closer, voice quiet. 'They argued about this on *that* day.'

Her emphasis lets me know she means the day Oak died.

'For a time I blamed him.' She shrugs, but I can see a sliver of grief in her sapphire eyes. 'Oak was distracted. I felt that without their quarrel, she would have survived – would have been focused on what she was doing and on her surroundings.' She dips her head, shaking it slightly. 'I no longer fault him. I understand now she was unlucky, as were many others in our House. But it still rattles me to see the prince. I don't think I'll ever see him without seeing Oak too.'

I nod, letting the information sink in.

This is probably why Alex reacted similarly to her – seeing Ivy's face and being reminded of her twin and his past love.

*Oh, Alex.*

'Thank you for telling me.'

Her mouth twists. 'I'm sure you would have found out

eventually.' She peers round, jabbing my side. 'You better go before you mess our plans up.'

'Me?' I say incredulously.

'Well, it certainly won't be *me*,' she retorts, rushing off in the direction of the Elder Nightshade's office.

## 50

The moment I set foot inside the infirmary, I smell the burning and nose-wrinkling stink of potions. I spot Fox, who waves in greeting.

'Hi Scarlet! How are you doing?'

She perches on a seat, her table covered in paper, wires and tubs of strange-looking creams. I take the chair beside her and allow small talk for a while as she sews some material together. Then I dive into the deep stuff. Olive, across the room, has already grabbed the attention of some Night-shades, no doubt giving them the same spiel.

'Fox, I need your help.'

She looks up from her work, her sapphire gaze curious, but she is content to listen. 'Yes?'

'I've discovered a prison camp full of dameer children, and I need some of your inventions to save them. Anything you can part with.'

She blinks, once, twice, before putting her sewing project down. She turns fully to me before saying, 'Pardon? Can you say that again?'

'Children have been going missing in Sapphire City. The families have been sworn to secrecy with the help of blackmail.' I hand over Mrs Kapper's note, the handwritten scrawl showing Fox exactly the type of warning the poor families have been threatened with. 'These kids are being taken to a camp in the middle of Gwenore Forest, where they are hidden from the outside world and used for their magic.'

Fox nods. 'Of course.'

She scatters papers around her desk in an attempt to find something. She begins to hand designs to me – devices, bombs and weapons. One piece flutters to the floor with her rough handling. I don't hesitate to pick it up.

Shivers run through me, my skull prickling with a strange sensation as my gaze roams over the paper.

'It can't be,' I mutter.

I straighten, eyes wide as Fox says behind me, 'What?'

I point to the depiction of a bomb, the one she was working on when I met her. In the corner is a design I recall seeing. We've spoken about it – joked, even.

*Looks like a flower*, I said, describing three triangles, each connected by one of their points, all facing the same direction.

*I thought it looked more like the head of a windmill*, Fox replied.

Now I see it in a new light, recognition flashing through me. I pick up a discarded ink pen from another table and begin to draw a rough circle around the whole design. In an instant, what used to be three triangles now looks like a carriage wheel with fewer spokes.

'Holy Hanrah,' I gasp. 'Fox, where did you see this? When did you draw it?'

The Nightshade can see I'm reeling, that whatever realisation I've come to is major. She flaps her hands in hopes of remembering its origin. I step closer, holding my breath, hoping – no, praying she can fit in this puzzle piece.

'Oh. I, uh ...' She squeezes her eyes closed, bouncing on the balls of her feet. 'An office. At Ivory Castle!' She snaps her fingers, proud for remembering. 'I was in a meeting with Prince Athos, I think.'

My hands clutch each side of her head as I lean in and kiss her forehead. 'Thank you, Fox! You're amazing! I need to keep this paper, though. Go to Olive. She'll explain what we need!'

I hope with all my heart my theory is wrong, but a deep, dark feeling inside me knows I'm not. Too many pieces fit together that I need to confirm it – to prove my suspicion before I can share it with anyone else.

Mira is panting hard by the time we arrive at the castle gates. A servant takes her reins as I launch off her back and leave her in the courtyard. I demand an audience with Prince Athos, but no one has seen him. I ask for Prince Alexander, and he comes rushing into the foyer several minutes later, flustered but glad to see me.

'What is wrong? I thought someone was dying under our roof with the amount of hysteria I heard,' Alex says, looking as pristine and immaculate as the last time I saw him in royal attire.

'I need to go to Prince Athos's office,' I say, clutching his arm and heading the way I know it is. 'Please. It's urgent.'

'Is this your way of asking for privacy? All you had to do was ask,' he says with a wink. But when I don't react, don't retort, his face falls slightly. 'What is this about, Scarlet?' He frowns, his blue eyes framed by pinched brows as he whispers, 'Is this about the children?'

'Yes.' I nod as he escorts me through his home, his pace quickening.

We come to a familiar door, framed in silver. Alex twists the handle and swings it open. I take no time to rush inside and look through every drawer, stack of files, notepads and even every book in his bookcase, trying to find what I need.

'Explain to me why you are ransacking my cousin's office,' Alex says, standing at the doorway as guard, his head popping out before glancing back at me. 'It's not very ladylike behaviour, even if you are a Raven.'

'You're not going to like it,' I warn, ignoring his attempt to ease my nerves, my fingers rushing through the pages of a newspaper for any scrap of evidence I can find upon Prince Athos's desk.

'I'm not easily offended,' he counters.

I sigh, peering up at him briefly. 'I think Prince Athos is the leader of the prison camps.'

Alex stills, light eyes narrowing slightly. 'Why do you think that?'

'Why? I don't know. I have no clue for his reasoning, but it all adds up. I have spoken to a Nightshade who works closely with the prince. Together they have invented various items throughout the years that seemed so unnecessary to me until now.' I list off the designs I remember Fox telling me about. 'Extendable chains, enchanted rope, blindfolds that render the wearer not only blind but also deaf.'

I watch the prince's mind spin as he recalls our visit to the prison camp. The enchanted rope – used on the kids while training so they could use their magic but were unable to run away. The blindfolds used on some of the younglings, that particular child who was practically shouting as if not realising he was loud enough to be heard from acres away.

'That's not all,' I continue, my words rushed, my heart pounding. 'Prince Athos claimed that several other people had found the camp. They had come to him about it, and he specifically said that each time he travelled into Gwenore Forest, the place had "miraculously disappeared".' I shake my head, furious I didn't see this all before. 'Do you know why that is? It's because *he* told the camp to move. *He* warned them before anyone could find them again. They've relocated so many times their plan is foolproof by this stage.'

'I'm sure that's a mere coincidence.' Alex shrugs, feigning nonchalance, but his shoulders are tense, his smile no longer visible as he crosses his arms.

'Then why is your cousin designing uniforms made of mermaid scales?' I counter. I hold up the designs Fox made, the materials that are needed – textiles that, when used in war, could be a game-changer. 'We both know mermaid scales are extremely valuable, and for good reason. Their tails are impenetrable to the sharpest of blades, and one of the best shields against forged weapons. Why would he need to make *new* uniforms? The royal army already has uniforms!'

My heart beats so fast, the pressing need for Alex to understand rising. But his expression hardly changes, his personal attachment to Prince Athos blinding him to the truth. And I know then I've lost him. I've lost him at this last hurdle.

'Please, Alex, you must believe me. I would not be saying this if I didn't think it was absolutely true,' I murmur, seeing his pale eyes gutter with hurt.

He averts his gaze, rubbing a hand over his face, then turns back to me.

'Get out.'

I blink. 'Excuse me?'

'Get out, or else I'll call the guards.'

He's serious. The most serious I've ever seen him. Sadness floods through me, that he'd throw me out when I've given him enough evidence against his cousin to prove I'm not clutching at straws.

I falter as I tidy Prince Athos's desk and put everything back where I found it before walking around it and heading for the door. Passing Alex in the doorway, I pause but refuse to look at him.

'When I save your brother from your future king, I'll expect you on your knees, begging for my forgiveness.'

Usually I'd expect an inappropriate joke, but he doesn't answer – not that I bother waiting for a response. I calmly stride away, back to the foyer and out into the courtyard, where Mira waits, and I settle into the saddle.

I don't make any suspicious movements past the castle, nor through the city. It's only when I arrive back at the House of Bane, hidden safely in the barn with Mira, that I bring out the envelope I've stolen from Prince Athos's office.

On the crisp white card is a red stamp – a carriage wheel with fewer spokes – or as I saw on Fox's desk, three triangles encased within a circle. I quickly rip it open.

It's addressed to someone I'm not familiar with. The cursive handwriting relays how many children have progressed to stage three and that they wish for an additional two to be advanced – whatever this means.

Finally, at the bottom, is the identifier I've been hoping for, the piece of evidence I've been looking for.

*Sincerely,*

*A.*


My smile widens as I shove the letter back into its envelope and force it into the front of my shirt for safekeeping. The prince had yet to send it off.

*And now he never will*, I think proudly.

'I've got you now, you bastard.'

51

I have to wait for Jack and Sol to return from their guarding duty in Gwenore before I can steal the Celestial away. In their place, having swapped late this afternoon, is Rusty and Peri. They offered to go next, knowing we females were dealing with other matters.

I don't need Sol to confirm or validate who the owner of the letter I found in Prince Athos's office is, but it's a relief to know that my team – the Hex – believes and stands behind me.

As I learned when first meeting the Celestial, he can see the memories of objects – in this case, he can see who held the note last.

'Prince Athos wrote this,' Sol confirms, handing the fancy stationery over to our guardian. 'He has impressive penmanship.'

Jack scowls at the letter. 'Stage three,' he murmurs, a quizzical expression on his tanned face.

I hum in acknowledgement as solace blankets me, and I thank the higher powers we've finally cracked the mystery of *who* is stealing children, even if the reason *why* still eludes me. Not that it matters right now.

'We must inform the Elder Nightshade of your find-ings,' Carmen insists.

Our mentors sit with us in the big dining room.

I shake my head. 'Ivy is there already, and Olive is rallying the Nightshades in the infirmary and most likely stocking up on every invention she can possibly find. The plan is already set in motion.'

Thea smiles proudly, a gleam of something in her pale features. 'Very well. Carmen and I will be in the healing quarters if you need us. We need to prepare ourselves for tonight. We have much to do before we take over guard duty.'

They exit, and I find myself collapsing into a chair beside Sol. Jack looks tired as he places the letter on the table before me. A night of watching the prison has taken its toll on him.

'Why don't you go and rest? I'll wake you up when it's time,' I offer.

Pale blue eyes roam over my frame before they flicker to the Celestial beside me. I ready myself for protests, for him to refuse to leave my side, but instead he nods. Surprise lightens me from within.

'See you both later,' Jack says with a wave.

Minutes pass before Sol meets my gaze. 'He's come a long way since his first day here.'

'He has,' I agree.

I gaze into the Celestial's golden eyes – stunning and full of hope. My smile grows at the sight of him glowing, and I take his hand. He only glows around those he's at ease with, and it always makes me happy to see I'm one of those people.

'You told me once that you find comfort in my presence.'

He lifts a brow, the edges of his mouth tugging upwards. 'I did.'

'You bring me comfort too, Sol. And I appreciate you immensely for it.'

He dips his head closer to mine, eyes wary even when he smiles. 'I appreciate you too. But why do you sound sad, like this is the end?'

'We are about to fight a prince and his army of soldiers – men and women who allowed the torture of children to unfold right in front of their eyes. Who knows what terrors they will unleash on us?' I sigh, looking out to the garden behind him, the vegetables bright in colour, the birds singing on this beautiful day. 'I suppose I want to make sure you know how I feel. Just in case.'

'Is that usual for Ravens?'

I shake my head. 'Ravens do not fear battle. Ravens do not fear death. But what *I* fear is leaving words unspoken when they are better shared.'

He absorbs my statement and nods in agreement. 'We'll be fine. Maybe a few scratches here and there, but I have experience patching those up.' He winks, and I chuckle at his ability to calm me even when the nerves threaten to tear me down.

'I'll hold you to that,' I say before allowing the Celestial time to rest his weary head. Soon we'll need all the strength we can get. Soon we'll be fighting the future king.

My body is weighed down with weapons – a belt of daggers, throwing stars and straps over my chest that hold a quiver of arrows on my back. In one hand I grasp a long bow I've taken from the weapons room in Hex Manor, while the other hovers over a small axe and satchel I have around the top of my thigh. Inside are small devices that, once I activate them, will explode – everyone here has them stored away, and they bring comfort to me in the face of what's to come.

To my right walks Olive, Sol and Rusty. To my left are Peri, Ivy and Jack. We head for the prison camp, where our mentors have been monitoring the children and making sure the guards don't relocate or hear of any news of our arrival. The element of surprise is what we need today.

'Are we ready?' Rusty asks in a hushed tone as we approach the shield, the pink shimmering faintly. The colour is similar to the pinks that streak through the sky, the stars beginning to wink into existence one by one and the sun lowering slowly into the horizon.

'Even if we aren't ready, we'll have to be,' Ivy responds with a glum face.

We all wear similar black leathers, attire that reminds me of the House of Raven, the uniform my family wears. We blend into the night except for our shocks of coloured hair, which we have covered up with hooded cloaks. I peer down at my mother's bracelet. Ruby's voice swirls through my head, readying me for this next trial. When I press the ruby jewel upon it, my body becomes encased in plates of armour, covering my limbs and vital organs with breathable metal.

*Stay focused and look for weaknesses. Everything and* everyone *has them. Once you find the fragile link in their armour, you can succeed in anything.*

'I'm sorry about Alex,' Jack murmurs, seeming to sense my dimming mood, his eyes lingering on my attire with appreciation.

I grit my teeth and force myself to clear my mind of any distractions. 'Don't be.' Alex is a lost cause which I've had to quickly accept. He doesn't want to believe his cousin is the monster in this narrative, and he certainly wouldn't want to fight him. 'We can do this without the prince.'

'We certainly can,' Olive pipes up, giving me a firm nod.

I stop before the shimmering pink shield, and the rest of the group follows suit, unable to see the barrier. I take one of my golden blades and cut open my hand. Watching the blood bubble in my palm, I take a deep breath, steadying my nerves for what's to come.

'Scarlet,' Jack murmurs alongside me. His hand rests beneath my elbow, sending warmth flooding through me. We've conquered so much together, and this will be something else to add to our growing list.

'It will be all right,' I assure him, loud enough for everyone to hear. 'We will show them exactly what it means for us to be the next members of the Hex – that justice will be handed out.'

I smear my hand across the invisible wall and watch as it crumbles.

52

No alarm is set off, no shouts alerting anyone of our arrival, and doubt creeps into my bones. Peering over my shoulder, I see Carmen and Thea step through the trees we hide in, their attire similar to the Hex's.

'Do they suspect anything?' Peri asks them, and they shake their heads.

'No,' Thea confirms, readjusting her hood. The sisters look like creatures of the night, their skin pale like moonlight, their hair and eyes as dark as the night sky. 'They are none the wiser. We have the element of surprise on our side.'

'Have faith, not only in yourselves but in your teammates.' Carmen's mouth is set in a grim line, her dark eyes roaming over the scene before us. 'Today will be the ultimate test, to see how well you work together in the face of danger.'

'It is natural to be frightened,' Thea murmurs, her voice low but sturdy. 'Fear is what makes us stronger. It will not conquer tonight, but it will help hone our skills.' She dips her head. 'Let us save those poor kids and bring them home.'

Ready and waiting for their signal are a mass of Nightshades, lingering in the shadows of the trees surrounding the camp. Their sapphire heads are bent in determination, their eyes burning blue with crackling nerves. It's been a long time since they've experienced such evil, the vampire coven who destroyed their families a past trauma, but they are here, defending their kingdom's youth regardless of their fears.

The Elder Nightshade holds a fist in the air, muttering a prayer under her breath. When her fingers splay out, they all move in unison, the command to strike clear. I spot Foxglove in the fray, her spear lifted, her body attired in brown fighting leathers as she rushes into war with her brethren.

One command, and everything turns to chaos.

The prison camp is dismantled in moments, the walls forced down with magic and brute strength. The barricades crash down with loud thuds as dust and dirt fill the air. Soldiers within are bellowing, finally ringing the alarm and fumbling to arm themselves while the blue army fills their camp. Carmen and Thea fight alongside the Elder Nightshade, their movements swift and formidable, their faces stern and calculating as they offer the distraction we need.

Battle cries fill the air, and I stand still as a statue, waiting for the right moment, watching as the soldiers are cut down. Children who are mid-lesson begin to scream and sob as they are suddenly swarmed.

Peri's hands flutter nervously. 'It's time.'

Without hesitation, the Hex splits up. My hand begins to bleed as we head towards the tents first, the majority of the children kept within. Jack has my back as we enter the fray, our bows at the ready, slicing through eye sockets and the throats of our enemies. I know that my guardian will replay this very moment, when he was the dealer of death, but right now we have no choice. The children are the priority.

'Duck!' he yells, and I fall to the dirt floor, a fireball shooting straight over us. It crashes into the tent I saw Sol and Olive rush into, but I do not go to their aid.

*They are capable. They will make it.*

The tent we aim for is empty, the men and women guarding it nowhere in sight. Jack and I rush to the caged figures, swinging our axes through the metal locks until they finally break. We help the younglings out onto wobbly legs and huddle them together, the older kids assisting to calm the younger ones down.

'You must escape. Go to the House of Bane if you can. Healers are there waiting for you with food and water. Go!' I command, slicing a line down the canvas that leads into Gwenore Forest.

They don't hesitate to leave, to escape this misery, even with obsidian chains hindering their movements.

I watch them go, their bodies fading into the darkness before Jack grabs my wrist.

'Next tent,' he orders.

We step out into the night, and the air is potent with magic. The ground is already covered in motionless bodies, and to my dismay, some have sapphire hair. My heart pumps like it's about to explode from my chest, and fear begins to creep up my arms, causing my hands to shake.

A young girl screams as a bull – no doubt a shape-shifter – races for Ivy. The Nightshade is on the ground, clutching her stomach, a long gash bleeding crimson over her attire. Peri's hauling her to her feet, none the wiser about the incoming attacker.

'Peril!' I scream, knowing if I run for them, I won't make it in time.

A wall of water hits the bull sidelong, crashing into the beast with such force it's flung straight into a tree, its neck snapped by the sudden assault.

The Silken's eyes widen, his expression ashen as he turns to my guardian.

*Thank you*, he mouths before I pull a stone-faced Jack away.

The second tent is not as easy as the first. Guards swarm us. Light and magic surround me the moment they realise who we are. I'm quick to shoot arrows. Eyes and throats are splashed with blood from my shafts as they slice through skin and muscle.

Once I'm out of arrows, I use my bow to smack a grimy face and release some teeth from the owner's mouth before using it as a javelin into a man who is extraordinarily strong.

'Left!' I shout.

Jack sends a burst of cold water into a male who is camouflaged. His body shoots through the canvas, creating a massive hole.

My knife finds purchase in a leg. A throwing star lands between the eyes of a female. A snap vibrates through my hands as I jump upon an assailant's back and twist her neck. She falls to the ground, and I find Jack staring at me.

'She was going to kill you,' I say defensively, hating the flicker of alarm that enters his eyes.

He nods but does not answer.

The tent is now clear, limp bodies covering the ground. I rush to the three children. This time they are on metal tables. They are quiet, their eyes closed, and their bodies are stone cold. They do not move, but they are not chained down, as I first thought.

I step towards the girl who is in the middle, her waves of blonde cascading over the table's edge. She's too young to be here, her pale skin bruised, the nails upon her small hands jagged, and some are completely missing.

'Thank the higher powers,' I mutter, looking down at one of the two fair-haired boys beside her and noticing they all have gold metal around their throats. My guardian's face creases with silent questioning. 'They aren't dead,' I clarify, hearing their hearts still beating.

'No. They still have a faint pulse,' Jack confirms, his fingers upon the girl's neck, only just fitting beneath the metal collar.

A shiver roams over my body as a gust of wind picks up. It enters the tent and lifts the canvas from over our heads, exposing us to the outside world. My eyes widen at the sudden exposure. My twin daggers fill my palms in seconds.

A strong voice that crackles with power lingers over-head. Jack and I peer up to find a figure floating in the air, his blue cloak rippling around him, the pearl-and-seashell crown upon his head glinting under the moon's rays.

'You have made a grave mistake coming here, Scarlet Seraphine,' Prince Athos says, a wide grin forming on his face.

## 53

I stumble slightly as the earth beneath our feet rumbles, an earth bender doing their best to fend off Thea in the distance. My chin rises to the heir of Teal-waters, the once kind and polite prince I met now replaced with a cold and scheming one.

'A grave mistake?' I echo with a snarl. 'I am here to correct your wrongs. These children deserve better than to be your slaves.'

'They are not my slaves,' the prince says, his body lowering, his feet finding purchase on the ground once more. From the look on my guardian's face, he also had no idea the heir could fly. 'They are my army.'

'Army for what?' Jack barks. 'There is no war here. You have an army already, of *adults*. Why take these poor kids? Why steal them away from their homes?'

Prince Athos tilts his head, coy and unyielding. 'You will never understand. You do not have the weight of a kingdom upon your shoulders. I chose them because they are strong for their age. I chose them because they can be influenced appropriately. They will be loyal to me as I am loyal to them.' He lifts a hand towards us, and I freeze. 'Come, my little slayers.'

A noise from behind grabs my attention. The three children rise from their tables, their eyes devoid of emotion, of feeling. They are all barefoot, their skin nearly translucent, and their expressions are sharp and devious. In a flash of bright orange, they disappear.

Prince Athos coos, bringing our disbelieving gazes back to him. The children have teleported from one place to another, I realise. The prince's arms wrap fondly around one who looks familiar. Somehow I know I've seen him before. My heart stutters, my mouth opening of its own accord.

'Ellis?' I blurt.

The heir's eyes brighten with amusement. 'You know my cousin Ellington?' Prince Athos slides an affectionate hand over the boy's ruffled hair, an adoring love in his gaze as he peers down at the collared child, talking to him softly. 'That's marvellous. This will be the perfect time to show off your work.'

'You're a monster!' Jack barks, making the prince shrug.

'You judge because you only see one side of this narrative. I see it differently.' He clicks his fingers, and the children all turn to him. 'You will take the guardian.' The other boy and girl are motioned towards Jack, their blue eyes upon him instantly. 'Make sure he is dealt with accordingly.'

The boy shoots a hand out, and Jack is flung back, spinning in the air before landing metres away in the dirt. Rusty runs to his side but pauses when he realises who we are up against.

'Jack!' I cry out.

The girl seems to bend the darkness around her, calling it to her side as she strides for my teammates. As she passes me, I go to grab her wrist, to stop her approaching, but a ball of what feels like fire slams into my hand. I hiss, clutching it to my chest.

'You have your own problems, Raven.' The heir tilts his head to his younger cousin.

Ellis begins to spark, his skin becoming inhumanly see-through while lightning crackles beneath it. He flicks a wrist, and a dazzling surge of white light escapes him. I jump to safety, rolling behind a pile of crates, and the stored apples inside tumble away as his power catches the corner of a box.

'Ellis!' I shout, hoping to knock some sense into him. 'I'm friends with your brother, Alexander!'

The boy does not react, as if deaf to my words.

'Lies!' the heir bellows. 'Incinerate her!'

The boy takes no time to rush me. His body is small and frail, but his movements are the opposite. Lightning bolts chase me, tiring me out far sooner than I'd expect from a child of his size.

Memories of my last Hex Trial follow me. My inability to fight back comes in waves as I do my best to escape from his magic, but he catches me, time and time again. The pain knocks the breath out of me, my legs wobbling as they struggle to keep me grounded. Lightning pulses through my veins, slowly weakening me.

'Ellis, this isn't you! Stop this!' I attempt, my chest heaving, my muscles screaming from the shocks.

'You can run, Raven, but you certainly cannot hide.' Prince Athos laughs while in the air, flying at a considerable speed to keep up with us. He watches the spectacle, nodding in approval as his other little slayers begin to win the upper hand with Rusty and Jack. He seems to tire of our cat-and-mouse dynamic, shouting his orders. 'Ellis, stop playing with her! I want her *gone*!'

To my disbelief, the boy begins to hover, his feet no longer in the dirt but floating.

*He can fly too?*

'What?' I mutter in astonishment.

'Stage three – the manipulation and absorption of magic.'

'Stage three?' I wonder as a burning bolt is aimed my way.

A procession of explosions erupts behind me – no doubt the Nightshades – and debris and limbs fall from the sky. I wince as a severed leg rolls by, the screams and shouts of battle filling the night sky.

'Stage three,' the heir confirms. 'Ellis has not one but *three* sets of powers. Taken from others and bestowed upon him.'

My mouth opens in protest. 'Taken? What happens to those you take from?'

'They usually die. The weak never do prosper.' Prince Athos shrugs as if we were talking about something as trivial as the weather.

My eyes study Ellis, who begins to spin, his body a blur in the darkened sky as I crouch in caution. *What is he doing?*

The prince tilts his head, considering. 'It's a feat, but with the help of dark magic and willing subjects ...'

I snort as he motions to the three children. Two boys and a girl with immense power and the ability to choose from various weapons in their arsenal.

'I made it possible. They'll be the perfect spies and assassins. They will infiltrate castles, bring down king-doms, and I will rule over them all.' His plans are more disgraceful than I could ever have imagined. 'My children will reign over all others, their growing powers under *my* control.'

I snap. 'You're delusional. Those families have suffered

for your fucked-up dreams. You cannot keep doing this. They do not belong here.'

'They belong to *me!*' Prince Athos bellows. 'They'll do as *I* wish. They do not have a choice.'

A scent so strong fills my nostrils, and I refrain from gagging. No creature or being has magic this potent in smell – not even Rusty, and that's saying something. Ellis lashes out a hand, and crescent moons of radiant light slice through the air towards me.

Pain like I've never felt before lances through my body. I kneel with the sudden agony, my Raven anatomy exhausted but still fighting to repair itself. My hand is still burning from his previous bolt, but now I feel like I've erupted into literal flames. I fall onto my side, unable to refrain from groaning in unexplainable torture.

I peer down to find my armour sizzling, smoke wafting from me. A glow radiates from my shoulder down to my hip. Another across my thighs. My cheeks feel suddenly wet, like liquid is dripping off them. I catch a drop with my hand, and it's crimson. I lift my fingers and find a huge gash from my temple all the way down my face to my jaw. My wounds feel as if lightning claws have slashed the air, and I've been caught in their wake.

'I told you not to waste your time, Scarlet. Now look at you.' Prince Athos watches as Ellis lowers himself, hovering above me with nothing but a blank expression. Does he understand what he is doing? Can he feel the torment he is causing me? 'You will die because you did not heed my warning. Your team will be slaughtered because of your pride.'

My mother's words ring through me as I begin to look for weaknesses. Prince Athos is too high for me to harm, but Ellis is not. The boy does not wear armour, but he is pure dark magic. He does not think, does not feel, and the answers to his defeat slowly fade away with my blood loss. I could throw a knife at him, to see if he is invulnerable in every sense of the word, but I cannot. My hands do not curl around my weapon belt. They do not reach for the one thing I could use to hurt this boy, this *child* who is being manipulated. He does not deserve that after everything he's been put through.

'Ellis,' I plead, my voice shaking with the effort to project my words. 'If you can hear me, Alex is waiting for you. He has been searching for you. He's never stopped.' I do not miss the slight flinch of his mouth, as if a shadow of a smile is trying to claw its way out. 'He would want you to defend yourself.' I feel my heart rate slow. 'But not like this—'

'Ellis!' Prince Athos orders. 'End her *now!*'

A ball of crackling light forms in his small hand, growing – shining brighter than a star as the seconds pass us. I cannot move. My body is useless, and my resolve is breaking. I can see it now, his power turning me to ash, a shadow of myself left in the dirt to be wisped away when the breeze picks up.

Ellis lifts an arm, ready to obey his master.

I close my eyes, not wanting him to see my fear, my terror. I do not want him to witness that when he ends me, in case he is still the master of his thoughts. A warmth starts at my feet, and I expect it to rise, to consume me. But nothing comes.

The young slayer does not strike.

I open my eyes to find him staring, frozen like a statue, waiting for orders. I glance towards Prince Athos, who looks surprised before anger fills his features. He flies down to the boy's side, his hands shaking with fury.

Looking down at the small area of warmth around my ankle, I notice my body is invisible. Gone. Non-existent.

*Alex.*

Prince Athos takes a discarded sword and swings it with little control, slicing it down, aiming straight for my chest. Something yanks at my leg, pulling me out of the way, and I miss the blade by only a second.

'Show yourself, Alexander!' Prince Athos seethes, his eyes turning savage as he searches the space in front of him. 'Come out and face me like a man!'

## 54

Arms encase me, warm me up, even, when my flow of blood is doing a good job of that already. I'm placed by the roots of a tree, the darkness within Gwenore eerie and intimidating.

'Scarlet,' Alex says breathlessly. 'You need a healer.'

'I can wait.'

'No, you can't,' he insists, pressing a hand into my chest and another upon my leg. It does not help that my face drips with gore, my vision going blurrier the longer we sit here. I know his attempts to stop the blood are no use. I'm fading away quickly, and he knows it.

'Save Ellis,' I urge, wanting to lift my hands and shake him, but even that is too hard. 'Please, for me, save your brother. Don't let this be in vain.' I tilt my head towards my wounds, my hands shaking uncontrollably as I feel the lasting effects of Ellis' magic. 'Stop your cousin before he hurts anyone else.'

'I can't leave you like this,' Alex growls.

'You can and you will. Go *right now*,' I snap. 'I will find a healer. I will be okay.'

'Promise?'

I nod, the lie coming easily. 'I promise. Now go. Ellis needs you now more than ever.'

I do not see him leave, his body disappearing instantly. What I hear, though, is taunts, shouting, cursing and crying. And then footsteps.

'What a shame,' a female says, coming from within the shadows, her pale face uncovered and hood nowhere in sight as I try to decipher who she is.

*The Raven who attacked me. The one who got away.*

'I was hoping for more of a fight to claim your death, but it seems someone has beaten me to it.' She kneels down before me and fingers the blood that oozes onto my armour. She licks her finger, smiling as if amused. 'I wanted to bring you pain, but you're fading fast, so I'll make this quick.'

She palms a blade and stabs me through my chest, aiming true, and I feel the piercing of my skin, my muscle, my *heart*.

'Try and get out of this, half-blood.' She chuckles to herself, proud of her efforts.

'Why?' I whimper, blood escaping my lips.

The female pulls a handkerchief from her attire and dabs at my mouth gently. 'The Elder Raven wants you dead. You embarrassed her, humiliated our leader in front of our House. She did not want you making a name for yourself, digging your way into the hearts of those you come across in the lands. She couldn't bear you being *loved*.'

She twists the blade, releasing a cry from me. My eyes are watering now, my body thrumming with agony, with torture. My breathing turns haggard, and I know I don't have long to live.

'I must go, but it was so nice talking to you.' The female waves, getting to her feet. She leans over to retrieve the knife from my chest – no doubt my undoing – but then an arrow of burning sunlight hits her straight through the skull. She falls over limp and lifeless, as many have found themselves tonight. Dead.

*She's dead.*

Sol is there, pressing against my wounds, eyeing the knife stuck in my chest.

'Mother of sunlight, Scarlet. What happened to you?'

I try to shake my head, but I can't. Instead, I cry, letting out my fear, releasing my anger and pain. 'I don't think you'll be able to patch me up,' I say, recalling our conversation in the big dining room.

He grimaces, remembering too.

My lip quivers, my cheeks stained with tears and blood. 'It hurts, Sol.'

'I know,' he murmurs, stroking my hair, trying his best to comfort me in my last moments. 'We'll fix you up. Just stay with me.'

My eyes flutter, my body beginning to shut down.

He shakes his head, cradling mine into his chest. One hand soothes me; the other clutches my bleeding heart, holding me together because I can't do it myself.

'Stay with me, Scar. Don't close your eyes. I've got you.'

My words fade, my mind doing the same as the blackness encroaches on my vision.

'Look after my guardian,' I whisper, feeling the very moment I lose the fight, the moment my heart gives out. 'Sol, I—'

I can't go on. All I can do is close my eyes and rest.

## 55

Blankets cover me, making me sweat. I go to kick them off, but the movement makes me wince. Somehow the birds sing louder, and the windows let in much brighter sunlight. I squint to find I'm in the healing quarters, and upon an armchair to my side is Alex. He does not say anything, only watches. His heart rate heightens, the blood pulsing through him making my head spin.

'Alex,' I breathe, relieved nevertheless that he is in one piece. 'You're all right.'

He nods without a trace of a smile.

'You came for me,' I add, remembering his saving me from Prince Athos.

My words seem to cause him pain, as he averts his eyes to the window.

'Of course I came for you, Scarlet,' he murmurs, getting to his feet. Suddenly he is right beside me, his scent filling my senses. 'Please forgive me. I did not listen to you. I was blinded by false hope, and I am a fool.' He bends down and gets to his knees beside my bed, looking up at me with eyes full of grief.

*When I save your brother from your future king, I'll expect
you on your knees, begging for my forgiveness.*

'This is unnecessary, Alex. Get up.'

'It is not,' he insists, clasping my closest hand. 'You
risked so much, and I was not willing to hear you out.'

My head dips in memory. 'I admit I was hurt. But I do
not blame you for it. Athos is your cousin. He is your
family.'

'Was,' Alex murmurs, getting to his feet and sitting
beside my legs. 'He *was* my cousin.'

My eyes widen. 'He is dead? How?'

'I cut him down. It's what severed the connection of
dark magic between him and Ellis – between him and the
other two slayers he kept.' He dips his blonde head, eyes
watering slightly as he opens his palms to me. 'I can't seem
to wash the blood away.'

I lean forward to embrace him, letting him breathe
heavily into my shoulder, hiding my grimace as my body
acclimatises to his weight. I expect the tears, but he does
well to hold them in.

'I won't tell you it was the right choice, only that it was
the necessary one.' I push him to arm's length. 'You are a
good person, Alex. This one act does not define you.'

'He turned out to be a stranger,' he murmurs. 'I didn't
know the man I killed.'

I wince, leaning back in the bed. 'He fooled us all.'

Sitting there, looking lost, I sympathise with the
dameer. I shuffle over to one side of my bed and pat the
space beside me. 'Come here,' I instruct, and he doesn't
hesitate. 'Let me console you.'

'I am here to comfort *you*,' he argues as I wrap my arms
around his shoulders while his arms circle my waist. He
lowers himself to lean his head against me. 'I knew you had
a soft spot for me.'

I smile and agree. 'From the moment I stabbed you.'

'What will your guardian think if he finds us like this?' he asks, a sliver of his old self shining through. 'We may have to fight over you. It would be rather romantic.'

'No one is fighting over me,' I retort. 'I am a beauty that can be shared.'

'A modest beauty, it seems.' He snorts.

'I am not boasting. I am simply stating a fact. I could sway wars with this face.' I turn to him, peering down with a restrained grin. 'Tell me I'm wrong.'

'I can't.' He chuckles, shaking his head.

'Exactly.' I grin, feeling the injuries to my face pull tightly. It stings, but I refuse to think about it. Instead, I focus on my friend.

We speak nonsense for a while longer before silence envelops us, and Alex's soft snores fill the room not long after. I stroke his hair, letting him rest. Letting the future king of Tealwaters have a moment of peace.

## 56

**D**inner is a grand affair, with bowls and plates full to the brim with food. It's the cooks' way of saying farewell before we head to our next destination. Our duty as Hex members sends us to the southern kingdom of Maya – the land of dragons.

I sit beside Olive and Rusty as we dig into warm bread rolls with soft butter. All the vegetables from Thea's garden lie in bowls on the table so as not to waste them, and a large variety of meats were purchased in the market this morning.

We talk about the battle, each of us spilling details the rest of us may have missed. We chat about Tealwaters and what we've loved about it and what we enjoyed about training in the House of Bane. We then talk of our expectations, what we had in mind before meeting each of our teammates and what we learned from our time here.

A part of me feels emotional, and looking beside me, I see Olive, too, looks ready to shed a tear. I reach for her hand and squeeze it, sharing a sad smile with the Severed. She, like many others here, has made an imprint on me.

They have welcomed me with open arms and have made me feel seen, made me feel like I *belong*.

When our stomachs are full and dessert is brought out, Thea stands up. She sits at the end of the table, while Carmen, who stands along with her sister, is at the other end. They lift their drinks up in unison.

'A toast to our first leg of the Honour Tour. We have learned a lot, and we will continue to learn more,' Thea says, and she takes a sip of her beverage when we all clink our glasses together.

We all repeat her words and drink. I meet Jack's eyes, and we share a smile. We've come a long way since we first stepped into this new kingdom. Our abilities to trust, to share, to love have grown immensely.

'A toast to those who fought for what's right, and to the souls we lost. Without them, my home would be in deep shit right now,' Ivy says, lifting her drink up before swallowing it whole.

'To those we lost,' I declare, and the words echo around the room as even our mentors repeat the tribute.

'You've worked well together, and I envision you only growing stronger,' Carmen says as she serves out caramel cake – Rusty taking two slices.

I reach for my piece and wince. The tightly bandaged wound across my chest makes my body ache.

As Ellis attacked me with dark magic, the wound will not fully heal. So along with my dragon burns, I'll have to live with these three additional scars that almost took my life. I grimace at the thought, the fear that ran through me as I faded away.

'Training will resume once we reach Maya,' Carmen continues, pulling me out of my dark thoughts.

Sol groans loudly, his playful smile making our mentor's mouth twitch with amusement.

'But if you ever keep something as big as this from us again –' Carmen slides her dark gaze to me with a stern expression – 'I will make your training hell for you.'

'What Carmen means to say is don't be afraid to tell us anything. We are your mentors but also your biggest supporters. We will have your back no matter what.' Thea smiles, giving me a bright beam as if to counteract Carmen's threat.

'To not keeping secrets,' I toast in jest, reaching for my drink again. My hand is a blur, and the glass flies off the table and smashes on the floor opposite where I sit. Ivy and Rusty peer down at the mess before them as I stand up and scowl with surprise. 'Whoops. I didn't mean to do that.'

Thea shares a meaningful glance with Carmen before waving a hand. The mess begins to clear itself up, a brand-new glass being filled for me in the meantime.

'We would also appreciate it if we were alerted to any royalty who approach you,' Thea says, resuming the conversation, as if I hadn't picked up on their slight change in demeanour.

*I wish for us all to be free of our curses, Scarlet, but some things are better left untouched. Dark magic can be life-threatening.*

I peer down at my scarred hand, nibbling my lip. I died and came back to life. I was resurrected like my mentor had said many others had tried before. Does that mean ...?

Olive nudges my side, jarring me out of my thoughts. 'We should probably brush up on our knowledge of the royal family. We were blindsided once, but never again.'

I nod. 'Agreed. I will also make sure I do not stab any more royals in the line of duty.'

'*You did what?*' Thea screeches, making me jerk away.

I laugh nervously. 'Kidding!'

Jack bursts into laughter, and Thea's worry is swallowed up by the chuckles around the table. Our conversation grows louder as the room progressively gets drunker and more out of hand.

Sol smiles demurely, watching Olive without restraint. I meet his eyes, and he winks.

*Are you okay?* he mouths, and I nod.

*Are you?* I mouth back.

He smiles. 'Wonderful,' he whispers, knowing I'll hear it.

I sit back and take everything in. My mentors are laughing at something, and my fellow Hex members are talking animatedly about what we can expect in the next kingdom – the topic of dragons being the most popular.

'Portals are against the law there,' Ivy states, facing the Briar. 'You know that, right? You'll be sent to prison for opening one, on the off chance a dragon escapes.'

Rusty dips his head, a sudden shimmer of sadness washing over his features before he schools them once more. 'I do, Ivy. Do not worry yourself.'

I lean back and stroke my full belly, peering over at my guardian. He appears as settled and content as I feel. His smile gleaming with happiness, his walls finally down around the group. We have finally found our people – those who understand us, and those who will stand with us.

*A family*, I think with a rush of giddiness. *I've found myself another family.*

Today is our last full day in Tealwaters. After lunch we all head for the barn in preparation for our travels. We will be taking one final trip to Sapphire City to buy last-minute supplies for our early start in the morning. Thankfully the Briar has visited Maya before so for the first leg of the journey, we'll be taking advantage of Rusty – creating a portal to the border – and then we will ride the rest of the way on horseback.

Before we can enter the stables, our mentors stop us in our tracks.

'We have a surprise for you all,' Thea announces, her excitement evident. 'As we continue your training, your predecessors have made sure to give you something you'll need in the next leg of your journey to becoming full fledged Hex members. They will be yours until your duty stops, and then they will be given to new owners.' She waves for us to finally enter, my curiosity piqued.

On each stable door is one of our names written on a piece of paper. Sol, Rusty and Jack on the left side. Peri, Olive, Ivy and me on the right side. I approach the stall designated for me and peel away the paper with my name on it. On the back is the name Red. I peer inside curiously to see a large stallion. He lifts his head, and I meet dark and curious crimson eyes.

'Hello, boy,' I murmur, opening the door slowly so as not to scare him.

He shuffles back as if to give me room. He's so unbelievably giant he takes up the whole stall. His hooves are bigger than my hands together. His ears are long and slick as they perk up, and his mane is plaited beautifully to show off his shiny dark red coat.

The horse nudges my stomach. He is strong, and I do my best not to stumble.

'Easy there.' I chuckle, handing over the apple in my pocket that I was saving for myself. It's shiny and red – Roux's favourite kind.

The stallion eats it with two bites. He seems to enjoy it, sniffing my hand for more.

'That's all I've got. I'll bring you some more tomorrow,' I promise him.

When he dips his head, I find a little piece of paper attached to his saddle with a strip of black ribbon. I rip it off and find small, precise writing.

*Scarlet,*

*Let me introduce you to Red. He's like us – part vampire – and has been an immortal companion for all our Raven predecessors. He understands what it's like to stand out but enjoys the attention.*

*He loves apples, carrots, sugar cubes and scratches behind his ears.*

Make sure you are firm with him. He can
be cheeky at the best of times and grumpy at
the worst.

Take care of him, and he will take care of
you in return.

Happy travels, and I hope to see you
someday very soon.

Sincerely,
Your aunt Brande

I blink seeing her unfamiliar scrawl, the handwriting strange but comforting. I lift my hand to scratch behind the beast's ears. He nickers with pleasure.

'Come on, everyone,' I hear Carmen shout through the barn. 'Let's get going before the markets close up for the day.'

Red is already tacked up, so I check his saddle is tight enough, shorten the stirrups, knowing my legs won't be as long as Brande's, take the reins from around his neck and tug him forward.

We are welcomed by the rest of the Hex. Rusty is on a large bronze stallion with hooves as big as Red's. Olive is upon an emerald mount whose hair is as good as – if not better than – her rider. Peri sits in the saddle of a gelding whose coat is a deep plum colour, shiny and perfect like his tail, which is plaited into three. Sol and Jack seem to have similar steeds, both with golden coats and sandy hair that is left free of restraints. And finally, Ivy sits upon a sapphire mare who pounds her hooves into the ground with impatience.

'Wow. How are you going to get on that thing?' Olive asks, looking at Red with bewilderment. 'He's massive.'

I peer up at Red and realise only then the same thing. If I have to keep finding items to boost myself up on while travelling, we are going to have a difficult time. As if hearing Olive's comment, Red shuffles and lowers himself to one knee. In moments, he's lying down, peering up at me as if to say, *Get on, then.* I swing a leg over and into the saddle. Once I give him a brief squeeze with my legs, he gets back to his feet, and I note the height I am at compared to the others.

'Why does the smallest person in the group get the biggest horse?' Sol wonders out loud, his question on every-one's face.

'You know what they say, Sol.' I shrug, keeping my face neutral. 'The bigger the horse, the bigger the—'

'You will not finish that sentence,' Carmen interjects, making me fight a grin.

Snorts of amusement echo around us, my guardian's the loudest, as Sol – the rider with the smallest horse of us all – frowns, realising what I was implying.

'I can prove you wrong if you'd like,' the Celestial protests, reaching for his trousers.

'That won't be necessary, Sol. Please keep that to your-self,' Carmen states, making us all howl some more.

'We have places to be, angel face. We won't have enough time to try and find it,' Olive chimes in, the laughter turning into roaring, my chest aching from shaking so much.

Thea smiles in amusement as she kicks her midnight-black mare into a walk. 'Is everyone ready?'

We all look around at each other, adjusting stirrups, taking up our reins and checking our saddles are all secure.

Then we follow her away from Hex Manor and towards Sapphire City.

The lavish carpet is a deep blue with silver stars dotted along it. Above are chandeliers made of beautiful crystal that shine down on us, making the elegant gowns of the ladies and luxurious attire of the men glitter like stars.

I follow the Hex into the theatre, other patrons gazing at us with wonder and new-found appreciation. We are escorted by a worker into the royal box, the seats grander than the standard seats, the velvet cushioning making the chairs extremely comfortable as we watch over the whole establishment.

'I feel like a princess,' Olive murmurs as she twirls on the spot, eyes lit up with delight.

'And you look like one,' Sol answers, ushering her into the seat beside him.

I smile, meeting Peri's gaze. He dips his head, looking more relaxed than I've ever seen him, before his eyes lift, his posture straightening.

I twist in my chair to find Prince Alexander.

'Welcome, everyone,' Alex says, the auditorium still loud as people find their seats. 'Thank you so much for coming tonight. I hope you'll enjoy your evening. Whatever you need, please don't hesitate to ask.' He waves his hands, and servers come by, handing over drinks of all colours, savoury treats and desserts.

I find a slice of chocolate cake next to my seat without prompting.

Alex meets my gaze and winks. 'Thank you, all, for your efforts. I cannot express how much it means to have our children back where they belong. We'll forever be in your debt.'

'Thank you, Your Highness.' Thea bows, and we all follow suit.

'Scarlet, may I have a word?' Alex asks, his hands twining together with what looks to be nerves.

I nod, finding Jack beside me utterly relaxed, a soft smile curving his lips as I stand up.

'Have I told you how stunning you look tonight?' My guardian smirks as he observes my every move. His ocean-blue eyes trail over the deep plum gown I wear, its bell sleeves made of silk and its body tight-fitting and more seductive than I'm used to.

'Perhaps you can tell me later tonight,' I whisper back, earning a gleam of excitement from my guardian.

'I shall.' He nods.

A shiver of contentment shoots through me. We may not be able to show our emotions in public but Jack and I have come to realise we can't stay away from each other. Yes we can only be truly ourselves in private but I'll take him in anyway I can.

As I make my way towards the prince, he leans against the railing on the other end of the royal box. He turns to me with a smile and embraces me when I reach him.

'This place is amazing. Thank you for treating us all on our last night,' I say in greeting.

'I wish I could claim this as my idea, but it wasn't.' He shrugs before waving his hand.

'Oh?' I spin on my heel to find the curtain to our box open, and a small boy walks in, nerves radiating from him, his blue eyes trailing along the floor.

'Scarlet, I would like you to officially meet my brother,' Alex says, trying to coax the boy closer. He kneels beside his sibling so they are nearer the same height. 'Ellis, this is Scarlet Seraphine. She is the friend I told you about.'

'I remember her,' Ellis answers, his gaze lifting to mine as I bend down. 'I'm sorry for what I did to you.' He glances at the scar across my face with obvious remorse.

I tilt my head, glad to see colour has come back to his cheeks and a bit of fat is returning to his gangly limbs. No doubt he has a long way to go to full recovery, but he's made a good start so far.

'Do not apologise. It wasn't you who did this. I know you would do no such thing,' I reply, soothing him with my voice, curling my mouth upwards in hopes of reassuring the young royal.

He dips his head, cheeks becoming stained with tears in moments. 'I did it. It was me, *my* hands.' He wavers, his breath catching as he shows me his palms. The gesture is too similar to when Alex showed me his, devastated to have killed someone for the first time.

Without hesitation, I grab his small hands and lift them around my neck. His body is so small and frail against mine, but I embrace the boy nevertheless, letting my warmth seep into him.

'I do not blame you, Ellis,' I murmur into his hair.

His grip on me tightens significantly, such that I can't help but wince.

I stroke his head like I did his older brother's once and urge him to believe me. 'I'll never blame you for this. You weren't in control of yourself.' My hand rubs his back, his body shaking as he cries. 'Will you promise me something?' I whisper.

He releases me, little hands still on my arms as he peers into my face. Tears streak his cheeks, and I wipe them away with a thumb.

'Anything,' he answers.

'Learn about your new abilities. Teach yourself how to wield them so you can learn how to *control* them. By doing this, you will never hurt anyone else again. Not unless you want to.'

'I don't want to,' he shoots back.

I bow my head. 'Then don't. But do not hide your magic away. Promise?'

He glances at Alex, who gives him a firm nod and a reassuring smile. Reluctantly Ellis agrees. 'I promise.'

Alex ruffles Ellis's hair before rising to his feet, his arm around his shoulder protectively. 'We should get you back now, buddy. The show will be starting soon.'

The boy peers up at me once again, a faint expression of hope lining his features.

'It was so lovely to meet you, Ellis. I hope we get to see each other again,' I say, offering my hand.

He grasps it, shaking gently.

'Perhaps you'll be able to show me everything you've learned about your powers then.'

He nods. 'I will.'

Alex escorts him away, promising to be back as I settle once again into my seat beside Jack. As the heir guessed, the theatre lights dim, and the people quieten down, a hush running through the audience. The stage curtain splits to reveal an orchestra, musicians and instruments covering the performance area. They begin to play a quiet melody, soft and sweet. My heart flies with the sound, the experience one I never would have had back in the House of Raven.

Suddenly a group of children come running onto the stage. They lift a banner up, the sign making me clutch my chest.



My throat constricts, and I tilt my head back to look at the ceiling in an attempt to stop the tears. Happiness and relief wash over me as I feel Jack squeezing my knee.

'We did it,' he murmurs, and I nod.

Alex slides into the empty chair alongside mine, readjusting the crown on his head as I peer across at him. He leans over, his voice low but clear.

'Thank you for being so kind to Ellis. He's been afraid of his own shadow since returning home.' He sighs, his worry evident. 'After what he did to you, he's been refusing to use magic, but I'm hoping you've changed that.'

'He's a strong boy. With you by his side, I have no doubt he'll be fine.' I smile reassuringly. 'Did he tell the king and queen what happened?'

He nods. 'Too many children experienced the cruelty of my cousin. Therefore, the option of a cover story was not viable. I told my aunt and uncle Athos died fighting for what he believed in. Ellis ...' He hesitates, averting his gaze. 'Ellis told them every detail. The collar he wore didn't wipe his mind. He remembers all the gritty details and did not hesitate to share them.'

*Good boy.*

'He's got fire, that kid,' I say approvingly. 'He'll keep you in line when you've been crowned king. I'm sure you'll need it.'

Alex chuckles, shaking his head. For a long moment, he stares at me, absorbing every detail of my face. 'I'm going to miss you, Scarlet.'

'I will miss you too, Alex.'

'I'll also miss your jokes, your attempts to get closer to me and your ability to get us into trouble.' He grins, watching me struggle to keep my laugh restrained.

'It's been an experience,' I agree.

'Can I expect a goodbye kiss after all this time?' he asks with humour.

'Perhaps in your dreams, Your Highness. Then you can visit my rooms in the middle of the night however many times you wish.'

His eyes glitter with merriment. 'I'd rather not be stabbed again – whether in real life or in my dreams.'

'Wise words for a future king,' I murmur.

The glee turns to worry in a blink. I can tell instantly he is doubtful of his capabilities now this duty of heir has been thrust upon him.

'I have faith you'll be exactly what Tealwaters needs,' I say. 'You'll be fair and kind, and you will be written into history books for generations to come. Just you wait and see. I'm never wrong.'

He swallows. 'You're right.'

'I know I am.' I nod.

The heir of Tealwaters leans over and kisses my temple. 'Thank you, Scarlet. For everything that you've done. I won't ever forget it.'

# EPILOGUE

ONE MONTH LATER

Lifting my chin, I behold Tarragon Castle above me as it expands across the mountainside, its large stone walls harbouring the most powerful family in Maya – the sovereigns and their children.

'This is incredible,' Olive murmurs, mouth open in awe, emerald eyes glinting with delight as we stare up at the sight.

I can't help but agree with her sentiments.

I edge Red sideways and peer down over the small wall, down the mountainside to the capital below. Scale City is full and thriving, its people loud and free, their opinions unleashed and brutal. Its buildings match the castle, dark grey rock that most likely came from the mountain itself. Along with the darkness are the kingdom's colours, orange and silver, in every shop window, on every food cart and even on the clothes the locals wear to brighten the place.

'They certainly show their pride,' Peri murmurs, violet eyes scanning the scene below us.

'Please follow us,' a Mayan guard announces, a spear in his grasp. He motions for some young boys to come take our steeds, their bright red hair and golden eyes a contrast to what we've been accustomed to in Tealwaters. 'Your horses will be tended to.'

I feed Red the last sugar cubes on my person before following the royal guards to the steps that ascend to the royal residence.

Peeking up at the extremely tall doors, I see depictions of dragons in battle, humans on their backs with sharp, intimidating weapons and fire covering the scene. I gulp, wondering if the people inside will give off the intimidating vibes their entrance emanates.

We are taken straight to a receiving room, a bare space except for two gilded chairs. The floor is dark stone, dull in colour but everlasting. A pair of thrones made of pure gold sit in the centre of the dais, stained-glass windows behind them displaying armour-wearing royals, their crowns large and obnoxious.

My eyes lower to find the thrones occupied, our arrival expected.

'How wonderful.' A dameer with long, shiny red hair smiles, his posture upon the throne relaxed but stern.

The Hex stays huddled together in this strange new place. I find myself peering around Rusty's body to see a gold-crowned king, his golden gaze elsewhere for now.

King Aiden sits comfortably, looking expectantly at the soldier before us, something lingering between them.

'I present the Hex, Your Majesty,' the guard announces, bowing at the hip.

We all follow the man's lead, dutifully folding our bodies until we are asked to stand once more.

'Welcome to Maya, fledglings. We have been patiently waiting for your arrival. I hope it wasn't too long a journey for you,' says a lady dressed finely in silver and covered in gold jewels around her fingers and neck. Queen Caida, I recall from memory.

*They seem pleasant enough so far*, I think with high hopes.

'No, Your Majesty.' Carmen speaks loudly and clearly for the Queen of Maya to hear. 'Our travels were without problems.'

'Good.' The queen nods, her features never changing from neutrality but her voice giving away her sincerity. 'Well, we would love an introduction, Carmentis.'

My brow lifts, but Carmen doesn't seem fazed by having her full name thrown out so casually. Instead, she waves a hand towards Sol, who is nearest to her. 'This is Sol Xavier, the Celestial of the Hex.'

The rulers nod in unison, both wearing small smiles at the mention of their own House, their golden eyes similar to the Celestial's. With the rest of the group, their expressions fade back to mild interest, their heads dipping in acknowledgement with each member until Carmen presents me.

'And lastly, Scarlet Seraphine, who is the Raven of the Hex.'

I see the monarchs stiffen when they hear my name.

'Raven of the Hex?' I hear the king whisper to his wife. Confusion enters his glowing eyes, and unease starts to build within my chest. 'Is she an impostor?'

'She could be the culprit we were told about,' the queen answers, voice hushed as her hand covers her husband's, digging her nails in.

'Guards!' the king shouts, panic passing through all our faces. 'Restrain her!'

I'm suddenly shoved forward and pushed to my knees

by several pairs of rough hands. They grab my hair, my arms and even wrap something cold and thick around my neck before chaining my legs so I can't stand up and run.

My throat tightens, my gaze falling to Jack, who's reaching out for me.

Ivy has grabbed him before he can intervene, her whispers fast and furious in his ear. 'Don't, or you'll make things worse.'

'What is the meaning of this?' Thea exclaims, her delicate hand hovering over her mouth in horror. She goes to approach me, but a guard with a javelin points his weapon at her – a warning to stay away.

'She is a lawbreaker,' the king booms, coming to his feet, his golden crown glistening in the sunlight streaming in through the window. 'Tell us your real name, girl.' His voice is commanding, and my heart races. Peri meets my terrified gaze, his own mirroring mine.

*What the fuck is going on?*

'Scarlet Seraphine, Your Majesty,' I answer, but my voice comes out quiet.

'Speak up!' a guard yells, making me wince as he tightens his grip on my hair.

My skull pounds with the sudden fear I'm going to be slaughtered and I'll be able to do nothing about it.

'Scarlet Seraphine, Your Majesty!' I practically shout as my heart pounds loudly in my ears.

Silence ensues as they decide my fate. The queen looks suspicious, something in her mind preventing her from approving of me. Is it because I'm a Raven that she does not trust me?

'State your purpose,' Queen Caida orders.

'I am the Raven of the Hex. I have been to Tealwaters to learn and train to take over from the Red Raven,' I reply quickly, my eyes darting around to see who else is about to pounce on me if I answer incorrectly.

'You have been with the Hex this whole time?' the queen asks before aiming the next sentence at my mentors. 'You did not pick her up recently?'

'No. She has been with us for months prior to our arrival here. She has been living in Hex Manor along with us all.' Carmen looks equally as confused as I feel, her hands open to show her sincerity.

My team nod frantically in answer when my mentor motions to them, urging them to agree.

'Very well.' The queen waves the guards away from me, and they release my hair and my neck, their biting hands letting go reluctantly.

Once freed, I get to my feet warily, keeping alert with them around me, still feeling caged in.

'Retrieve her,' King Aiden tells the guard closest to him.

I expect him to come for me, to haul me closer to the royals, but he doesn't. He leaves the room entirely.

'There must be a misunderstanding,' the king says, giving us a broad smile again. He sits back down and makes himself comfortable once more. Everything about him and his wife seems fake to me now, reminding me of adders waiting to strike.

'Ah, here she is,' Queen Caida declares, arms open as if everything is better now.

I certainly don't *feel* better, and now I'm here in this hauntingly beautiful castle, I want so badly to escape it before they accuse me of anything else.

Every gaze in the room turns towards the figure who enters the great hall, her steps echoing through the space. With every stride, my heart tightens, stopping me from breathing properly as I absorb what I'm seeing. She moves alongside the steps by the sovereigns and displays a proud smile, revealing sharp and malicious fangs.

'Who is that?' I hear Rusty ask, earning mutters of uncertainty back.

As the female turns to face us, I feel my hands curl tightly into fists.

*Do not be afraid. Do not be afraid.*

I hold her stare, lifting my chin in hopes of looking confident.

'Why does Scarlet look like she's about to mark us as her territory?' Sol asks, trying to break the tension. He senses my stiffening body and wisely doesn't comment further.

'Do you know her?' Olive nudges me.

I don't look at the Severed but hold the female's bright red gaze from across the room. I refrain from shaking, hating how my feelings are churning right now.

'Yes,' I bite out.

Jack, ever the saviour, explains. 'That's Ember Seraphine, Scarlet's sister.'

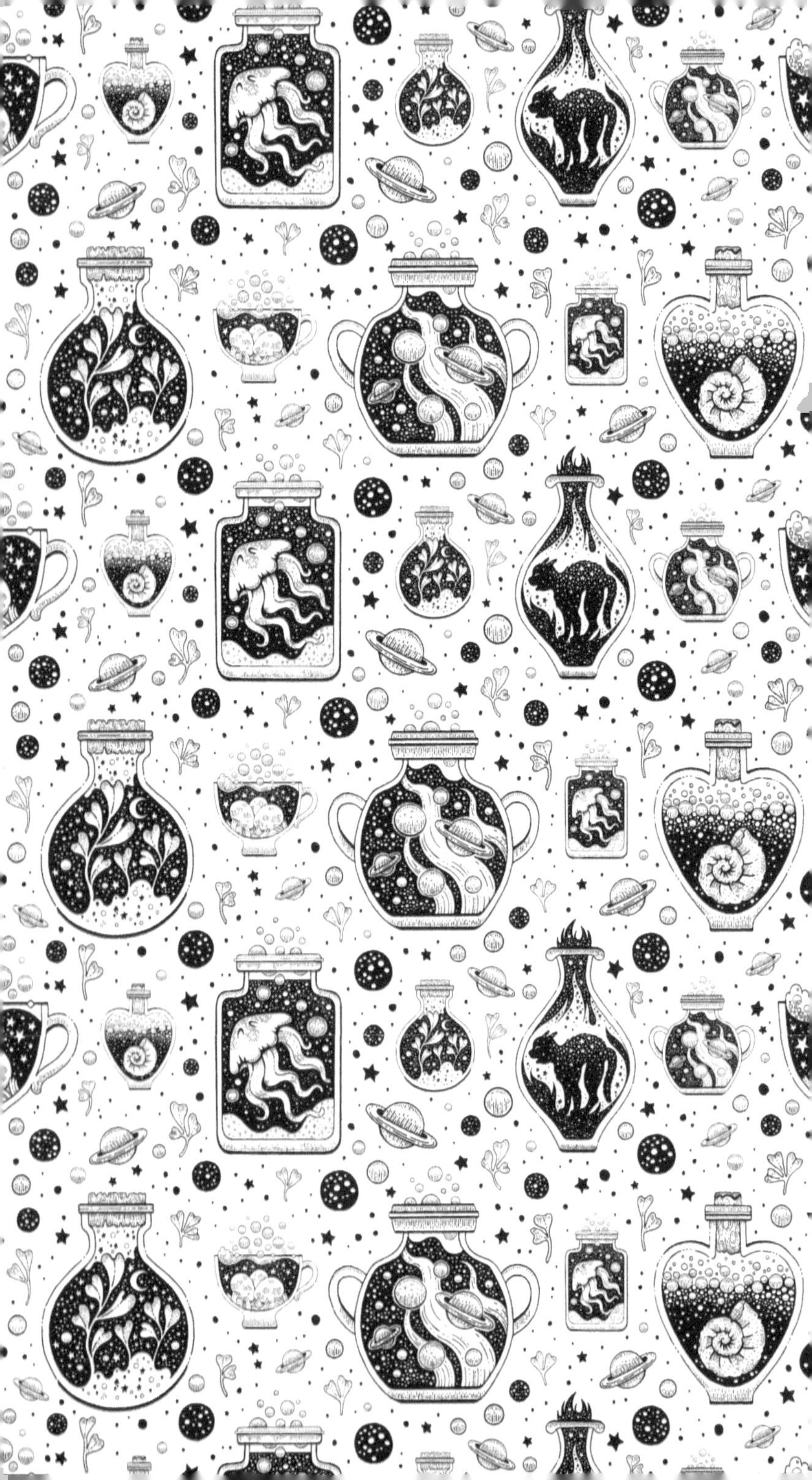

# AUTHOR NOTE

Hi there!
I hope you enjoyed reading
THE SAPPHIRE CROWN.

It only seemed right that Scarlet was able to escape the dreaded House of Raven and explore more of the world. She has so much potential and I can't wait to keep writing her story...

Thank you so much for purchasing The Sapphire Crown. Please consider leaving a review or recommending it to a friend.

Thanks again,
Hannah x

# ACKNOWLEDGMENTS

It has been a long time coming but The Sapphire Crown was a journey I couldn't have gotten through without these people.

To my family — as usual your support and help is most appreciated. You listen even when you have no clue what I'm talking about and that's enough. Thank you.

To my beta readers — Teresa and Vee, you ladies continue to support me in more ways than you realise. My stories grow with your feedback and love for my series. I'm forever grateful for you both. Thank you.

To my editor Leonora — who brings my books to another level of awesomeness (yes that is totally a word). Thanks for sticking around, I know Scarlet's story is in safe hands with you. Thank you.

To my writer friends — when I need help you are always there and I couldn't do this without you. Talking all things bookish business and plots and characters is a dream I never knew would come true. Thank you.

And lastly to the readers — for those that loved The Crimson Scar and write to me about your favourite characters, you make my day and keep me writing Scarlet's story. I have received so many messages, and posts of readers/book clubs loving my debut that it makes my cheeks hurt from smiling. Thank you.

# ABOUT THE AUTHOR

Hannah is a huge lover of tea, a passionate writer and an avid reader who claims buying books and reading books are two completely different hobbies. She is also the author of The Crimson Scar series.

As a Bachelor of Criminology and Law, Hannah has spent years reading and writing fantasy stories with morally grey characters, villainous crimes and lots of blood.

**Want to know more?**
Visit: www.hannahpenfoldauthor.com
Socials: hannahpenfoldauthor

www.ingramcontent.com/pod-product-compliance
Lightning Source LLC
Chambersburg PA
CBHW020255120726
47904CB00001B/211